AUSTRALIAN HAUNTINGS

Borgo Press Books by JAMES DOIG

Australian Gothic: An Anthology of Australian Supernatural Fiction (editor)

Australian Hauntings: A Second Anthology of Australian Colonial Supernatural Fiction

Ghost Stories and Mysteries, by Ernest Favenc (edited by James Doig)

AUSTRALIAN HAUNTINGS

A SECOND ANTHOLOGY OF AUSTRALIAN COLONIAL SUPERNATURAL FICTION

JAMES DOIG, EDITOR

THE BORGO PRESS

MMXIII

Classics of Fantastic Literature
Number Fifteen

AUSTRALIAN HAUNTINGS

FIRST BORGO PRESS EDITION

Published by Wildside Press LLC

www.wildsidebooks.com

ACKNOWLEDGMENTS

I am very grateful to Douglas A. Anderson, Leigh Blackmore and Mike Ashley for supplying stories and information, and to Professor David Ritson for giving me permission to reprint his father's (Max Rittenberg) story, "The Sorcerer of Arjuzanx." I am also grateful to Neil Cladingboel for his tireless editing over three volumes.

CONTENTS

INTRODUCTION
THE COLONIAL GHOST STORY

As the title suggests, the majority of stories in this collection involve ghosts or hauntings. The ghost story is by far the most common type of colonial weird tale. This is not surprising, as the ghost story was extraordinarily popular in the nineteenth century, and its structure and dynamic reached a standard form in the middle decades of that century. The ghost interacts with the living in order to exorcise or ameliorate past sins or unrealised promises. A consequence of this limited dynamic is that the vast majority of ghost stories are conventional and unremarkable, and the Australian ghost story is no exception—most are commercial offerings of little merit. Occasionally, however, an exceptional writer extends the possibilities of the form and takes it to a new level.

The typical colonial Australian ghost story is exemplified by the first known supernatural tale set in Australia, "Fisher's Ghost" or "The Ghost Upon the Rail" (Gelder, 1994, 2007) a well-known tale by John Lang (1816-1864) in which the ghost of a murdered man leads the authorities to his killer. The story survives in several versions, the earliest appearance of which was anonymously in *Tegg's Magazine* in 1836. The basic plot of justice obtained through supernatural means is extremely common in colonial supernatural fiction; Mary Fortune, a prolific writer of crime stories, wrote several stories in this vein which appeared in the *Australian Journal*. One of these is "Mystery and Murder" (Gelder, 2007), published in 1866, in which Mr

Longmore, a successful merchant and well-known resident of Hobart, recounts to a detective how the apparition of his wife appeared to him at the foot of his bed. The wife had eloped years before with a ship's captain named Walter Cuvier, "a most disgraceful and low rascal". The ghost leads the detective to her body—she had been stabbed to death by Cuvier and buried in a shallow grave in the grounds of her husband's house, presumably while on her way to seek forgiveness from her husband for her dreadful behaviour. Again and again in the stories in this anthology we shall see similar scenes played out—of a crime committed, and revenge or redemption obtained through supernatural means. In what follows I will describe colonial ghost stories in relation to an aspect of the Australian experience or environment against which they are set.

The Australian Penal System

The great colonial novel of the Australian penal system is Marcus Clarke's *His Natural Life*, which describes the ordeals of Richard Devine, later the convict Rufus Dawes, who is unjustly transported to Port Arthur in Tasmania. When a group of convicts escape from Port Arthur they are ill-equipped to deal with the harsh environment of wilderness. When they run out of food they start cannibalising each other. The last remaining escapee, Gabbet, is picked up by a whaling vessel with a half-eaten human arm hanging out of his swag. Dawes survives in the version of the novel originally serialized in the *Australian Journal* in 1870; however when Clarke substantially revised the work as *For the Term of His Natural Life* for book publication in 1885, Dawes and his love interest, Sylvia, drown in a cyclone, a much bleaker ending. Clarke is intent on describing the terrible depredations of the penal system; there is no scope for a happy colonial future.

For all of its gothic trappings *His Natural Life* has no supernatural or fantastic elements; there is enough real life horror to obviate the need for otherworldly fears. Other writers of the penal system followed his example, most notably William Astley who wrote under the pseudonym "Price Warung". Astley wrote powerfully of the physical horrors of convict life in stories like "How Muster-Master Stoneman Earned his Breakfast" (1890) and "The Liberation of the Three" (1891), both anthologised in Neil Stewart's *Australian Stories of Horror and Suspense from the Early Days* (1978). However, there is a small body of supernatural tales that touch on convict life. Hume Nisbet's "The Haunted Station" (*The Haunted Station and Other Stories*, 1894; Gelder, 1994, 2007) is arguably the best-known colonial Australian ghost story, and it draws heavily in its outline from *His Natural Life*. The narrator is a young doctor, who is wrongly convicted of murdering his wife. Saved from the gallows by influential friends he is transported to Western Australia. While working on a chain gang he escapes with two fellow convicts and after a breathless pursuit in which one of the convicts is recaptured, the other shot dead, and the narrator shot above the elbow, he arrives at a remote station house. From the moment he lays eyes on it he senses an overwhelming uncanniness about it:

> I felt the weird influence of that curse even as I crawled into the gully that led to it; a shiver ran over me as one feels when they say some stranger is passing over your future grave; a chill gripped at my vitals as I glanced about me apprehensively, expectant of something ghoulish and unnatural to come upon me from the sepulchral gloom and mystery of the overhanging boulders under which I was dragging my wearied limbs.

He naturally takes the house to be deserted, but closer inspection reveals the skeletons of a mother and her daughter in an upstairs bedroom, and down in the servant's quarters, the bare bones of three domestics with shattered skulls, still clothed in their bloodstained nightdresses. Clearly a terrible slaughter had taken place there years before which had remained undisturbed until now.

In the climax of the story, which takes place, inevitably, during a stormy night, the murdered woman's husband arrives, a stereotypical gothic villain, with pallid complexion, thin black moustache, blood-red lips and fiery eyes. Weeds and slime trail from his saturated clothes as if he has spent a long time submerged in water. The revenant relates the terrible history of the events that occurred there—of treachery, murder, and revenge from beyond the grave. When the storm is at its height the woman and her ghostly child manifest themselves and the narrator, by this time in a paroxysm of fear, flees the house, not a moment too soon, as it is destroyed, like Poe's house of Usher, by a fork of lightening.

Squatters, Drovers, and Aborigines

In Australian history, squatters were people who occupied large tracts of crown land in order to graze livestock. In its original derogatory context the term was usually applied to the illegitimate occupation of land by ticket-of-leave convicts or ex-convicts. However, from the mid-1820s, the occupation of Crown land without legal title became more widespread and was often carried out by those from the upper echelons of colonial society. As squatters became wealthy entrepreneurs, the term came to refer to a person of high social prestige who grazed livestock on a large scale. A society of bush workers developed—drovers, stockmen, shearers, superintendents—to work the stations. Naturally, the hardship and lawlessness of station life became a popular subject for Australian writers who seized on the dramatic possibilities of life far from the civilising influence of the cities. Many of Australia's best-known colonial writers wrote about bush society—the conflicts, tragedies, loneliness—often with humour and pathos, for example the bush ballads of A. B. "Banjo" Paterson and Adam Lindsay Gordon, and the short stories of Henry Lawson.

In R. P. Whitworth's "A Strange Story", published in the *Australian Journal* in 1895, the narrator and his cousin, Jim Welsh, come to Australia to make their fortunes as squatters, preferring the adventurous life on a cattle station to a tame sheep run: "...the headlong galloping through crashing timber, and down stony defiles and steep gullies, the camping out beneath the giant gum trees in the solemn bush, the cracking stockwhips, the cabbage-tree hats, the blue shirts, the breeches and boots, and the other glories that render the life of the stockman so desirable." The cousins acquire 70,000 acres on the upper Goulburn River in Victoria and set to work. Things go well for them at first, but soon a tribe of aborigines in the area start spearing their cattle indiscriminately. Fearing that they might soon start to kill colonials, Welsh decides to ride to the nearest neighbour to discuss what to do. A few hours later, after an uneasy sleep, the narrator sees an apparition of his cousin: "Coming slowly up the path, not twenty yards from me, and gliding rather than walking, was a form, the form of my cousin, Jim Welsh, whom I had seen start for Carfrae's some hours before. Pale to lividness, shadowy, ethereal, with a look of pain on his erstwhile handsome face, and a crimson blotch of blood welling from a deep gash in his breast." The narrator's worst fears are confirmed when he finds Welsh's corpse in a "gloomy" gorge, stuck through with a spear. "A Strange Story" is a conventional English ghost story, down to the dismal, gliding spectre that portends unnatural death, transposed to a striking Australian setting. It produces a melancholic effect in the thwarted optimism of the young English men, one of whom is destroyed by the hazards of the new land.

Another conventional trope is the ghost that repays a favour. William Sylvester Walker's "The Wraith of Tom Imrie" (*From the Land of the Wombat*, 1899; Doig, 2011) is related by a station hand named McIlwaine around a campfire in traditional ghost story fashion. Twenty-five years earlier he and his friend, Tom

Imrie, stop at a bush hotel while droving cattle. While they are playing cards a murder takes place; Tom Imrie pursues the killer on horseback and shoots him dead, but then unaccountably turns the gun on himself and commits suicide. McIlwaine visits Tom's mother in Sydney to tell her the news of her son's death, and from her he learns that the man Tom killed was her own brother, which explains why he committed suicide. Soon afterwards McIlwaine is droving rams through the same country when he is bitten by a deadly snake. He passes out, but is roused by Tom's dog, Joker, which would not leave Tom's grave. Tom's ghost appears and guides McIlwaine to a pool of water, saving his life.

Similarly, in Edwin M. Merrall's "The Spectre of the Black Swamp: An Overlander's Story" (Doig, 2011), first published in the *Australian Journal* in 1875, the narrator, a drover, tells of events that took place many years earlier on a remote cattle station in New South Wales. John Warsfield is the "dashing" station overseer or superintendent who mysteriously disappeared while droving cattle to a neighbouring station with Mike, a "low-browed, brutish-looking" stockman. At about the same time Mike's wife disappeared and it was generally believed that she eloped with the boundary rider who left about the same time. Soon afterwards a headless rider is seen in the vicinity of a drovers' camp called Black Swamp. Years later, Mike is employed by the narrator on a droving job in the same region. Although they are warned not to camp overnight at Black Swamp because the headless rider will disturb the cattle, the narrator dismisses the story. With supernatural punctuality the headless rider appears at the stroke of midnight. The apparition, a "horrid presence" with "two luminous eyes", accosts the narrator, and then attacks Mike in his tent before rushing down to the swamp shrieking with triumphant laughter. In the morning a bloody trail from Mike's tent leads them to a headless skeleton concealed in the swamp and Mike confesses to the murder. He had intercepted a letter from Warsfield to his wife asking her to elope with him to Sydney; when he did not show up she left instead with the boundary rider. The droving party camp at Black Swamp another night so that the sceptical superintendent can investigate the apparition for himself; the revenant reappears and again attacks Mike who dies of fright.

Again, this is a formulaic ghost story, a typical tale of supernatural revenge in which the ghost realises justice for a past sin. The author also preserves familiar notions of social hierarchy with the dashing superintendent contrasted with the brutal stockman, though some moral ambiguity is introduced—is not John Warsfield culpable for having designs on the stockman's wife? Nevertheless, traditional views of hierarchy and literary form are central here; indeed, the author places the tale firmly in a venerable literary tradition by introducing the familiar supernatural form of a headless ghost, common to British legend and folklore and best known in literary terms in Washington Irving's "Legend of Sleepy Hollow". The headless horseman also appears in "The Phantom Horseman", published in the *Australian Town and Country Journal* in 1881, and like Irving's exemplar, the phantom turns out to be a fake. Again the action takes place on a remote outback cattle station where there is a tradition of the ghost of a murdered man, which appears every Christmas Eve. The phantom horseman dutifully appears, but it turns out to be a drover—his horse has bolted while he is unsuccessfully trying to remove a blanket that has knotted itself around his head.

A Christmas Eve legend figures also in Frances Faucett's "A Bushman's Story" (*Thou Must Write. A Bushman's Story*, 1886; Doig, 2007) when a young squatter, travelling alone one Christmas eve, finds that purgatory has emerged from the "grand silence" of the bush: "It was a city of the dead—they were dead men who walked in its streets—who had raised its stately towers—who sought in this great white dome the objects they had striven to attain all their lives." The ghostly people stream silently along its streets and the squatter is drawn irresistibly to join them. On a bridge he is accosted by ghouls that rise up from the river, presumably denizens of hell, but he manages to escape. The city disappears in the mists and the squatter never returns there again.

Arguably the most important Australian colonial writer of weird fiction was Ernest Favenc (1845-1908). He wrote numerous stories of the supernatural for the popular magazines of the day, including *The Bulletin*, and many of them draw on his experiences as a station hand and explorer.[1] In "The Boundary Rider's Story" *(My Only Murder and Other Tales*, 1899; Doig, 2007) Favenc's theme is the greed and lawlessness of the bush. During a terrible storm a boundary rider arrives at a bush pub with the news that he has seen the revenant of a Chinaman who had earlier been found dead with his throat cut. It turns out that the station contractor has murdered him for his paycheck. The contractor is found with his throat torn out and a terrified expression on his face; the Chinaman's grave has been disturbed, and when it is dug up the check is found clutched in his hand. Indifference for human life was often expressed in the senseless killing of aborigines. In "The Ghostly Bullock Bell" (*The Bulletin*, 1893), the sound of the spectral bell makes one of the drovers recall how, as a young man, he caused the death of his brother. In "Doomed" (Gelder, 2007), published in *The Australian Town and Country Journal* in 1899, one of a party of five young squatters fires into a group of aborigines for a lark, killing an aboriginal woman and her baby. Before she dies she curses the squatters and each in turn suffers a premature death; the last thing they see is the woman carrying her baby. More often, though, it is the aborigines who are the threat, and in these stories the casual and often brutal racism of many colonial writers is starkly apparent.

See for example, Favenc's "In the Night" (*The Bulletin*, 1892; Doig, 2011) and Rosa Praed's story "A Disturbed Christmas in the Bush," in which hostile natives threaten a homestead. Another example is Sophie Osmond's "The Story of the Stain" (*Phil May's Winter Annual*, 1901; Doig, 2011). Osmond, an

1. A collection of Favenc's weird tales, *Ghost Stories and Mysteries*, is available from Borgo Press (2012).

Australian novelist who is now all but forgotten, wrote three weird tales for Phil May's annuals between 1901 and 1904. In "The Story of the Stain" a family renovating an old homestead are concerned when a stain appears in the kitchen and cannot be removed. One of the daughters has a vision of three men in the house being attacked by aborigines; one of the men with his dying breath implores her to "Find it! Find it! For God's sake! Send it to her! She has been waiting all these years." Upon tearing up the kitchen floor they find a bag containing a bundle of letters from a woman named Mary Elwyn in England. Investigations reveal that her husband, George Elwyn, went missing in Australia years before and the discovery of the letters finally allows her to make closure.

Rosa Praed's celebrated tale, "The Bunyip" (Gelder, 1994, 2007; Doig, 2010), first published in the anthology *Coo-ee: Tales of Australian Life by Australian Ladies* (1891), also involves typical station workers; we can recognise them instantly:

> …there was something striking about the appearance of the men, in their bright Crimean shirts and rough moleskin trousers and broad-trimmed cabbage-tree hats, as they lounged in easy attitudes, smoking their pipes and drinking quart-pot tea, while they waxed communicative under the influence of a nip of grog, which had been served out to them apiece.

The first half of the story is a meditation on the Bunyip, or Debil-Debil, the legendary Australian monster that haunts remote lagoons and swamps. According to the narrator, "it is the only respectable flesh-curdling horror of which Australia can boast." The Bunyip is more than just a sea monster, but a supernatural being that lures people to their doom by "a certain magnetic atmosphere" that spreads "a deadly influence for some space around." It is especially said to haunt a particular lagoon that exerts a particular melancholy fascination on the narrator:

I liked nothing better than to go with my brother on moonlight nights when he went down there with his gun over his shoulder to get a shot at wild-duck; the creepy feeling which would come over us as we trod along by the black water with dark slimy logs slanting into it, and reeds and moist twigs and fat marsh plants giving way under our footsteps, was quite a luxurious terror.

Of course, this is the very same "pleasing terror", to use M. R. James's phrase, that the weird tale is meant to evoke, and it corresponds with the "weird melancholy" that Marcus Clarke saw as so distinctive about the Australian forest.

The weird atmosphere is even more pronounced in the second half of the story, when the group hears a strange wailing cry in the swamp. They realize it is a lost child and go in search of her: "It was a dreary, uncanny place, and even through our coo-ees the night that had seemed so silent on the plain was here full of ghostly noises, stifled hissings, and unexpected gurglings and rustlings, and husky croaks, and stealthy glidings and swishings." They find the girl, but too late—she has been dead several hours. Praed leave us with the question, if the girl was already dead, who, or what, made the strange wailing cry?

The Gold Rush

Gold was discovered in New South Wales in April 1851 and in Victoria in July of the same year and sparked a mass movement of people that rivalled the gold rushes in the United States a few years earlier. The gold rushes had wide-spread social and economic effects: new found wealth, an upsurge of republican nationalism, racial suspicion and conflict caused by the migration of people from Europe and Asia to the gold fields, and the threat to law and order caused by the greed and corruption of gold diggers. Many stories and ballads were published that focused on the sensational aspects of life on the gold fields, and a number of these have supernatural or fantastic elements.

A typical example is "The Ghost from the Sea" (Doig, 2007) by J. E. P. Muddock. James Edward Preston Muddock (1843-1934) was a commercial writer for magazines who was particularly popular in the last decades of the nineteenth century. He wrote many stories and novels under the name Dick Donovan. He spent some time at the Victorian goldfields before travelling extensively in Asia; he returned to Melbourne in 1868, but left soon afterwards for London and a writing career. "The Ghost from the Sea" appeared in his collection *Stories Weird and Wonderful* (1889), and is set in Melbourne during the gold rush. Muddock makes his theme clear from the opening paragraph:

> This period in the history of our Australian colonies is a startling record of human credulity, human folly, wickedness, despair and death. The [gold] fever was confined to no particular class of people. Clergymen, bankers, landowners, shipowners, merchants, shopkeepers, sailors, labourers, classical scholars and ignoramuses alike fell under the fascination. The worst passions of our nature manifested themselves; hatred, envy, jealousy, greed, uncharitableness. The parsons were no better than paupers; the classical scholars than the ignoramuses. The thin veneering of so-called civilization was rubbed off, and the savage appeared in all his fierceness at the cry of "Gold! Gold!"

The story is written in a journalistic style as if Muddock is reporting true events. Mr. and Mrs. Harvey are a young couple living at a Melbourne boarding house. Harvey goes to the gold fields and rumour has it that he has struck it rich, which is confirmed by the couples' profligate lifestyle when he returns. When he returns to the gold fields his wife is brutally murdered and Mrs Harvey's jewellery and other valuables stolen. The police and unable to trace the killer and when her husband returns he is broken by the news of her death. Some time later, the boarding house owners, Mr and Mrs Jackson, travel on board a clipper to England. Mr Jackson spends his time drinking in his cabin and appeals to the startled captain that a mysterious woman is trying to lure him overboard. The captain and crew see strange lights aboard the ship which they cannot explain. Finally, during a storm while passing Cape Horn, the light is seen again which on this occasion transforms into the apparition of a woman; Jackson rushes from the cabin doorway and the figure beckons him over the side of the ship. Subsequently Mrs Jackson loses her reason and is confined to an asylum in England. The clear explanation is that Mrs Harvey has obtained supernatural revenge on her killer. A very similarly plotted story is Favenc's "The Haunted Steamer," which was published in *The Town and Country Journal* in 1901. Again a man is forced overboard by the spirits of the people he murdered. Both stories appear to owe a good deal to F. Marion Crawford's classic ghost story, "The Upper Berth" (1886).

If gold fever led inexorably to greed and murder, the goldfields themselves were places that bred superstition and fear. A. G. Hales' "The Spectre of Kurnalpi Gold Field" (*Camp Fire Sketches*, 1902) is, unusually, set in the Coolgardie gold fields in Western Australia. When a dog takes off with the bone of a dead man whose grave has been disturbed by greedy prospectors, the diggers are suddenly overcome by superstition, especially after they all catch a fever from the rotting corpses they have unearthed in the search for gold: "It was horrible, but the most horrible part of it all was that nearly every man in his madness raved of a spectre fox-terrier hunting him over hill and gully, with a bone in his mouth, by moonlight." Subsequently the prospectors desert Kurnalpi, which becomes a ghost town. A literal ghost town appears in Guy Boothby's "A Strange Goldfield" (Doig, 2010) in which a small party of prospectors stumble upon an abandoned mining town. They make camp outside the town where they meet a "hatter" who has evidently lived by himself in the area for years; when they ask if he is lonely he tells he has many friends in the town, which comes alive after dark. The party investigates and find the madman is telling the truth: "...we could distinctly hear the rattling of sluice-boxes and cradles, the groaning of windlasses—in fact, the noise you hear on a goldfield at the busiest hour of the day. We moved a little closer, and, believe me or not, I swear to you I could see, or thought I could see, the shadowy forms of men moving about in the moonlight." The party break camp, vowing never to return.

In "Little Liz" (*Shadows on the Snow*, 1866; Doig, 2007), B. L. Farjeon also emphasizes the "weirdness" of the Victorian gold rush:

> When the Victorian gold-fever was at its height, people were mad with excitement. Neither more nor less, I was as mad as the others, although I came to the colony from California, which was suffering from the same kind of fever, and which was pretty mad, too, in its way. But Victoria beat it hollow; for one reason, perhaps, because there was more of it. The strange sights I saw and the strange stories I could tell, if I knew how to do it, would fill a dozen books.

"Little Liz" is the young daughter of an uneducated prospector with a heart of gold, who is consciously modelled after Dickens' Little Nell, even down to her beloved dog of mixed breed and stout heart. Farjeon lays on the sentimentally in thick strokes and when the inevitable happens and she goes missing on a rich gold field discovered by her father, we expect the worst. Supernatural forces appear to lead her father and his companion to her murdered body, thrown down an abandoned mine. Her father kills the murderer, a villainous and cowardly prospector, but is himself mortally wounded—father and daughter are buried together and a fence is put up around the grave.

In Ernest Favenc's "Jerry Boake's Confession" *The Bulletin*, 1890; Doig, 2011), a man suspected of murdering a popular mine owner and stealing his gold is taken to the scene of the crime and chained to a tree for the night where he is overcome by superstitious dread:

> And then—well, then, a sight that would never leave him; the moon was young and sickly then, but its light was strong enough to show the dead body of the murdered man, with the bloody smear on his face. Would morning never come? Presently the moon would set, and then the darkness would be horrible. Who knows what hideous thing might not creep on him unawares. The air seemed thick with an awful corpse-like smell; had they buried the body there, where it was found? But this thought was too maddening—he would go frantic if he entertained it. Why did not the bleak shadow shift; the moon was getting low now?

The man confesses and is hanged.

If good people often come to a bad end on the lawless and immoral gold fields, others are rewarded for their good deeds. In William Sylvester Walker's "A Voice From the Dead" (*From the Land of the Wombat*, 1899) a seaman, Tom Trevittick, on board a clipper on its way from England to Melbourne tells Boyd, the narrator, that he has seen a vision of his dead father holding a tin water bottle in his hand, which he takes as an omen of his impending death. He gives Boyd his mother's address in case he is killed on board the ship. On safely reaching Melbourne Trevittick sets off to the gold fields to seek his fortune. Three months later Boyd himself sets out for a new gold fields in the remote outback about which evil rumours abound. On the way he comes across a dead body and a tin water bottle; scratched on the bottle are words identifying it as Trevittick's, with instructions for the location of a gold reef. With the help of other prospectors he finds the reef and becomes rich. Later he returns to England where he seeks out Trevittick's mother, buys her a cottage and provides her an annuity for the rest of her life.

"The Red Cap Spectre of the Robertson" (*The North Queensland Register*, 1896; Challis and Young, 2010) is interesting as one of the few early stories to feature the ghost of an aborigine. Three prospectors are fossicking for gold in a remote part of Queensland; one of them is startled when he sees the ghost of an aborigine on three occasions. The fossicker, of Irish background, relates the experience to his mates: "His eyes looked loike coals ov fire at the bottom ov a deep hole, and there was a piece ov a broken spear sticking out ov his breast, and his white pants were all red with blood in front, and be the same token, he had a red cap on his head."

Later the fossickers learn the story of Pat Courbett who was murdered some twenty years early. Courbett was a fossicker who always travelled with a black boy; he struck gold and carried a large amount of it with him in saddlebags. He was found dead with two spears in him, and the black boy had disappeared. Soon afterwards the fossickers find the remains of the black boy in a cave near where the ghost was seen; he too had been speared and had holed up in the cave where he eventually died. The fossickers find Courbett's gold in the cave; they give the boy a decent burial so he can rest at last. The story is certainly above the average of its kind, and is full of local colour and authentic detail; the author, E. Downs, does not appear in any bibliography or literary history, and he or she does not appear to have published anything else under that name.

Mining

Whereas the gold rush stories described above are about a type of frontier society characterized by lawlessness and a breakdown of civilization, mining stories are about the unknown—the physical act of penetrating to places beyond our knowledge.

In James Edmund's "The Prophetic Horror of the Great Experiment" (*The Lone Hand*, 1909; Doig, 2008) a party of adventurers, including a professor of extinct languages, decide to sink a shaft as far into the earth as possible; the narrator sets out their aim:

> We were looking for the unknown—for the hidden mysteries of life, and the story of the buried past. We were seeking for the original home of gold and precious stones—the great deposits whose merest fringes have been found by the seekers after treasure; and for the fires which are supposed to burn for ever in the earth's centre. We wanted to investigate the ancient myths about an interior world in the hollow globe, where subsidiary planets revolve in a toy firmament, and strange races of humanity, or races that are apart from humanity, have their being.

In fact, the party reach Hell, literally. Suspicions are first aroused when the drill breaks through to a vast underground chamber from where the professor hears snatches of Hebrew, Sanskrit and Coptic, but their worst fears are realized when they find attached to the retrieved drill a horned tail, severed at the root. The irate Devil appears at the entrance and they make a dash for the surface; fortunately the tunnel caves in and most of the party manages to escape, leaving behind the Muslim labour force, which is left to face the consequences. George Locke, the London book dealer and bibliographer, thought the story "imaginative and a cut above the average" and felt that Edmund would have made an excellent addition to the Lovecraft Circle, but the story reads more like farce, a typical Australian tall story, than genuine cosmicism. Edmund, who edited of *The Bulletin* from 1903-1914, wrote another bizarrely titled mining fantasy, "The Plans and Specifications of the Lost Soul Mine," about a cursed mine in Goulburn Valley, Victoria, that destroys all who try to work it. Again, the story reads like farce, a meditation on the futility of mining, and the narrator, who ill-advisedly purchases the mine, is grateful when it is taken off his hands by a successful law suit against a previous owner.

Edward Dyson is a notable Australian writer of realist tales of mining and factory communities. In "The Accursed Thing" (Doig, 2010), published in *The Bulletin* in 1922 an old fossicker working an abandoned mine is threatened by what seems to be a remorseless creature of nightmare:

> The thing filled the space about the shaft as with the convolutions of a monstrous writhing snake, and was advancing towards him, surging slowly. He lit his candle and retreated the length of the excavation, whimpering like a child in his horror of the oncoming force, which he realised as a living, sentient, passionless brute-thing bent upon his destruction.

Drawing on an indomitable will to survive and fortified by his long-abandoned faith, the fossicker manages to dig through to a parallel shaft where he is saved by other miners. One of the miners explains that the Thing was in fact thick, rubbery mud formed by recent flooding, but the fossicker will not believe him and refuses to return to the mine.

The Bush

In colonial fiction the Australian bush is often presented in a similar way to the woods and forests of English and European folklore and supernatural tales—as a quasi-living entity, often overtly malevolent, in which natural laws are suspended and civilization cannot penetrate. The archetypal example of this sort of story is Edward Dyson's "The Conquering Bush" (Wannan, 1983) in which a stockman's wife loses her mind on a remote station: "…she was absorbed in a terrible thought. The bush was peopled with mad things—the wide wilderness of trees, and the dull, dead grass, and the cowering hills instilled into every living thing that came under the influence of their ineffable gloom a madness of melancholy." She is eventually destroyed, drowning herself and her young child in a nearby waterhole. Perhaps the best known of this type of story is Henry Lawson's "The Drover's Wife" (1892) in which a woman alone in the bush with her four children must overcome a snake lurking beneath the floorboards of the bush hut. While she waits for the snake to emerge she recalls other threats she has had to overcome in the bush—fire, flood, a mad bullock, a sinister tramp and so on. As morning approaches the snake appears and she is able to kill it, thus saving her children, an unheralded hero. Another acclaimed story in this vein is Barbara Baynton's "A Dreamer" (1902; Gelder, 1994, 2007) in which a young girl is lost in the bush; she stands in "uncertainty, near-sighted, with all the horror of the unknown, that this infinity could bring." The natural world—the trees, the wind, the creek—is like a malignant force that obstructs her way home. These are non-supernatural, psychological stories, representative of the literary realism that Australian authors preferred over romance. Nevertheless, they indicate something of the numinous and "weird melancholy" that are features of romantic fiction.

The story of a child lost in the bush is a common one in colonial fiction. We have already examined "The Bunyip" and "Little Liz", but there are many others. In Hume Nisbet's "Norah and the Fairies" (*Stories Weird and Wonderful*, 1900; Doig, 2007) a lost girl is supported by her fairy tale imaginings as she gets progressively weaker and delirious; finally, in a scene that outdoes "Little Liz" for syrupy sentimentality, her death is attended by a Snow Queen and fairy court who escort the girl up to heaven in a silver car drawn by white horses. William Hay's "Where Butterflies Come From" (*An Australian Rip Van Winkle and Other Stories*, 1921; Doig, 2007) explores how the apparent gullibility and naivety of children can reveal a deeper truth. When Isbel Yawkins' uncle tells her that butterflies come from a magical butterfly tree out in the bush, little Isbel goes in search of it...and finds it. Normally, however, childish fears of the bush conjure up frightening images as in Marcus Clarke's "Pretty Dick" (1870) who imagines "the shapeless Bunyip lifting its shining sides heavily from the bottomless blackness of some lagoon in the shadow of the hills." The lost child symbolizes the European colonist helpless against the elemental forces of nature, and in "Pretty Dick" and "Norah and the Fairies" nature proves too strong a force.

Exploration

Another common colonial narrative that often had supernatural or fantastic elements concerned explorers and exploration, such as lost race literature, a popular sub-genre of fantasy that developed from the extraordinary popularity of H. Rider Haggard's novels of African exploration and adventure, *King Solomon's Mines* (1885), *Allan Quatermain* (1887), and *She* (1887). Like Haggard's novels, tales of Australian exploration are characterized by masculine heroics and an imaginative vision of the Australian outback that combines both an optimistic view of its limitless potential and an exaggerated fear of the horrors that might lurk there.

The best weird tales of this type came from the pen of Ernest Favenc, himself an explorer of note who wrote a definitive *History of Australian Exploration 1788-1888* (1888). In "Spirit-led" (*The Bulletin*, 1890; Doig 2007) two drovers in a north Queensland settlement run into Maxwell, whom one of them knew years before as a man who had cheated death. Maxwell had apparently died of a cataleptic fit; when he was about to be buried he suddenly awoke, his hair turned completely white from the experience. When one of the drovers saves Maxwell's life, he tells them the story of his "death". While he was dead his soul apparently travelled to a remote part of Australia he had never visited before. He found himself with a strange companion who pointed out to him a boulder with an inscription in Dutch, "Hendrick Heermans, hier vangecommen, 1670"; further along they see a rocky outcrop with gold showing through. After this experience, Maxwell felt an irresistible urge to return to his body, which he succeeds in doing after his soul flies through a sort of twilit purgatory. Now Maxwell believes that the land he saw is in this part of Queensland, and he invites the two drovers to join him to search for the gold reef. The three find the boulder with the inscription, much more weathered and overgrown than Maxwell saw it, suggesting that he had gone back in time. They press on and find the gold reef; however, they hear a strange cry back in the direction of the boulder and Maxwell, strangely disturbed by the sound, returns to investigate. A few minutes later the drovers hear a couple of gunshots and they race to see what has happened. They find a skeleton in Maxwell's clothes; they are horrified when the skeleton implores them to help him—it is Maxwell, his body decayed to a state of decomposition it would be in had he died years before. One of the drovers ends up in an asylum, a raving lunatic, while the other looks after him in the hope that he will recover. This is an interesting story that mixes various ingredients: contemporary spiritualist notions of spirit travel; Dutch exploration in the seventeenth century and traditional stories of European sailors being stranded on the continent through their misdeeds or by misfortune; and the opening up of the interior of the continent through exploration, motivated by the search for gold. The strength of Ernest Favenc's tales are revealed here—they are based on personal experience, of places he has seen and stories he has heard, enhanced by his interest in Australian history and legend. In this sense Favenc has something in common with the English tradition of the antiquarian ghost story exemplified by M. R. James and the American regional supernaturalists like Sarah Orne Jewett. Favenc weaves his tales from the stuff of Australian history and tradition in much the same way that M.R. James drew from his knowledge of British antiquity, or Jewett from the landscapes and traditions of New England.

Similarly, in Guy Boothby's "With Three Phantoms" (1897; Gelder, 1994, 2007) it is the desert that claims a team looking for traces of Ludwig Leichhardt's ill-fated expedition. After four years in which they were presumed dead the leader of the team arrives at a north Queensland settlement on Christmas Eve; he tells the assembled company how he was saved from certain death in the desert by the ghosts of his three companions who led him out of the desert. The long ordeal proves too much for him and he dies of exhaustion on Christmas day.

William Sylvester Walker was another author of talent who depicted the fantastic nature of the Australian outback. His best known weird tale is "The Evil of Yelcomorn Creek" (Gelder, 1994, 2007), which was collected in *When the Mopoke Calls* (1898). It first appeared in a slightly shorter version in the *Centennial Magazine* in March 1890 as "The Mystery of Yelcomorn Creek." In this story an old shepherd named Baines recounts how, in his younger days, he explored outback Queensland, prospecting for opal with an aboriginal guide named Bobbie. They find a tunnel in a rocky outcrop that leads to a lost valley, "like the garden of Eden." In the valley Baines hears a faint "coo-ee", a ghostly cry of "quivering despair," that heralds his discovery of an aboriginal grave site. The grave contains hundreds of graves with exposed bones, and stone tomahawks and boomerangs scattered about, clearly the scene of a massacre many years before. As Baines explores the valley he hears the ghostly "coo-ee" more frequently, and when he returns to the campsite he finds that Bobbie has died of fright. That night Baines sees "the skeleton-painted wraiths, tall and weird, of those warriors who fought and fell in the dim long ago." He faints at the sight of the ghosts, and when he recovers the following day he buries Bobby, seals up the tunnels entrance, and leaves that country forever. Baines withdraws from the world and becomes a shepherd, retreating from his ambition to become a successful opal prospector for a life of solitude and introspection.

In these stories the interior is a taboo area, the preserve of ghosts, madmen, and monsters. By travelling willingly into the interior, explorers are taking on more than the conventional dangers of the desert, but a cursed landscape that holds the promise of a fate worse than death. This contrasts with the more positive vision in lost race romances, in which the interior is seen as a land of opportunity.

Australian Fauna

European artists, too, had difficulty coming to terms with the Australian landscape and native fauna: the strange, diffuse light of the bush, the blinding glare of the outback, the bizarre animals that seemed travesties of the natural world (when Bernard Shaw saw a platypus for the first time he looked for the tell-tale marks where duck and mole had been sewn together) were beyond the experience and skill of colonial artists and it was many years before they were accurately portrayed. Ernest Favenc effectively exploits this notion of Australia as a country of evolutionary and natural oddities in his "Haunt of the Jinkarras" (*The Bulletin*, 1890; Gelder, 2007; Doig, 2007, 2010). In this story aboriginal tales of the Jinkarra, a native bogeyman invoked by parents to frighten wayward children, turns out to be real—a race of subterranean troglodytes. With its low brow, shaggy pelt, rank odour and tail, the Jinkarra is an evolutionary throwback, a scientific oddity. The story is cast as the diary of an overland telegraph worker, who with another man, the only survivor of an expedition in which he had been found and kept alive by blacks, go in search of a ruby-field in northern Australia. In an outback mountain range they find a cave complex in which the Jinkarras live. However, it is not the Jinkarras that pose a threat to the ill-fated explorers, but the land itself. The bushman falls down a cliff in the cave, while the narrator, after surviving rising floodwaters in the cave, is claimed by the desert while trying to return to civilization.

Most stories of this type involve a monstrous specimen of an existing creature. Arthur Bayldon's "Benson's Flutter for a Fortune" (*The Tragedy Behind the Curtain and Other Stories*, 1910) involves huge stone fish that menace divers searching for treasure; again the scientific unnaturalness of the creatures is emphasized:

> The bravest man would have quailed at the sight of that heaving, misshapen abortion of crab and fish. First a mouth like that of a filthy sewer, then a scaly incarnation of everything abominable and evil, weaponed with spikes, that are slowly erected as the dull, loathsome eyes fastened on me…God! The whole gallery is full of the monsters. Everywhere they are crawling—down the walls, over the shell—the very floor is beginning to lift. The water is curdling beneath myriads of threshing tentacles.

In "Worse than a Shark", which appeared in the *North Queensland Register* in December 1897, the monster is a giant octopus, while in Alex Montgomery's "The Deicides" a giant man-eating archer fish dislodges unwary natives from the rocks by spitting sea water at them and then consumes them whole. More satirical are Saul Spring's "The Passing of the Colossal Kangaroo" (*The Lone Hand*, 1920) and Phil Robinson's "The Gladstone-Bag Kangaroo" (*Phil May's Annual*, 1892) about a hunter who stumbles across a race of super intelligent kangaroos. More in the tall story vein is J. A. Barry's "Steve Brown's Bunyip" (*Steve Brown's Bunyip*, 1893) in which the legendary monster of the title turns out to be an escaped circus elephant.

Conclusion

While often derivative, the stories considered here are interesting in the way in which the Gothic form has been transposed to a new, alien environment. The outback, the desert, the bush are imbued with forces that are inimical to European explorers and fossickers. Colonists struggled to cope in the harsh landscape and climate and were frequently claimed by it; most famously the explorers Burke and Wills in 1861, and Ludwig Leichhardt, whose expedition to traverse Australia from east to west disappeared without trace in 1848. The land itself seemed a malignant force that exacted a terrible revenge on those who challenged it or wandered thoughtlessly into it. Thus, in many of the stories described here, characters range across a landscape in which the supernatural can erupt at any time. Characters frequently fall victim to the bush; indeed, often it is children, symbols of innocence and European naïveté, who are claimed.

Most Australian writers of the supernatural followed the model of the English ghost story, which had reached a standard form by the middle decades of the nineteenth century: a ghost interacts with the living in order to exorcise or ameliorate past sins or unrealised promises. A consequence of this limited dynamic is that the vast majority of ghost stories are conventional and unremarkable, and Australian colonial ghost stories are no exception—most are commercial offerings of little literary merit. However, some writers were able to extend the form and make a genuine contribution to the genuine; Ernest Favenc for example was particularly conscious of the Gothic possibilities inherent in the Australian landscape and its heritage (Doig, 2012). His interest in and knowledge of Australian history and legend coupled with his first hand experience of the remote outback gave him unique insights into the colonial experience. In stories like "Spirit-Led," "A Haunt of the Jinkarras," "The Boundary Rider's Story," and "Doomed" he modernised the Australian supernatural tale. This anthology reprints a number of powerful vignettes that he wrote for *the Bulletin* during the 1890s.

Bibliography

Challis and Young, 2010: Angela Challis and Marty Young, *Macabre* (Brimstone Press, 2010)

Doig, 2007: James Doig, *Australian Gothic: An Anthology*

of Australian Supernatural Fiction 1867-1939 (Equilibrium Books, 2007; reprinted Borgo Press, 2013)

Doig, 2008: James Doig, *Australian Nightmares: More Australian Tales of Terror and the Supernatural* (Equilibrium Books, 2008; reprinted Borgo Press, 2013)

Doig, 2010: James Doig, *Australian Ghost Stories* (Wordsworth Editions, 2010)

Doig, 2011: James Doig, *Australian Hauntings: A Second Anthology of Australian Colonial Supernatural Fiction* (Equilibrium Books, 2011; reprinted Borgo Press, 2013)

Doig, 2012: James Doig. *Ghost Stories and Mysteries*, by Ernest Favenc (Borgo Press, 2012).

Gelder, 1994: Ken Gelder, *The Oxford Book of Australian Ghost Stories* (Oxford University Press, 1994)

Gelder, 2007: Ken Gelder and Rachael Weaver, *The Anthology of Colonial Australian Gothic Fiction* (Melbourne University Press, 2007)

Stewart, 1978: Neil Stewart, *Australian Stories of Horror and Suspense from the Early Days* (Australasian Book Society, 1978; reprinted Hale & Iremonger, 1983)

Wannan, 1983: Bill Wannan, *Australian Horror Stories* (Currey O'Neil, 1983)

JERRY BOAKE'S CONFESSION

by Ernest Favenc

The Bulletin, 8 March 1890

Ernest Favenc was born on 21 October 1845 at 5 Saville Row, Walworth, Surrey, the son of Abraham George Favenc, and his wife, Emma, née Jones. His father was a merchant by trade and his occupation appears to have sent him to different locations, as Favenc was educated at Temple College, Cowley, in Oxfordshire, and in Berlin. With his two sisters, Edith and Ella, and his brother, Jack, Favenc came to Australia in 1863. After a few months working in Sydney, Favenc moved to a cattle station owned by his uncle in north Queensland where he worked as a drover. He spent the next sixteen years in north and central Queensland working on stations, usually as a superintendent. By 1871 he was writing fiction and poetry for the *Queenslander*, and in 1878 Favenc was placed in charge of an expedition, financed by Gresley Lukin, the proprietor and literary editor of the periodical. The expedition, which became known as the *Queenslander Transcontinental Expedition*, was tasked with surveying a route for a railway line from Brisbane to Port Darwin.

Favenc's journalism and his successful land speculations in the Northern Territory in the early 1880s allowed him to marry and settle down in Sydney. On 15 November 1880, Ernest Favenc married Bessie Mathews, whom he had first met in Brisbane in the mid-1870s, at St John's Baptist Church, Ashfield, Sydney. The 1890s were Favenc's most productive period as a writer, and his best tales of mystery and the supernatural were published between 1890 and 1895, five of which are printed here. By this time he was working mainly for *The Bulletin*, which was edited by J. F. Archibald whose preference for the short, unadorned bush yarn influenced Favenc's style. Favenc continued writing into the new century, but his alcoholism affected his productivity and the quality of his work. By May 1905 Favenc was seriously ill in Royal Prince Albert Hospital, and later in the year a bad fall that broke his thigh confined him to St Vincent's Hospital. He died on 14 November 1908 in Lister Hospital in western Sydney.

Perhaps one of the most popular fellows on the then newly-opened H— Goldfield, in Far North Queensland, was Jack Walters. Everybody knew him, and everybody liked him, and there was great chaff and much popping of corks 'ere he started down to C— with the avowed intention of getting married. Walters had shares in one or two good mines, and had a tidy sum of money with him when he left the field amidst the congratulations of 'the boys' on his approaching nuptials. Jack was a friend of mine; when he was temporarily crippled by a blasting accident I used to write his love-letters for him.

Three days after he left, Inspector Frost and his black troopers, who all knew Walters, rode into the township. Naturally, the first question asked was, had they met Jack, and how far he'd got on the road?

"Never saw or heard of him," was the unexpected reply,

"perhaps he was off the road."

"No, he said he was going down easy and expected to meet you."

"Hum!" said the inspector, "I'm going back tomorrow, and I'll keep a sharp lookout for him."

Fifty miles from H— was a creek with permanent water and a good feed, a favourite camping-place. Frost, who had told the troopers to watch for signs of Jack, had almost forgotten the matter, to which, after all, he did not attach much importance, when a shrill whistle from one of his boys a short distance off the road to the right attracted his attention. The boy had dismounted, and was standing gazing at something on the ground. Frost rode up, and had almost anticipated what it was before he reached the spot. Screened by a few bushes from any chance traveller lay the body of a dead man—Jack Walters. His head was pillowed on his riding-saddle, his blanket was thrown over the lower part of his body, and his packsaddle and bags were close by, where they had evidently been put overnight. He had been shot through the temple, and in his hand he still held a revolver. To all appearances it was one of those motiveless cases of suicide that now and again puzzle everybody.

A careful examination was made, but nothing seemed to have been disturbed; no money save some loose silver was found. Frost collected all the camp paraphernalia, took careful notes of the position of the body and all the surroundings; then, leaving one trooper to guard the remains, despatched a boy back to H— with the news, and instruction to the police there to come out and take the body—he himself had to proceed on his journey. Casting one more glance around, he noticed a newspaper lying some distance away. Such things were commonly found on old camping grounds, but he walked over and picked it up. It was the *H— Express*, the journal of the mining township he had left. He looked at it idly for some time, thinking more of the sight he had just witnessed than of the paper in his hand, when he instinctively noticed the date, which suggested a train of thought. Walters had left the field three days before Frost's arrival there. The Inspector remembered that fact well, because there had been some debate as to the spot where they should have passed each other. Three days would make it Monday, and this paper was issued on Tuesday. How had it come into the dead man's camp?

Frost went back and looked at the corpse before the troopers had covered it up with boughs. The revolver taken from the stiffened fingers, he remembered, was but loosely held—it was not in the iron grasp of a dead man's hand, clutched hard at the moment of death. No doubt remained that the case was not one of suicide, but cowardly, cold-blooded murder. Somebody had left the diggings the next morning, had ridden hard and overtaken Walters at the creek, had shared the hospitality of his camp, and had shot him for the sake of the money he had with him. Where was the murderer now?

Frost, who had gold to take down to the port, did not tarry long between the scene of the murder and C—. The second day saw him closeted with the police magistrate, who had just received a telegram from H— informing him of the arrival of the native police with the news of Frost's discovery. Hardly had Frost told his tale before another telegram arrived—"Jerry Boake left here after Walters. See if he is in C—."

Jerry was a pretty notorious character, and, strange to say, Walters was one of the few men who had befriended him when everybody else had thrown him over.

A very short inquiry elicited the fact that Jerry was in town; also that Jerry was in funds, and had given the barmaid at the 'Rise and Shine' a gold watch and chain. Interviewed, the barmaid produced the gold watch and chain, which were at once recognised as the property of Walters, who had bought them as a present for his fiancée. Jerry was arrested, and, absurd as the statement may seem, was actually wearing a ring well known to belong to Walters. He denied his guilt stoutly, stated that Walters had given him the ring and the watch and chain to bring down, and that when he was drunk he gave it to the barmaid. Jerry was remanded to H—, and Frost himself started up in charge of him.

The dusk was setting in when they reached the bank of the creek where the dead body had been found. The party from H— had been there and removed it. Frost pulled up, and looked round. The prisoner, manacled to a trooper, was close to him.

"You're not going to camp here, are you?" stammered Jerry Boake, with pallid lips.

"Why not?" said Frost, sternly. "*You* know nothing about this place, do you?" And without another word he rode straight to the scene of the murder, and got off his horse.

"Turn out," he said briefly.

The troopers dismounted, and began unpacking and unsaddling. Frost undid the handcuff from the trooper's wrist, and refastened it on the prisoner's.

There is only one way in the bush of securing a criminal charged with such a crime as Jerry's, and who would stick at nothing to escape. A light trace-chain is used, and the prisoner tethered securely to a tree. Without a word, Frost, chain in hand, walked to the tree beneath which the body had been found, and beckoned to the troopers to bring the prisoner. Jerry approached; he had summoned up all his hardihood, and called up a look of defiance on his face, but he couldn't control the trembling of his now pallid lips. Frost secured him, and the black trooper brought him his blankets, and sat down a short distance off to watch him.

Darkness closed in, the camp fires blazed up, food and tea were given to the prisoner, and with an air of bravado he pretended to eat; but though the food passed his lips not a bite could he swallow. The tea he drank greedily, and asked for more. The day's journey had been a long one, and the tired men soon dropped off to sleep one after another—but for one man there was no sleep that night. For all that the camp was so quiet, he had an idea that he was being watched, and it gave him a miserable kind of moral support to think that there was someone else awake as well as himself. It would be an awful thing to be the only waking man in that camp.

He had got to the full length of the trace-chain, and must

have lost consciousness for a few moments, for, while his heart beat until it nearly choked him, he saw a black shadow under the tree—a dark shadow that was not there before. With an effort he stilled his trembling nerves, and forced himself to gaze at the object. Pah! The moon had risen higher and changed the position of the shadows, that was all. But supposing a man with a bloody smear on his forehead and half-closed dull eyes were really to come and lie down on that spot, while he himself was chained there not able to get away, what an awful thing it would be!

Would morning never come? he thought. Why must he think, think, think, and all about the one thing; his own incredible folly? A few pounds in gold, a few days of drunken 'shouting' and now—it must be a nightmare, surely—he could not have been led away to do such a madly insane deed. He disliked the man mostly because he owed him many kindnesses, but that was not why he killed him. No, it was for the few miserable pounds he was carrying. That horrible black shadow seemed to stop there, although the moon's position had changed. Why did it stop there? Perhaps there was a stain of blood on the ground; he would force himself to go over and see. No, he couldn't do that, he would stop where he was and try to think of other things; but he couldn't. Always the same thought, the same hideous picture—a man asleep with his head on a saddle, and another standing over him with a levelled pistol. And then—well, then, a sight that would never leave him; the moon was young and sickly then, but its light was strong enough to show the dead body of the murdered man, with the bloody smear on his face. Would morning never come? Presently the moon would set, and then the darkness would be horrible. Who knows what hideous thing might not creep on him unawares. The air seemed thick with an awful corpse-like smell; had they buried the body there, where it was found? But this thought was too maddening—he would go frantic if he entertained it. Why did not the bleak shadow shift; the moon was getting low now?

Just before daylight Frost was awakened by one of the boys

at the door of his tent. "Marmee, that fellow Jerry sing out along of you!" Frost got up and went over to the place. The moon had set, and the night was dark; he told the boys to make the fire.

"My God! Mr Frost," said a piteous voice, "take me away from here, and I'll tell you everything." Frost undid the chain, and led him to the fire. He afterwards said that the look on the wretch's face haunted him for months. Jerry Boake made a full confession—and was hanged a few weeks afterwards.

THE TRACK OF THE DEAD

by Ernest Favenc

The Bulletin, 23 April 1892

What's the matter with you; why the deuce can't you sleep?"

"I don't know," returned Alf; "got a touch of insomnia tonight. If I do go to sleep I have the most awful dreams all about men I used to know, men who are dead now."

"Oh, for heaven's sake don't start such talk at this time of night. Sit by the fire and smoke your pipe quietly," I answered, wearily, as I turned my back to the blaze and drew my blanket around me.

"Right you are, old man," he replied, good-naturedly, and I dropped off into unconsciousness.

I awoke with a start. The fire was out, or nearly so, and the camp was silent. Just above the horizon the spectral last quarter of the moon was hanging, throwing ghostly, dim, long shadows around. It was the hour before dawn, the uncanny hour when all the vital forces are at the lowest ebb. Some great general is reported to have said that the only courage worth a hang was three o'clock in the morning courage. Whether anyone ever did make the remark or not, there is a deal of truth in it.

I roused myself a little and looked around. Alf was sleeping on the other side of the fire, and where he had set his bed down was now in deep shadow, and I could make nothing out. I tried to go to sleep again, but it was useless. Perhaps a smoke might send me off; so, seeing a spark still smouldering, I arose, and blowing the end of a still glowing firestick into a blaze, I lit my pipe, and then, holding the lighted stick up, looked over to where my companion should have been sleeping.

His blankets were tenantless.

May I never experience again such an uncomfortable thrill as went through me when I made this discovery! I put my hand on the blankets where they had been thrown aside. They were cold and the dew had gathered on them; he must have been gone some hours. I listened long and intently, but the night was silent. For a man to wander away from camp in the middle of the night, out in the Never-Never Spinifex country, and remain away for hours, is a most uncanny thing. If he had heard the horses making off he would have called me ere leaving; if—but I exhausted all conjectures before daylight dawned. I could do nothing until then.

The light came very slowly, or so it appeared to me. We were camped at the foot of a Spinifex rise, on a narrow flat bordering a creek. When the light was strong I could see the horses feeding quietly some short distance away, and picking up my bridle I soon had one caught and saddled, and firing off my rifle two or three times without eliciting an answering shot, I started to look for my missing mate. After some trouble I picked up his track leading straight up the ridge, which, near the crest, was sandy, and the prints of his footsteps were clearly defined. The Spinifex was scantier here, and as I gazed intently down I saw something that made me pull up and hastily dismount to scan the tracks closer. Alf, was not alone, somebody was walking ahead of him.

Step by step I followed leading my horse, but I could make nothing of the foremost track, for Alf's almost covered it every time. At last they diverged, and the two ran side by side. It was a bright morning, the sun just glinting under the stunted trees; what little live nature there was in that lonely spot was awake and joyously greeting the day; but I rose up from my examination of that awful footmark with the dew of superstitious terror on my forehead. No living man had made that track.

I had to follow on scarce knowing what to think or expect. I tried to persuade myself that the footprint was that of some attenuated old gin, lean and shrunken as a mummy, but that was against reason. The track was that of the skeleton of a man; and Alf was not following it, but following whatever was making it.

With varying fortune, now finding, now losing the trail I kept on for about two hours; then, halfway down a slight incline, I came upon the object of my search. He was sitting on the ground talking to himself, I thought at first, but when I got closer I saw he was addressing some object on his lap. He was nursing the head and shoulders of the remains of a human being. He lay at full length amidst a patch of rank green grass fertilised by the decayed body, a skeleton with fragments of rotten clothing still clinging to it. Alf had his arm under the skull as one would support a sick man, and was murmuring words of affection. He raised his head as I approached but evinced no surprise.

"This is my brother Jack," he said. "Fancy his coming to the camp last night to show me where he was. We must take him into the nearest station and bury him, for he can't rest here, it's too lonely."

I could not answer. Alf's mind had evidently given way and I could not reason with him. He carried the body back to our camp and I commenced a ghastly ride to the nearest station over seventy miles away, with a madman and a corpse for companions. The third day after starting we arrived at Ulmalong, then the outside station, and here I learnt the story of Alf's twin brother.

He had been a stockman on the place when it was first settled, and had ridden out on his rounds one day and never returned. There was little doubt that the skeleton we brought in was his, but what led the living twin to its resting place? I held my tongue about the 'track' for they would only think I was as mad as poor Alf.

After we buried the remains Alf relapsed into almost constant silence. He was quite harmless and they found him some light work to do about the place, but he died, prematurely aged, in about a year's time. He was buried with his brother.

BLOOD FOR BLOOD

by Ernest Favenc

The Bulletin, Christmas Edition, 17 December 1892

Silence everywhere, the spell of heat on everything. Kites, which had been soaring on strong pinions away back in the dry country, swooping down on the grasshoppers, have had to come in to this lonely waterhole tired out and worried, and now sit dozing on the branches of the motionless coolibah. One who had left it too long has had only sufficient strength to reach the water and flounder in, and stands with bedraggled feathers moping at the edge of the muddy pool. There is no animal nor human life to be seen—just a round clay hole, a few withered polygonum bushes, and some gnarled and warped coolibah trees. Around lies a bare plain with a bewildering heat-mist hovering over it.

The slow, hot hours creep on. The sodden kite standing near the water suddenly topples over and falls dead; at times one of the others flops heavily down from its perch, takes a few sips and flies back again. These are the only sounds, the only living movements that break the stagnant monotony.

There is neither track of man nor beast to be seen, but for all that what was once a man is lying there beneath one of the shadeless tress. It has been lying there for over six months, so there is nothing very repulsive about the poor corpse but its shrivelled likeness to humanity. When it staggered in there alive the hole was dry, and it sank down and died. Since then a quick and angry thunderstorm has passed and partly filled the hole, too late. But no prowling dog has found the body, not even the venturesome crow has been to inspect it; the desert has protected it from white tooth and black beak, and it lies there dry and withered, but the form of a man—and a white man, still.

This is the story of that unburied, unwept, untended corpse. It is a story of thirst, of treachery, of revenge.

Years ago, when stations were valuable and all things pastoral looked bright ahead, three men pushed out beyond the bounds of settlement in search of new country. Two of them were fast friends, although there was a considerable difference in their ages. The third was simply on the footing of ordinary friendship and of about the same age as the elder of the other two. The party was completed by a black boy.

Far beyond the lonely waterhole where the weary kites sit watching the silent dead, they came on to good country—fair, rolling downs and deep permanent holes. At one of these they fixed a camp and inspected the country on all sides with a view of dividing the runs fairly. One day the younger of the two friends and the third man went out together. They took a long excursion northward and finding no water, made, the next day, for a small hole they had passed on their way out. Fatal mistake—the hole was dry, with the body of a misled dingo rotting at the bottom, and with thirsty, tired horses, and nearly empty bags, they were now fifty miles from their camp, the nearest water.

They turned out for a short spell and lay down to catch a few moments of slumber. The young man slept soundly, dreaming of long, cool swims in a river; of watching it sparkling and leaping amongst the rocks; then he awoke suddenly to find himself companionless in the desert. He raised himself on his elbow and looked around. The clear starlight showed him nothing; he was actually alone; his mate and all the horses were gone. He went to where they had hung the waterbags on a tree. They were gone, too. He comprehended it all. His treacherous friend had taken the two freshest horses and the remnant of the water, and started for the camp, trusting that one would get there where two could not. The other two horses had probably followed of their own accord, to die in their tracks.

He had no hope that his companion meant to come back with succour. A man who could do such a deed would never suffer his victim to bear witness against him. He had the choice of two deaths—a lingering one where he was, or a quicker one in a desperate attempt to gain the camp. He chose the latter. He had no expectation that his own old friend would come to his relief, for he guessed he would be deceived by some specious lie.

When the end came, as it soon did, and he fell for the last time, he prayed with his dying breath that the man who had wrought his death might die as he did.

Late that night the survivor, with one remaining horse, reached the camp, and told the anxious occupant how his friend had died of thirst; how he had helped him on to the last, and only left his body when aid was useless and his own life in jeopardy. "I must start at daylight and bring his body in if possible," was the answer at last. Then one lay down to sleep the sleep of exhaustion, the other to watch and mourn.

Overtired men seldom sleep soundly. Some rambling words from the haunted sleeper roused the watcher's attention. He listened, as the dreamer restlessly babbled out his secret. He understood it all, and for an instant his hand was on his revolver; but no. He would have proof, then—

Next morning, with the black boy, he was on his way before the stars the paling. Proof was easily forthcoming by the tracks. The body of his young friend lay by itself on the plain; no horse-tracks led to it, none from it. He had died by himself, and the story of staying with him to the last was false. What use in following the trail back further? He returned to the camp with vengeance in his heart.

It was easily done. The other suspected nothing. One morning the two rode out together for a last look to the southward before returning. Twenty miles from the camp they stopped at a scanty belt of timber; beyond was nothing but a boundless plain.

"Get up one of the trees," said the avenger. "You may be able to see a little better from that elevation."

The other dismounted and complied. He stood on the highest limb, no great height, and looked all around; nothing visible but the blue mirage. He looked below. His companion was a hundred yards, or more, away leading his horse. He stopped for an instant and turned in his saddle, and the words smote on the listener's ear hotter than the blazing sunbeams: "As you served that poor murdered boy, so I serve you. If by any miracle you survive and I hear of you again amongst men I will take your life wherever I find you." Then he turned and rode away, deaf to calls and entreaties.

Stumbling over the plain, nor cursing in impotent rage, now begging and praying for mercy, the guilty man followed the silent figure leading the horse. Followed it until his sweat-blinded eyes could see no longer, and the poor, abandoned wretch felt the lonely horror of the desert encircle him, for he knew he should never see the face of his fellow man again.

He reached the camp during the night. It was deserted. The threat was carried out to the letter. Aye, more, for a ghost sat there by the dead embers, that he only could see, but it drove him forth into the night, and with desperate, hopeless purpose he made for the haunts of men. Who knows what he suffered before his dying footsteps led him to the dry hole, and he crawled under the nearest shade to pant his life out?

* * * * * * *

Next morning the recruited birds take wing for the drought-smitten plains once more, leaving the body of their comrade to keep company with that of the murderer.

IN THE NIGHT

by Ernest Favenc

The Bulletin, Christmas Edition, 17 December 1892

"Steady now, old man; do you feel better? Here! Hold hard! *I'm* not a nigger."

The wounded man had struggled desperately as though still struggling with his foes.

One dead white man, speared through the body; one with his head cut open, whom the speaker was trying to revive, and four dead blacks, lying on their faces with outstretched arms—the posture in which niggers usually die who meet with a violent death. The sun had set, and darkness was rapidly closing in. Presently the wounded man regained his senses somewhat.

"How's Joe?" he asked

"If Joe is your mate, I'm afraid it's all up with him, as it would have been with you if I had not come. Not but what you had done pretty well before I came. I can only account for one," and he motioned towards the dead.

"Yes; I remember. Joe was speared at the start. He was picking wood for the fire. How did you come here?"

"I've been after horses all day, and was on my way home when I heard the row. I got here just as you had this crack on the head; and the niggers cleared. I suppose you fellows were bound for the Cloncurry?"

"Yes. Poor old Joe! Are you quite sure he is dead?"

"Quite sure. Now, what's the best thing to do about you? I

suppose you can't rise?"

The other shook his head wearily.

"It's fifteen miles to the station. The boss has got a buggy in there, and we'll bring it out for you if you are game to stop here alone while I go. I'll be back by daylight. There's no fear of the blacks turning up again, I know the run of these fellows."

"I'm game," said the wounded man faintly.

"Right. I'll load your revolver up for you, and be back as soon as I can. Keep your pecker up, you're safe enough here."

With this rough but kindly consolation the stockman departed, and the survivor of the two men who had been suddenly attacked by the natives when camping, was left alone. Not a pleasant position, but nerves are not supposed to be known in the outside country.

There was a first-quarter moon, and the shadows soon got darker and darker beneath its feeble light. The man with the broken head had quite recovered his consciousness but he still felt dizzy and weak. It was an awful time to wait until daylight. Supposing the niggers came back again after all! Then he recalled all the stories he had heard of the blacks mutilating the dead bodies of their enemies. If they came back at all it would be for that. Supposing he was unconscious when they came and they commenced on him! He must watch all night to prevent that. Poor Joe, his mate, he wouldn't like him to be cut up by the darkies.

Surely, he thought, one of the bodies had moved. The moon gave such a sickly half-light now it was sinking that it was impossible to make certain. Yes, it was a dark figure creeping up to Joe's body, not one of the dead ones, for he could still count them—one, two, three, four. A live nigger crawling up to hack Joe about. He took aim and fired. That dropped him; he could see him writhing in the streak of light that broke through a rift in the trees. Go and finish him, to save another shot. On his hands and knees he crawled over, picking up a dropped club on the way. Then the silence of the night was broken by fierce and heavy blows, and he crawled back to his tree and fainted.

The moon had set when he opened his eyes again, but, by the pale light of the stars, he saw, to his horror, another black shadow approaching the dead body of his mate. Another successful shot and, full of rage, he again crept over and used the formidable club. But the savages were not to be deterred; one after another the dark forms came creeping up, to fall beneath revolver and club, until at last the man's senses left him.

The day had broken, but the sun was not yet up, when the stockman and another man drove up in the buggy. They jumped out, and hastened to the apparent sleeper, but he was dead.

"Have the niggers been back and killed him?"

The stockman shook his head. "I can't make it out—look at this club in his hand covered with blood and—"

The two stood up and gazed curiously about. One, two, three, four black bodies and one red heap.

"He wasn't like that when I left him," said the stockman, hastily; "he was speared clean."

The head was pounded out of recognition, the body and limbs smashed by maniacal blows; the corpse of the wretched Joe was beaten out of all semblance of humanity.

"There have been no blacks here since I left."

"What can be the meaning of that club in his hand?" was the reply.

A STRANGE OCCURRENCE ON HUCKEY'S CREEK

by Ernest Favence

The Bulletin, 11 December 1897

The heat haze hung like a mist over the plain. Everything seen through it appeared to palpitate and quiver, although not a breath of air was stirring. The three men, sitting under the iron-roofed verandah of the little roadside inn, at which they had halted and turned out their horses for a mid-day spell, were drenched with perspiration and tormented to the verge of insanity by flies. The horses, finding it too hot to keep up even the pretence of eating, had sought what shade they could find, and stood there in pairs, head to tail.

"Blessed if there isn't a loony of some kind coming across the plain," said one of the men suddenly.

The others looked, and could make out an object that was coming along the road that led across the open, but the quivering of the atmosphere prevented them distinguishing the figure properly until within half-a-mile of the place.

"Hanged if I don't believe it's a woman!" said the man who had first spoken, whose name was Tom Devlin.

"It is so," said the other two, after a pause.

Devlin walked to where the waterbags had been hung to cool, and, taking one down, went out into the glaring sunshine to meet the approaching figure.

It *was* a woman. Weary, worn-out, and holding in her hand a dry and empty waterbag. Although only middle-aged, she had that tanned and weather-beaten appearance that all women get, sooner or later, in North Queensland.

With a sigh of gratitude she took the waterbag from Tom's hand and put the bottle-mouth to her lips, bush fashion. There is no more satisfactory drink in the world for a thirst person than that to be obtained straight from the nozzle of a waterbag.

Tom regarded the woman pityingly. She was dressed in common print and a coarse straw hat, and looked like the wife of a teamster.

"Where have you come from, missus, and what brought you here?"

"We were camped on Huckey's Creek, and my husband died last night. I couldn't find the horses this morning, so I started back here."

"Fifteen miles from here," said Devlin. "We are going to camp there tonight, and will see after it. You come in and rest."

He took her back to the little inn, where she could get something to eat and a room to lie down in. Then they caught their horses and started, promising to look up the strayed animals and attend to everything, according to the directions the woman gave them.

The three men arrived at Huckey's Creek about an hour before sundown. They examined the place thoroughly, but neither dray, horses, nor anything else was visible. The marks of a camp and the tracks bore out the woman's story, but that was all.

"Deuced strange!" said Devlin. "Somebody must have come along and shook the things, but what did they do with the man's body? They wouldn't hawk that about with them."

"Here's the mailman coming," said one of the others, as a man coming towards them with a packhorse hove in sight.

They awaited his approach, standing dismounted on the bank of the creek. The mailman's thirsty horses plunged their noses deep in the water and drank greedily.

"I say, you fellows," he called out, "you didn't see a woman on foot about anywhere, did you?"

"Yes," replied Tom, "she is back at the shanty."

"Wait 'til I come up," said the mailman. When his horses had finished he rode the bank to the others.

"Such a queer go," he said. "About five or six miles from here I met a tilted dray with horses, driven by a man who looked downright awful. He pulled up, and so did I. Then he said, staring straight before him, and not looking at me, 'You didn't meet a woman on foot, mate, did you?'

"I told him no, and asked him where he was going. 'Oh,' he said, just in the same queer way, 'I'm going on until I overtake her.'

"'You'd best turn back,' I said. 'It's twenty-five miles to the next water; and I tell you I'd have been bound to see her.' He shook his head and drove on, and you say the woman's back at the shanty?"

"Yes; it's about the rummiest story I ever come across. The woman turned up at Britten's today, about 1 o'clock, on foot, and said that her husband died during the night; that she could not find the horses, and had come in on foot for help."

"I suppose he wasn't dead, after all, and when the horses came in for water he harnessed up and went ahead, looking for his wife, in a dazed, stupid sort of a way."

"I suppose that is it," said Devlin. "Are you going on to Britten's tonight?" he asked the mailman.

"Yes."

"You might tell the woman that her husband has come-to, and started on with the dray. After we have had a spell, we'll go after him. He can't be far."

"No," replied the mailman, as he prepared to ride off. "He looked like a death's-head when I saw him. So-long."

The men turned their horses out and had a meal and a smoke; by this time they were talking about starting when the noise of an approaching dray attracted their attention.

"He's coming back himself," said Tom.

The dray crossed the creek and made for the old camp, where the driver pulled-up and got out. The full moon had risen, and it was fairly light.

"Don't speak," said Devlin; "let us see what he is going to do."

The figure unharnessed the horses with much groaning, and hobbled them; then it took its blankets out of the dray and spread them underneath and lay down.

"Let's see if we can do anything for him," said Devlin, and they approached.

"Can we help you, mate?" he asked.

There was no answer.

He spoke again. Still silence.

"Strike a match, Bill," he said; "it's all shadow under the dray." Bill did as desired, and Devlin peered in. He started back.

"Hell!" he cried, "the man *did* die when the woman said. He's been dead forty-eight hours!"

THE WRAITH
OF TOM IMRIE

by William Sylvester Walker

From the Land of the Wombat (1899)

Alas for this grey shadow once a man!
                                    —Tennyson

Yet this way was left,
And by this way I 'scaped them.
                                    —*Ibid.*

William Sylvester Walker (1846-1926) was born
at Hartlands, Heidelberg, near Melbourne, on 16 May
1846. He was educated at Sydney Grammar School,
where he was a contemporary of Sir Edmund Barton,
Australia's first Prime Minister, and continued his
studies in England at Wellesley House, Twickenham,
and later at Worcester College, Oxford. As a university
student he won the Worcester challenge skulls, played
for the college first eleven cricket team, and was nomi-
nated for the University Trial Eights. He lived in New
Zealand for fifteen years where he worked as a journalist and was editor of the *Marlborough Press* and
later the *Blenheim Times*. It was in New Zealand that
he began to write poems and short stories for popular

periodicals of the time. Walker was the nephew of "Rolf Boldrewood" (whose real name was Thomas Alexander Browne), the great Australian colonial writer and author of *Robbery Under Arms* (1888), who evidently did not approve of his writing. He had three sons, two daughters and two step-daughters. In 1921 he took up residence with his family at Soroba House, Oban in Argyllshire, Scotland, and he died there at the age of eighty in 1926.

And so you don't believe in ghosts, you fellows?" said McIlwaine, the squatter, one night as we sat around the cheery pine-log fire at Yerilla. "I do, and I will tell you my reasons. It is not the first time in my life that I have seen one, and I've heard that ghost-seeing runs in our family.

"I saw the ghost of a man, a horse and a cattle dog one night as plain as I see each of you now, but the dog turned out to be real afterwards, and I don't believe that he saw the ghost; anyway, he didn't act as if he did. He was very serviceable to me, that dog. Twenty-five years ago, before some of you were born (you may well look, Jemmy, but it's true), I was cattle-droving 'store' cattle from up north, and my chum was a man called Tom Imrie.

"We camped one night on the Lower Tarcoo, and Tom and I left our head man and the others with the cattle and rode on to a bush hotel to put in the evening. There were about a dozen fellows there, a rather mixed lot; and some one was playing a concertina awfully well as we rode up. I never got that imitation peal of bells out of my head. 'Oranges and lemons, say the bells of Saint Clements,' sort of thing. He played the different changes and triple bob majors, crashes and all the other thingummybobs nearly as well as George Cass himself, whoever he was. I did not know the player then, but I had cause to do so afterwards.

"There were two other drovers in a private room at the hotel, who had a mob of cattle ahead of ours. So we chummed up and had a game of whist."

"McIlwaine plays whist everywhere, anywhere and where he can, so beware," remarked Jemmy uproariously.

"You bide awee, ma fren, and I'll knock spots out till ye," rejoined McIlwaine.

Jemmy made a pantomimic gesture, expressive of contempt, and McIlwaine resumed:

"Well, as I was after saying, if that infant hadn't interrupted a man of my age, the name of the place was Bylo. The usual far-back sort of a township, only the hotel and public stockyard. And the hotel was combined with an all-round store, where you could get a variation from a suit of clothes to a frying-pan, haberdashery and hardware mixed. The police had not yet arrived, though there were any amount of long, loafing crawlers in the district, the usual sort who stay about a place of this description, that promises to be a town some day. They usually get cleared out in time, before decent people come. And there is generally a death or two before that happens—innocent and guilty alike. The police were wanted. I tell you, and not very long after our arrival either. We tied our horses up to the verandah posts, along with a lot of others, on first arriving, and it was there I noticed the concertina. We stayed about an hour playing whist with the drovers, and taking an occasional glass together.

"You must know that in the big knock-about room, next to the one we were in, a lot of young fellows were gambling, and drinking pretty freely also. Some of them I noticed were jackeroos, 'jaast like ma young fren, Innocence, here,'" laying a mighty paw upon Master Jemmy's shrinking flesh and causing an awful hullabaloo, so that we had to wait until things assumed an aspect of order again.

"Well, these jackeroos that I was telling you about were mixed and various 'poddies,' 'cleanskins,' 'two tooth,' some of them 'four,' and maybe one or two just lambs unshorn, like Jemmy; knew just enough to say 'baa'. It was a wild, Godforsaken sort of district, right out on the back blocks beyond the New South Wales border, and young fellows learn bad things quick enough, unless they stick to their work like men.

"One fellow amongst this lot who were gambling looked pretty 'old in the horn'. I spotted him when I passed the door, for I went out once to look if the horses were all right. He was the concertina player. Sort of sharp, by his appearance. He might have been anything from a cattle-duffer to a horse thief, but he looked like a 'spieler'. He was pretty hard bitten.

"All of a sudden, whilst we were going on with our game (I had the ace, four, five and three of hearts, trumps, I mind, in my hand, and it was my turn to play), there was a fearful shindy! Shouting, swearing, stamping, chairs and tables knocked down and a rush. We jumped up and, just as we got to the door, the very man I have been describing tore out like a maniac, took the first horse he came to and galloped off. The rush of the others coming out after him all of a heap frightened the other horses to such an extent that they all pulled back at once and broke every individual bridle in that crowd. My word, that fellow on the horse did scratch away past the pine ridge on the up-river road.

"Tom was a pretty hot-tempered fellow. He managed to catch his horse somehow, got a bridle from somewhere, and was away after the fugitive before I could say 'Jack Robinson'. We had seen a still form lying in that other room as we came out, and some of the fellows were shouting 'Murder!'

"At last I got my horse, and a fresh bridle out of the store, and one of the drovers, another young fellow and myself, started in pursuit. Off we went. The tracks kept on the road, and after a hard ride of about six miles we suddenly came upon two dead bodies—the spieler-looking concertina man and poor Tom! The first had a bullet through his head, as near the centre of the forehead as it well could be.

"Tom was a sure shot with a revolver, and always carried one. So did the other man it appeared, for we found the two pistols close by, just a little way off each body.

"But though there was only one barrel of the alleged murderer's pistol discharged, Tom's had two, and the wound Tom had died from was in the right temple. Apparently he had shot himself. I was terribly cut up. The whole affair was so awfully sudden and unexpected that I could scarcely collect my wits together. We had the bodies brought carefully back to the hotel, and despatched a special messenger for the police, 100 miles away. But we had to bury all the bodies next day on account of the heat. I stayed to give my evidence, of course, but I put on two more hands, and could trust my head cattleman to look after the 'mob'.

"It came out that the man who had committed the murderous assault upon the poor young jackeroo was not well known. He was a stranger, but was named, according to his merits, 'Flash Jack,' and was reputed to be up to any blessed thing, from petty larceny to cattle-duffing, according to my informants. The story went that the jackeroo had several one-pound notes knocking about. One of them was a new one. They were all pretty well boozed, and Flash Jack had got hold of this new note somehow. The new chum accused him of stealing it, and threatened to strike him with a hunting crop he carried. The man swore horribly, and in the scuffle which ensued he wrenched the hunting crop from the young fellow, and hit him such an awful crack on the head with the heavy brass handle of it that he just collapsed to the floor and never spoke again. The heavy end of the whip had sunk right into his brain! The police came at last, a sergeant and a constable, and went carefully over every 'in' and 'out' of the case; after which they put all the witnesses who remained, and myself, upon our oaths before Mr Fielding, the police magistrate, and owner of Yankalilla station. (Good brand that—J. F. conjoined—was in those days.) Gone off colour since the old man died, and left the property to his son. *He's* too fond of town, and leaves the station too much to others. Never knew *that* game pay, unless the manager is a partner, or the overseer is a real worthy man.

"Well, it was all finished fair and square, and what is left of those three bodies, whirled to their death in a sudden gust of passion, lies there to this day. I don't suppose the bones would come out of the ground, even if their ghosts wanted to walk, and say a few things they hadn't time for on this earth, eh? We buried them on the rise of the big pine ridge. There's a much bigger cemetery there now, for I passed it only last year.

"Tom's cattle dog, Joker, would not leave the grave until I led him away on a chain, but after a day or two I began to get the poor beggar to eat a little, but I had to keep him on the chain, or he would have gone straight back and most likely died there at the grave.

"When I had delivered the cattle all right I found myself down in Sydney for a spell. I of course made my first visit to Miss Imrie, as I was in duty bound to do. She was Tom's sister, and used to keep a home for him all ready when he came down from the bush to town. She lived at the top of Woolloomooloo, in one of those quiet streets on the left going out to Pott's Point. Nice comfortable little cottage, with a diminutive garden in front. I rang the street-door bell, and was shown into the drawing-room. Miss Imrie appeared. Nice lady-like girl. I had written the sad news to her myself from up country, so that she had had some considerable time to get over it, for I had been two months on the road with cattle since I wrote that letter. She was dressed in deep mourning, and knew me at once, and we commenced to talk over matters. I knew, of course, that her affairs would not be so comfortable for her after the loss of her brother. Sort of unprotected like. But she had many good friends in Sydney, and I knew that they thought a lot of her. She had a small legacy of her own, just enough to live on. I had brought all Tom's money that was owing to him with me, having got it from our employers, and I handed it over to Miss Imrie then and there.

"'And do you think my poor brother, Tom, shot himself?' said she. I told her 'yes,' but that it might have been by accident (I did not think so myself). What could I say? But if he had, I couldn't tell the reason, any more than the man in the moon.

"So ran my thoughts. I knew well enough that Tom meant to lake the man so as to hand him over to justice, fight or no fight. He was a most determined chap. But he would never have shot him unless the other had been so desperate as to fire at him first. And then perhaps he might have had to do so to save his own life. But the other shot, the one which killed him—a shot from his own weapon apparently—*that* was inexplicable. Miss Imrie broke in upon me at this point in my reflections.

"'Will you describe the man who was supposed to be shot by my brother, Mr McIlwaine?' she asked.

"I nodded, and described him exactly. She got paler and paler as I went on, but when I described what was undoubtedly a birthmark, which I had seen on his chest, and which bore an exact similarity to a fallen autumn leaf, she slid off her seat and fainted!

"I rang the bell at once, and the housemaid came, and between us we brought her back to consciousness. The girl, of course, had heard of Tom Imrie's sudden death, though her mistress would naturally enough conceal the real facts. She (the housemaid) would probably think that we had been talking over the matter, and that that had been the cause of her mistress' indisposition. She knew me, too, as I had been there on one occasion to tea during Tom's lifetime. I took my hat and my departure, feeling that I could be of very little use, but I gave the girl a tip as I left, requesting her to give Miss Imrie a message, saying that I would call again if she wished, on hearing from her that she felt sufficiently well to receive me. I also asked the maid to express to Miss Imrie my very great sympathy for her in her sorrow, which I shared also.

"I went to my hotel, and two days afterwards received a letter from Miss Imrie telling me the most awful thing you can think of. I remember the words well enough. They burnt themselves into my brain!

* * * * * * *

"That man you described was my other brother! We hadn't heard of him for years. Poor Tom! Now I can see the reason for his own rash act. Please don't call again. I can't bear it. And may I ask you, on your honour as a gentleman, never to mention this subject to a living soul, for my sake, and for the sake of those who are gone?"

"Of course, I complied with her wishes, but it was as equally plain to me now as it had been to Tom's sister after the dread revelation of the fatal birthmark. The man's shirt was open at the breast when we found the two bodies, and I saw the mark then and afterwards.

"Strange to say, the refrain of an old drinking song came into my head the moment I saw that fallen leaf mark, and there it droned away in my head, pathetically, in the presence of the dead:

> Fades as the leaves do fade,
> Fades as the leaves do fade,
> Fades as the leaves do fade,
> And dies in October.

"But the result had not been brought on by the 'small beer,' the prelude to this particular part of the chorus. It was strong liquor, and much of it, which had been the prominent cause of the whole thing. And that tune that droned in my head, the man himself, 'Flash Jack,' had played on the concertina in the hotel verandah, the others joining in the chorus, on the previous interlude to the ghastly tragedy.

"And there he lay himself, and another, both cut off like the leaf, and—Alas, poor Tom!

"Tom must have seen this mark in a far worse and more awful light than ever I did. His own brother! He must have opened his shirt to feel if the heart beat, after the first deadly shot in self-defence and in the heat of passion.

"He probably would know nothing at first. His brother would be altered with a long beard on. They had been parted for long. He had, at the time he started after him from the hotel, no knowledge of his whereabouts, or even existence. What 'Flash

Jack's' antecedents may have been, of course, I do not know, but it may be taken for granted that no idea of fratricide had ever entered Tom's head. The man's altered looks, after a long lapse of years, his unrecognised appearance, with long hair and bush clothes, his face twitching with evil passions, the wish to shoot Tom probably working in his mind. So the shots had been exchanged, Tom's with sudden and deadly effect. Then can you fancy the awful reaction, the terrible conviction, and the dread confirmation of the appalling horror of the unwitting deed? Then the sudden despair and anguish, amounting to a passion, a fury, a morbid madness, and culminating at the last in a quick self-annihilation? God knows what he thought! I knew the poor fellow's character pretty well—good ideas, kind heart, but stubborn and determined, moved too much by sudden impulse. A man who, once having decided his course, would carry it out unflinchingly, never thinking of the consequences. And he took his own life, after all! I thought he would have lasted for many happy and prosperous years.

"I left Sydney and started up country, as I had another cattle-droving job from O'Hooligan's on the Tarcoo. I should have a chance of seeing to poor Tom's grave, and, strange to say, it had been arranged for me to take delivery of O'Hooligan's cattle at Bylo, the very place where the whole unfortunate affair had happened.

"This new duty was much more satisfactory in detail, to my mind. Four hundred prime fat cattle for the Adelaide market. It paid better, but took a long time on the road. But there is not the anxiety, if the season is good, that one experiences with 'stores'. I had two of my best men with me, and would have to purchase an American waggon and a pair of horses.

"The three of us made Belala, on the Gunyahgo, and we were lucky enough to complete our purchase of waggon and horses there.

"I found, on arrival, a letter awaiting me from Harper of Fassifern, asking me as a favour to travel fifty merino rams, very valuable animals out of the Belala stud flock, from thence to his place, Fassifern, on the head waters of the Tarcoo, the next station but one from O'Hooligan's. Luckily, I had plenty of time to spare. It had been a dry season, but all my horses were in good order.

"One of the Fassifern black boys had ridden in with the letter. His name was 'Boro'. I sent the wagon with my head cattleman down the Gunyahgo and across from Brandyville to Bylo, to await O'Hooligan's draft. I had a clear fortnight, and I didn't want to disoblige Harper, as he had drafts of cattle in prospect from Fassifern, and he always gave me a job of droving when he could.

"So I accepted the rams willingly enough, the more especially as, after having delivered them safely at Fassifern, I could go down the Tarcoo to Bylo, see O'Hooligan on the way for final instructions, take over the cattle, and make a fair start from Bylo. Also there was the welcome prospect of putting a few more pounds into my pocket."

"Always there or thereabouts when 'dibs' are served out!" muttered Jemmy from his corner.

"Ma certie, ye heathen, a thocht ye were deid," snapped McIlwaine *en parenthèse*, and went on.

"I took the Fassifern black boy, 'Boro,' with me of course. He might just as well work for his 'tucker' instead of crawling back, and stopping a night or two at the blacks' camp. That was the worst bit of work I did on the trip.

"I thought he might be useful tracking in case of mishap, as the rams were worth over £1000. Well, this black boy, 'Boro,' I did not cotton to. He was all a 'waddygalo,' but a 'waddygalo' of the worst tribe—Eepai. You can pick out 'Combo,' 'Eepai,' 'Murral,' and 'Cubbai'. They have the same types of face, that is to say, a 'Combo' resembles a 'Combo,' a 'Murrai' a 'Murrai,' and so on; but a 'Combo' is the best of all for physique and good intentions. If an 'Eepai' learns anything it is roguery or devildom.

"But with regard to this 'Eepai'—'Boro'—I reckoned I would smarten him up a bit before I had done with him.

"He needed it. One boot, one spur, about a yard of torn blanket for his 'swag,' no shirt, a fearful and wonderful hat with no top to it.

"You know the way some of these 'myalls' ride. So did 'Boro'; one big toe on one side of the stirrup iron—the inside—next toe on the other, and the foot and all the other toes outside; the one boot thrust well home into the opposite iron. Doesn't look pretty. But then old Harper never did have any ideas about black fellows, never kept them neat and tidy, never had them properly clothed. If one doesn't keep some sort of hold on these 'nigs', and train them properly, they never will be fit to be seen. I'm particular about it, but the untidiness is in them, and therefore, if you don't keep a good look out on a trained 'nig', he will disgrace your teaching if he gets a chance. Why, one of my own boys, 'Tommy,' a Tarcoo black, about fifteen, broke out on one occasion—lapsed into savagery, as I should term it. I got him from his mother. She was old Biddy from the station camp. It was my first trip with him and he's all right now.

"I was in at Brandyville. Tommy was in charge of my horses. Used to run them up to the town stockyard every morning. I had him nice and neat, riding-breeches and boots, cabbage-tree hat, spurs regular, not one-sided, and a very nice little darkie he looked. Hair properly dressed by the barber, too. He got his meals at the hotel and a small glass of ale with his dinner. He preferred to sleep, however, the first night, at the blacks' camp without my leave.

"Next morning up he comes at breakfast time. 'Horses all right, Tommy?' 'Yowi' (yes). He had someone else's hat and shirt on—nothing else. Positively indecent. Dirty too. Hair anyway. Face all over wood-ash.

"'Where are your breeches, Tommy?' 'Mine been break him trous belongin' to mine!' Quite a new state of things. The little brute was entirely demoralised. Never had any morals until I took the trouble to instil them. This wouldn't do. Was I to go about the country with a nigger in this untidy state? Certainly not. 'Whose hat and shirt have you got on now, Tommy?'

'Nother pfeller, black pfeller, Charlie, cousin belongin' to mine.'
'Where are your *own* clothes?' 'Mine been give 'em alonga 'nother pfeller, black pfeller!'

"Tableau! '*Give* 'em away.' The suit had cost me about three guineas, and the cabbage-tree hat another ten-and-sixpence, to say nothing of the spurs and boots. But you know their horribly irresponsible style, and how it riles one.

"I took him straight down to the blacks' camp by the car, and demanded instant reparation, under a threat to the old chief that, unless he complied with my wishes immediately, I should 'yabber alonga policeman'. That 'fetched' him!

"He collared half a dozen youngsters, and brought them up, yelling fit to wake the dead. One had had Tommy's hat, another his boots, and another his spurs, at one time or another, but had halved or given away the articles to others, every one of the kids wishing to wear something belonging to my black boy.

"So these young 'nigs' were sent to collar the others, and a furious hullabaloo then took place, mixed, with chivies round the gunyahs, over and through the fires, and in and out of the creek; and it wasn't until we had collared every kid in camp, with the assistance of old Jimmy and his harem, that we found the missing articles—a boot on one, a spur on another, and so on. I don't know whether they thought I should be willing to take Tommy out of the town in a state of nudity or not, or whether I should just get him some more outfits, until I had clothed the lot of them, but my determined move euchred them all together. So I made Master Tommy put on his duds one by one, 'til he arrived at hat and boots, with a circle of worshippers round him, telling the frightened youngsters that if I caught them again dividing my black boy's raiment amongst them I should have them all hung by the policeman on the big windmill at the town stockyard, concluding:

'Then you baal jump up white fellow, hang alonga sky, wokkaratchies (crows) eat 'em up.'

"You never saw such a scare. And old Jimmy, the chief, quite believed it, and yabbered and howled like blazes to all the 'gins' within a quarter of a mile. Then they began to bring in the rest of the missing articles, but two little wretches had torn Tommy's good Crimean shirt in half to make, as they explained after much browbeating and threatening, 'two little pfeller blankit'. And one of the junior members of Jimmy's seraglio appeared with the collar worn as a necklet. That collar was her sole apparel. However, things simmered down after a bit, and I gave old Jimmy half a stick of Barrett's twist, and bought Tommy another shirt. I made him sleep in an outhouse near the stable in the back-yard after this, but one morning early I caught two other urchins 'coiled' with him, the whole lot under his blanket. They were also 'cousins,' and had arranged to work with him in relation to the horses, hoping, I have no doubt, to get stray bits from the breakfast that my lord did not want himself.

"But it ended in these two others having a separate 'mess,' which I paid for. The hot tea with their breakfasts must have comforted their small 'tums,' and I never like to put obstacles in the way of praiseworthy energy. So Tommy slept warmer at night, and I was the richer by two first-class trackers.

"Eventually I took these boys with me, and they turned out well, and were very useful. And my boy, Tommy, never dared to speculate after this with his clothes. Everything depends upon how you bring them up.

"But, as I was saying before my digression, this boy, 'Boro,' of Harper's, was to come with us, and I did not like the look of him one little bit. He was a holy terror of uncleanness and carelessness.

"We left the Gunyaligo with the rams, and I meant to cross the dividing range with them, straight to Fassifern, steering about north-north-east by the sun.

"Mick Brady was my white man, a regular old stodger with cattle, slow, but sure and steady, well up to every wrinkle on the roads.

"He had been with me for years. We made a creek the first night, and I camped the rams successfully by a big 'waterhole'. Mick had his old one-eyed cattle dog, 'Bally,' with him, and I had 'Joker,' who had taken to me wonderfully. We had about fifty miles to make from this water-hole to Fassifern, and a long stage next day of fifteen miles. Next day proved to be very hot, and we made slow progress. At noon we let the sheep 'camp' as usual. I made sure of finding good water over the range at a place I knew of, or I never should have taken this route, but it was a straight track of my own from Belala to Fassifern.

"I let the rams have a good rest and feed, intending to take them on to the water during the night if necessary.

"'Boro' had our water on the packhorse, and I tell you both Mick and I needed a drink badly at mid-day. We had four big waterbags. The horses felt the heat too, and they just got a 'washout'—a mouthful apiece. We started on again at about four o'clock in the afternoon, ten miles to go to water. We kept on 'til dark and camped again four miles farther on. It was the middle of summer, and a horrible sort of haze had set in which would obscure the moon. There would not be much of that luminary in any case, only about a third of the night, but I had calculated on it. As we rounded the rams on to a nice dry 'rise' to 'camp' for the night, I missed 'Boro'.

"Just before we had rounded up we had passed a low spur of the range we had to cross. I had seen him there last, but what with being absorbed with my reflections about poor Tom Imrie's case, and upon my own business, I had given little thought to him. Mick, of course, had been actively employed in heading the sheep in the right direction, and had had his eyes on the flock.

"Well, we lit a fire and sat there waiting for the young brute to come up, so that we could get enough water for our tea to boil the 'billy'. Not a sign of him an hour after, and I began to get uneasy.

"From thinking he had been delayed in cutting a 'possum' out, a conviction was formed that he must have met with an accident. Old 'Chockaroo,' the packhorse, was a demon to kick if anything went wrong with the 'swag' on his back, and, for all I knew, he might have kicked 'Boro's' head off also. So I told my ideas to Mick, got my horse, which was hobbled, and started to where I had last seen him. Not a sign of him! And the sky got so cloudy, that it very soon got too dark to do anything. So I found my way back to camp. Here we were, in a pretty pickle, no water, and both of us very thirsty.

"Nothing could be done 'til daylight. The sky was now completely overcast, with a sort of cottony-woolly haze, which looked as if it meant another blazing hot day on the morrow.

"I resolved to hang it out. About six miles more would do it.

"So we two got a small round pebble apiece, rolling them round in our mouths to increase the flow of saliva. And all that blessed night we didn't get a show to move, and it would have been just madness to attempt a start, for you couldn't see the sheep fifteen yards off, and as to where your horse would go to it would be impossible to judge. My eye, it was a weary watch.

"To make matters worse, Mick's horse smashed his hobbles, and, of course, made back straight to the last water. I just managed to catch mine, as I heard the row.

"Mick's horse must have come a cropper by getting his hobbles across the stump of an old burnt mulga tree. I shouldn't have caught 'Black Jack' if I hadn't run full butt into him, and he would have been sure to have followed Mick's horse. It was black dark 'til the moon rose, but that made very little difference.

"I took the precaution to put a halter on 'Black Jack' and tie him to a tree, hobbles and all. I couldn't afford to lose him. However, I got him a big heap of mulga boughs, and made him as comfortable as circumstances would allow, but the poor old chap wanted a drink as much as I did, and didn't bother about eating.

"Morning broke dull and cloudy. I had had plenty of time to think over my plans, and determined not to be beat. I would try and find 'Boro' and the water-bags, and then come back on my tracks and join Mick. I might find 'Boro' and I mightn't. The horses, if loose, would be sure to make back to the last water. If I had had anything to carry water in, I would have gone on to the other side of the range, and brought some water to Mick, but all our belongings were on the packhorse.

"The young blackguard had evidently bolted. He had probably ridden well clear, and then jumped off and let the 'yarramen' go. I knew he daren't turn up at either Belala or Fassifern on horseback without us. Well, I came to the place where Mick's track and mine of yesterday were going to camp. A little farther on I got the two others. 'Boro's' horses, ridden, I could see that. If he had been off their backs they would have been apart more than the half length of the head-stall rope. Of course I had given instructions to Mick to keep steadily on; he knew the way 'Boro's' horses' tracks swerved off our direction of yesterday, then towards the range, and then up and over the first hill. He was probably making towards some blacks' camp. When he knew the country he would let them go—having dismounted— and probably by this time they would be back at Belala. Well, if they were, they would be sent on from the station, and some one with them to see what was the matter with us.

"I paused to think. Should I go back to Mick and take the chance of getting to the water with the sheep, and let the horses be?

"'Boro' had gone, also three horses, and all our waterbags. No doubt of that. I was awfully thirsty, but I could not now leave Mick and the rams. I turned and rode slowly back. My thirst was increasing, and my mouth was dry and harsh. Just as I passed a large cotton bush, a minute later, one of those confounded blue-grey Tarcoo snakes made a dash at my horse's legs. You know well enough what those deadly brutes mean—death in about twenty minutes for a man. 'Black Jack' gave a plunge, and fell clean over, throwing me just clear. He was so startled that he fell for the first time in all his life, I believe. The next moment he was up, off and away, as if the devil had kicked him.

"In the scrimmage and flurry, for we were all floundering about in a lump, I felt a sharp puncture on my wrist. I was certain I had been bitten. I examined it carefully. Sure enough, two punctures, with a small drop of blood in each. The death mark! I got my knife, cut the place out pretty deep, sucked it furiously, and tied a ligature just above the wound (the direction nearest to the heart), with a silk cracker I happened to have in my pocket. Oh, the agonies of mind I felt! Death staring me in the face! But I reflected that I had taken all reasonable precautions, *and* at once. The flow of the blood and the sucking *might* have removed the deadly virus. So I staggered on, half-dead with thirst, bruised, sore and very sick and nervous. 'Black Jack' had sprung into a crab hole in his fright and gone clean over nearly on top of me, right on to the rough stony ground. I had made sure that I saw the snake dash at me afterwards, and that I had put my hand on it!

"I began to feel like a man in a dream, and staggered on and on, not knowing in the least what I was going to do, or where I was going.

"So," I thought, "it has come to this at last. Cut off in my prime by a beastly accident; bitten by a snake, and if the poison has taken hold of my blood, I shan't have very long to live. It's destiny, I suppose—my fate! This is the end planned by a higher Power from the very first moment that I was born! I am not the first or the only one in this world who has had to suffer in the same way, and they had to meet their fate, and must have felt very much as I do now. Death, the end of all things! I wonder what poor Tom felt before he pulled the trigger of his revolver? Hundreds of men and women, thousands of them, perish every year by awful accidents—drowning, burning and shipwreck, plague, pestilence and famine.

"Some are annihilated in a moment. Others die fearful deaths. Well, life has been very pleasant to me, in spite of its many ups and downs, and I must meet death like a man.

"I had better write a few lines describing how I came to my end. I began to hastily jot down the details in my pocketbook, and whether it was with the worry at my repeated bad luck, the unavoidable accident, or terror at the approach of grim, unflinching, unalterable Death, I half lost my senses. I was vaguely conscious of staggering on, choking with thirst, and fighting with something or some one, I could not tell what. I had a sort of idea that my name was Robert McIlwaine, and I had to do something, but that it would be no use because I was dead. Then I must completely have lost consciousness, for I remember nothing until I came to myself lying at full length in a thick scrub. I vaguely wondered what it was all about. What was I there for? How did I come there? Who was I? Then I fainted again. Then—but how long a time after I have no idea—a thought came upon me that I was dreadfully oppressed with thirst. Then I became conscious that there was a weight on my chest, and that 'Joker' was licking my face. I gradually came round, and, after a period during which my mind refused to work at all clearly, I began to understand that it was really 'Joker' who was by me. I must have been asleep somewhere. No, I was dead and 'Joker' was a ghost. He must have died too, then, to be with me? Was this heaven, this scrub? No, I was dead, I had had a sharp fall with a horse. I had been bitten by a snake. What was 'Joker' here for? He ought to be with Mick and the rams. He must be a ghost. I feebly felt him. No, it was 'Joker' right enough. I found myself sitting up somehow, and I realised that it was moonlight.

"'Joker' was whining. I managed, I never knew how, to stagger to my feet, and grasp a sapling to keep myself from falling down again. Oh, this dreadful thirst! I had suffered from it once before, when I had started on a very hot day and ridden thirty miles away from the river to where I expected to find water, but it had dried up. That was thirst, but I got relief then, for I found the lid of an old tin 'billy' which some idiot had pricked full of holes, but I plugged these with bits of green polygonum and then milked my mare 'Flirt' for she had a foal at home. But I shan't get relief from this! No water anywhere. This thirst! I can't speak, I can't even make a noise! I shall go mad! *Who* am I? *Where* am I? Bitten by a snake and dying, and no water. Oh, God! What can I do? I can hardly walk! Two steps and a frantic clutch at another sapling. Dying, oh, my God! I made a feeble step or two forward, poor old 'Joker' whining with delight. I got a firm hold on the next sapling and rested panting. As I looked up again, as I live and am here to tell you all, I saw a little open glade, with the moon bright on it, and Tom Imrie sitting on his roan horse, as I often remember him doing, half-turned round in his saddle towards me. He pointed with a gesture of authority right across me. I looked steadfastly at him. He was only vapour, so was his horse. I could see the trees through both of them. But his gesture was very clear, commanding yet kind, and his index finger pointed straight in one direction.

"I remember trying to say weakly, 'Hallo, Tom, old chap,' but no sound came, and I thought: 'Yes, I'm dead. That's Tom. We are together again. This is the other world!' But Joker jumped upon me, almost pushing me down. Tom was still there, he and his horse. I saw what he meant. I was to go where he pointed. *Must* go, to save my life. *Must* go! I made a line slowly in the direction he indicated, and before I had gone six yards I saw a pool of water—a good clay pan!

"I managed to reach it, fall flat down, and drink a little. And I have a dim consciousness of shouting and singing, and then a long period of rest.

"When I came to myself again it was daylight, warm and sunny. And there was 'Joker' with a bandicoot he had caught. My senses were a little better. Where had Tom gone to? I remembered. Tom showed me the water. Came out of his grave to do it!

"Poor old Tom and 'Joker'! Good dog, 'Joker'. I felt ever such a little stronger. Oh, the snake! What time is it? Time must have passed! Moonlight and sunlight. I was too weak to rejoice; I couldn't take it in yet. I was close to the water; I drank some more, then lit a fire, cooked the bandicoot on the hot embers, and ate it ravenously, slaking my thirst with the life-saving water. I was coming round, but the thought of the snake struck through me like white-hot iron every now and then. I have, personally, a nervous horror of snakes. Some fellows don't care a button for them, and will catch them by the neck and handle them, but to me they are a terror. Well, I wasn't dead after all. And slowly my thoughts came back, and I began to want to go back and find Mick. 'Joker' never faltered. I was in a gully, a good bit off the track, or tracks, we had made. I hadn't the slightest idea of my whereabouts, but he took me in a straight line to more water. Caught a 'paddy melon' and we cooked that. I came up with Mick two days afterwards, a little dazed still. He had got the rams to water all right after a very severe and thirsty trip, but had been terribly uneasy about me. So he sent 'Joker' off to find me.

"You can't beat a rough cattle dog with one blue eye and one brown one. Best breed of the lot. And so you see, boys, why I don't like to make a mock at ghosts. Poor Tom Imrie! I saw him as plain as I see you, ghost or no ghost. I am quite open to argument that I was off my head for a bit. I don't deny it. I know I was, but where did the idea come from—the positive conviction that I saw Tom Imrie at a critical point in my lifetime when I should have gone mad and died of thirst unless I *had* seen him? Was not the idea providential in itself, if I had not been guided? Therefore I believe in this sight of Tom Imrie's ghost as the one means of preserving me, and I hold it sacred. But whether I really saw him or my poor excited over-wrought brain brought the fancy that I did, I cannot tell you. I simply narrate the impression and belief left. And 'Joker' was a bit of a ghost too at first. He turned out real. And the vision showed me the water. We finished our journey with the rams all right. I hunted all over the Fassifern Camp for 'Boro,' but never saw him again.

"The horses were all found and sent over, water-bags and all. We went down the Tarcoo afterwards, arranged matters with O'Hooligan, and made a most successful trip to Adelaide with the fat cattle, topping the market.

"Then I went to Sydney, and found that Miss Imrie had gone to England, but I kept true to my trust and never said a word that would prejudice my old friend Tom's case."

"No, I suppose not," said Jemmy, "you've simply been letting the cat out of the bag the whole bally time!"

"What? You think I have given him away all through, do you? Well, none of you fellows know Tom Imrie or his sister either, for they don't exist. I never told you the real names, and the facts of the case are completely forgotten. It happened too long ago to come to light, as only the actors in it can say anything, and there's not one of them near the district now. What do you say to a game of whist?"

HULK NO. 49

by J. A. Barry

The Queenslander, December 1893

John Arthur Barry (1850-1911) was born in Tor-quay and was apprenticed to the Orient Steam Naviga-tion Co. at the age of thirteen. He found himself in Australia during the gold rush and joined the Palmer diggings in North Queensland in about 1870. Over the next few years he was engaged on various outback occupations such as droving and boundary riding. In 1879 he accepted a position as overseer and station-manager, probably at a property near Scone in New South Wales. In 1893 he visited England and there published his first collection of short stories, *Steve Brown's Bunyip*, for which Rudyard Kipling provided some introductory verses. He soon returned to Sydney and continued writing popular tales of sea adventure. He remained a bachelor, and died of chronic myocar-ditis at his home at North Sydney on 23 September 1911, aged sixty-one.

There was a big crowd of officers and men "looking for a ship" one damp, foggy morning at the old Tower Hill office in London. A barque for the Cape, two or three steamers, and a four-master for Calcutta filled up before I could get a show at all. At last "A second mate and eight ABs for the West Indies!"

was sung out. Lots of seamen still hung about, but not a man except myself stirred.

"Now then!" shouted the doorkeeper again, "here y'are! Who's for the Cumberland—three pound a month, and a six months trip, all in the warm weather?"

"Not me," replied a big, grey-bearded, mahogany-faced seaman, drawing back. "I likes a light in my fok'sle, I does. An' I ain't taken' any stock in stinkin' ghosts wot can't leave a poor shellback alone in his watch below!"

This much I heard as, passing in, I found myself in the presence of the captain of the Cumberland and the shipping-master.

"What's the matter with the men, Mr Jackson?" the former was saying. "They simply rushed the other vessels, and now they won't look at mine."

"Oh," replied the other, "I expect some of them have got hold of the old story about the barque. I remember once or twice, years ago, the same thing happening. I should have thought, though, that by now the thing had died out. Probably one of the men outside has sailed in her and told his mates the yarn. It's said that to keep a lamp alight in her fok'sle's an impossibility— that—or—in fact, a ghost comes and blows it out." And old Jackson grinned and looked rather sheepishly at us.

"What rubbish!" exclaimed the captain—a pleasant-faced man of about 30—laughing heartily. "And I'm to lose my ship because a pack of idiots have got some old woman's story into their thick heads! Why, the Cumberland's been laid up for years, and has, they tell me, only just come out of dock after a good overhauling, as sweet and fresh and clean as a new pin."

"That's so," replied Jackson; "and the very reason she lay idle for so long is the one that stops the men signing to her now. Before your present firm bought her and altered her name she was known as the Carlisle, and was in the same trade as she's going to run in at present."

"The deuce!" exclaimed the skipper. "I've heard of her. But, Mr Jackson, if the devil himself comes and blows the fok'sle lamp out every night, I'm going to sail her if I can get a crew.

And, at any rate (turning to me), here's one to start with."

My business was soon finished; only, finding that I held a master's certificate, Captain Habden offered me the position of chief in place of second mate, the man who was to fill the former billet having unexpectedly resigned at the last minute through his wife's illness. I liked this well, and signed without a question. Indeed, neither for Jack nor his masters were these the days for hesitation. Besides, I took to the frank, good-humoured face of my new skipper, seeing no sign therein of what fate had in store for him.

"Would you mind having a work with the men, Mr Forbes?" he asked me presently, "and trying to reason with them a bit. Fancy an old ghost story like that getting hold of Jack at this time o' day to the extent of making him refuse a good trip and a comfortable ship when both are such scarce matters." So out I went into the dirty waiting room, foul with tobacco, and thick with the rank smoke of the weed.

"Now, my lads," I commenced, without any preamble, and knowing my marks, "what's all this nonsense? Because some fools, a dozen years ago, hadn't enough sense to keep a lamp alight, are you going to lose money, and let the old woman and the kids go hungry? Come now, I've signed as mate of the Cumberland; aren't there ten bullies, not afraid of their own shadows, that'll keep me company. I'll help you to trim your lamp, if you want help. I came in through the hawse-pipes, not through the cabin door, and haven't forgotten how to cut a wick yet, as well as turn in a deadeye, if need be."

At this there was a laugh; and I think if it had not been for the big fellow I have mentioned before I would have got my men at once, for I saw several pocket their pipes and shake themselves, preparatory to making a move. But the grey-headed sailor, stepping forward, and chewing viciously on his quid, said, quietly enough, "I'm one o' them fools, mister, as you're speakin' on. I sailed in the old tub ten years ago, when Hellfire Jack Brown was skipper on her. There was a curse put on her them days—not the trip I was aboard. P'raps it's off now. Any way, I ain't goin' to make one to find out. Mind ye, I'm not sayin' anythin' agen the barque, mates. Mebbe her'd be better to han'le if she had double tawps'is 'stead o' they big whole uns. But she's tight an' dry, or was in them days, an' no doubt she's right enough still. It was the bloomin' ghost as knocked us—none o' yer half an half happaritions, but a gennywise forty-power stinkin' speciment. He came inter the eyes of her, in the shape of a blasted fog bank, and doused the glim every time we lit it. An' cold—lor! you could 'ear our teeth a-rattlin'. An' stinkin' worser'n tanyard and bilge water mixed! Well, o' course we clears like redshanks, an' Hellfire trying to bounce us as we'd seen nothin'! But it warn't good enough. Then the old man hisself, down he goes. An' when he comes up agen he looks more'n sick, altho' he never lets on a word. Nor he didn't cuss an' haze us, as he used to do, any more. An' he doesn't hobjeck when we rigs a fores'l over the after hatch and camps there durin' the rest of the passidge. We wants our discharges at Kingston; he wouldn't give 'em to us. So we takes chokee instead, an' glad to git it. An' the ship goes round to Savannah la Mar; there the new crew clears; and there, never havin' got over the chill he catched in the fok'sle, Hellfire dies. It was four months afore a crew could be got to take the barque home; an' when she came to the dock they was camped same as we'd been—on the after hatch. Wages out o' the port o' London is three pun' a month. An' if 'twere thirty pun, mates, Joe Harris (that's me) 'd think twice afore he shipped on that there Cumberland, helias Carlisle. Nor—"

"Come, come, my lad," I broke in impatiently, "belay all that. Your slack jaw's as long as the main-t'gallant halliards. One would ha' thought you'd had time to outgrow your fright since all that happened. I don't want any croakers in my watch. But I dare say some of these other hearties 'll come and help me keep the barque's fok'sle lamp alight. Why, hang me if it wouldn't make a man believe he's put back a hundred years to hear the way you talk! Now, then, you tarpaulins, I'll give you five minutes to come along and sign. I don't hanker after Dagoes or Lascars or Dutchmen; but the Cumberland's got to have her crowd; and, you know, I can get her one in five minutes over at Green's Home." And, so saying, I went into the next room.

"You talked to 'em like a father, sir," remarked the old shipping-master approvingly. "We've heard it all through the side window here. If that kind of jaw don't fetch 'em, nothing will. And here they come!"

Sure enough, a dozen or so of my late audience came shuffling in, grinning and nudging each other and cracking dim jokes in husky undertones. They were, too, I was glad to see, all British. For, inveterate growler as he is, and insubordinate at times, and apt to give more trouble all round than the subservient "Dutchman," or the sneaking Dago, I confess to a strong preference for the British sailor-man, with all his faults. Blood's thicker than water, for one thing; and you know that when you've got a crowd of English speakers you've got something that'll stick to you and to your ship through thick and thin, and not crawl below out of the hurly-burly, or holystone the decks with their knees and call upon Saint Antonio to do their work for 'em.

We got all we wanted out of the mob, including one to act as second mate and boatswain. And, business over, old Jackson came and had some lunch with us. During the course of the meal we got him to tell us what he knew regarding the legend of the lamp, which, after all, didn't amount to very much.

"One trip," said he, "the Carlisle had a real bad crowd. But amongst them was a half-witted sort of chap that old Brown had picked up to act as 'Jimmy Ducks' and slush about generally just for his tucker. Well, one night he neglected to trim the fok'sle lamp, and a couple or perhaps more of the brutes—regular packet-rats they were—kicked and pounded him, so that he presently died. They got scared then; and, giving out that he was ill, they kept the body for three or four days in one of the bunks. Then they hove it overboard, and swore the poor wretch had committed suicide. Well, that very night the lamp went out. Nor, despite all attempts—and, between ourselves, I don't think they made many—could ever a lamp be got to burn in that fok'sle again. I remember one of the crew telling me that a single experience of the cold and stench combined when the apparition appeared was quite enough for any average man. Indeed, crowd after crowd either ran away or went to gaol sooner than sail in her; and what with delays and court work, the vessel used to eat her freights. So they laid her up for sale. But, until your owners bought her, no one would look at such a losing concern as a haunted ship. Why, it's over five years now since she first took up her quarters in 'Rotten-row.'"

"Well," said Captain Hebden as we rose from table to go aboard the barque, "surely the curse is run out by this time, and the spectre laid. I suppose, Jackson, you never put any faith in such a cock and bull story, anyhow?"

But the ancient mariner scratched his baldpate doubtfully as he replied.

"Well, I don't know, captain. I've seen some curious things at sea in my time. However, you'll be able to give me your opinion on the matter when we meet again. And I hope you won't come up the river, as I've seen the barque do afore now, with a spare main'sl rigged across a lower stu'nsl-boom over the after-hatch to serve instead of a fok'sle."

"Not much danger!" laughed Captain Hebden gaily. "If I can't follow my profession without being molested by nasty, freezing, evil-smelling ghosts—why, I may as well give it up. No, Jackson, I've got too many barnacles on my hide to be scared by anything in that line."

"So old Hellfire thought," retorted the other with a boding shake of the head; "but they say it killed him."

But the captain only laughed again, and, bidding the shipping-master goodbye, we made for the docks. We found the Cumberland (the first fight of her for both of us) a sound, wholesome looking barque, strongly built after the fashion of twenty years back; square in the stern, and bluff in the bows; no double raids, donkey engines, patent capstans, or other modern fallals about her; but still a homely, comfortable seeming kind of creature of a ship, such as builders don't turn out of hand in those days of iron, steam, and steel. The stevedores were stowing the last of the cargo in the square of the hatchways. The riggers had the sails bent and furled, gear rove, stays and back stays well set up, and everything aloft ataunto; and with her shining white lower masts, brightly scraped upper spars towering to gilt-trucked royal poles, and the big spread of her square yards she looked, to the eye, coming down, took in her great beam, massive bulwarks, and shining brass work, a notable contrast to the sharp-nosed, gim-crack iron clippers that surrounded her. A tub the moderns might sneeringly call her; but, very certainly, she was the sort of tub whose decks you might walk in slippers whilst their lee-scuppers were breast high with green seas. On her main deck she carried an enormous longboat, fit child of such a buxom mother, and intended to cruise around the islands amongst the planters for rum, molasses, and sugar with which to return to the anchored barque, and fill up the capacious maternal interior. Technically, this boat was known as a "drogher." But it took a lot of room; and, in addition, there was a host of spare spars, big water-casks, etc., that gave the decks somewhat of a lumbered-up appearance.

We were to haul out at high water that night; and, even now, the men were straggling down, more or less sober, and dumping their round-bottomed bags and their chests into the dark hatchway that led to their quarters below.

I was kept too busy for a time to think of anything outside my work; but, after we brought up at the Nore with a westerly wind in our teeth, and I went aft to turn in for an hour or two, I laughed to myself when, glancing down the fok'sle scuttle, my eye caught the gleam of a brightly burning lamp, and my ear the dull, peaceful, rumbling notes of men's voices. Before daybreak the wind came round with plenty of westing in it, and, calling all hands, we got up our anchor, made sail, and wallowed away down channel with a wake like a paddle-steamer; steady as a pyramid, dry as a baker's oven, and with half-a-gale of wind roaring and hooting in the bellies of our topsails.

"Fok'sle lamp burn all right last night, Mr Forbes, d'ye

know?" asked the skipper at breakfast with a twinkle in his eye.

"Yes, sir," I replied.

"At least, I've heard no complaint, so far."

"Ah," said he, laughing, "I thought that long spell in the docks would have taken all the energy out of the best and staunchest ghost going."

And until we got clear of soundings it really seemed as if the captain was right; for his sake I only wish it had been so. But then the trouble began in earnest; and if I hadn't so many available witnesses to back me up I don't know that I'd care about putting what happened us into cold print. We had just cleared the Channel. It was four bells (six o'clock p.m.) in the second dog watch, a fine, bright cold evening, with a jump of a head sea on, and the Lizard light barely visible on the port quarter. As I stumped the poop to and fro from binnacle to break—having just relieved the second mate to let him get his supper—happening to glance for'ard, I saw, one after the other, the watch below come bolting up through their scuttle as if propelled from a catapult. It was not yet so dark but that I could distinguish the passionate gestures with which they told something to the little group of the port watch, that at once surrounded them, before, racing aft, they bundled up the poop ladder, at the head of which I met them. In each of the five faces fear and bewilderment strove for the mastery, and all five bodies shivered and trembled as with ague.

"If you please, sir," at once began an elderly man named Jones, his brown face turned to a nasty slate colour, and his words jostling each other as they came out, "we can't stop down there," jerking for'ard with outstretched thumb. "We was just havin' our supper when a stinkin', freezin' THING comes an' douses our lamp. We all seen It, so there's no error. An' we all felt It—leastways the cold an' the stench of It. Poof! It's in my mouth yet!" And he spat over the side, imitated scrupulously by his mates. "No, sir," he went on, raising his voice as he saw me grinning at him, "we ain't no fools, an' we knows our work as sailor-men; but we ain't a-goin' to stand no such larks as them.

Harris was right arter all. The ship's harnted; an' you can't expec', sir, as ornery flesh an' blood 'll put up wi' a bloomin' ghost as comes foggn' an' stinkin', strong as a whole churchyard full o' corpuses, into a man's fok'sle whiles he's a-eatin' of his bit of supper."

The fellow was perfectly civil, and I saw at once that, so bad a scare had they all got, the time had passed for an ordinary tongue-thrashing to have its usual effect.

"Ay, ay, Bill's right," remarked another in the pause that followed. "An' Mr Forbes'll remember his promise to help keep the fok'sle lamp trimmed." This speech was received with a deep growl of approval. It was the starboard watch—good men all, and the last I should have thought to be easily frightened. And I felt puzzled. But clearly it was a time for action, not talk. The captain was napping, and I did not want to bother him about such rubbish; so, calling the second mate, who was smoking an after-supper pipe on the quarter-deck, I gave him charge of the ship while, followed by the men, I went for'ard and down the hatchway. Rather to my surprise, not a soul offered to accompany me.

"Now then," I asked laughingly, as I stood halfway down the ladder, with my head over the coamings, "isn't anybody coming to help me do Jimmy Duck's work?"

None of the second mate's watch made answer. But one of my own men, a little fellow called Daniels, belonging to the Isle of Wight, replied cheerily:

"Ay, ay, sir. I'll come if old Nick hisself's there. Wheer another man's game to go I ain't afeard."

So down we went. It was black as pitch: and getting to the foot of the ladder, I struck a long wax vesta and glanced around. It wasn't a very cheerful place. Along one side ran twelve bunks, six on top, six below. Underneath them were lashed chests; on the opposite bulkhead hung suits of oilskins; on the floor was a wooden tub containing a big lump of salt beef, and another one full of biscuits; from a capsized hook-pot the tea had flowed in a dark stream; close to it lay a square bottle of vinegar, out of which the liquor still ran when each heave of the barque canted it forward; about the chests were scattered plates and pots; disorder everywhere testifying to a very hurried evacuation. All this I noted before my match went out, and while my companion struck another. Taking it from him, I approached the lamp that swung from the ceiling nearly amid ships. It was just the ordinary tin receptacle, full of oil, from which projected a couple of long spouts for the wicks, that one still sees in many "sailers'" forecastles, where it has not been superseded by the kerosene-fed, closed "hurricane." Applying the match to one of the wicks, it "fizzled" and would not light.

"The idiots!" I exclaimed. "The cotton's wet as a soaked swab! They've been too lazy to trim it! Bring the thing on deck, Daniels, and I'll get the steward to fix it properly."

Taking the lamp aft to the pantry, I left my companion sitting on the hatch, and whistling with a fine assumption of devil-may-careness as the rest came round him.

"An' ye saw nothin'—nothin' at all, Dan?" I heard one of them say as I returned and lit the lamp under shelter of the hood that drew over the scuttle.

"Ne'er a thing," replied Dan calmly. "What should us see? Come on, you star bowlines, an' finish yer suppers; the mate an' me 'll purtect ye while yer stows 'em away."

"Garn!" replied one of the taunted watch in a tone of exasperation. "Why, blast me if I'm ever going to get warm again; to say nothin' o' the stink o' rotten corpses as is in my nose yet! Damp wick! Ho!" and the speaker snorted indignantly.

Hanging the lamp on its hook, it burned clearly and with a good bright flame.

"There, now," I remarked complacently, seating myself on a chest and filling my pipe; "what could be better than that? We'll stay awhile to make sure; and then we'll call those babies up there to finish their supper. And—" But, here, glancing at Daniels, I caught him staring open mouthed past me into the darksome corner right for'ard, known as the "eyes." Following his intent gaze, I saw, coming slowly towards us, a sort of thick mist shaped like a human figure with outstretched arms, while the air, hitherto warm and close, grew icy cold with a chill in it that seemed to freeze my very marrow. And as if this were not enough, a horrible stench pervaded the fok'sle—a grisly, putrid stink that brought corrupt and festering corpses into the mind's eye. As the Thing glided past a pricking sensation of horror swept through me; I broke out all over in a cold sweat, my teeth chattered like the rattle of a dynamo; and for a minute I thought I was going to faint. Then, all at once, came darkness and a comparatively clear atmosphere.

For a while, panting, spitting, and shaking with the awful cold, I couldn't speak. Then I called Daniels. Receiving no answer, I struck a light. But I was alone; Daniels had disappeared. Pulling myself together, I struck another match, unhooked the lamp, and slowly went up the ladder on deck, having received the worst scare I ever got in my life, and studying only how not to show it. It was dark enough by this, and I nearly stumbled over a man sitting and groaning, with his back against the fore-hatch.

"It's Daniels, sir," said a voice: "Daniels a-throwin' up ov his soul-bolts, an' not by chalks so jolly cock-a-noopy as he were just awhile agone, when he in-wited of us down to finish our suppers."

Taking no notice of this, I said, as calmly as I could, to the clustered forms around, "That fok'sle of yours, lads, is a bit unhealthy just yet. It's the fumes from the new paint gets working in a man's brains, I expect. However, we'll have the matter cleared up presently. Now lie aft, and get a good nip of grog each."

Very thankful was I for the darkness that enabled me to escape the searching, inquisitive eyes that I could feel boring, as it were, into me. Afloat or ashore, the officer that gives way before his men is done spent—has outlived his usefulness. And, had it been daylight, I could hardly have answered for myself, so heavy and unexpected had been the shock to me. In the lighted alleyway near the pantry I met the captain. At sight of my face he started back, saying, "Hello! You look as if you'd seen something that didn't agree with you! Or are you not feeling well? What's the matter?"

I told him my story. At first he laughed, and cracked a joke or two at my expense. But, seeing that I really was nervous, shivering, and unstrung, he became grave, filled me out a stiff nip of rum, and said, "This is awkward, Forbes. We've got no place to put the men. Of course, it's all imagination on your side as well as theirs. Somebody's playing tricks down there. When you feel better we'll try and settle the thing, you and I. In the meantime the men can have their supper aft here on the hatch. I'll tell the second mate to keep all hands there while we're away. Yes, of course, there must be something in it, or you wouldn't pitch such a story. But it's capable of rational explanation, I think. Just tell the steward to get the riding-lamp trimmed while I fetch my revolver. Put a pair of scissors in your pocket to cut the wick with, should it go out again; and when you're ready let me know."

"Now, truth to say, I had but little stomach for a second edition of the business. Still, seeing the captain so alert, cheery, and confident put heart into me, making me half willing to believe that my imagination might have had some share in the thing. Therefore, by the time he'd fixed up his revolver, and I'd taken another stiffener of rum to warm my chilled body, I was ready for the adventure.

As we passed out the second mate was calling the roll at the quarterdeck capstan, and the cook was bustling about the afterhatch with plates and dishes by the light of a similar lamp to the one I carried.

"All present, Mr Williams?" asked the captain, pausing a moment. "All here, sir," replied the second mate. "Except the men at the wheel and lookout."

"Call the lookout aft, too," ordered the captain. "He can keep it on top of the spars awhile, 'til we return."

This left us the whole fore-part of the ship to ourselves, and lonely enough it felt as we walked along the deserted deck and descended the fok'sle ladder.

A riding-lamp is globular in shape, of uncoloured thick glass, protected by rings of stout wire, can only be opened by unscrewing the bottom, and is impervious to wind or rain. It is a heavy lamp, made usually of copper, and is generally hoisted well up the forestay of a vessel at anchor.

Hanging it carefully on the iron hook in place of the other one, we sat down on a chest, close to each other, our eyes fixed steadily on the gloomy space for'ard, where the sides of the barque narrowed into the stem—the spot whence the Thing had appeared before. The last of the top tier of bunks, I knew, lay there; and I asked myself with a shiver if it might not be the one in which the corpse of the murdered man had been kept so long.

The air was close and stuffy, within it a predominant smell of new paint; the big lamp, swinging fore and aft to the motion of the ship, flung great blobs and splashes of white light athwart the dimness; now and again a heavier sea than usual would smite the bows with a sound as of giants slapping giants' cheeks; a huge polished cockroach crawled out from under a chest and investigated the dark stains of tea and vinegar on the floor; and the empty oil skin suits opposite us rustled and swayed to and fro in the shadow of the bulkhead like a line of hanged men swinging in a breeze.

I was anxious—anxious to justify myself in my captain's sight, and the time seemed endless. But not more than a few minutes could have passed ere the air grew cold. I nudged my companion's arm. On this occasion there was leisure for scrutiny, and, knowing what was to happen, I felt steadier and calmer. At first all that was visible seemed a thick, filmy filling of the dim fore-part of the fok'sle—something like fog or smoke of a dull-grey colour. Then, gradually advancing, it took to our eyes human shape, becoming still more opaque as it did so. And at this stage I heard the revolver click to full-cock, while the cold grew so intense as, in spite of us, to set our teeth rattling. The Thing, by now, was only some four or five feet from us, a little to the right, and approaching with a slow gliding motion. There were the head, trunk, outstretched arms, legs, all the members perfect, even to the fingers; but, otherwise, all a dull vaporous blank—featureless. And the shocking, rotting, corpse-like odour made us gasp again for breath.

"Get between it and the lamp, Forbes!" whispered the captain with a shake in his voice. But I hesitated, thinking I was close enough. Whereupon, without waiting, he started from my side, throwing himself right in front of the phantom, then some three yards from the lamp. In a moment I saw the form close on him; the long grey arms curled round his neck—the light and he were both blotted out, two pale splashes of flame leapt from the darkness, two dull reports sounded, and something fell heavily to the deck. Then the cold and the stench vanished, leaving me sick and shaking.

Striking a match, I saw the captain lying flat on his face, one arm underneath him, the other outstretched and still grasping the pistol. Raising him, I found that, though sensible, he was shaking as with ague; also that his clothes were as soaking wet as though he had been towed overboard all day. Otherwise he was apparently unhurt.

"Shall we wait any longer?" I asked.

But, in place of answering, he staggered to the ladder, the water dripping in little rivulets from him, and his feet squelching in their boots. I had to take his arm to support him along the deck and to his cabin. Nor this time was any evasion of the dozens of inquisitive eyes possible; and all hands and the cook very soon had their tongues clacking, trying to guess what had happened to "the ole man" down in the fok'sle.

In spite of dry clothes and hot toddy, it was fully an hour before the skipper got over his shaking-fit; and even then he looked miserably ill and broken up. His fingers, too, constantly wandered to his throat, and he complained of a choking sensation there."

"Are there any marks about my neck, Forbes?" he asked more than once.

"None, sir," I replied, after looking.

"Well," said he, "I'll swear I felt them—ice-cold claws that gripped as if they meant to strangle me, and only let go when I fired. I'll never get over it, Forbes," he continued. "All the sun in Jamaica 'll not make me feel properly warm again. It's in my bones. Fix the men up as well as you can. I don't think any of us will care to go back in this ship. I know I shan't."

Well, we managed to rig up a sort of fairly comfortable shanty by righting the great longboat that reached across the main hatch from the galley to the mainmast. And in this the crew lived for the remainder of the passage.

In spite of all reticence it got about that the skipper had fired at the Thing and grappled with it; and his condition emphasized the result. Indeed, by too time we reached Port Royal he had to be carried to the hospital, so ill was he. And then, before we finished discharging cargo, he died. I would have taken the Cumberland home could I have got hands. But not a man in the island would sign in her if offered £20 a month. Eventually she was sold, and dismantled, her decks ripped up, filled fore and aft with coal, and towed round to Morant Bay, where she still lies, known only as *Hulk No. 49.*

MISS CROSSON'S FAMILIAR

by Rosa Praed

Stubble Before the Wind (1908)

Rosa Campbell Praed (1851-1935) was born in a slab hut on a remote station in south-east Queensland. In 1872 she married Campbell Praed, the younger son of a notable English family, who had been sent to Australia to make his fortune. The marriage was a disaster—they had no interests in common, and from the start, Rosa found sex repugnant, in stark contrast to her husband (she locked him out of the bedroom when his demands became too much). Rosa spent a miserable couple of years on Curtis Island, where her husband had bought a station, but things looked up when they moved to England in 1876. Rosa had long dreamed of going to England to pursue her literary ambitions, and her dreams were realised when her first novel, *An Australian Heroine*, became an overnight sensation when it was published in 1880. A string of bestsellers followed and she found herself fêted by celebrities such as Oscar Wilde and the Prince of Wales.

Always interested in spirituality and reincarnation, she became heavily involved in occultism, especially theosophy, and blended these interests into her novels and stories. Rosa's life was marred by personal tragedy. Not only was she tied to a loveless marriage, but her daughter, deaf from birth, went insane and was committed to an asylum, and her three sons predeceased her, one by suicide. Her one consolation was her partner of many years, Nancy Harward, a medium whom Rosa believed to be the reincarnation of a Roman slave girl. Rosa died on 10 April 1935 in Torquay. "Miss Crosson's Familiar" was published in *Stubble Before the Wind* (1908) a collection of connected stories, three of which are supernatural. The story references "The Ill-Omened House," which I reprinted in *Australian Nightmares*.

Miss Crosson lived in a house some streets distant from that of Ill Omen, and oddly enough, her abode had a very similar association. I do not know why this should have been unless there are certain magnetic currents which draw together ghosts of the same genus. As far as I ever heard, these two are the only houses in Elchester with an uncanny reputation, but it is certainly true that they were said to be haunted by the same order of spirit. That particular evil genius, which, it was supposed, incited to crime dwellers in the House of Ill Omen, was reported to be the spirit of a valet who had there committed murder and suicide, while in Miss Crosson's villa the malign influence was likewise a manservant's ghost, which appeared to have accompanied the owner of the place thither.

Probably I should never have made Miss Crosson's acquaintance had it not happened that my friend Nora Mitchell and her husband and children came to live in the house next that of Miss Crosson—their respective gardens being divided by one wall; and in later years, when books brought me an increase of income and I was less tied in London by journalistic work, I got into a way of paying the Mitchells frequent visits.

Nora Mitchell was a friend of my younger days, her father, the Honourable and Reverend Theodosius Chisholm, having been rector of Chalford, near Elchester. I had indeed been, in a sense, connected with a painful episode concerning her father's death, and with a curious mystic experience by which Nora had been warned of the event. A year or two afterwards she had married Colonel—or as he then was, Captain Mitchell, and when he retired from the Indian Service, it had been quite natural that the pair, with their two sons and seventeen year-old daughter Una, should make a home at Elchester.

My friends were people of comparatively modest means for their position, and the street where they and Miss Crosson lived was not in the old and aristocratic part of Elchester, but in a newer region, and was composed chiefly of villa residences very much on the suburban pattern. Like all the rest, their house had its three storeys, its two bow windows, and its prim, box-edged flowerbeds in front, with the ornate railing and screen of lilac and laburnum that prevented passers-by from staring in at the dining-room and drawing-room windows. The largest space of ground lay at the back of each dwelling. Here, a stone wall separated the various territories, and these were laid out more or less ornamentally according, in different cases, to the taste of the tenant. Most of the enclosures owned a good-sized beech-tree—the site had been a park—which afforded pleasant shade in summer and gave a gratifying suggestion of ances-tral acres. The Mitchells' predecessors had thrown their back garden almost entirely into lawn, so that Una and her brothers enjoyed the benefit of a large croquet and tennis ground. Miss Crosson, however, being, as it seemed in the Mitchells' first year of occupancy, quite alone in the world, did not of course want a tennis-court. Her plot was laid out in shrubbery at the bottom and, near the house, in grass, with narrow gravel paths bordered by standard rose-trees.

Miss Crosson spent much time in her garden, and from my bedroom window which overlooked the back, I could not fail to see her as she paced her paths, snipped her roses, and pottered about her "graveyard." She had a small cemetery stretching along in the shadow of the wall—a collection of tiny mounds, marked by little wooden crosses, which we supposed contained the remains of deceased pets. It appeared a large assortment, considering that one very seldom saw an animal about her. We did notice, during a visit longer than usual which I paid the Mitchells, some cats and several dogs—a dachshund I remember, a terrier, and, I think, a spaniel. But as none seemed to stay more than a day or two, I concluded they were stray dogs and cats attracted by the profusion of scraps which one might almost have fancied had been laid to lure them. Thus I credited Miss Crosson with a benevolence she was far from possessing, assuming that after the waifs had been fed they were duly returned to their respective owners.

Miss Crosson spent much of her time in her garden, and her favourite occupation in it seemed to be the tendance of her graveyard. When she was not engaged upon her little mounds, which were all carefully grassed and clipped, I would see her pruning her roses and lopping her shrubs, sometimes with quite savage impetuosity, or performing various gardening operations in which she displayed an equally feverish energy. Then at other times, she would walk up and down her paths with an abstracted air while yet she cast stealthy glances around her in a furtive fashion that struck us all as eccentric, and, Una Mitchell declared, gave her quite a creepy feeling. It was her demeanour when walking in her garden that made Nora suspect Miss Crosson of being a little queer in her head. She was always alone, yet from her manner one might have imagined that she had a companion invisible to the ordinary eye. Frequently she would appear to be carrying on a conversation with this unseen companion, and would halt, shake her head remonstratively and gesticulate with her lean fingers as if she were trying to convince an opponent in some heated argument. Then she would show signs of great agitation, would seem to be pleading, denouncing, and at last, apparently vanquished, would move on, her head bent in, as far as could be judged, the deepest dejection. Again, she would come out upon occasions wearing a sort of defiant air, her bright black eyes fixed challengingly before her, her spare form erect, and a look of fierce resolution upon her sallow, witch-like face, which was framed in elfin masses of iron-grey hair. To me there was a horrible fascination in watching Miss Crosson from my bedroom window. Often, after a few minutes of firm pacing to and fro, during which she took no notice of anything or anybody, she would suddenly start and throw frightened glances behind in that furtive way of hers, as though she feared somebody was dogging her steps. Indeed, speaking generally, the expression of her face gave one an impression that she was watching or listening for something outside ordinary consciousness. I have seen her break off in the middle of a sentence, an intent and fearful look in her eyes, and no matter how noisily the young people's tongues wagged around her she would sit silent and oblivious of all that was passing. I have noticed her too, when at dinner, pause suddenly, her knife in her hand, and with a nervous gesture, check, as it were some invisible prompter, and wait to continue her meal 'til she had, apparently, debated and decided some moot point that beset her mind. The more I saw Miss Crosson the more did she give me the notion of a person fighting against some almost unconquerable prepossession.

In time, I did get to know her. So strong was the queer interest with which she inspired me that I allowed Nora no peace 'til she had effected the introduction and established a visiting acquaintanceship with Miss Crosson. I fancied that the old lady fought a little battle over us with her inward monitor, for it was with mingled eagerness and reluctance that she met our overtures. The difficulty would have been greater had it not been for the arrival, during my visit, of her niece Margery, a bright, charming girl, for whom Una Mitchell at once conceived a romantic friendship. Margery Grieve used to come pretty nearly every afternoon that summer and play tennis in the Mitchells' court with the young people they collected about them. It was some time, however, before Miss Crosson could be induced to drink a cup of tea in Nora's drawing-room.

On the first occasion a rather curious incident occurred which after events impressed upon my memory.

Nora had a favourite collie which was accustomed to take up a position, winter and summer alike, upon the rug in front of the fireplace in the drawing-room. He was the mildest, most sociable of beasts, and had constituted himself a sort of master of the ceremonies, it being a family joke with the Mitchells, that, by the number of paces Scot advanced in greeting a visitor, the status of that visitor might be accurately determined. Never had he been known to show anyone admitted as a guest the smallest discourtesy or unfriendliness, though, if Scot were on the watch, woe to the unauthorised intruder. Scot had never taken to Miss Crosson. He would growl when he met her out of doors and show signs of animosity for which we could not account, as the old lady was evidently desirous of being friendly with the beast. This time—the first when Miss Crosson had broken bread in the Mitchells' house, it was plain that a battle waged in Scot's breast between his sense of courtesy to a visitor and his instinctive dislike of that visitor. In truth, he deserved credit for the self-control he exercised, and it was interesting to see how he retired without belligerent demonstration from his customary position upon the hearthrug, allowing Miss Crosson to seat herself in peace upon a couch which was set at right angles with the fireplace.

She accepted the cup of tea Mrs Mitchell handed her and diffidently responded to our attempts at conversation, when the entrance of a caller drew off Nora's attention. Presently the newcomer, who was an enthusiastic gardener, begged her hostess's permission to look at a plant in the conservatory. Margery Grieve and Una Mitchell were busy discussing some affairs of their own, and thus it happened that the burden of talk with Miss Crosson fell upon me. Our conversation was a mere interchange of commonplaces—the weather; the services in the cathedral; the state of various people's green-houses, and such like local topics usually discussed with Elchester townsfolk. I thought Miss Crosson difficult to get on with, and her manner excessively peculiar. She was so nervous that she upset her cup of tea as she gave a sudden start and a quick alarmed glance sideways at the couch on which she was sitting. It was then that the dog Scot exhibited a remarkable uneasiness. He growled, came forward, pricked his ears, showed his teeth, retreated as if in fear, then, gathering courage, sprang towards the couch barking furiously. It really seemed as though he wanted to attack some obnoxious person seated there, but who was invisible to our eyes. At first I thought it was Miss Crosson to whom he objected, but when she moved to a chair, he took no notice of her and, in spite of Una Mitchell's rebuke, continued his onslaught upon the unseen foe on the sofa.

After a minute, he suddenly slunk back, trembling as if he had been beaten. His limbs quivered, his face wore an expression of abject fear and he suffered Una to put him quietly out of the room.

We hastened to apologise to Miss Crosson for the dog's behaviour. She was trembling too: her lips moved silently: she had gone back to the sofa, and, had not the thing been impossible, we should have supposed she was expostulating earnestly with someone on the couch by her side. Her niece Margery looked very uncomfortable, and Nora, only vaguely aware of some slight disturbance ending in Scot's expulsion from the room, partly covered the situation by finding fault with the dog. At that moment two more visitors were announced, and in the slight confusion of their reception, Miss Crosson had time to recover herself. A few minutes afterwards she took her leave, followed reluctantly by Margery Grieve.

I remarked that the younger of the new visitors—a girl lately come into the neighbourhood, and a *spirituelle* creature, with particularly lucid eyes—gazed after Miss Crosson in a half-shocked, half-puzzled manner. As the door closed upon Margery and her aunt, this girl looked first at the friend who had brought her, and then from Mrs Mitchell to me. A question seemed to frame itself upon her lips but she checked it.

Nora made some little speech about Miss Crosson's unsociable ways and evident shyness. "You seemed surprised," she added, turning to the girl, "at meeting her here, actually taking tea with us!"

"Oh, that was not what astonished me," replied the girl. "Of course I don't know anything about your friend the old lady; in fact I hardly noticed her. It wasn't that which made me stare so rudely. Please forgive me, Mrs Mitchell."

"What was it then that made you stare?" Nora asked. "Not little Margery, I am sure."

"Oh, no." The girl hesitated, then exclaimed with an embarrassed laugh. "But it did seem odd to see a gentleman get up and leave a drawing room without taking the smallest notice of his hostess or of anybody else in the room, and to let the door be opened for him by a lady too! But you didn't seem to mind his rudeness."

It was now our turn to look surprised.

"Gentleman!" Nora repeated in amazement. "What can you mean? My husband is away in Scotland and my two sons went to the other side of the county this morning. You could not have seen any gentleman in the room."

"But surely," cried the girl, "when we came in, there was certainly a man sitting on the sofa beside the elder of those two ladies who went out just now. And he never spoke at all, except once to her in so low a voice that I could only see his lips move. He got up when she did and went away with her."

Una Mitchell turned to me. "Scot saw him," she said in a low voice. "And Scot didn't like him."

"What sort of a man was he?" I asked the girl.

"I can't say that I liked his face," she answered, "it had such an unpleasant expression. But he seemed a respectable sort of person—rather big, dark and clean-shaven. Only, his clothes didn't look right somehow. I really thought he was wearing a dress-coat with grey trousers, and I wondered for an instant if he could be a French man come from a wedding. To tell the truth," she went on, "he didn't seem to me quite a gentleman. If he hadn't been sitting there I should have taken him for the butler."

"Ah, well, I don't keep a butler," said Nora, "so if he was one he must have belonged elsewhere." The girl laughed whimsically. "It doesn't matter at all my saying that, and you won't be angry when you know." She glanced at her friend. "I'm certain from their mystified faces that I've been *seeing*."

"Seeing!" echoed Nora, bewilderedly. "Oh, you don't mean—?"

Her lips whitened and quivered. I knew that she was thinking of a certain psychic experience of her own.

"Seeing—*what?*" she asked solemnly.

"Thought-forms, spooks, dead people," explained the other lady, airily. "Etta is the most uncanny being you ever came across. She's always beholding things in the astral; she's clairvoyant, you know. I used to be frightened at her. Now I find it immensely amusing when she describes Joan of Arc sitting in the hall and Mary Stuart hanging round my drawing-room. We tried the other evening to get her to explain about the Casket Letters, but Etta couldn't make her understand. Poor thing! Perhaps she had forgotten."

Una was half-tickled, half-awed.

"I have never seen a clairvoyant before!" she said. "It seems very wonderful."

"Oh, it is quite a common faculty," replied the young lady who was called Etta. "The race is developing a sixth sense, that is all. But it's just a little confusing sometimes, and I didn't feel sure at first which plane I was on—the astral or the physical."

None of us had anything to say and Miss Etta continued: "I think that gentleman may very probably have been a deceased relative or something of your friend's, and that very likely she was as unconscious of his presence as you were. I shouldn't fancy, though, having him round me much. He didn't look good."

The incident dropped then and conversation went off on other tracks. It came up again naturally, however, at dinner, and Colonel Mitchell and the boys made great fun of Miss Etta and her astral seeings. I must own that I had a very uncomfortable feeling about the whole matter, and so, I could see, had Una. But Miss Etta soon went away from Elchester, and nothing more was heard about spooks and the astral plane. As for Margery Grieve, we had decided that we would not tell her anything about Miss Etta's "seeings," though there never was a less morbidly-inclined girl.

The most miserable thing about the business—if indeed there was any connection between Miss Crosson's ghostly companion and the fate of Nora's dear collie—was that a few mornings afterwards Scot was found lying dead in front of Una's door, where he always slept. No sound had been heard in the night and the dog's body bore no trace of violence. Scot's death seemed inexplicable and it appeared unreasonable to suppose that Miss Crosson had anything to do with it. Yet one little circumstance in the case—though we could hardly say why—had for us a horrid significance. Miss Crosson sent in to ask whether we would allow the animal to be buried in her garden cemetery and offered to put up a stone to his memory. We declined the offer, wondering why it had been made, and Scot found his last resting place in a sunny grave under the cast wall of the Mitchell territory. There, with many tears, Nora and Una laid their faithful pet.

It was a short time after this that we remarked how ill and worried Margery Grieve began to look. When our sorrow over poor Scot's untimely end had somewhat abated, Nora asked Margery to tea and I made an opportunity for taking her up to my bedroom and talking to her about the change in herself and about her life with her aunt. I tried in a roundabout way to get her to tell me if she were happy, for it seemed a settled thing now that she was to live with Miss Crosson.

She answered falteringly that she was happy. Oh, yes, she did not mind at all living with her aunt, and it made such a difference, she said, our all being so kind to her. Only, of course, she added, it had seemed a great change coming from a merry family circle to companionship with one so silent and reserved as her aunt.

I gleaned that Margery was the youngest of many daughters and that she had been sent here "on a long visit to Aunt Sarah," partly because of rumours which had reached her father—Miss Crosson's brother-in-law—of the old maid's failing health and lonely ways, and partly, I opined, with the view of a possible inheritance. Margery was a sweet, simple girl, and I felt certain entertained no mercenary designs on her own account.

She admitted that Aunt Sarah was peculiar and rather depressing and that she had very few friends, but Margery said that she was sorry for her and would like very much to make the old lady's life happier if that were possible. "Not that Aunt Sarah seemed really unhappy," Margery added, "but she was so very strange and unsociable."

Presently, touching Miss Crosson's offer to have Scot interred in her own pets' graveyard, I inquired how there came to be so many animals buried in the garden, since I never saw about the establishment any but stray cats and dogs, which, it seemed, were always sent back to their proper homes, as they invariably disappeared after a day or two. To my surprise, Margery burst into tears, and my questioning at first only elicited from her the information that the lost cats and dogs were put into the cemetery.

"But, my dear, I should have thought the right thing would be to communicate with the police, and get them restored to their real owners, who would probably be grieved at losing them."

"Oh, but that's just it!" Margery cried in deep distress. "They don't belong anywhere. The dogs come from a dogs' home."

"A home for unclaimed dogs!" I said, much puzzled. "I can't imagine Miss Crosson taking the trouble to get them from there; and if she does, and cares for them, why should they die?"

"She doesn't care for them. She hates them. She—" Margery's agitation increased. "Oh, I feel I must tell you or somebody—it's so dreadful. I can't bear it any longer; it makes me so wretched.... Don't you understand? The reason why you never see animals about Aunt Sarah for more than a day or two at a time, is that because as soon as they come to her, they—

they die."

"But why should they die?" I repeated. "Tell me, my dear, how can this be?"

"You will scarcely believe it; I couldn't myself make it out at first." Margery spoke with evident relief, once the ice had been broken. "Oh, I have been so puzzled, so miserable; and now that I know, I am frightened."

The girl trembled. Clearly she had had a nervous shock. I soothed her as far as I could, and did my best to draw forth her confidence.

"It is only since two or three days that I have really known," she said. "I had guessed, but would not let myself believe the truth. Two nights ago I saw with my own eyes, and I could doubt no longer. It upset me so terribly, that now I simply dread the nights, though of course I lock my door when I go to bed."

I urged her anew to tell me everything, and the story came out brokenly.

"You know when I first came here," Margery said, "It seemed to me such a strange sort of house, and I found Aunt Sarah so unlike anybody else. I didn't seem able to get fond of her, though I wanted to—and though she is always kind and generous—giving me presents and letting me send things to my sisters, who haven't much money to spend on their clothes. Then too, I'm not obliged to be a great deal with Aunt Sarah. I always have the mornings to myself, because Aunt Sarah doesn't get up 'til luncheon time. And she never minds my going out in the afternoons without her. She likes working in her garden. She—she plants things on the graves—"

Margery shivered.

"Yes, I see that from my window. Go on, dear. About the pets?"

"Ah, those graves! I daresay you haven't noticed, because there are so many under the wall, how there get to be more and more of them. I was so puzzled. There would come cats and dogs—one by one—and Aunt Sarah would have the poor creatures in with her, and seem to gloat over them for a day or two;

and then suddenly in the night, each one would disappear; and after a while I noticed that when one disappeared there would be a new mound in the graveyard, but nobody said anything about it. I thought at first that perhaps it was the cook who didn't like animals, and that she poisoned them or sent them away, and that it was all my fancy about the new mounds which had no head-stones. I supposed that the others were really graves of Aunt Sarah's pets. But one day I saw stains of blood upon the gravel walk.… And then—the other night—I saw." Margery became more and more agitated. "The moon was shining brightly; I could not sleep and I kept hearing the poor thing yelp. It was a dear little fox-terrier, and it cried so pitifully. I think it must have been tortured. I got up and looked over the balcony into the garden, and there it was.… Oh! Oh! And it was Aunt Sarah herself who killed it."

The girl's voice had sunk to a horror-stricken whisper.

"My dear Margery, there must have been some good reason. Perhaps the dog was mad. Otherwise the thing would be too shocking. Could you have been mistaken?"

"No, no; I couldn't have been mistaken. And I am positive the dog wasn't mad. Just before dinner Aunt Sarah had been nursing it. And if you had seen her face in the moonlight! It was dreadful—like the face of a fiend.… I don't know what to do," Margery went on in a burst. "I must have talked to you or Mrs Mitchell today about it all. I cannot help feeling that there is something horribly wrong with Aunt Sarah. Lately she has been more strange than usual. She looks from side to side so oddly, and stops what she is doing, as if somebody had spoken to her, and she were listening. Last evening at dinner, she picked up the carving-knife and examined it, and put it down again, listening all the while. It really seemed that she was having things about it explained to her. I could scarcely bear to sit there. And haven't you noticed how often she appears to be talking silently to some-body? I have wondered sometimes if it's possible there could be a ghost beside her. Do you believe in familiar spirits who follow people about and tempt them to do wrong things?"

I assured Margery that the pure in heart need never fear such visitations, and spoke, with a confidence I did not wholly feel, of the barrier fast set between human beings and the powers of darkness. Thus I succeeded partially in turning the girl's mind from the more gruesome aspects of the case. But all the same I thought of the other girl, Etta's, seeings, and of her description of the "respectable sort of person—not a gentleman exactly; and who did not look good"—the man whom Etta had seen sitting on the couch beside Miss Crosson, and who had followed the old lady out of the drawing-room, invisible to all except the one who had eyes to see.

"I believe in mental illness, however," I said to Margery, "and in the effect of nervous strain upon the mind. I think your poor aunt must be out of gear both in body and brain. She ought to see a doctor without delay. Can you think how this may be managed?"

Margery shook her head dubiously.

"Well, in the meantime, let me advise you to write to your father at once and tell him all you have told me. Ask him to come to you as soon as he possibly can."

"I have written to father," answered Margery. "I posted my letter this morning. But it is not the least use trying to get Aunt Sarah to see a doctor. She detests doctors and was saying the other day that Dr Gleeson has never dared to set foot within her house since he called to introduce himself when she first arrived."

"We must get over that," I answered decidedly. "Dr Gleeson shall find some pretext for calling again. I'll go round and explain things to him. As for you, my dear, do you feel comfortable about tonight, or would you like to remain here? We can invent some pretext for that, I am sure."

"Oh, no, I couldn't think of troubling Mrs Mitchell," the girl exclaimed, "and there is no need. I daresay that I have been stupid to make so much of the thing. I feel ever so much happier now that I have told you. Perhaps it was partly my imagination—that dreadful look on Aunt Sarah's face. The moonlight may have deceived me." But she shuddered as she spoke.

I impressed upon her that she should lock her door on going to bed, and this she promised to do. Presently she got up to rejoin the others, having made me promise that I would not say anything to Nora or Una at present about her fears. "Daddy will be here tomorrow," she said, and added remorsefully: "I feel a traitor to Aunt Sarah, who is really most kind to me. Only yesterday she gave me a cheque to send the girls. I would gladly do anything I could for her, and yet I know that if it hadn't been for Una and for the kindness of you all here, I couldn't have borne to stay on for as long as I have done."

At the door as she was going out, Margery paused.

"There's one thing that has been worrying me dreadfully," she said. "Oh, do you think it possible that she—that it could have had anything to do with Scot's death?"

"I do not think so," I replied, though I must confess that the idea did cross my mind. "It seems quite impossible that anybody could have got into the house without our knowledge. Scot would certainly have barked. He slept at Una's door, which is next to mine and I am a very light sleeper. That night, I remember, I was particularly wakeful."

She seemed relieved. "I am so glad to hear you say that. But it was odd, wasn't it? Poor Scot!"

Yes, the whole business was odd. It perplexed and troubled me. I could not help feeling nervous on Margery's account, and was sorry that I had promised to keep silence to Nora about what she had told me. I went round to Dr Gleeson's house but found that he was not likely to be in until late, so merely left a message that I would call early the following day.

It was a good thing that Tom Mitchell was tired after his shoot the previous day, and that he overslept himself the next morning, so that instead of being in the breakfast-room as usual at half-past eight, he was shaving in front of a window which looked straight across to Miss Crosson's balcony. The old lady had added this balcony to her house, and her bedroom gave on to it by a French window. This window was open, and as Tom stood with his razor in his hand before his dressing-table, he heard suddenly a wild shriek and thought that he recognised the voice of Margery, for whom he had a distinct tenderness. Immediately upon the cry, came a crash of falling china and the over-turning of a piece of furniture. Then Tom saw Margery dart in terrified fashion through the window of Miss Crosson's room on to the balcony and through another window into the house. A moment later, she was followed by a maniacal figure in a white nightgown with grey witch-locks streaming down her back and some gleaming weapon in her hand.

At first Tom could hardly realise that this was Miss Crosson herself, but not a second passed before he was flying out of his room, down the stairs and out into the garden. I saw him from the side window of the dining-room rush to where a ladder stood against the wall dividing our demesne from that of Miss Crosson, vault the wall and disappear. It was the work of a few moments to summon the man-of-all-work and despatch him also over the wall, while Nora and I ran by the longer route to our neighbour's garden.

There we beheld a strange sight. Tom had seized Miss Crosson in her pursuit of Margery, who stood white and trembling a few paces off. He held the demented old lady by her wrists, and she struggled and snapped at him in a paroxysm of frenzy. The large knife he had wrested from her hand was stuck point downwards in one of the tiny graves beside the wall. It was a curved bread-knife with a sharp, broad blade—a truly, murderous weapon.

The madwoman was overpowered at last and Dr Gleeson sent for. He pronounced her a raving lunatic, and, as soon as Margery's father arrived, steps were taken to place her under restraint.

"I have been afraid for some little while that things were wrong," the doctor said to Nora. "There was a look in Miss Crosson's eyes once or twice when I came across her that made me suspect mischief. I watched her walking by herself and apparently holding an imaginary conversation—one might have fancied that she was talking to a ghost—which I considered a very bad sign, and only yesterday I was casting about in my mind what I had best do. Not having been consulted professionally, of course it was difficult for me to put myself forward, but I felt that for the sake of poor little Miss Grieve, some action should be taken."

Margery's story was that Miss Crosson's maid being ill that morning, she had herself carried up the old lady's breakfast-tray and had found her sitting up in bed gesticulating curiously and talking to herself. At sight of the tray an uncontrollable impulse seemed to take possession of her. She jumped up, snatched the bread-knife, aimed with it at her niece, and the girl had barely time to evade the attack by making her escape through the window.

Later on, it became known that quite recently Miss Crosson had written to a friend of her youth confiding a secret trouble which preyed upon her mind, and would, she declared, drive her to do some desperate deed. The friend was in India and did not receive Miss Crosson's communication in time to warn the old lady's relatives. In that letter, Miss Crosson told how for years she had been haunted by the apparition of a dead man, a late butler in her family, who had been dismissed for acts of cruelty to animals, and having afterwards developed homicidal mania, had died in an asylum. Miss Crosson's description of her familiar tallied exactly with that given by the girl Etta of our phantom visitor. He talked to her, Miss Crosson said, and prompted her to kill animals at first and then human beings. In the beginning he had visited her only at intervals; latterly his presence had become practically continuous and his evil promptings more and more insistent. It was, in fact, a tale almost similar to that of poor Beatrix Bray's tragic obsession.

THE GHOST OF
BRIGALOW BEND

by "Wanderer"

Western Mail, 16 December 1898

"Wanderer" was the pseudonym of a prolific West
Australian author who wrote short stories and journalism for the *Western Mail* and other newspapers around
the turn of the twentieth century.

"Say, Tom, I want you to go out to Brigalow Bend. The roan
bull has strayed away from his mob, and Christy says he cut
the beggar's tracks going in that direction. I'm awfully sorry
to have to send you today, but I can't help it. You're the only
man on the station who can track the brute in that country, and
he's too valuable to lose. The boss gave £200 for him only last
month."

The speaker was George Dalrymple, manager of Violet Bank,
a cattle station on the headwaters of the Dawson, where I was
employed as overseer. I had just ridden up to the hut after a hard
morning's work, and was looking forward to a luxurious swim
in the big waterhole, followed by an afternoon's spell, for it was
Christmas Eve, and all hands were to knock off at dinner-time.

"Bless the bull!" I exclaimed ("bless" wasn't exactly the
word), swinging myself from the saddle. "It's a bit rough on a
man to lose his Christmas dinner and all the sport afterwards

for the sake of that beast. Why in blazes didn't Christy go after him himself? He might have found him easily if he'd taken the trouble to look."

"He did run the tracks as far as he could, but after a while they led into that patch of rough country beyond the Box Flat, where he lost them altogether. You know Christy's not a star at that game. I'm certain you'll find the bull somewhere about the Bend. He camped there one night on the road up, and tried his best to break away with some scrub cattle that sneaked up during the night. At all events he's gone in that direction, as I said before, and he must be found, Christmas or no Christmas. I wouldn't send you if I could help it, but who else is there? All that country round the Bend would puzzle a blackfellow since the Brigalow got a start on it, and if it comes to tracking you're the man for the job. You can sleep in the hut tonight if you go straight to the Bend, that is, if you're not scared. I think I've heard you say you don't believe in ghosts?"

"Not I," I replied. "I might have been afraid of old Lanty in the flesh, but I don't think his spirit can hurt me, even if it does 'walk.' I've never seen a ghost either, nor do I believe any man who says he has."

Dalrymple looked at me curiously for a moment, and then said, "Perhaps you're right, but—well, never mind. I was going to say something, but I'll wait 'til you come back. You'd better make a start as soon as you've had some dinner, and perhaps you may pick the bull up before sundown. If not, you can go on to the Bend."

Of course, I had to obey orders. So, with a hearty malediction on imported cattle in general and the roan bull in particular, I departed to saddle a fresh horse and roll up my blankets, so as to be prepared for two or three days' camping out. Then there was a supply of tucker to be procured. I sighed as I thought of the feast our cook was making ready for next day's dinner. I would be out of all that, as well as the subsequent festivities. I could only carry some bread and meat, and, of course, the indispensable quart-pot. Accordingly, having made all my other preparations, I invaded the kitchen in search of the necessary eatables.

"My word," said the cook, when I had explained my errand, "that's a bit o' bad luck right enough. I tell you what, though; you shan't go without a bit of my puddin' after all. It's been boilin' all day, so it'll be fit to eat by this time. I'll take it out o' the pot an' cut you off a hunk; then if you take a four-quart billy with you you'll be able to warm it up, or you can fry it on the coals. Eh, how will that do?"

"First rate, doctor," I replied (a cook is called "doctor" or "poisoner" in the bush, accordingly as his dishes are excellent or otherwise.) "I'll be camping in that old hut at the Bend tonight most likely, so I'll want something extra good to keep my courage up."

The cook stared at me open-mouthed when I mentioned the hut.

"You're not goin' to camp in that infernal shanty?" he gasped.

"Of course I am," I answered, laughing heartily at his awe-stricken expression. "I don't take any stock in old women's tales about ghosts or such-like rot. If there was a murder committed there, what then? Some swagman suffering a recovery camped there soon after the crime, I suppose, and mistook the little fellows who were chasing him for the murdered man's ghost. I'm surprised to find you as superstitious as the rest, upon my soul I am."

"I've heard a lot of 'em talk like you," replied the cook, shaking his head solemnly, "but they all changed their tune after they'd tried sleepin' in that hut. Do you mean to tell me a good buildin' like it would be allowed to stand empty if there wasn't somethin' uncanny about it? No bally fear! You ask the boss. He'll tell you he wouldn't camp there for a year's wages. You're only been here a few months, an' don't know how many's been scared pretty nigh out o' their seven senses by old Lanty's ghost. You'll sing another song when you come back, I'll bet a dollar."

"All right," said I, "I'll bet you a sovereign neither Lanty's nor any other man's ghost can make me camp in the open when there's a comfortable bunk to sleep in. Not but what I'd prefer the open air myself in summer time, but I mean to sleep in that wonderful hut tonight, just for spite. I mustn't dawdle here any longer; I've got thirty odd miles to ride. Give me that duff, and make your mind easy about Lanty. From all accounts he's gone to a place where the climate's so hot that he'd perish if he attempted to show his nose back here."

The "doctor" cut off my share of plum pudding, and wrapped it up in a bag, grumbling to himself the while about "youngsters who fancied they knowed more than men old enough to be their fathers."

"If the ghost does come, doctor," said I, weighing the parcel in my hand, "I'll just bash him in the forehead with this, and I'll guarantee it'll lay him effectually." Then, dodging a rolling-pin and sundry other handy utensils, I beat a retreat towards my horse, followed by such a blast of profanity as made me quite certain our worthy "dough-banger" had served his apprenticeship to bullock driving.

At the time of which I write—a year in the early seventies—there was no finer cattle country in Australia than on the Dawson. Fairly open, splendidly grassed and watered, and comparatively easy of access, it was indeed a paradise for the herds that roamed, free and untrammelled by hateful wire fences, over it's broad plains, or sought a noonday shelter in its cool forest glades. But even then the deadly Brigalow had begun to lay its grip upon the land. Slowly at first, then, as its seedlings became more widely scattered, by leaps and bounds, the useless scrub overspread forest and plain alike, telling no uncertain tale, to those who watched its almost miraculous growth, of abandoned homesteads, starving cattle, and ruined owners. In no part of the world—and I have wandered in many lands—have I seen such an alteration in the appearance and prosperity of a district as has taken place within the past twenty-five or thirty years on the Dawson. For scores and scores of miles, where I can remember wide, rolling downs, with here and there an islet of shady forest, the country is covered with

Brigalow scrub so dense as to be absolutely impenetrable to either man or beast. Nothing lives there, save, perhaps, an occasional kangaroo-rat. Where thousands of cattle found herbage so luxuriant that it grew rank in spite of their cropping there is now not one single blade of grass, for the Brigalow is merciless; no other herb or plant may grow beside it. Some day, perhaps, a plan may be devised for ridding the country of this scourge. At present it defies man's puny efforts; and, if cut down or grubbed up, bursts with the next rain into a fresh and vigorous existence, twenty young trees springing where one has been destroyed.

As I jogged along northward on this Christmas Eve, however, the possible extinction of both cattle and squatter did not trouble me much; indeed, had I known for a certainty that one of the former—the roan ball to wit—was about to "peg out," I would have rejoiced exceedingly. As the cook had observed, I had not been long on the station; in fact, I had only recently returned from a trip with an exploring party in Central Australia, and I had been looking forward to having a real good time at Christmas. The men on Violet Bank, from the manager down, were a very decent sort, and they had "spread themselves" in making preparations for the festive occasion. It was too bad! Instead of enjoying a good dinner, with a sing-song, or, perhaps, a "buck dance" to follow, I would be stuck in an old deserted hut all by myself, with nothing to enliven me but the prospect of a visit from old Lanty's wraith. True, I had brought a bottle of whisky with me out of the case provided by the manager, but what was that I was too young to find any pleasure in drinking "Jack Smithers," and I could scarcely expect the ghost to join me. He would be "spiritual" enough already.

The frequent mention of Lanty's name recalled to my mind the story of his tragic end. The yarn, as it was told to me, ran thus:

Some ten years earlier, the hut to which I was now proceeding was occupied by an old shepherd—the run was under sheep at the time—whose violent temper and readiness in using the sheath-knife which he always carried, had earned him a most unenviable reputation in the district. Lanty Moore, as he was called, was a typical "old hand," scarred deeply both in body and soul by his experiences at Port Arthur and other penal settlements; a drunken old wretch when he had the chance; quarrelsome and blasphemous at all times. No hutkeeper could live with him, and he would have been speedily sacked but for his undoubted skill in the management of his flock. No other shepherd on the river lost so few sheep or kept his charges in such tip-top condition. Therefore Lanty's employer bore with his vagaries as best he could, sending him one hutkeeper after another as fast as he frightened them away. At length, however, he met his match. On coming home one evening with his flock he found a new mate installed in his hut, which was built on a bend of the river where one of the first patches of Brigalow began to spread. Hence the name Brigalow Bend. The new arrival was a youngish man, quiet and inoffensive to all outward appearance, but with a lurking devil in his long, narrow, black eyes, which portended an exceedingly stormy time for whosoever woke him up thoroughly. He, too, made but a short stay, but his departure was due to somewhat different circumstances from those which had caused his predecessors to make themselves scarce. The very morning after his arrival Lanty began to give him a taste of his quality. He found fault with the damper, swore the mutton was rotten and the tea "not fit to sluice out a sewer in hell." The newcomer listened for a few moments in silence; then, when Lanty paused for breath, said:

"I've heard tell of you, my joker, an' I kin see I was told no lies. There's only one way o' dealin' wi' your sort. Coma outside an' take your shirt off!"

Lanty glared in speechless astonishment. Who was this whippersnapper who bearded him thus? The idea of a crossbred gum-sucker talking fight to him! Then the torrent of his wrath burst its bounds, and he sprang at his challenger, grinding out a stream of blistering profanity from between his clenched teeth. Smash! The hut keeper's right caught him square between the eyes, and Lanty staggered back against the rough slab wall half-dazed by the blow. In a few seconds he recovered, and, whipping out a murderous-looking sheath-knife, again rushed to the attack, his eyes red with the lust of blood, his face blotched and mottled with passion.

Quick as thought his antagonist snatched up a heavy iron bar which did duty as a poker, and, springing lightly aside to avoid the thrust which Laney aimed at his heart, brought his weapon down with tremendous force on the shepherd's unprotected head. No skull however thick and tough, could withstand such a blow, and Lanty fell forward without a groan, bespattering floor, table, and wall with blood and brains. Then the slayer coolly rolled up his swag and made his way to the head station, where he recounted to an awe stricken circle of listeners the particulars of his crime just as I have set them down here.

The manager, knowing the dead man's insatiable appetite for rows at all times and seasons, believed the hut-keeper's story; and, holding that the latter had not been guilty of murder, but had committed justifiable homicide, advised him to make tracks before the police got wind of the affair. At first he talked of giving himself up and seeing the thing through, but finally took the manager's advice and departed without beat of drum.

Soon after he had disappeared men began to whisper that his story was a fabrication; that he had known Lanty before, and had followed him to this out of the way spot for no good purpose; that instead of killing the old man in fair fight he had taken him unawares and brained him as he lay asleep. Certain indications in the hut pointed to the probability of this hypothesis, but by the time suspicion of foul play had hardened into something like certainty, the murderer had vanished, nor could a trace of him be found in the district.

Eventually the matter was hushed up, and old Lanty laid to rest in a grave not far from the hut he had occupied so long. But he would not rest, at least so report said.

The next occupant of the hut only remained there one night, turning up at the station in the morning with a fearsome tale of how Lanty's ghost came and stood over his bed at midnight, brandishing a spectral knife in his shadowy hand, and using language which left no doubt in the rudely awakened listener's mind as to the identity of his unearthly visitor. The man's story was received with derision, and another sent to take his place; but he, too, was back at the homestead before dawn in a state of semi-collapse from fright, and scarcely able to stammer forth an entire corroboration of his predecessor's assertions. Then the manager himself, with a fortitude born of superior education and incredulity, braved the terrors of the lonely hut. What he saw or heard there no one ever knew, but certain it is that nothing short of actual force could induce him to cross its threshold again. There it had stood ever since, untenanted save by birds and creeping things, its sturdy slab walls and bark roof showing but few traces of the ravages of time.

Twice or thrice, when passing that way, I had peeped in at the half-open door and conjured up a vision of that sanguinary struggle, until I almost fancied I could see the massive figure lying prone upon the earthen floor, with shattered skull and grey, blood-bedraggled locks, while over it stooped the murderer, leaning on his bar, gazing with stony calmness on his awful handiwork. Although I had laughed to scorn the idea of Lanty's shade threatening to slit men's weasands with a diaphanous whittle, and, as a matter of fact, did not believe it possible for a disembodied spirit to revisit the scene of its former joys and sorrows, still I would not have dreamed of camping in a place which boasted such an evil reputation had it not been for the doubt as to my courage implied in the manager's suggestion. Now, however, it was necessary to act up to my boast of scepticism, or else back down and acknowledge myself as credulous as others; rather would I ace a thousand ghosts.

Having come to this heroic determination, I shook up my horse and cantered steadily on towards the Box Flat, across which the bull was said to have passed. On reaching the Flat, I picked up his tracks without much difficulty, and ran them for three or four miles, until they led into the rough, broken country spoken of by Dalrymple. To follow them here required slow, patient work, so, as they headed steadily northward, I resolved to leave them, push on to the hut, and make an early start in the morning.

* * * * * *

The sun was barely half an hour high when I rode into the clearing in which the deserted humpy stood. As my gaze rested on its dark, weather-stained walls, and then travelled round the bolt of dull, greyish-green scrub which put out the last level rays of sunlight, my heart grew chill, and a shiver, such as is said to pass over one when a stranger treads upon the spot destined to be one's grave, shook me from head to foot. For an instant a sensation of actual bodily terror took possession of me. Then, with a laugh—somewhat forced, I am afraid—at my momentary weakness, I sprang from my horse, and unbuckled the swag which I had carried before me on the saddle. In five minutes I had transferred all my traps to the shelter of the hut, scaring a colony of paddymelons, which had taken possession of it, into fits by my sudden entrance, hobbled out my horse with one ring, and gathered an armful of dry wool for my fire. Then, taking my quart-pot and the billy, which I had brought at the cook's suggestion, I descended the sloping bank and filled them out of the river, which ran, dark and sluggish, around the bend. My horse had already made his way to the water, and was now climbing slowly up the bank, cropping the green river grass as he went. He whinnied as I passed him, and I paused to pat his firm, glossy neck, feeling, as even I had never felt before, the bond of sympathy and companionship which so closely unites the bushman and his faithful slave. The man of cities and civilisation can never really know his horse. It is only in the mysterious solitude of the bush that biped and quadruped are so drawn together that each unconsciously assimilates certain of the other's nobler qualities, and thus they come to understand each other perfectly.

In a very short time I had such a fire going on the wide hearth as had not been seen there for many a year; in fact, it was so fierce that I could scarcely get near it to lift off my quart-pot. It made the old shanty hot and close too, being mid-summer, but it looked cheerful, and, besides, I wanted to clear out any stray snake or centipede which might be planted in the chimney. While the blaze leaped high I took advantage of its light to sweep the dust off a rude bunk which ran along the wall facing the door. I had half a mind to take my blankets outside when I saw the accumulation of dirt and cobwebs on which I had to lie. It would have been much pleasanter in the open air, with a good, leafy tree to keep the dew off; but then I thought of the ridicule which awaited me on my return to the station if I showed the white feather. There was nothing for it but to go through with the job I had set myself, so I made my bed on the unsavoury bunk, with my saddle for pillow. As I unrolled my blankets out dropped the bottle of whisky, which, up 'til that moment, I had entirely forgotten. Good old Andrew Usher! Never did the sight of your familiar name bring more satisfaction to the most inveterate "swiper" than it brought to me that Christmas Eve. I had a corkscrew in my pocket-knife, and in less time than it takes to tell I was reviving my drooping spirits with a "first mate's nip"—four fingers, and "damn the water!"

"Aha!" I exclaimed, rubbing my epigastric region with one hand, while I held aloft my pannikin in the other, 'Come one, come all' as one of those poet Johnnies says; "come the whole population of shadowland, they shall not see me flinch; no, not so much as an eyelash! Gee-whiz! What's that?" as a rattle of chains, followed by a long-drawn sigh, came from just outside the door, filling me—despite my bravado—with that indescribable sensation which thrills through the sleeper who awakes suddenly in the dead of night with the firm conviction that something is in the room.

Next instant my horse poked his head through the doorway, and I felt inclined to kick myself for my momentary "funk." The poor brute, doubtless feeling lonely, had crept up to the hut unheard while I was lighting the fire, and it was the rattle of his hobbles, as he moved a step nearer, which had given me such a start. I stroked his velvety muzzle, and gave him a piece of damper, after which he turned away contented and began feeding.

After I had eaten some bread and meat, I tackled the plum pudding, which I had warmed up in the billy. Whether the "doctor" had made a mess of it in the first instance, or I turned it into a "sod" by boiling it a second time, I know not. Anyhow, I narrowly escaped losing two or three of my front teeth in the first mouthful. Oh! But it was solid! Still, I finished it. When one is young and a bushman to boot, one's digestive powers approximate to those of the ostrich, and, as I had in my time wrestled with even tougher triumphs of the culinary art, I did not anticipate any evil results from my "set to" with this master-piece. Another jorum of hot whisky—just to assist in the disin-tegration of that awful duff; a fresh armful of wood on the fire; a fragrant cloud rising like incense from my old briar. I began to feel quite festive, and, as I stretched myself on old Lanty's bunk, and watched the flames leaping up the wide chimney, I was as jolly and comfortable as a possum in a hollow log.

I am usually a splendid sleeper, but on this occasion I wooed the drowsy god in vain. First I tried lying on one side, then on the other, then on my back; but it was no use. After two hours' turning and tossing I was as broad awake as when I lay down.

"It must be that infernal duff," I soliloquised, sitting up and beginning to fill my pipe anew. "Perhaps I didn't take enough whisky to soften it? I'll have another nip!"

I had another, and yet another, but sleep seemed as far off as ever. Finally, I gave it up as a bad job, and, having made up the fire, lay down again with my hands behind my head, and, like another wanderer of old, "wished for the day." All this time I was smoking, and as smoking begets thirst, I naturally moist-ened my throat occasionally, taking care, as I thought, to leave a decent nip for the morning. Picture my astonishment, therefore, when, on putting the bottle to my lips about midnight, to drink a merry Christmas to myself, I discovered that it was empty!

Not a drop left! Surely I must have had a visitor! Perhaps the ghost? I laughed loud and long as the idea struck me. Then my mood changed.

"'Pon my soul it's a bit strong," I muttered, addressing the heap of embers on the hearth. "If old Lanty wanted a drink he might have asked for it like a man instead of sneaking it in this fashion. If the villain would only show himself, I'd quick tell him what I think of him."

As I ceased speaking a shape arose between me and the fire, misty and indistinct at first, then taking form and substance, 'til its outlines showed up clearly against the flaming background. My eyes travelled slowly up the patched moleskins and blue shirt—worn, as all "old hands" wore it, outside the trousers—'til they rested on the face. My blood froze, my flesh crept, when I would have spoken my tongue refused its office and clove to the roof of my mouth. The thing glared at me in silence, its deep-set eyes glowing in their cavernous sockets like halls of fire. Then it raised a shadowy hand, and, pointing to its skull all bruised and battered and covered with clots of blood, from which a constant drip, drip fell to the earthen floor, a sepulchral voice issued from its pallid lips, which lent a new terror to its fearsome presence.

"Ye see the track o' yer bar, slim Jim," said the voice. "Ye waited a long time for the chance o' settlin' me, ye crawling white-livered cross between a Jew lizard an' a black snake; but dash, dash ye to blank! I've waited longer for you. I'd have ye to know that I'm turnspit in the devil's kitchen, where I'll have the pleasure of roastin' ye an' bastin' ye with vitriol for ever an' ever, ye blasted cur! My master's given me leave of absence to come an' fetch ye. Ha! Ha! Ha! I was beginnin' to think I'd never get the chance to scour my knife on yer brisket, but it's come at last!"

The thing—Lanty's astral shape as its language eloquently proved—advanced towards me, a long, glittering blade poised high above its head. I tried to scream, but no sound came; to lift my hand, but every muscle was paralysed. Nearer and nearer it came; I could feel its burning gaze eating into my very brain.

Beside my bed it paused, the up-raised arm swung still higher; one last flourish of the shining steel, and then—

Crash! I rolled off the bunk on to the floor with a yell that might have been heard at the station, and lay there half stunned, gibbering like a maniac and shaking like a dog in a wet sack. Every moment I expected to feel that horrible knife between my ribs, but the blow never fell. Presently I took heart of grace, and glanced fearfully around. I was alone! Of my ghostly visitor not a trace remained, save the empty bottle and a strong smell of sulphur!

Certain scoffers to whom I have told this "ower true tale" have received it with many nods and winks and would-be witty innuendoes concerning the effects of too much whisky and plum-duff mixed, but these be Philistines to whom aught savouring of the supernatural is *caricre*.

I am, and always will be positive, that old Lanty's ghost paid me a visit. I could never imagine a light supper of plum pudding and good Scotch whisky capable of conjuring up such a hideous vision; and if I did find a hole burned in my blankets by the pipe which dropped from my panic-loosened jaws, it does not account satisfactorily—to me—for the odour of brimstone so suggestive of the culinary establishment in which the apparition claimed to be *chef.*

THE SPECTRE OF THE BLACK SWAMP: AN OVERLANDER'S STORY

by Edwin M. Merrall

The Australian Journal, 1 November 1875

Edwin Merrall's only other known work is a paper presented to the Victorian Branch of the Royal Geographical Society of Australasia in 1887 titled "An Unknown Portion of Victoria".

It's many years ago—commenced the overlander—since I became acquainted with the Box Forest station. This station was owned by a Sydney firm, and was worked by a manager, being a cattle station, but very few hands were employed on it, and they, for the most part, had been in the service for many years. Indeed such a length of time has elapsed since the period to which I refer, that I have now but a faint remembrance of any of the employees with the exception of two. These two, however, are all that are requisite for the understanding of this story, and I shall briefly describe them.

John Warfield was what we cattle-men call a "super"—that is, an overseer acting under the manager. He was a dashing young fellow, of about seven or eight-and-twenty, and very popular. Good-natured to a fault, and courageous to recklessness, he always took upon himself the carrying out of any enterprise which presented more than the usual share of danger. The life of an overlander is not altogether one of cakes and ale, and he consequently had plenty of opportunities for the indulgence of his fancy. I remember once being blocked with a small mob of cattle with Warfield, on the banks of the Hunter. The river was flooded, and as the rain came down unceasingly, there was no possibility of the floodwaters running off. So we paddocked the cattle, and took up our quarters in an adjacent town.

But the flood came down upon the town that same night, and, before morning, one-half of the buildings had been swept away. That was a dreadful night, and is but too well remembered by many a desolate hearth. Many lives were lost, and more would have been sacrificed to the insatiable waters but for John Warfield, whose reckless courage found a legitimate and noble sphere of action on that occasion. Amongst other acts, he swam out with a line to a submerged house, on the roof of which some half score of naked and frozen individuals were clinging. They were all safely rescued by means of the communication he established at such a great risk, and the building fell almost immediately afterwards. For his disinterested conduct on this occasion he received the gold medal of the Humane Society; and of this badge he was very proud, and always wore it suspended by a ribbon round his neck, but, of course, out of sight.

This, then, was the kind of man the super Warfield was. The other man whom I have very good reason to remember, was called "Mike." But I do not think that was his real name, indeed he himself admitted that he had at various times been known by so very many different cognomens that he could not now state with any degree of certainty what his real name actually was.

He was a low-browed, brutish-looking animal, and an out-and-out bad character, no matter how viewed. Very ignorant, very brutal, and very passionate; in short, a man who was completely the slave of his feelings, which were purely animal. He was merely a stockman on the station and had been there a long time. Of course, he was generally disliked, but his skill in his craft was admirable, and his knowledge of the surrounding country, which was very rough, was invaluable, and well worth the wage he drew.

I had only been a few days on the Box Forest run, when Mike drew a twelve months' cheque and started on a trip for Sydney, it being an understood thing between the manager and himself that his billet of stockman should be kept open for him.

Mike was back again in a fortnight but he didn't come alone. He brought with him a wife. This young woman he had picked up at some low public-house, I believe, and her general character was much on a par with his own, and she soon became notorious on the Box Forest station. I suppose, however, that Mike cherished for her a strong animal attachment as he soon became bitterly jealous, and the object on whom his jealous suspicious settled was no other than John Warfield.

As the affair in question had no interest for me, I paid but little heed to it, and am not therefore in a position to say, from personal observation, how far Mike's suspicions were justified. But he could not very well make any disturbance about it, and affairs went on as usual, although all the station hands ware well aware of the thorn in Mike's side.

It was at this time when the manager despatched Warfield a small mob of choice cattle for a Victorian station and ordered Mike to accompany him. The cattle in question consisted of just a few quiet beasts which two men could manage easily enough.

In addition to a spare horse which Warfield took with him, he was mounted upon his favourite bald-faced cob, as nice a little bit of blood as one could wish to see.

After they had effected a start we heard nothing more of them for about a month, when some returning overlanders called at the station and informed us that it was feared an accident of some kind had befallen John Warfield, as he had most unaccountably disappeared, and that Mike was travelling down with the cattle alone, and instituting such inquiries as he could for his lost companion.

The manager instantly despatched me to ascertain the meaning of this extraordinary intelligence, and I managed by dint of hard riding to overtake Mike just as he arrived at his destination with the cattle. He had been fortunate in securing the services of a chance traveller, and he explained to me that before he had done so he had been nearly worn out with day droving and night watching, a fact which his haggard and care-worn appearance fully testified.

Mike was very much surprised that no tidings had been heard of Warfield, who left him, as he said, at the Black Swamp for the purpose of selecting the route ahead, and also to notify to the squatters that travelling stock were about to pass over their runs.

I forthwith instituted a systematic course of inquiry all along the route travelled, but could not glean the slightest information respecting the missing Warfield. In this search I was assisted by several neighbouring squatters, who were personally acquainted with the lost super, but our efforts were all in vain and we were reluctantly compelled to receive the conjecture, which some of his friends put forward, that he had, in all probability, been drowned whilst attempting to ford one of the numerous creeks or rivers which intersected the route. And this hypothesis was rendered the more plausible from the known recklessness of his character. And so, after some weeks of anxious and untiring search we gave it up, and left the fate of John Warfield and his cob shrouded in mystery.

Mike had been as diligent in the search as myself, and we both returned to the Box Forest homestead in a somewhat gloomy frame of mind; at least, this was my state; for I esteemed poor Warfield very highly. But Mike's troubles were not ended. Immediately on his arrival he was confronted with another disappearance—the disappearance of his wife.

There was, however, no very great amount of mystery connected with this latter event, as the lady in question had been observed to saddle up her horse on the morning of her disap-pearance, and had further, as the unfortunate Mike discovered, conveyed away their most valuable portable effects.

Some of the station hands connected her departure with the

simultaneous disappearance of the boundary-rider, and they further suggested—by way of substantiating their theory—that her ladyship had succumbed to the blandishments of the boundary-man, by way of consoling herself for the absence of her liege lord.

But remembering the manner in which Warfield's name had been associated with that of this woman, the probability occurred to me of her having joined Warfield somewhere, in accordance with some preconcerted plan, and that the pair of them had gone off together; and I straightway mentioned this suspicion to the manager. But he shook his head at it.

"Warfield," said he, "would be the last man to neglect his duty in that way. He would never leave the cattle on the road, as has been done in this case. If the cattle had been safely landed, I should not doubt it in the least; but as affairs stand, I say no, decidedly no. And," continued the manager, "there is another thing to be taken into consideration, and that is that the station is indebted to Warfield in a couple of hundred pounds."

But, notwithstanding this opinion, a lurking suspicion of the correctness of my idea still possessed me.

I have already stated that Mike was generally disliked, and even distrusted; and more than one of the station hands—with that blunt uncouthness which characterises certain of their class—exhibited a most marked and very significant hostility towards him; and, indeed, in a general way declared as plainly as mere deportment could declare, that they suspected Mike of foul play in the matter of Warfield's disappearance.

Mike, in a certain way, was by no means deficient in perceptive faculties, and he very naturally cowered under the unspoken but none the less terrible imputation, and somewhat abruptly announced his intention of quitting the station.

For my part I honestly pitied the man. Circumstances had placed him very awkwardly from the start, and the mingled distress and chagrin he exhibited on learning his wife's flight would have excited commiseration in the breast of a savage, and I felt quite glad of a discovery which he made, and which went a long way to confirm my theory, that Warfield had eloped with his wife.

This discovery was simply a portion of a letter, which Mike said he had found in his hut. The letter was in the unmistakable writing of Warfield, and was clearly a proposal of elopement to Mike's wife. The greater portion of the letter had been torn off, and what remained revealed nothing further than—as I say— the mere proposal of elopement.

As my original supposition had been already circulated amongst the station hands, the discovery of this fragment which her ladyship had incautiously left behind her, served in a great measure to convert them to my theory, and we all—with the exception of the manager—expected to hear again of John Warfield.

But Mike still adhered to his resolution of leaving the station, and he left accordingly.

My business, too, with the Box Forest station was now concluded, and I also left, after having received a promise from the manager that in the event of Warfield's applying for his money I should be apprised of the fact.

* * * * * * *

Many years had now elapsed since the mysterious disappearance of John Warfield, and not the slightest tidings had been heard of him. During the whole of this time I had been in a remote part of the country, and now found myself with a small mob of cattle in hand intended for a Southern destination. Before I could start it would be necessary to procure an additional hand to assist in their transport. I was assisted in this matter by the squatter from whom I had purchased.

There was a shepherd, he said, on the station who had been accustomed to droving, and with whose services he was about to dispense. I, therefore, in company with the squatter, set out to interview this man.

"I must tell you," said the squatter, as we rode along, "that there is something peculiar about him. Whenever he sees a horse approaching he immediately falls down upon his knees and commences to tell his beads. That's all I know about it, and there does not appear to be much harm in it. Every man, they say, is eccentric upon some particular point, but this shepherd of mine is clearly a maniac as regards this little matter."

The singular information of the squatter was almost immediately after confirmed. No sooner did the shepherd see us approaching than he was down upon his knees praying with apparently great fervour.

He was very pale, and appeared very much agitated as we rode up, and we naturally recognised each other. He was my old acquaintance, "Mike," of the Box Forest station.

I briefly stated my object, and offered him liberal pay for his services.

He inquired the destination of the cattle, conned over the route to be taken, and finally accepted the situation.

I loitered for a few moments in his company, hoping he would refer, in some way, to the missing Warfield, or to his own fugitive wife, but he referred to neither, and curious as I was to ascertain if my old suspicion was correct, I refrained broaching the subject, as I feared to awaken unpleasant reminiscences in the old man's mind.

We effected a good start the following morning, and continued our journey without anything worth mentioning transpiring until three-parts of the way had been covered when, from information received relative to the state of the cattle market, I resolved to alter our destination.

As Mike appeared to be well contented with his billet and as I had engaged to pay his expenses back to our starting point, I did not deem it necessary to inform him of the alteration of our destination and he did not appear to discover it himself until we were within one day's stage of the Swamp, and then he rose up to me, and in a somewhat flurried manner, inquired if we hadn't got out of our course.

I explained the alteration of our destination, but Mike didn't at all appear to relish the prospect of camping on the Black Swamp. It was there where he had lost Warfield and I could readily understand the man's objection to the spot, which was very natural. But, for all that, I had no inclination to be left upon the road, single-handed, with a mob of cattle. So, in reply to his request, I plainly announced my determination not to release him by any means from his engagement.

But he didn't like the prospect at all. Indeed, he appeared to be quite frightened, and it was only by sheer dint of moral form that I ultimately overcame his reluctance.

It was about mid-day, when a man who had charge of a large mob in our rear rode up to us. Mike went ahead with the cattle whilst I stayed behind to converse with this man.

"I'm coming up," he said, "a few days' stage behind with eight hundred head; and seeing your tracks ahead of us, I just rode up to let you know. We must be careful not to box the mobs. There's no drafting-yards within a hundred miles, and a cutting-out match on these plains will be the devil's own job, especially as I'm short-handed."

I explained that we only had about eighty head, but admitted the advisability of avoiding a box.

"You'll be on the swamp tonight," continued he, "and the mob is bound to break off, that much you know. So if you pitch your own quamby on this side, you might manage to let them break away ahead. If they come back upon us with any sort of a rumpus they'll rise our mob as sure as fate."

"Why is our mob bound to break?" I asked.

"Why, don't you know? The Black Swamp is one of these confounded haunted camps. You can't have been long on this trail, or surely you would have known that."

I explained that I was not regularly in the trade.

"But what's the camp haunted with?"

"Well, they say a bald-faced cob and headless rider rises every mob that camps there."

"Well, but surely you don't mean to say that you believe in such an absurdity?"

"Well," he answered, "you see I've never camped there yet, and so I shan't say much about it. You'll be there tonight, and I'll be there tomorrow, so we'll both be better able to talk about it afterwards. But I've a private opinion that the bald-faced cob and headless rider is nothing more than a 'will-o'-the-wisp.'"

"If the cattle won't stay on the camp," said I, "why camp there at all?"

"At this time o' year we can't help it. There's no water for a day's stage on either side. I," continued the drover, "attach far more importance to this affair than you appear to think it worth. But there never was a mob camped there, that I've heard of, but didn't break. It's scarcely a month ago since Scotch Jock's mob—three thousand head of Queensland cattle—was scattered to all points of the compass. It took them nearly a week to re-muster, and then they were forty or fifty head short. So you see your camp is bound to rise tonight, and if you can only just manage to head them off our direction, you'll do well."

And so speaking, the drover returned back to his cattle.

I confess that this conversation with the drover affected me considerably more than the subject seemed to justify. But that was mostly owing to the description given of the swamp. A bald-faced cob, and headless rider! Why, it was a bald-faced cob which Warfield was riding when he disappeared! I pondered over the matter for come time, but dismissed the subject as being altogether unworthy of serious thought.

What the drover had said about the camp was sufficient to convince me that the cattle were frightened off the ground by a natural phenomenon of some sort, probably a will-o-wisp, as he had suggested, and the original sight of which had suggested to the terrified imagination of some ignorant and superstitious stockman the image of a bald-faced cob and headless rider; and having been thus unfortunately christened, the excited imagination of nervous night-watchers never failed to apply the likeness immediately on sight of the phenomenon.

But I deemed it advisable to say nothing to Mike upon the subject. He was uneasy enough upon the matter of camping there already, and the smallest hint of this ghost would be sufficient to scare away my stockman completely.

We safely landed our cattle on the camping ground, and pitched our tent. Shortly after sundown Mike turned in, as I resolved to keep the first watch myself, intending to call him at two o'clock.

It was a beautiful summer's night. There was no moon, but the excessive brightness of the stars shed a soft radiance over the plain.

I spent several hours dreaming with my eyes open, and stargazing. I watched the southern cross swinging round and falling down in the western heavens, and I saw the Pleiades rise over the eastern horizon. The appearance of this latter constellation reminded me that it was near midnight. I drew out my watch, and, with the aid of my lighted cigar, saw that it wanted but a few minutes to twelve.

"Now," soliloquised I, "is the time for the unquiet spirit of the swamp to put in an appearance. 'This is the witching hour of night, when churchyards yawn and graves give up their dead.'" And then I surveyed the dark clump of cattle quietly reposing on their camp and chuckled.

But I was reckoning without mine host; for whilst still chuckling, a white object suddenly arose from the swamp and rushed the cattle, who immediately rose their camp like a flash, and came thundering towards me in wild terror. To spring upon my horse and gallop out with intent to block them was the work of a moment.

Looking beyond the cattle I could see the white object which had started them, apparently miles away on the edge of the plain, but, before I could crack my whip it was back again upon the mob with the rapidity of a cannon-ball.

The cattle divided right and left, as the spectre shot through them and rode right down upon me.

I have no objection to admit being horrified, for the spectre presented to my terrified eyes the unmistakable image of a *headless rider seated on a bald-faced cob.*

My horse propped, snorted in terror, reared, and fell back upon me, and what then took place seemed more like some delirious nightmare than anything else.

I was not hurt by the fall, but the horse was lying like a log upon my leg, and prevented my moving even if I had the power to do so. But I had no such power, nor even inclination. My very faculties appeared to be under a spell. I fancied hearing the distant rumble of the footsteps of the flying herd, but that died away immediately afterwards, and I became conscious of being enveloped in a dense, opaque mist, which paralysed all my senses and shut out surrounding objects. This horrid presence pressed me down, and I was dimly aware of two luminous eyes bending over me.

I did not appear at all frightened, but felt inert, physically and mentally, as if the blood in my veins had been turned to lead.

How long this dreadful thing had possession of me I can't say, but its presence was suddenly withdrawn, and all my senses and faculties returned to me immediately. At this moment the horse, too, recovered from the stupor into which he had been thrown, and made a desperate attempt to rise. I, however, was on the alert to prevent him. This horse was an extremely vicious and dangerous brute, and I knew well, if I allowed him to get up, he would, in all probability, dash out my brains before I could get clear of him. So I threw my arm over his head and held him down, and was just about to cooee for Mike to come to my assistance, when my voice was arrested by hearing a series of the most dreadful shrieks and shouts. They came from the direction of the tent, and, turning my head with difficulty in that direction, I saw that the tent was enveloped in a dense white mist, which towered high above it.

Remember, it was a moonless midnight, and things could be seen but indistinctly through the gloom. But I swear I saw a ghastly, shapeless horror emerge from the tent, and rush down towards the swamp with screams of triumphant laughter, and trailing behind it my shrieking stockman. They almost immediately disappeared in the gloom, and the laughter and shrieking terminated abruptly.

Could I have got free the probability is that I should have made swift tracks behind the cattle. But I was pinioned by the horse securely enough, and was compelled to endure some hours of strange terror and suspense.

And thus I lay 'til daybreak, but there was no appearance of Mike. I had just resolved to let the horse get up, and to take my chance with him, when I heard the approaching hoof-strokes of horses, and shortly after, the super, who had charge of the cattle behind, and two of his stockmen, rode up. They saw my situation in a moment, and, dismounting, held the horse, and released me at the same time. Although somewhat stiff and cramped, I was unhurt.

"If you don't kill that brute of a horse he'll kill you one of these days," remarked the super, and then he proceeded to state that our mob had come back upon him and boxed with his.

"So the bald-faced cob and headless rider rose your camp, did it?" asked one of the stockmen.

"Something very much like what you describe startled them," I reluctantly admitted.

"You recollect boss," continued the stockman, turning to the super, "that we stipulated for no watch on the Black Swamp; so, if there's to be a watch tonight, you'll have to keep it on your own hook."

We led the way down to the tent, in order to discuss the best mode of procedure with reference to the boxed cattle. As I entered, I was struck with dismay on discovering Mike lying upon the floor covered with blood. We hastily lifted him up, and discovered that he had burst a blood-vessel. Blood was slowly coming from his mouth and nose. But this was not altogether sufficient to account for the dreadful appearance which he presented. He was wild-eyed and haggard beyond description. But in reply to our startled interrogations, he only lay back and groaned.

"By heavens! What's the meaning of this?" suddenly exclaimed the super, who was standing at the tent-door. His tone expressed so much astonishment, that I immediately joined him, and stood looking at the broad and bloody trail he pointed out, much as would be made by a body being dragged over the ground.

We proceeded in startled silent wonder along this significant trail which led us to the edge of the swamp, and there stopped. At this termination the little clump of growing rushes was unusually luxuriant; one of the stockmen, gathering a handful, tore them up by the roots, and then curiously pottered away at the exposed mould. A bone was revealed, then another, and finally, as we all assisted in clearing away the sod, a human skeleton was exposed to view.

"By heaven!" exclaimed the super, springing to his feet, I verily believe we've yarded the secret of the Black Swamp."

At this moment something glittering upon the breast of the skeleton attracted my attention. I picked it up and found it to be the gold medal of the Royal Humane Society, on which was engraven the name of John Warfield. I may also add that a feeling of something more than astonishment pervaded our party on discovering that the skeleton was headless.

One of the stockmen turned upon his employer with a hysterical laugh, "what do you think of the headless rider now, boss?"

But the super could only shake his head dubiously, as if the matter were altogether beyond his comprehension.

We returned back to the tent, and found old Mike cowering in the corner, the same as we had left him. With one of those inspirations which so often fall upon men in situations like the present, I sprang forward and seized him by the arm.

"We have found the remains of Warfield!" I almost shouted. "Confess, you villain, that you murdered him."

He turned his stricken eyes upon us, gave a few gasps, and struggled to his knees.

"You've found him, have you? Well, I'm mighty glad of it. Yes, I killed him."

Notwithstanding my question, I confess to being somewhat taken aback at this straightforward answer to it.

"Yes," he continued, "I confess it. I killed him on this swamp: cut off his head with the axe whilst he was asleep and buried him in the swamp. And now I feel better than I have done for the last fifteen years—since the moment I done it, I've suffered dreadful," he continued. "He was here last night. I thought he 'u'd have killed me; I wish he had. Perhaps he has, though, for I feel mighty weak."

The self-confessed murderer sank back on his blankets, and shivered from head to foot; and the blood again oozed from his mouth and nostrils.

We stood at the tent entrance, regarding him in dismay.

"What did you kill him for?" I at length inquired.

"Well, he was going to run away with my wife. I stopped a letter he wrote to her. Don't you mind seeing part of it? I tore of the other part. I told you I found the letter in my hut after I came back, but I got it before I started with the cattle. They were going off together after he should come back from Victoria, but I determined he never should come back. That's why I killed him. But she never waited for him, but went away with the boundary-rider."

A fresh flow of blood here interrupted him, and we drew off to consider the best course to pursue.

We decided to leave the guilty man in the tent, whilst we went back and brought up the cattle in one mob.

We notified this intention to Mike, but he protested against the arrangement with hysterical vehemence.

"For God's sake, don't leave me alone," he said. "If you do, I'll run away."

We smiled at this, for the man was too weak even to rise himself upon his feet.

"I've suffered already," he said, "more even than I deserve. But don't leave me alone, for God's sake."

The super suggested that I remained on the ground whilst he and his riders would bring up the boxed mob.

This was agreed to, and they departed for the cattle.

I carried up a billy of water for Mike, who, in reply to a question of mine, stated that he had also killed the bald-faced cob.

"I couldn't get the animal," he said, "away from the spot where I buried Warfield so I was obliged to kill him, too, for fear of his betraying me;" and, beyond a few delirious mutterings, he spoke no more during the whole of that day.

The double mob of cattle were safely landed on the Black Swamp camp before sundown, and all hands agreed to sit up that night and keep a general watch.

Leaving the wretched Mike in sole possession of the tent, we made a fire outside of "cattle chips," the only fuel procurable on these plains, and laid in a supply of the same material; and we filled all the billies with water, and spread our rugs around the fire, and in this way prepared to keep vigil; but it was an understood thing that, in the event of the cattle breaking away, no pursuit should be made.

I shall never forget that watch on those midnight plains. It was a most lovely night, and the soft lustre which the stars shed around seemed to hallow even that desecrated spot.

Our conversation, which was confined for the most part to the startling revelations of that day, and of many events connected with that revelation, was carried on in semi-hushed tones. Our pipes were in constant requisition, and the billies of scalding tea simmered around the smouldering fire, whose familiar presence there served to reassure us.

The super was a remarkably intelligent man, and his conversation for some time past had been directed in the endeavour to disrobe the events of the past night of their apparent supernatural garb.

He boldly maintained that when my horse reared at sight of the "will-o'-the-wisp," and fell over on me, I must have been terribly shaken, and was probably, although unknown to myself, unconscious for a short time; as for the shrieks of the guilty Mike, on sight of the "will-o'-the-wisp," they were, of course, true enough; but those shrieks, he further pointed out, were only heard by me when the presence of the spectre left me, or, in other words, when thorough consciousness returned.

As for the apparition dragging Mike from the tent, and the trail of blood which led us to the discovery, he accounted for that by stating his opinion that the conscience-stricken murderer, really believing that the victim had been present with him, had actually crawled down to the grave to ascertain if the sod had been disturbed.

"I really believe," continued the super, "that this wretched man, whilst under the influence of terrified fascination, crawled after the receding *ignis fatuus* down to the swamp. Owing to the relative positions occupied by yourself and the tent, your line of sight struck the course taken by them diagonally, and not at right angles, or you would have seen they were not close together—one dragging the other apparently—but some distance apart."

It is needless to say that this plausible reasoning was stoutly combatted by everyone there present with, perhaps, the exception of myself.

The half-dozen stockmen were by no means content to have the terrible spectre, which for so many years had reigned over the Black Swamp camp, so easily disposed of.

"The only remarkable thing I see about the affair," continued the super, "is the manner in which the guilty man himself led us on to the discovery."

But his audience was not appreciative, and still murmured their dissent.

The super, the better to enforce his argument, rose upon his feet.

"Now, look here," said he, "I trust this thing, whatever it is, will show up tonight. I'll investigate it anyhow."

"Well," said I, drawing forth my watch, "it wants but a few minutes to midnight, and that's the time, you know."

The watchers looked nervously over their shoulders, but not the least sight or sound disturbed us, and the super continued, "I intend to face it—no matter in what aspect it comes."

At this moment a tremendous commotion shook the tent and the wretched Mike rushed out from it with the wild cry of—

"Here he comes!"

The miserable man was bent nearly double, his hair was literally standing on end, his eyes darting from their sockets, and in blind terror, was rushing right into the fire.

The super was standing with his back towards the tent, and when that dreadful cry burst upon him he vacated his position with amazing celerity; clearing the fire, the billies, and the men lying beyond it with the agility of a kangaroo.

I started up just in time to save the guilty Mike from plunging headlong in the fire, but so great was his onset that I stumbled and fell with him, and as we fell I felt that convulsive twitching of his limbs, and heard that choking-rattle which always precedes dissolution, but even in that dread moment my eyes were riveted upon the tent; and so, indeed, were those of all the party, and thus we stood, sat, or kneeled—each in the attitude in which we had been surprised, without moving a muscle for the full space of a minute.

The super was the first to recover himself and move towards the tent. We all followed, but saw nothing. We looked around in every direction, but neither sight nor sound disturbed the death-like stillness of the plains. The cattle were lying quiet upon their distant camp, everything around us was quiet—as quiet, indeed, as the man we had left by the fire.

We continued our vigil until daybreak, but nothing disturbed us.

The following day the remains of the self-confessed murderer were interred by the aide of his victim, and we drew up a rough statement of the affair—minus the few apparent supernatural surroundings—and forwarded it to the authorities.

But the Black Swamp is no longer haunted. The unquiet spirit is now at rest, and the overlanders hail the camp as the best on the southern cattle trail.

CHRONICLES OF EASYVILLE

by Patrick Shanahan

The Australian Journal, 1 March 1875; 1 October 1875

Patrick Shanahan is known only for his "Chronicles of Easyville", a series of short stories set in the fictional Victorian town of Easyville that were serialized in *The Australian Journal* in 1875.

Easyville! The beauteous, the romantic! So far away from the busy turmoil of the city, and yet not too far for the rusticated student who may desire to visit the Victorian metropolis occasionally. Who first planned thy limits? Who first arranged thee into streets and byways? Who first built for himself a habitation within thy limits, thou paragon of Victorian villages?

It is five o'clock p.m. The coach from Melbourne comes grinding over the flinty highway, laden with passengers and luggage. What a grand sight the antiquated mail coach is, thundering along the hard stony ways with its steaming horses, its dandy driver, its motley cargo of passengers. The clashing of iron-shod hoofs, and the loud rumbling of wheels!

But it has passed, and I turn me within the walls of my hotel, to hear the loud voices of drunken quarrymen, farmers, cattle-dealers, and such like, "blowing" in the best colonial style. I pick up a newspaper, 'tis a bound copy of yesterday's *Argus*. I have no taste for politics, little for news, and so disregard the "leading daily." I perambulate my room, for I am a lodger of a week's acquaintance with Easyville folks, and have retained a room solely for myself. I examine the chamber and the pictures which decorate the walls, and finally settle down on a sofa, to drown my *ennui* in sleep. But what is the packet which attracts my attention as I lie reclined, at the farthest end of my chamber. In a dark nook I first beheld it, a dried, crumpled fold of papers tied with stained and faded pink silk ribbon. What can it be? Probably some title deeds! lost by some former tenant of this chamber! Perhaps it might be a draft for £10,000 on some of the banks. I will see. I open it carefully—slowly—and what do I find?

A bundle of MSS. containing sketches of Easyville, written by some lounger for amusement, and entitled "Chronicles of Easyville," by a visitor. The first paper which attracts my eye is this:

The Strange Unknown

What a charming little town is this Easyville! How compact; how nicely arranged into streets; and, above all, what an enlightened population it possesses. I have been "taking stock" of them as I stroll along Gossip-street, and I confess that I have seldom, if ever, met with a more intellectual lot of mortals. I watch them every day, as group after group passes beneath my window; and, sooth to say, they are a rare galaxy of "stars." We have the bush politician, the bush lawyer, the bush doctor. We have poets (male and female) and artists ditto. We have musicians galore, and—well, I must not omit to say we have a few clergymen; but they are certainly in the minority, although Easyville possesses three churches and two schools.

There goes a local J.P., with his hat set jauntily on one side of his neatly-combed head. Behind him, puffing a cigarette, and walking as hurriedly as if the safety of the Easyville folks depended upon his speed, struts a coxcomb of the first water—a new arrival from the Victorian metropolis, and by all exterior appearances, an ass!

But I see today a new arrival at Easyville. I have been noticing him as I sat at breakfast this morning. He passed by my window twice or thrice, as if in meditation, and he seems to be a strange individual.

And I—pardon this fault—am a curious personage: I am on fire to know who this stranger is, albeit this curiosity of mine is a sin against courtesy. I must know him; he seems so totally unlike the common folks of Easyville. I put on my surcoat—for the day is cold and inclined to be rainy—and walk abroad. I seek out this "strange unknown", and meet him at the Hotel Square.

Of course, the meeting is accidental. I bow. He returns the salute; and I stop to ask some questions relative to the place, being a stranger. He replies as best he can; and I am convinced that he is an extraordinary individual; and, after surveying him closely for ten minutes, I invite him to my lodgings. He acquiesces; and so, kind reader, we become acquainted.

Now, dear reader, I cannot introduce you to this individual, because I know not his name or nation. He wished to preserve an *incognito*, and the "strange unknown" is the only name he bestowed upon himself. To all appearances, he is a Frenchman—a fine handsome fellow, with dark hair and whiskers, and an eye of that deep penetrating sort that looks *through* its objects, and is never off its guard.

I will detail an account of our first acquaintanceship, as nearly as possible.

We had tea and demolished a bottle of port. My friend became a little more talkative, and told me his business at Easyville. He was a travelling artist, and painted well. Some of his pictures might have graced the walls of our colonial picture galleries, and have met with few equals from colonial artists. One especially—"The Love Test"—which he showed me, was really a masterpiece of colouring and expression. It represented a young

Tyrolese and his maiden lover standing beside the mouth of the black ravine, overhung with trails of ivy and fern. The maiden stood, or rather clung, to her lover's neck, imploring him to remain at home; for he was about to go abroad. He pointed to the bleak, cold ranges of his native country, as if asking, "What was to be done there to gain a decent living." He was a fine, handsome youth, and from his belt hung a dagger, which his fair partner essayed with hand to grasp, in order to put herself to death rather than part with him, while with the other she clung to his neck. A glance sufficed to show what idea the picture meant to convey, and I confess I was charmed with it.

"You see, monsieur," he said, addressing me, "that picture is expressive of a passion, which, though I painted the ideal on canvas, I never believed to exist in one-half of human nature."

"You do not think, then," I replied, "that there is such a thing as love capable of standing a test like that represented in your picture?"

"*Parblieu*! No monsieur, I *know* it."

"You have had experience then?" I continued, hoping to draw him out further.

He shrugged and looked vacantly at the window for some time, but made no response.

"I have a reason for preserving an incognito," he said, after a few moments silence; "but though brief our acquaintance, monsieur, I confess I like you better than any of your species that I have met with in my life.

"My species! What do you mean?"

"You are a man are you not?"

"I hope so. So are you, I presume?"

"*Pardieu!* No, I am a—"

"A what?" said I, in surprise.

"A demon!" he yelled, and in an instant he had gone.

"My God!" I exclaimed, after I recovered myself thoroughly. "The fellow is a lunatic; and yet I never saw aught so strange! This is a sort of madness not easily explained."

I went to bed, and remained all night awake, thinking of this mysterious stranger. There was something unearthly about his looks, I thought, after one surveyed him closely.

Next morning I was strolling through Gossip-street square, and I met the Strange Unknown. He smiled and seemed as placid and cool as if we had parted in the most courteous manner on the previous night.

I confess that I did not half relish his acquaintance this time; but before I could offer an excuse for going, he took my arm and led me along the street, saying, "You see, monsieur, I am a strange character altogether."

I confess that I thought him such.

"Well, monsieur, I wish to ask you one question. Will you be kind enough to reply and trust to my honour. I can hold your secrets (as you think they are) for I know them already if I choose to tell them to others. You love a young lady not twenty yards from here?" and he pointed with his forefinger to the house, where I confess dwelt the object of my love.

Thunderstruck at his supernatural knowledge, for so I deemed it, I replied that I did, and asked him how he learned it.

"You slept none last night, monsieur," he continued, without replying to my query, "and tonight you will meet with a mishap."

"You have a rival in that quarter, and your 'lady love' knows not that you love her, otherwise...." Here he paused.

"Go on," I exclaimed, breathless with agitation.

"You will learn the rest, monsieur, soon enough. I shall be with you when you expect me not. I trust you will be fortunate. *Bon jour*!" And he left me.

I went to my lodgings ruminating over my adventures with this strange individual. Who could he be? No doubt he *was* a human being. I never believed in the supernatural, but here my unbelief got a home-thrust. This man, whom I never saw 'til I arrived in Easyville, could tell me secrets of my past life, and point out the very girl whom I loved. I went to bed, and tossed to and fro in hope of sleep, but it fled my eyes. I rose up in desperation and dressed; I walked into the street. "Some fatal fascination is about the fellow," thought I; "I will cut his acquaintance;"

and such I intended to do. But imagine my horror at beholding the individual—the mysterious stranger of three days' acquaintance, again. He came up to me as I strolled up and down the street. It was about midnight.

"Not in bed?" he exclaimed, with a sardonic smile on his thin lips.

"No," I muttered. "I wish the devil had you, for I verily believe you are not human."

But he only smiled—"You will see me again before you go to bed; good night," and he vanished.

I stood confused for a few minutes. "He is some juggler," I thought, and he intends to victimise me. I turned into my room, and arming myself with a pocket pistol, I sallied into the street again. This time I met him not. I walked on as far as the end of the township, and sat down to enjoy a smoke. Two men came hurriedly towards me as I lay, half-reclined on the grass. The stopped in front; they were both masked and carried bludgeons. I leapt up as they stopped before me.

"Who are you?" I asked.

"Oh, 'tis you, is it?" said the two in a breath. "Let him have it, Jack!" said one, and they sprang at me, sticks in hand.

I leapt backwards, and fired straight in front of me; but I missed, and aiming at the nearest of the two with the butt-end of the pistol, I knocked him senseless. But scarcely had I done so when I received a blow on the skull from his comrade which stretched me, senseless and bleeding, on the ground.

* * * * * *

When I recovered I found myself where I lay, with my face and clothes covered with blood, my pockets rifled, and my watch gone. I essayed to rise, but being weak from the loss of blood, could scarcely do so, when a friendly hand helped me; and turning to see who it was, I beheld the mysterious stranger.

"I told you we would meet again before you went to bed. I hope you are not injured. I knew of this. I couldn't prevent it, but came in time to give you assistance, monsieur," said he.

"You knew of it—and why not let me know" I asked, turning fiercely on him. "You were aware that I was to be robbed, and maltreated, and—"

"I told you you would meet with a mishap tonight."

"You *are* a demon," I shrieked, "be gone!" And he left, smiling.

* * * * * * *

Ten days later I was sitting in the parlour of my love's mansion, chatting away and smiling at my happiness. It was the first time that I dared to speak of love to woman. But now I had already asked her hand, and she half-yielding, half refusing, deliberated. It was a dreadful moment for me. She turned her head away as if confused; her eye rested on some object, she quailed even as the bird beneath the fatal glance of the serpent. She uttered a low, agonising shriek, and fainted.

I left her to her friends to restore her, and, rushing to the door, sought for the object of her terror. But I met with none. Two hours later, I met the "strange unknown." He smiled one of his demoniacal smiles, and told me of the occurrence just described. "I know it," he muttered with a horrible grin; "but you will lose sight of me for a long time, monsieur—I leave you a *souvenir*. The picture which you fancied so much, the 'Love Test,' is yours. I left it at your lodgings," and so saying, he departed.

* * * * * * *

Three months later, and I was in Sydney. I was walking down Pitt-street. I had been to the theatre on the previous night, and, having indulged in ardent spirits, was rather unwell. I had left Victoria almost a month previous, and was seeking an engagement on the staff of a daily journal published in Sydney. My engagement with Miss C., at Easyville had been broken off;

she had assented, after the occurrence previously mentioned; but for some trifling cause we became alienated, and I determined never to visit Victoria again. I had forgotten, or tried to forget, the "old affection" of past days, and was musing on my future prospects, when, turning the corner of the street, I came suddenly on the strange, mysterious individual whose acquaintance I first cultivated at Easyville. He was attired in the same fashion as usual. The same demoniacal smile was on his thin lip; the same inexplicable look of mysterious intelligence was in his dark brown eye.

"We meet again, monsieur," he said, with an easy air; "I hope you are well. I expected to meet you here. Come and have a glass of wine."

I followed him mechanically, as if some mysterious agency impelled me. We sat in a back parlour of the hotel, and sipped our sherry.

"I am going to the continent, monsieur," he said, "and am glad I met you. You are likely to need me ere long, but I cannot be of any service to you *now*, seeing that your love has discarded you; nevertheless, this may be worth seeing, if only in remembrance of past affection." And he showed me a *carte* portrait. I stared at him in astonishment. It was a well-executed portrait of Miss C., of Easyville; and, as I was aware that he was a total stranger to her, I marvelled how he became possessed of it.

"You wonder how I came to have it!" he said, with a grim smile, evidently knowing my thoughts. "I cannot tell you though," he added; "but, if you will, I will show you the original; that is, if you allow me to do so, *here,* tonight."

Overwhelmed at his suggestion, I agreed.

Night came, and I was sitting with legs towards the grate, reading a volume of Bulwer Lytton's, when the strange unknown entered.

He had the same easy, nonchalant air about him, and carried a small parcel under his arm. He seated himself beside me, and after a few minutes' hesitation, asked if I wished to see the original of the *carte*? Half incredulous of his power, I replied in the affirmative, resting assured that Miss C. was at Easyville.

After muttering something in a language unknown to me, and making three signs with his right hand, he said, "Behold her!"

I turned abruptly, and lo, before me stood the fair, graceful figure of my quondam love, Miss C. It was for a moment only, and she vanished.

"By heaven!" I exclaimed, leaping upright. "Thou art a devil to do this!"

"Steady, monsieur!" he smilingly replied. "It is only the shadowy resemblance—the spiritual essence of the fair Miss C. The real clay original is—"

"At Easyville, of course," I replied.

"Yes, monsieur; but in the grave there!"

And he was right.

* * * * * * *

It is five years ago since Miss C. died, and today I stand looking from my chamber window at her once beautiful mansion. The very window, when I first beheld the "strange unknown" walking up and down Gossip-street, six years ago! How altered all things seem since then! I am in the "sere and yellow leaf" now, my heart crushed, my hopes blighted, and my health impaired.

I have been thinking of this "strange unknown" today. I never saw him since the memorable night in Sydney. I expect to see him again. There is a fatal link that binds me to this man, or demon, whatever he be, and I cannot sever it. Today, I strolled to the cemetery at Easyville. I saw Miss C's grave, and wept over it. Tomorrow finds me on board ship for Europe.

I never loved but once, and that love was unrequited. I take the picture of the "Love Test" with me. I am a ruined, broken-spirited man now. Fortune seems to turn against me, and I am haunted with visions of the "strange unknown."

I never speak of him—or of my strange adventures with

him—to any. They would laugh at my silly story; but I feel that there is some fatality about the man, or demon, that I am subservient to. I hope I may never meet him again.

The Haunted House

Moreton Hall is the oldest and largest mansion in the vicinity of Easyville, and it stands upon an eminence not half a mile from the township, half hidden amongst the recesses of a thickly clustering pinewood. A little creek runs at the western end of the wood, and a broad avenue, skirted on either side with lofty pines, leads us to the old mansion. Years ago the Hall and its lands were the property of a wealthy old Scotch gentleman, who died on the premises, and was buried in the village cemetery. The property fell into the hands of his nephew—for the old gentleman was a bachelor. The heir to Moreton Hall estate was a wild profligate young man, who spent his easily acquired wealth in betting, horseracing, and such like, and eventually became bankrupt. To add to his misfortune, he became addicted to drink, and from being one of the leading men of society in the neighbourhood, he fell into a state of dissipation and degradation, from which he hopelessly endeavoured to extricate himself. The rich and respectable shunned him, the poor despised him. Friendless and moneyless, and despicably clad, he left the neighbourhood, and sought to earn a livelihood in the metropolis, by manual labour; but death put an end to his misfortunes, for on the third day after his arrival in Melbourne, he was found dead in one of the low houses of Little Bourke street. He was buried at the expense of the Government; and his name forgotten amongst men.

He had scarcely been dead a week, ere strange rumours were circulated about Easyville that Moreton Hall was haunted. The new proprietor of the old mansion was a native of Sydney, a member of the legal profession, who had retired into private life, and hoped to live his life comfortably at the hall; but somehow he was disappointed; the servants asserted that the place was haunted; strange unearthly noises were audible at unlawful hours, and screams were heard ever and anon about the "witching time" of midnight. Fear took possession of their hearts, and the proprietor was forced to believe that there was something in it. Whether he heard the strange noises or not, he never said; but eventually the servants at Moreton Hall left one by one, and when strangers were brought in their stead, it was the same thing. They in turn declared that the house was haunted, some even averring that they saw the ghost stalking along the passage. The report spread, and the superstitious added their own to the mass of strange intelligence concerning the Hall. The proprietor left in turn, and let the place to a young farmer, a recent arrival from Gippsland. This man was newly married, and on the first night of his advent to the Hall his wife declared that she saw a man walk with folded arms and drooped head along the passage leading to the parlour. The young farmer, alarmed at this piece of intelligence, and knowing nothing of the report circulated concerning the place, instantly essayed to search for the intruder, whom he suspected to be some burglar. Armed with a revolver, he hunted up and down the place from one chamber to the other, holding a lighted candle in one hand and a revolver on full-cock in the other, but without success. He then retired to bed, and had scarcely done so, ere he and his partner heard the footstep of a man—a slow measured tread— along the passage. The young man, who was a courageous fellow, instantly leaped up and, armed with a revolver, rushed after the supposed burglar; but imagine his consternation when he found the doors all locked, the windows barred as he left them, and no trace of the twice sought for burglar. Determined to make the discovery, he called up his wife, and having attired themselves, they seated themselves by the fire, with a lighted candle on the table beside them. Again they heard the footstep along the passage, as if coming towards the chamber wherein they were seated, eagerly listening. A strange fear took posses- sion of the pair as the footsteps approached them. The husband grasped the revolver, but it fell from his hand on the table, the wife looked at him with eyes distended with terror and alarm, and as a cold rush of air penetrated the room and blew out the light, she uttered one load shriek of terror and fainted.

When she recovered, she declared to her husband that she saw the figure of a man, attired in shabby habiliments, standing with his arms folded, and his eyes set fixedly, fearfully gazing at her, at the next moment the cold rush of air alluded to penetrated the room, and she saw no more.

The young farmer left the premises on that very night, and took his lodgings at a neighbour's house, to whom he related the whole of the strange affair. Of course the Easyville folks had heard the strange reports concerning the place from various other sources, and they advised the young man to leave the hall instantly, as no one had ever remained for any length of time in the place at night since Harry Greville, the young profligate roué, died.

The young farmer took their advice and decamped; and for upwards of four years Moreton Hall was without an occupant.

At last a tenant in the person of an old sea captain, with a servant, rented it for a month. He had been apprised of all the danger of seeing an apparition within its walls after nightfall; but he laughed at the strange piece of intelligence.

Armed with an old cutlass and, having his servant at his elbow, the captain waited for the ghost of the witching hour. Nor did he wait long in vain. As the hour of midnight came, the footsteps of a man approached from the farther end of the passage, and stopped abruptly in front of the chamber wherein the captain and his servant were located. This was the same chamber where the young farmer and his wife were seated when the latter beheld the ghost of young Greville. At this moment, the captain's servant (an Irishman named Clynch) uttered a loud scream and rolled from his seat senseless on the floor. The captain threw a jug of water over him, and, with his eye fixed on the door, waited patiently.

The captain was in no way superstitious; he believed that the whole cause of the strange reports, etc., originated with some natural design, some trick of an intriguer for his own purpose. But his opinion soon changed when he beheld in the doorway the figure of a man, dressed in a suit of grey habiliments, with his arms folded on his breast, and his eyes glaring wildly.

The courage which supported the captain on former occasions did not desert him now; so calling on the ghostly intruder to speak and declare his errand, he was somewhat astonished to see the apparition point to a small nook adjoining the fire-place, and disappear without uttering a word. The captain roused his servant into a state of consciousness, and they searched the nook in question. It was a small aperture in the wall, wherein a stove had once been placed, but which had long been unused. In this aperture the skeleton of a human being (to all appearance that of a woman, from the length of the hair still attached to the skull) was found doubled up, as if it had been placed or compressed in that manner, in order to conceal it within the small compass accorded to it. To drag this skeleton from its place of concealment was the work of a few moments; and, on the following day, the captain communicated with the authorities, and a minute search was made in and about the premises of Moreton Hall.

The skeleton was recognised as that of a young woman who was the paramour of Harry Greville, and who suddenly disappeared from the place a year or so previous to his downfall. He had circulated a report that she had gone to England; and the report was credited. The fact was, the unfortunate woman was murdered by him and hidden in the aperture in the wall, a place where no one would have sought for aught concerning her fate. But his shade could not rest 'til the affair was cleared up; and, strange though it be, it is an acknowledged fact that Moreton Hall no longer possesses the repute of being haunted since the memorable discovery of the skeleton, and at the time I write this it is tenanted by the local attorney, a gentleman to whom the reader is referred for the credence of the above marvellous tale.

L'envoi

So ends the "Chronicles of Easyville," which I found carefully tied up in a packet at my hotel lodgings. I made researches
and inquiries amongst the residents of Easyville, and found
that "the Strange Unknown," "The Dan O'Toole," "My Friend
D'Arcy," and "Tim Mulvaney," are no fictitious characters, and
now as I sit leisurely smoking my pipe, I can see "Moreton Hall"
in the distance, and I marvel much at the strange story of its
having once been haunted. Of Paul Selwyn, "The Wronged and
the Wronger," I may say that there is a picture of his (painted by
him a year before his death) hanging in the parlour of my hotel
lodgings, and entitled, "A glimpse of the Snowy Mountains."
They tell me that the landscape artist was a constant visitor at
"Mac's Hotel" (my hotel lodgings), and painted this picture gra-
tis for my landlord. There is an *on dit* report current in Easyville
also that "My friend D'Arcy" is at present in Melbourne, and
contributes occasionally to the weekly journals. So be it. In the
meantime I beg leave to bid adieu to the reader, and conclude
my postscript with a verse of one of D'Arcy's songs:

> *"When a man has fleeced his pockets out,*
> *How gruff a "pub" looks I know;*
> *Because a man should never "shout"*
> *Unless he's got the "rhino."*
> *And when a yarn, spun out too dry,*
> *Grows dull in any quarter,*
> *What should a fellow do? Well, why,*
> *Of course, to cut it shorter!"*

POINT DESPAIR

by H. B. Marriott Watson

H. B. Marriott Watson (1863-1921) was born in Melbourne, educated in New Zealand, and settled in England in 1885 where he took up journalism. He was assistant editor on *Black and White* and the *Pall Mall Gazette* and eventually published over fifty books. He collaborated with James Barrie on the play *Richard Savage*. He also penned several supernatural stories, including "The Devil of the Marsh" and the vampire tale "The Stone Chamber." His short story collections *Diogenes of London and other Fantasies and Sketches* (1893), *The Heart of Miranda* (1899), *Alarums and Excursions* (1903), and *Aftermath: A Garner of Tales* (1919) contain the odd supernatural tale. The following story comes from an early Australian anthology, *By Creek and Gully* (1899), and concerns a Maori massacre.

A generation has slipped away since the Great Massacre, and even in this district in which I live, scarcely a hundred miles from the theatre of that abominable tragedy, the facts are almost forgotten, at least blurred to a fading patch of colour. It is remarkable how swiftly time passes; and what was yesterday a fear, tomorrow will become a reminiscence somewhat agreeable to talk over. Yet upon my mind are scored deeply the recollections of that horrible scene.

In the year of the Great Massacre I was in my eighth year, pretty sharp for a child, though somewhat undersized. My escape came about in this way. I had left Point Despair about eleven in the morning in the company of a lad, somewhat over my own age, who was returning to his people at Murimuru, some twelve miles distant. The road was plain and easy, running for some miles along the coast; moreover, living alone with my uncle, I maintained a certain licence in my expeditions. Consequently, I asked no leave to slip forth and accompany this playmate a certain part of his journey. It was a bright, warm day; we had some sandwiches in our pockets, and there was the sea smiling with a thousand lures at our feet. The suggestion was irresistible; we stripped to the skin, half way to Murimuru, and idled most of the afternoon in the water. It was not until my companion was suddenly pricked by his tardy conscience, and marched off, declaring he must make Murimuru with all speed, that I turned to retrace my way to Point Despair. The road as it reached the point, dipped into a sparse piece of bush, through which it twisted irregularly for a mile or more, and ere I had issued from its shadows the dusk had fallen.

It was not at once that I was struck by the singular quiet which ruled the flat, for I was occupied at the moment with lively fears about my length of absence; but half way to the post-house some uneasy appreciation of the stillness brought me up, and almost simultaneously I noticed a column of thin smoke rising at the back of Willis's lean-to. With that the significance of the silence went out of my mind; there was plainly a fire forward, a most unusual event in our small settlement, and, my anxiety forgotten, I broke into a run, thrilling under the stimulus of a new sensation. I had barely passed the lean-to in the dull twilight when I stumbled and went sprawling over something in the pathway. The thing gave way under me, shifting a little aslant, and I cannot tell you my sensations when I perceived it to be a dead body. The light was still sufficient to see by, and ere I withdrew with a pant of alarm and terror I recognised the face, which was now staring up at me, as that of Willis himself. The spectacle was horrible. I carry it still in my memory, as vivid and as ghastly as on that evening thirty years back. God knows how barbarously the wretch had been done to death, or perhaps the innumerable and dreadful wounds had been inflicted after the release of that poor spirit. My mouth fell open, and my eyes watched the dead man's fearfully, drawn with a nameless attraction. It was the first time, I had ever encountered death, and I had no power of motion in my limbs. My legs shook, I stood transfixed; the stare of those dead eyes held and terrified me, But presently the tide of reflection returned; I took my gaze from the corpse and let it go round the vicinity.

I was alive now, on wires of fear, ready to jump off at an instant's sound. But no noise came save the low, persistent murmur of the sea upon the shingle. Even then I had not conceived the fate which had fallen on the settlement. The horror had been so extreme that it had dulled my nerves, but as the blood flowed anew from my heart a certain reaction set in, and I was able to gather my wits together. I supposed that this Willis, who had never been popular with me for a sourness of temper, had met with an abominable accident, and that I was the first to come upon the tragedy. The news, shocking as it was in all the horrid circumstances of its presentment, roused in me an alacrity, and I hurried to be off. I turned from the still and stupid body, which as it lay had somehow a look of obscene importance, and I scuttled towards my home with all speed.

As I did so the dark and moving shadows of the column of smoke saluted my eyes once more. Vague and distant in my mind was a restless wonder of this appearance. I had a momentary presage of a wider fear, unintelligible but colossal, and then I was running for life with the terror of that defiled body at my heels.

The house in which I kept my uncle company was little more than a shanty, and lay about the middle of the four-and-twenty houses which constituted the township of Point Despair. The settlement held no street; it had not reached the dignity of order, and few of the plots were enclosed. A kitchen-garden, containing a handful of gooseberry-bushes, a few currant-bushes, and rows on rows of cabbages and potatoes, for the most part surrounded each dwelling-place. Macfarlane's house alone had the luxury of a verandah, and was, in addition, fenced with posts and rails, against which grew a hedge of *pinus insignis*. Here it was that I stopped for the third time. For the front door, flung wide, was squeaking in the breeze and a figure in a woman's dress lay in a heap on the verandah.

The sight sunk me back into my abject fears. I would have fled past it on the feet of panic, had not a horrible fascination mingled with my terror. I had come direct from one corpse upon another. The bare fact of this sequence appalled and benumbed me, and yet once more I was drawn insensibly to inspect this second horror.

It was not so dark but I could make out every particular of that mangled heap. I remember that I pored over it stupidly, noting every ghastly detail, but comprehending little. My imagination suffered under a surfeit of the earlier horrors, and could digest no more. She lay with an arm clutching at her side; it may be she kept some secret in that final moment, or perhaps it was merely by an instinct of defence. I could peer at the body so, but I should have shrieked out to have touched it with a fingertip. When I left the verandah I had no proper sensations and no settled thoughts save a desire to get home. So incapable was I of further impressions that the body of a child in the pathway conveyed no meaning to me, though I was conscious that its name had been Sally. I merely accepted it as a natural part of this strange and rather terrible condition. I stepped over the child, backed away from it cautiously, keeping my eyes upon it, and then swiftly resumed my former gait. It might perhaps have leaped upon me. I knew not what would happen.

The smoke was rising from the ruins of the store, which stood only a few paces from my uncle's cottage. The flames had not worked much harm, as the fire been unskilfully kindled, for the roof alone had been consumed, and the walls were still solid, but smouldering. Even the windows, though they were broken, showed still a few packages of grocery. The sight of the store, filled, as I pictured it, with innumerable sweets and treasures, struck me with more interest than the dead bodies, and for a moment I awoke to a thrill of excitement. But it was only mechanical, and I hardly paused to wonder as I dashed through the patch of cabbages to the door of my home. I had no thought of finding my uncle also dead, but the image of the woman returned persistently, and I glanced involuntarily about to see if perchance the body lay here also. As I entered by the door, which stood open, and my resounded familiarly upon the wooden flooring, something of comfort warmed me suddenly, and yet something of trouble too. I went clattering through the rooms, calling upon my uncle, a quaver in my tones.

The sound of my voice, solitary in the dusk alarmed me further. No uncle answered me: there was no reassurance from the falling night. Indeed, the only noise that reached me came from the shore a mile away, where the waves of the Pacific moaned by day and night perpetually. It inspired me now with fresh terror to hear this melancholy sound, of which as a rule I passed unconscious, save on nights of storm. Inside the house it was more obscure than in the open road but in two rooms I could swear that there was no sign of my uncle. One corner of the third was wrapped in deeper darkness, and upon this I stared with dilating eyes. I dared not enter and inquire there. Somehow the conviction grew in me firmly that there sat my uncle in the evil blackness of that corner with a grin upon his face, and on his body all the gross marks of those dead creatures I had seen.

I had ceased calling, and the silence frightened me even more than my lonely voice. Terror crept over me, at first gently, and then with a rush. It held my face blanched and fixed towards the darkness, lest something should spring from it upon me. The rickety table by which I stood shook under my trembling hands, and the harsh grating and creaking completed my horror. I yelled like a cat, and like a cat fleeing from the room dashed out of the house, down the garden and into the road.

I ran on heedless of my direction until my wind was spent,

and then, the original impulse of fear being lost in breathless fatigue, I stopped, and found that I was on the sandhills that filled the mile between the sea and the houses of the Point. The air was warm, and I was now all a-sweat from my running. I could hear the water roaring louder than before upon the beach. Inwards, where the bush lay black, in the rear of the houses, was a, dreadful quiet. Somewhere across the dunes a *weka* called and was silent. The moon came out and shone faintly, for the night had already fallen as it is used to fall suddenly from southern skies. I was alive in a graveyard.

It was some time ere I was able to drag myself back to the houses. Indeed, I think nothing short of a new terror would have made me return. As I lay crouching in the "scrub" of the dunes my ears and eyes were preternaturally alert. The sand was covered with thin, rough tussock-grass, which shook and sighed in the wind. These sounds again discomfited me, and more particularly as the wind grew. A first breath of trouble, as it seemed to me, stirred through the long culms and set them gently whispering, as it had been the lamentation of a little child. Then with a slowly growing volume of wailing the reeds rocked and swayed in anguish, and it was as if the groans of that whole company of dead were expressed in my ears. The horrible tragedy, as I now conceived it, was enacted before me in these noises. As the wind rose I heard the shrieks of the poor women barbarously handled, and the screams and prayers of the dying returned to me; and as it fell so I conceived again a silence to fall upon the settlement, which was the final stillness of death.

This impression made such a mark upon me that the beats of my heart quickened to a gallop, and I began to see life start from the inanimate bushes and creepers about me. What nameless things I imagined were haunting those trembling and invisible bushes I have now no notion, nor indeed had I at the time. The dunes were alive with crying ghosts, and I was alone with them. I was stung once more into action, and with despair in my heart I crept from the open seaward space into the settlement again.

I took up my post now as distinct from the houses as I could manage to be, without being actually beyond the precincts of the township. A space, still unoccupied, and the common playground of children, spread out before the store, and upon a slope in this, where the ground rolled up against a patch of bush, I sat in a heap of furze and watched the night. Some sparks of fire lingered in the beams of the store, and broke out into flame from time to time, revealing thick clouds of smoke that still rolled upwards to the moon. I took a certain comfort in this companionship, and after a time my terrors had so nearly subsided that I began to feel hungry; for I had eaten no food since midday. Though my spirit was returning, and my fancies were gone, I lacked the courage to approach my uncle's cottage, or even to explore the store, in which I was sure to find some food. I endured the pangs with fortitude rather than face the unknown terrors across the threshold. But presently I remembered the wild fuchsia-tree which grew in the bush at my back, and with some of the *kanini* berries I stayed my appetite. The scene was so peaceful, and my refuge among the ferns was so warm that I grew even cheerful, and was soon whistling softly to myself; and when at last my extreme thirst compelled me to make a journey to the creek, two hundred yards away, I set out upon the expedition with scarcely any reluctance.

A house with a garden which in our wilderness had always been held quite magnificent, stood upon the verge of the creek. I had made the distance swiftly and in a respectful silence, but having taken my drink without accident I resumed something of my normal ease and security and strolled back more leisurely, whistling the catch of a song. But at the gate of the house I was brought suddenly to a halt, my heart stood for a moment still, and I was rooted to the earth with the fear of what I saw. Something was moving under the white light in the rude track before the gate, crawling and crawling, as it seemed, towards me. It was not until the clouds streamed from the moon and the light grew clearer, that I realised the cause of my stupefaction. It was the body of a woman, stirring feebly, and as soon as I had perceived this my fright left me and I drew closer and looked down upon it. I recognised her at once as Mrs Stainton, a young woman of comely appearance, who since her advent to Point Despair three months before, with her newly-married husband, had shown me much kindness. She was still alive, and as I stood over her, not knowing what to do, she groaned and opened her eyes upon me. She lifted her hand and beckoned to me feebly; but I was reluctant to approach, and eyed her from a yard, or two away. I saw her part her lips and struggle for speech. Her body writhed, and features were contorted with her efforts. Her uplifted arm shook and fell.

But still I held aloof. In truth, I feared to approach lest she should take hold of me. She made a little upward motion of her head three times, as though she were striving to rise upon her elbow; but if it were so, the attempt was vain; her body quivered and her head sank back, and with a tiny sigh she was still. I waited a moment and then bent over her.

"Mrs Stainton!" I called, "Mrs Stainton!"

She returned no sign, and with alarm I perceived that her eyes were still open and were staring at me. I got up and ran away from the spot hastily.

Once in my lair among the bracken I felt safe and comfortable. The repugnance of the dead bodies did not pursue me thither. I was covered up from the eye of heaven in the long ferns, and in my warm seclusion sheltered from the wind by the patch of bush at my back. I soon began to nod. The walk of the afternoon had tired me and the mental disturbance of the last two hours had added to my weariness. I do not think I should have attached any importance to the very presence of the murderers at their work, if the tragedy had been re-enacted before me. Curled up, with my knees to my chin, I passed gently to sleep.

I awoke some hours later with a dismal squalling in my ears. I sat up with a start in that sudden panic that seizes on the dreamer while yet he is halfway to his senses. My heart thumped and my eyes strained through the cloud of darkness. Presently I recognised the sound as the mewling of a cat hard by. It came from the pines behind me, and drew gradually nearer; so that in a little while it had approached quite close to my refuge, where it stood; as I could see now in the twilight of the dawn, crying desolately. I jumped to my feet and put out my hand.

"Puss! Puss!" I called softly.

The cat darted away, limping on three legs, and I heard the sound of something trailing through the grass. I followed still calling on it.

"Puss! Puss! Poor Puss!" I said in a condoling whisper. It stopped forlornly before a heavy log of wood which barred its way, and threw a scared glance at me. I made a little rush forward, but the creature spat passionately at me, and gathering itself together, with an angry growl scrambled up the log, dragging a broken leg. It vanished with a screech of pain into the undergrowth.

I groped my way back towards the bracken disconsolately. My nest was difficult to discover, for I was still drowsy, and I wandered for some minutes ere I lighted upon it. I had scarce found the bush by which it was marked when my foot stumbled upon something, and being very stiff and sore from my hard bed, I fell forward rather heavily. I put out my hands to save myself, and they touched the cold flesh of a dead body. I screamed and fled blindly, escaping into my hiding-place, where I lay trembling. Those terrible things had followed me even there; there was no escape for me. I listened for the footsteps. Would it approach? The chill of something worse than death struck my heart as I heard a slight movement in the grasses beyond the bush. I would have torn open the earth with my hands to bury myself. I cried out, calling on my uncle, who lay dead somewhere himself. Then there came a swishing sound; a cracking followed; and then with a sibilation of the tussock, the Thing slipped out of the detaining grasses and rolling with a soft thud from spot to spot, went down the little slope. I heard it pause in the hollow below, and silence once again prevailed.

* * * * * * *

The sun was far gone in the sky when I awoke with the noise of horse-hoofs clattering in my ears. From the rise I could command a view of the road from the point where it ran into the bush; and along this a horseman was cantering leisurely towards me. Save for the wounded cat and the last few moments of that flickering spirit the night before, this was the first live thing I had set eyes upon since my return; and, once assured that it was no marauding Maori returning to his terrible work, I jumped to my feet, and scampered to meet the rider. The body in the hollow caused me a little gasp of fright as I passed it, all but treading on it again in the long grass. But even this reminder of my fears availed nothing against my sudden burst of joy. I ran down the road and met the horseman ere he turned the corner by the first cottage.

"Mr Stainton! Mr Stainton!" I called in excitement.

He threw a nod at me, but he did not draw rein.

"That you, Johnny?" he said. "What brings you up early like this?"

Even as he spoke and passed by, without waiting for an answer, a nameless and delicate fear came over me. I saw him now heading his horse for that house; and outside that house I saw what was waiting for him beckoning me again with crooked fingers. For a moment I stood paralysed behind him, and then, a deeper instinct moving in my boyish mind, I ran at the heels of his horse, shouting in a treble:

"Mr Stainton! Mr Stainton!"

He must not, I felt dimly, be suffered to come wholly unprepared upon the remains of that tragedy. But my cries were ineffectual; he waved his riding-whip as in greeting, without looking back, and cantered on. I stood for a space of time, not knowing what to do, whether to go forward or to retreat. Then, broken by my doubts and the dreadful thing my instinct scented, I took the latter course and hid in the bushes again. It must have been a quarter of an hour later that I perceived Mr Stainton coming back from the creek. He was riding fast, and his horse shied before the house with the verandah at something in the path.

When he came abreast of me I rushed out, calling to him again"

"Mr Stainton! Mr Stainton!"

He turned his face towards me, and I saw that it was stricken ghastly white. His fingers shook on his bridle, and he stared at me, paying me no heed.

"Mr Stainton, take me with you," I moaned. "Take me with you."

It was as if he saw me not. He went by like a flash, unheeding, with his grey face evil with terror; and down the road I ran, sobbing and crying after him, 'til he had vanished into the bush and I was all alone again.

Yet this desperate and unavailing act had accomplished one thing. I had passed in my flight the limit of the township, and was now beyond the graveyard. Recognising this at last I dashed into the bush, and that lamentable flat became lost to my sight.

Caetera desunt.

A NEW SPECIES

by Robert Coutts Armour

The Red Magazine, June 1921

Robert Coutts Armour (1874-1945/56?) was born on 14 September 1874 in Brisbane to Robert Armour and Maria Coutts. Maria died on 20 October 1879, when Robert was four, and his father died on 4 June 1895 shortly after leaving Brisbane for England. The following year, Robert successfully sued for the wrongful detention of the title of his father's property in Queen Street Brisbane, claiming the property and £1000 damages. It is not known exactly when he moved to England, but he was certainly living in London in 1899, sustained by the proceeds of the sale of the Queen Street property. In the 1901 census his occupation is given as artist, and he is living with his wife, Edith, at 14 Dancer Rd, Fulham, whom he had married around 1899. By 1911, Armour and Edith had moved to a three-room house at 6 St Luke's Road, Clapham, in London, and he was working as a litho-graphic artist. By 1912 he was writing short stories for Harmsworth's *Red Magazine* (he illustrated one of his own stories in the August 1914 issue). In all he pub-lished about 100 stories for Harmsworth's *Red Magazine*, *Yellow Magazine* and *Green Magazine* under the pseudonyms Coutts Brisbane and Reid Whitly, most of them science fiction and fantasy stories. From 1921 Armour became a prolific author for the Amalgamated Press' Sexton Blake Library. The year of his death is uncertain.

Eternally battered by demoniac seas, ringed by reefs wicked as a shark's teeth, outermost of the Outer Hebrides, the isle of Eiarn is but seldom visited by man. The sea-birds own it. Their ceaseless crying cuts shrilly across the boom of the waves breaking at the foot of basalt cliffs, or thundering into the recesses of caves worn by ages of unremitting hammer strokes. They brought Porter to Eiarn.

He was a little grey man, very lithe and active, brown of face from incessant exposure to all kinds of weather, with a twinkle in his grey eyes and the infernal patience of a cat hidden somewhere behind them.

Indeed, there had been need of that last quality before ever he got to the island, for he had waited nearly two months until the launch which he had chartered dared put out; and even then they had lain for a day and a night in the lee of the place ere the cargo she carried could be landed. Provisions enough for half a year had been hurried ashore, and in hot haste the launch's crew erected the hut Porter intended to make his home for the next three months. It was very small, but strongly made of sections which bolted together, with a roof that offered no hold to the wind and a well-fitted door, calculated to resist the pelt of hurricane driven rain. It was placed in a niche a little below the flat summit of the island, and well ballasted with heavy stones.

"I reckon ye'll no get blawn awa' there Maister Porter," said the skipper, as he finished his labours and drew back to observe the result. "Man, it's no' me that's envying ye. This is no' canny place. There's tales, ye ken—"

"Oh, I've heard all the yarns," replies Porter. "The sea folks come here, don't they—mermaids and mermen and all sort of thing? Well, I dare say I shall be glad of their company. I'll ask 'em to tea, eh?"

"Mebbe it's you they'd be wanting for dinner," the skipper chuckled; and then since the sea was rising once again, hurried his fellows aboard.

Half an hour later the little vessel was out of sight down to leeward, and Porter was monarch of all he surveyed.

His first feeling, so he says, was one of elation. A keen ornithologist, he had long dreamed of this expedition. This solitude peopled by a multitude of birds, was paradise enough for him. He had his cameras, a gun and a little rifle for collecting specimens, egg blowing apparatus, preservatives for notebooks, a full equipment, and inexhaustible material. He was happy.

The weather held fine for something more than a fortnight, during which he was busy from sunrise 'til far into the night, grudging the time, spent over meals because he knew well that such favourable conditions could not last long.

"Then there came a gale from the northward,—a regular snorter," he says. "I thought I knew something about wind, but that was an experience I'd hardly care to live through again. I dared not venture more than a few steps from the hut, lest I should be torn off the rock and slung into the sea. The air was full of spray, so that I could hardly see my feet, and the row was appalling. The whole island quivered, and grew nervous lest the rock under which the hut lay should topple bodily on top of me. I put in a lot of time piling up big stones around the hut and on the roof. By the time the gale abated it had the place nearly buried in stones. At a little distance it looked like some Palaeolithic dwelling, and nothing short of an earthquake could have shifted it."

Calm succeeded the hurricane, comparative calm that is, with a light south-westerly wind that brought rain, and only a moderate groundswell. Porter seized the opportunity of neap tide to explore certain low-lying ledges which he had not ventured to visit before, and wandered a good way from the strip of beach in the tiny cove, or recess, that was the landing place, 'til the turn of the tide warned him it was time to return.

"I was disappointed, for I had hoped to reach the mouth of a cave which I could see from the cove. There were certainly nests in it, and I wanted to observe the habits of the troglodytes. But there was no sense in risking a wetting, or perhaps an uncomfortable night in the open, so I took one or two photographs and turned about. The ledge was narrow, and I had to go slowly. I came to a corner, and was in the act of slipping round it, when I had a queer sensation that something was looking at me.

"Perhaps you know the feeling? I remember a fellow at the Travellers' telling a yarn of how he was stalked by a lion on the veldt. He said he would have fallen an easy prey to the brute if he hadn't suddenly felt its eyes boring into his back, as it were. Well, this was exactly the same thing. I felt eyes upon me, and a chilly creeping of the skin along my spine.

"I turned as sharply as I could. There was nothing on the ledge, absolutely nothing, nor on the face of the rocks above. Nothing could have scaled that scarp. Then I saw a ring of ripples spreading across the face of the smooth water in the cave-mouth, as though something had just dived there. I waited a minute, but saw no more, so went on and reached the cove all right.

"There is a steep path up from the beach, and the flat ledge behind it, to the hut. I paused at the foot of it, took a final look round, and started up. Then I had the feeling again! I whisked about, with no better luck, for though I thought I saw something vanish from the midst of the cove, the sea was too lively to show any ripples there.

"I climbed the path, puzzling over the matter. Some of the diving birds have an uncanny way of disappearing when one turns towards them, but I had had them stare at me often enough before without feeling it, and, besides, the bird that could have made such a disturbance as those ripples by the cave must have been a monster such as I had never heard of.

"I concluded that it must have been a seal, and then it occurred to me that I had seen none since my arrival, though the island seemed an ideal spot for the creatures. This was the more curious in that I had not seen many along the coast of Lewis, and on the trip out. But perhaps they had gone northward for the summer, leaving one old, solitary bull, who, grown cautious through years, would take no risks. On the whole, I thought this the most likely notion.

"I spent the rest of the afternoon developing an accumulation of plates, and went early to bed to rise with the sun. That was the finest day of my whole stay. The sky was cloudless and the sea nearly calm, so I ventured to bathe.

"What I had called the beach of the cove was in reality a sloping shelf of rock, with shingle in pockets and crevices. It dipped suddenly, so that after wading three or four steps I was in deep water. I swam out for perhaps a hundred yards, turned over on my back, and floated. Except for the gentle heave of the swell, the sea was perfectly smooth.

"Then suddenly I saw a swirl on the surface close to me, the sort of eddy that is caused by a big fish swimming just below the surface, and a moment later had that same old uncanny feeling that I was being observed from behind.

"I turned over, but once again too late. There was a ring of spreading ripples, but nothing more. I did not wait. I am no great swimmer, but, I fancy I must have covered the hundred yards to shore in something close to record time. I think, though not sure, that the Thing accompanied me on a parallel course, until I stood upright and splashed up the shelf.

"I began to dress in a hurry, blundered into my trousers, and, losing my balance; thrust a foot against a sharp stone, cutting it rather badly. I had splashed the rock freely with my blood before I succeeded in stanching the wound. I sat down on a rock to finish my toilet, cursing the ill-luck that would confine me to the neighbourhood of the hut for several days to come, when, round the buttressed end of the island came a fishing-boat. She was well out, but, on seeing me wave, turned towards the cove, dropping her sail to negotiate the reefs about the entrance.

"There were four men aboard her, and it seemed to me that they were reluctant to come ashore. The two who were rowing hung on their oars, while the man in the bow shouted a string of questions, of which I understood nothing, since he spoke Gaelic. I noticed that the man steering had a gun across the thwart beside him—a somewhat unusual piece of furniture for a fishing craft.

"I beckoned hospitably, and made invitation as I hobbled to the water's edge. Finally, the boat came in, disembarked the bow man, and backed out quickly while he waded ashore in a mighty hurry, bursting into a flood of speech as he reached me.

"I fancy he was urging me to come aboard at once, to which I could only reply by shaking my head and pointing to my hut. When he saw the blood on the rocks and noted my wounded foot, he looked very concerned, much more than the matter warranted, I thought, and when at length I made him understand that I would have him come up and taste my whisky; he insisted on half carrying me over the lower part of the path. So far as I could make out, he thought the bloody trail I left on the stones an uncanny thing.

"When we got to the hut, he examined the door before he went in, nodding approval of its strength. While I poured out whisky he caught sight of my gun, and brightened a little, but on examining some cartridges, shook a desponding head, and by vigorous signs signified that he thought the charge No. 8 was the heaviest shot I had—far too light. As for the little rifle, he snorted contempt over it. Certainly a 22-calibre bullet is no great missile, though I have always found it sufficient for my purposes.

"Over the whisky he waxed eloquent. Indeed, it clarified his language signs so much that I understood clearly he wished me to come away with him at once, though it did not suffice to make me understand the reason why. I replied by showing him, on the calendar, the probable date of my departure, some nine weeks later, at which he threw up his hands in despair.

"Finally, seeing me adamant, he took his leave, but not before he had chopped a lead sinker, from his pocket, into slugs, with which he charged a cartridge in place of the despised small shot.

"From the door of the hut I saw the boat slide in and take him aboard, and at once shove off. In a few minutes they had caught a slant of wind, which took them out of sight in a short while, leaving me in a very low mind. In vain I reminded myself that these simple fishers believed all manner of weird legends that every rock of the thousands along coast was the haunt of some watersprite or mermaiden, that seals were the descendants of folks drowned at sea, and that once a year, on the Eve of St. John, they doffed their skins and danced on the beach in human form from midnight to dawn.

"Very likely Eiarn was haunted by some bogey, some baseless fabrication of the Celtic imagination, I told myself. What is more natural amidst perilous seas, where the red dawn comes up like blood, and all manner of queer sounds echo along precipices wreathed in sea mists?

"Yet even as I laughed half-heartedly, I knew that something more tangible than kelpies or witchwork lay behind the fisherman's evident anxiety. There is something very concrete about lead slugs. A man doesn't bother to hack up a good sinker merely on account of hypothetical merfolks.

"Could it be that the Thing was the cause of his perturbation? Had I had a narrow escape? And, above all, what under heaven could It be?

"I had time enough to ponder over the problem, for there was no going far that day. I redressed my wounded foot by the door of the hut, fed myself, and so sat me down again, staring at the cove, fancying at times that I could see something moving swiftly across it, a little below the surface, reflecting that, after all the dredging and netting that has been going on systematically for well over half a century men knew precious little about the inhabitants of the sea.

"Undoubtedly the ocean holds many species of which we have, so far, neither specimens nor record. The great sea-serpent may yet be proved no myth of bibulous sailor men, and the kraken not altogether a figment of the imagination.

"So went my musings, until a fog crept up I sat just within the doorway, the tiny and blotted the cove, the path, and everything but the ground on which I stood, out of sight. I went into the hut, and got out Campbell's *Myths and Legends of the Western Highlands*, which I had brought for light reading, and was soon deep in tales of warlocks and witches who could raise storms and go to sea in eggshells.

"I sat just within the doorway, the tiny window of the hut being useful only as a ventilator. The fog stood like a wall beside me; through the obscurity the eternal crying of the birds came fitfully, a thin wailing as of lost souls, that made a very fitting accompaniment to my reading. The light was fading. I was on the point of closing my book and rising to make tea, when, without a sound, something loomed up out of the fog within a couple of yards of me—a wavering indefinite thing that looked near as tall as a man.

"A sickening reek swept to my nostrils. Then I yelled in sheer panic, and at the sound of my voice the Thing vanished. I heard a rattle of stones, no more: the fog stood blank as before the visitation.

"'But there can't be anything!' I found myself shouting to vacancy. 'There's nothing here which could do that!'

"Which is—or was—perfectly true. Nothing of the apparent size of my phantom visitor able to climb the steep path from the sea existed in those waters, so far as natural history books recorded. A seal might have made the ascent, but, allowing for the magnification of the fog, this must have been the great father of all the seals, something of the dimensions of the elephant-seal, whose habitat lies half a world away from Eiarn.

"Thus, having convinced myself by a few seconds' reasoning that what I had seen couldn't exist, I leapt inside and slammed the door, shooting the bolt with a pang of regret that it was so frail a thing, then fortifying it with the heaviest packing-cases. In short, I was for a while in the bluest of funks.

"Only because I had seen something inexplicable in the fog? No. Rather it was the result, the culmination, of all that had gone before, and, most of all, the fisherman's anxiety for my safety. This Thing must be deadly, or that big, red-bearded man would never have made so much fuss. I shoved the cartridge he had loaded into the breech of my gun, and prepared several others in like manner using a leaden paperweight. When I had done this I felt happier. I was ready to protect myself.

"The evening wore on. Nothing happened. Finally I put out my lamp and turned in, all standing, dropping off to sleep almost at once, strange to say. Some hours must have passed before I was awakened by a noise outside, the sound of one of the stones I had piled against the walls falling with a rattle. A moment later another followed. Assuredly the Thing was trying to climb upon the roof. I lit the lamp, and as the rays streamed from the window I saw—or thought I saw—something dark move swiftly across the illuminated patch of fog outside.

"There was no more noise, but though I lay down I could not sleep again. When wan daylight came at last I could stand no more, but opening the door, peered out, my gun ready. Nothing! Except that some shreds of the blood-soaked handkerchief I had left lying by the door when I removed it, were scattered over the rocks.

"I went a little way down the path, and found more shreds here and there. The Thing had come up and gone back to the sea that way. I grew foxy. I would at least have notice of its coming, and be ready for it. So I piled a wall of small stones across in such a fashion that not even a rabbit could have passed without bringing them rattling down. Since there are no rabbits on Eiarn, there was little chance of a false alarm. Afterwards, I prepared a flare of straw and packing paper soaked with oil.

"I endeavoured to occupy myself with my notebooks, with little success, the gun between my knees bringing my thoughts back continually to what might be lurking in the fog close at hand. I don't think I ever spent a more uncomfortable day, and I was glad when at long last it began to grow dark, for I felt certain that my visitor would return.

"Leaving the window open, but shading the lamp so that only a glow could be visible from without, I settled to my vigil with ears pricking to every whisper of sound. At nine I ate my simple supper. At ten I gave up the pretence of reading. By twelve I had grown sulky, telling myself that the Thing would not come that night. And, only two or three minutes later, I heard my alarm-wall fall.

"I had rehearsed exactly what I would do, and did it without a hitch. I lit my flare, flung it through the window, then opening the door, sprang out and let drive a barrel down the path.

"There was a commotion of rolling stones, a sort of coughing bellow, a swirl of the fog, and something dark and indefinite blundered past up the hollow and so to the plateau beyond. I fired the second barrel into it as it passed, eliciting another roar.

"Then followed a great outcry from the birds as they rose before the disturber of peace, but since there was nothing more to be done I got me in again, reloading as I went.

"Slowly the racket among the bird folk died away; there was silence, save for the usual nigh noises. For the time the enemy was routed.

"But I did not sleep. The gully running past the hut was the only way down to the sea, so far as I knew, and the creature might return at any moment, paying me a visit in passing. However, I was no longer nervous, but rather eager to have another shot at the beggar. Chiefly I was consumed by curiosity, my glimpse of the Thing having in no way enlightened me. I had seen only a dark bulk which might have been anything, a blur shapeless as a puff of smoke.

I puzzled myself 'til daylight, then, since nothing seemed likely to happen, snoozed for several hours. The mist was gone from the upper part of the island when I awoke, though it still hung thickly above the sea. Determined to follow up my quarry and make an end of the mystery, if I could, I snatched a hasty breakfast and hobbled out.

"There was no difficulty in following the trail. A pool of blood where I had built the little wall, and many splashes all up the gully showed that I had hit hard. On the plateau above the trail was still plain. The creature had ploughed straight over the close lying nests, crushing eggs and fledglings in its passage.

"It seemed to have gone blindly for a little way, then steered towards the edge of the cliff, along which it had gone for a considerable distance, evidently seeking a path down. I walked very warily, expecting to come upon the brute at any moment. Several times I halted before a clump of boulders and threw stones. Nothing showed, however, and the trail ran on until I had come to a place almost immediately above the cave I had mentioned. There it plunged into gully so steep that I hesitated to negotiate it with my lamed foot for handicap.

"But after hesitating a little, I ventured so far as a large rock that jutted from the face of the cliff about thirty feet down. The descent took me some time, but at last I was securely seated in a crevice, and able to scan the remainder of the gully.

"As I had thought, it did not go right down, but ceased at a broad ledge some fifty feet above the sea. The mist still hung about the ledge, while I could only catch an occasional glimpse of the dark water below. The vapour swirled with the light breeze, now blotting out the ledge altogether, now thinning 'til it was only a gauze veil, through which I could see boulders and lichen patches wavering indistinctly.

"Something moved on the ledge, something long and large, so like in colour to the rock it lay upon that only the movement revealed it for a living thing. At which moment the mist thickened again, and I saw no more.

"Waiting was my game. I trained my gun between my knees, and watched the eddying drift of the wreaths for a full half-hour at least before they thinned once more; then, as the grey, humped form loomed out again, let drive both barrels.

"From aloft it looked as though a section of the ledge lifted a little, then rolled over into the sea. I had a clear sight of what seemed a webbed paw flailing out in a vain effort to hold on— then there came a mighty splash, and with it a rush of something which flung the water aside like the bow of a destroyer. The sea foamed, I could see two dark forms battling furiously, see the spray discoloured with blood—and then the mist closed down once more, leaving me as far from a solution as ever.

"For several minutes longer I heard the battle, then quiet fell, and when the mist cleared at last, before a gust, there was nought to see but a patch of stained water, which slowly cleared. Though I waited a long while, I saw nothing more.

"That afternoon my fishermen returned, bringing with them, for interpreter, their minister, a pleasant young fellow who spoke English with the Highland clearness of accent. He came ashore, accompanied by the red-beard who had first visited me, while, as before, the boat shoved off and the man in the stern kept his gun at the ready, precautions that no longer seemed ridiculous.

"The minister opened fire as soon as he was within hailing distance, by explaining who he was and why he came.

"'Angus Macpherson here came to me in great distress because he could not make you understand the grave risks you run by remaining here,' he began. 'So I had to come perforce, as it were. Have you been molested? What is all this?'

"He had halted before the first of the bloodstains, while Angus, in great excitement, poured out a torrent of Gaelic.

"'That is the blood of one of the grave risks,' I replied. 'I can give it no other name, since I have only had the merest glimpse of the creature.'

"'And Angus cannot tell what it is, either,' he said. 'There seem to be several. One of our boats has been missing, and the men declare that it was attacked by these things. Remnants of the craft that have been picked up show the marks of terrible teeth. This isle is supposed to be a haunt of the brutes. You had better leave with us. The opportunity may not occur again for a long while.'"

"Well, I left. Solitude is all very well, and birds are extremely interesting, but they may be studied under less exacting conditions. If I had to be continually on my guard, I should be able to do little more. Therefore, we carried my baggage to the boat and pushed off, not without many a backward glance towards the dark mouth of the cave which, I suspect, held the secret of the island."

Here ends the material portion of Porter's narrative. There

has been no further light on the matter, though several mysterious disappearances of fishing craft have been laid to the door
of the terrors of Eiarn.

Marine zoologists are puzzled. One suggests a new species
of seal, larger, more, ferocious than the gentle beasts we know
of, carnivorous and bloodthirsty. Another gloats on the prospects of discovering a novel sort of alligator which has taken
the sea for its province. A third boldly plumps for something
altogether new and strange, an amphibious shark-tiger, product
of heaven knows what evolutionary process in the mighty deep.

And, while the expedition that is to solve the riddle is being
got ready, Mr Porter wanders the halls of the United Services
Museum and all other places where slaughter weapons are
displayed, meditating an armament. He does not propose to
return to Eiarn without precaution.

DE PROFUNDIS

by Robert Coutts Armour

The Red Magazine, November 1914

About the junction years of the nineteenth and twentieth centuries, writers of popular fiction were seized by a prophetic fervour of destruction. I think the scientists pointed the way with interesting speculations about such matters as the heat-life of the sun; an eminent French astronomer amused his leisure with a romantic, dithyrambic story of the human race's end; various cheery people of varying authority decreed the speedy exhaustion of the world's coal-fields; and a host of sprightly authors made haste to entertain us with accounts of great cities overwhelmed, and our painful built-up civilisation obliterated by dire and diverse means. Man warred with Terra, Ocean sent forth her devouring monsters, nation hurtled against nation, the Yellow Peril loomed terribly, new diseases devastated the whole world, leaving only a few choice spirits to the task of re-peopling it—and whilst we enjoyed this feast of speculation, the forces prepared for our undoing were already marshalling. Whether any one of those ingenious scribes anticipated what came to pass I am unable to say, though, for irony's sake, I trust it was so, and that he has had ample, opportunity to revise his theories in the face of facts.

It may seem strange, but the calamity came without any warning, the few isolated incidents that might have served being misunderstood or disregarded. I myself was witness, after the event, of one such, in this wise.

I had been making holiday in Cornwall, tramping the coastline or occasionally diving inland, in an irresponsible fashion that would have shocked the laborious writer of itineraries. The weather was unusually fine and warm, so, having a large waterproof poncho, a bag of provisions, and a little kettle, I gipsied very happily 'til the eve of the inevitable day when I must return to London. Being by then wise in the selection of a camping ground, I got me at sundown to the sheltered side of a little wood, ate my supper, and, wrapped in my poncho, lay down to enjoy a pipe before going to sleep.

It was my last camp in England, perhaps the last I shall ever make there. At the present time, of course, such a proceeding would be stark lunacy even in the most desolate place. In front of me, looking inland, the ground rose with a gentle swell, dipped and rose again to the horizon quite bare of cover, there being no trees of any growth in that part of the West Country. They were all cut down long ago, I have been told, at the time when every Cornishman turned mole and burrowed after tin, and certainly they must have needed forests to prop the workings with which the country is honeycombed. In the field before me was the shaft of one ringed by a high stone wall, and with it for text I speculated drowsily whether, in the far future, the wood underground would have rotted or turned to coal. Then an old horse came and looked over the hedge at me in a friendly way, and the tips of his ears twitching against the sky were my last waking memory.

I awoke once in the dark with a confused sound of hoofs and a long, wailing cry ringing in my cars, but all was quiet. I attributed the noise to a trick of dream, sniffed distastefully a faint, acrid odour drifting on the slow night breeze, and, turning over, slept without stir 'til the sunlight crept into my eyes. Within half an hour I had sluiced myself at a runnel, eaten breakfast, and was ready to face the road, the rail, and the Big Smoke.

My direct route lay through the field in front, and climbing on the gate I stood at gaze, seeing that close beside the walled shaft-mouth lay something which, I was absolutely certain, had not been there overnight—a large skeleton.

I noticed, too, that my friendly horse was nowhere in view, though the boundaries of the field were all in sight, and, exceedingly puzzled, approached the bones. They were fresh, *raw*, though not a particle of meat adhered to them, and unmistakably equine. I went back to the gate, the only exit, examined the ground beyond it, which was soft enough to show a track, and made sure that the beast had not gone out that way.

The conclusion was obvious. Within a few hours a big, strong animal had been done to death, and clean picked! It was incredible, yet there was the skeleton, without a toothmark, still held together by its ligaments, and perfect as an anatomist could desire. I began to be a little afraid, but being of a fairly practical turn set about searching after further facts, and ran against more incomprehensibility.

From the gory patch about the skeleton to, the wall around the shaft, ran two tracks, worn through the turf to bare earth, about four or five inches wide and as much apart, one of which continued in a red stain up the perpendicular face of the stones.

Now, I offer no excuse for my conduct in the face of the mystery. Certainly the wall was high, and had been effectively pointed no great while before, but I could easily have climbed it. Only—I didn't want to climb. Without weighing matters I concluded instantly that the power which could so deal with a horse might very easily treat me in like fashion, left the unhealthy precinct on tiptoe, and ran 'til I came to a cart-road. Decidedly the spirit of research was not in me that morning.

At the time I felt I was doing shamefully, but looking back I see that I acted with common-sense. Had I searched further I should have lost my life as vainly as one who throws himself to a school of sharks; yet my self-esteem barometer went down and down, so I mentioned the phenomenon to no one, but got to town, and to work once again determined to forget an inexplicable incident.

In those days I had just entered on a series of experiments having for object the discovery of some volatile fuel to replace petrol, and my little laboratory contained so many samples of oils, tars, and essences that, despite ventilation, it usually smelt like the interior of a submarine. I suppose, strictly speaking, mine was a dangerous trade, and certainly the top floor of an old-fashioned office building in Fleet Street was scarcely a fitting place in which to distil inflammable liquids. But it happened that the den was my own, the property having belonged to my people for near a century, and with the near prospect of eviction, when the ground lease expired, I didn't wish to squander money on other premises.

I had but few visitors and only one intimate friend, Henry Mayence, a short, broad, immensely strong man, devoted to motoring, and consequently keenly interested in my attempts to cheapen his pastime. He used to bring all kinds of absurdly unsuitable material, ranging from camphor to burgundy-pitch and palm oil, though apart from this foible he was entirely levelheaded. I returned from Cornwall at the beginning of June; twelve days later—on Friday, the 13th, to be precise—I heard his familiar step on the landing, the heavy thump of something weighty banged on the floor, and opened to find him in the act of upending a large iron oil-drum which smelt vilely of crude petroleum.

"So you're back," he grunted. "That's a good job. Didn't want to lug this thing home again. Out of the way!"

He pushed past unceremoniously with the thing in his arms, and, depositing it within with another crash, condescended to explain.

"Right stuff at last," he said. "Wales. They've struck it—regular lake. I've got an option. You try it. It's heavy, but—"

"But, confound you, I don't want a hogshead!" I objected. "It'll stink the place out. Phuff!" I had been at work all night, and so was irritable. "Why on earth couldn't you bring a little?

A bottleful would have been enough."

He grinned placidly.

"Because this is going to be a big thing, sonny, and you'll need it all. Besides, what does another flavour matter among so many? Open the windows."

"And kill the sparrows? You'll jolly well have to take it away again! Hang it, man, I'll be run in for causing a nuisance!"

"All right," said he soothingly; "perhaps it is a bit too thick. Didn't notice it on the car. Horrid business, that of the policeman, Kingston way!"

"What business?" I asked. "I haven't been out yet."

"Devilish rummy! Found the poor beggar behind a hedge, uniform on—helmet, too. Beastly! And I may have spoken to him—been held up thereabouts more than once. Poor chap!"

"What are you gibbering about? Was he murdered?" I demanded irritably.

Mayence shivered.

"Ghastly, I tell you! Nothing but his clothes, only bones left inside 'em. Ugh!"

"What?" I shouted. "D'you mean to say—Why, down in Cornwall—"

And forthwith I told him briefly what I had seen.

"Same thing," he said, nodding emphatically. "A horse don't matter, but a man! And a lot of other people are missing, too. Wonder you didn't hear the boys yelling the specials outside."

"I did," said I. "But I'm so used to that, I didn't take notice. Hallo! There's another edition, or—"

We sprang together to the window opening streetwards and craned our necks.

Right opposite, building operations were in progress, and a great hole had been dug in the earth, from which, as we looked, the workmen came crowding and jostling, howling gigantically, in a frenzied hurry to reach the narrow door in the hoarding along the street front.

"Lord!" ejaculated Mayence. "What in thunder's up! Look at that chap!"

A man, who had, I suppose, been in the deepest part of the excavation, came clawing frantically up a ladder, reached the level, put his hands to his head with the gesture of one suddenly smitten to death, reeled, and fell backwards into the pit.

A cloud of dust flew up and hid everything for an instant; then something which looked exactly like a wave of treacle— a brownish-black, shiny, wet-looking, lapping tide—flooded up over the edge of the hole, and flowed out towards the men jammed in the doorway.

They must have felt its coming and redoubled their efforts. A section of the hoarding gave way, falling outwards on the front ranks of the swaying crowd that had collected instantaneously, and, as they gave back, the fear-minded workmen charged forth, tripping, stumbling, and striking out fiercely at everything in their path, driven by blind, panic terror. Close on their heels through the gap, over the hoarding's top and through every crevice of the boards, came that amazing fluid mass.

Everybody shouted, abruptly everybody faced about, turning to fly, and I had an impression of the crowd as a heaving, whirling maelstrom, with pinky-red faces for bubbles and a tossing spray of straw hats adrift for foam. I saw a tall man—a Press photographer, I presume—struggle free and present his camera at the oncoming treacly tide, stagger, fall, and lie motionless.

Subconsciously I wondered if he had got his picture, and whether I should see it in the morrow's papers. The treacle swept on and over him—ay, and over many another. Men faltered and fell in rows, even as they fled. A tubby man, with flashing glasses that stayed miraculously firm on his nose, swarmed halfway up a lamp-standard, lost his hold for no apparent reason, and fell, limp and lifeless.

The street within our view cleared, the din retreated a little, and I could hear Mayence.

"Alive!" he shouted "Alive! The stuff's alive, I tell you— alive!" He used language quite unprintable. "And deadly—look at that 'bus!"

It had been at a standstill, unable to move through the swift-gathered throng. Its top was crowded. The driver stretched a hand to put in the clutch, drew it back sharply, lifted it to his mouth, and sagged forward over his wheel.

"What is it? Great heavens, what is—"

Somebody sprang into the room behind us, and banged the door. It was Vidal, a quiet, little, oldish man who, in an office on the floor beneath, practised the nearly extinct art of wood-engraving for such scientific journals as needed clearly detailed pictures, instead of the cheaper dot and smudge variety. Usually he was staid and self-contained, but now, and little wonder, he was livid and shaking with terror.

"They're coming up!" he screamed. "Shut that window! We're done for! I saw 'em once before, but nothing like this!"

Mayence grabbed him by the shoulders and shook him roughly.

"What?" he shouted. "What the blazes is it?"

"Ants!" quavered Vidal. "Millions of trillions! They're stinging everyone to death; keep 'em out!"

It was well for us then that Mayence had piloted racing automobiles; a practice that breeds quick thinking. He didn't stop to question the truth of the statement, but shook his man a trifle harder.

"Will paraffin keep them off?" he demanded.

Vidal nodded.

"Perhaps," he said hoarsely.

"Lucky I brought a big 'un, then!" growled Mayence, and leapt at his oil-drum. "Rags, Tom, a brush, paper—anything! Bathe in it!"

In a twinkling he had the bung out and tipped a pool of thick, yellow, evil smelling, crude petroleum on the floor by the door, spreading it with his handkerchief over every crevice.

"Mother Partington, Atlantic Ocean!" he grunted, snatched a towel, and stuffed a soaked strip beneath the door. "Window, you cripples! Buck up!"

We worked like demons. As a motive-power there is nothing to excel fear; and yet though we wrought swiftly, smearing the sashes and every visible joint in our defences, the ants were already darkening the panes ere we had finished.

"Kill them! Quick!" shrieked Vidal suddenly, pointing. "There!"

From under the skirting-board a score of large ants, near an inch and a half long, came boldly at us, travelling rapidly, halted at the edge of the puddle in which we stood, and sped swiftly back again.

"Don't like it, by jingo!" Mayence shouted exultantly. "Magic circle, spread it out!"

It was done. Panting, soaked with oil and sweat, hardly able to breathe because of the stink, we stood up, saved; perhaps the sole surviving witnesses of that first outburst, since it would appear that parties of the ants invaded every building, slaying relentlessly every human being they encountered. Us they let alone after the first trial; and presently, when the panes cleared, being nearly suffocated, we ventured to open the window.

Speech became possible.

"Don't lean out!" Mayence warned me. "Some of the brutes might drop on you!"

Standing on a chair well withdrawn from the casement, I looked forth. Within my circumscribed view I could see the dead photographer and several of the others on the further side, the top of the 'bus with its lifeless load, and a taxicab wedged into a shop window, its engine still running, the driving wheels slithering and grinding on the pavement. At several open windows men hung or sprawled. The air reverberated with a vast noise; the voices of fearful thousands roaring from every point of the compass beat painfully on the ears; but silently, the cause of it, the river of ants, still flowed from the excavation, each yard of it an army, dividing into streams, which went their way west and east without pause.

"Jumping Jupiter!" exclaimed Mayence, mounting behind me. It's unbelievable! It's—it's a hallucination."

"It isn't," said Vidal. "I saw something like it in Venezuela once, when I went with a collecting expedition. They kept on for a day and a night, and though they weren't so poisonous as these, everything had to get out of their way or perish. Perhaps they've come out in other places, too."

A duty we had neglected came to my mind, and I jumped from my chair and rushed to the phone.

"Exchange!" I yelled. "Are you there? Are you there?"

There was no answer, though I called again and again. My belated attempt at warning was useless.

"Death everywhere," murmured Vidal.

"Or else the gels have scooted," suggested Mayence. "Don't be too infernally gloomy."

"Perhaps it's the beginning of the end for the human race," persisted the little man.

"Rot!" cried Mayence. "It's horribly bad, of course, but that couldn't happen. A lot of damned insects!"

"And they'll soon be settled," said I. "Squirt acids or poisons on them, or—"

"Or set a dog at them," sneered Vidal. "D'you think they'd stand still and let you do it? Look at the pace they can go. And they've got brains, I'm certain. What if this has all been arranged? Why, I'll bet they're all over the town—other towns, too; perhaps other countries."

We cried out at this monstrous suggestion, yet—though, of course, we didn't know it at the time—he wasn't far out in his estimate of the abominations. He warmed to his dismal theme.

"Even if they're driven back underground for the moment, how are you going to keep them there. Nice job it'll be to make every house antproof. And walking about in armoured clothes, or soaked with anticide, will be pleasant, won't it?"

"But they die off or go to sleep in the winter, don't they?" I suggested.

"How d'you know this kind will? Anyhow, they've got lots of time before them. How many of us will live 'til the first frost? How about harvesting, and tending sheep and cattle? We'll all starve if we're not killed. It's a conquest, an arranged business, I tell you. Perhaps some of us will be kept as slaves. There are species who have others to wait on them—"

"Will you shut up?" roared Mayence. "We're in the devil's own pickle, without being driven daft by your maunderings! What d'you reckon we'd better do, Tom? Stay here 'til the siege is raised?"

"How about the river?" I asked hopefully. "The oil keeps the beasts off. If we soaked ourselves, we might get there all right and find a boat."

"Probably a few thousand others have found it already," he chuckled grimly; "and a few billions of our little friends appear to have gone in the same direction. It's risky every way."

We all stared gloomily at that ceaseless torrent of venomous life, pouring, pouring silently, swiftly, with an ordered purpose. Against uncountable myriads so devilishly endowed, what had man to oppose? I could think of no adequate defence.

"Perhaps you're right, Vidal," I said. "One hopes of course. But—"

"Have you got anything to eat or drink?" Mayence interrupted. "We must keep our pecker up."

"Biscuits, whisky, soda—that's all," said I, producing them. And we ate and drank unpleasantly, each mouthful being tainted with the all-pervading petroleum, then stared out of the window again.

"The noise is dying down, I think," said Vidal at length. "But what's that racket overhead?"

Mayence listened.

"Somebody breaking the law. An aeroplane coming—over there, see? By jove! It's the old training 'bus, the biplane at Hendon. What the dickens are they after?"

Moving quite slowly, the 'plane hove in sight, skimming dangerously near the housetops, one of the two men in her apparently searching the ground with field-glasses. Mayence snatched up the linen overall I wore when working, tied a sleeve to a walking stick, and thrust it outside, waving 'til the airman saw it, and, putting a big megaphone to his head, shouted something which was drowned by the rattle of the engine. Slowly the machine swung about over the pit, a small, dark object fell from it, and—"crash!" a mighty spout of dust flew up, concrete foundation walls and scaffold-poles crumbled and rocked, tinkling glass fell in showers. The man in the plane had dropped a bomb into the ants' portal.

With the explosion their columns broke, thinned, and vanished into doorways, the drains and crevices; in twenty seconds they were all under cover. The 'plane circled out of sight, returned, and this time we caught something of what the megaphone bawled to us: "…in a dozen places…going to shut 'em down… all right soon." We waved an answer, they shot away, and in a few minutes we heard the smack of another bomb, followed at intervals by others, each more distant.

"A dozen places!" exclaimed Vidal. "What did I say? It's an organised invasion. A fat lot of good those chaps have done. See!"

The side of the crater made by the explosion began to heave and crumble, a dark spot appeared and grew larger, and long before the sound of the last detonation came to us the ant river was flowing again, steadily as though it had never been so rudely interrupted.

Mayence mumbled disgustedly, and faced about. "Question is, what are we going to do? Stay and starve, or take the risk of going out?"

"They won't touch us," said I confidently.

"Don't be too sure. Some of them, maybe, will sacrifice themselves on the off-chance of getting a bite home. At all events, I'll go out first and reconnoitre." But at this Vidal and I protested, and in the end we drew lots. The short match fell to me, and I confess to feeling horribly uncomfortable, but I managed to conceal my feelings whilst I was smeared anew with the abominably smelling oil; my boots were soaked 'til they squelched at every step; face, hair, cap, and gloves, all were saturated, and Mayence finished me off by tying a dripping duster around my neck. "In case they drop on you from aloft," he explained. "Now you're all right. We'll get ready while you're gone."

I opened the door gingerly. At the edge of the landing was a group of ants, several score, big fellows, with their heads turned towards me; simultaneously, they darted forward, came almost to my feet—and retreated. Instinctively I squashed the hindmost. "All serene!" I cried. "They won't face it," and slithered down the first flight to find another and larger vidette, which behaved exactly like the others. I had no more fear after that, but went on confidently as a medieval knight in armour of proof hewing his way through a mob of peasants.

On the first floor I peeped into the office of Wardell, an advertising agent, and saw what was left of him lying back in his chair, a half-open sample tin of insect killer on the floor beside him; evidently he had bethought him of this defence at the last moment. The ants were swarming all over him, and I turned away hastily, feeling very sick; it is a shocking thing to see a man you have known and swapped drinks with in process of disintegration. Yet the sight served to diminish the shock I received when I found the entry and the lower stairs completely choked with bodies. I went back and reported, and, since there was no other way, we at last let ourselves down by a rope from the window of Wardell's room, after lowering the precious oil-drum, now half empty, and set foot in a Fleet Street transmogrified to the semblance of a battlefield.

Perhaps a soldier hardened to slaughter could have supported the spectacle, but to us it was near overwhelming. Remember that the view from my office was circumscribed by projecting buildings on either side, and that the portion of street it commanded was abandoned at the first outrush, so that what we had seen before was as nothing compared with what confronted us.

Looking westward, the street was filled from side to side with a horrible barricade, vehicles of all sorts piled and wedged together in inextricable confusion, for a base; and over, under, between, shaken together and trembling to the throb of the engines still working beneath, were piled the dead.

From the accounts since collected it would seem that on this fatal day the ants emerged from the earth, not in a dozen, but in scores of places, from each of which they diverged on either hand, killing as they went, 'til they met the columns of their fellows, and so ringed Central London in a cordon of poison, whilst from other points within the circle other hordes spread devastatingly 'til hardly a nook or corner remained unvisited.

Of the millions of folks so surrounded, comparatively few escaped, and those, curiously enough, mainly by the underground railways, which were let alone for some time; but the majority of the people fled panic-stricken from one army only to encounter another, and most often met their fate struggling amidst maddened crowds.

Horror left us dumb for a little, then Mayence, hugging his oil-drum, turned towards Ludgate Circus, and we followed in silence. With us, on either hand, marched thousands of ants at a respectful distance, and so we came to Bridge Street, and the first survivor, a telephone linesman, slung in a travelling cradle from the cables crossing the road. Intent upon our steps, we were startled by his hoarse cry from aloft: "Hi mates!" he called.

"Can you let yourself down?" answered Mayence. "We've got stuff to keep them off. Come along."

The man became frantically busy with a coil of wire.

"Righto!" he yelled. "Just a minute."

There was a sudden commotion amongst our escort, a thin brown thread shot up the façade of the building directly below the poles supporting the telephone wires.

"They know!" exclaimed Vidal. "They're after him. Quick, man, or they'll get you yet."

Mayence stood ready with his oil, the linesman dropped the end of his cable almost to out feet, unbuckled the strap which held him in the cradle, wound his cap about the wire, gave one unearthly scream, and fell smashing to the pavement. I think he was dead before he reached the ground.

We trudged on towards the river without a word; pity, horror, terror, all capacity for emotion seemed numbed to exhaustion, and we moved mechanically. Blackfriars Bridge was choked by another dreadful barricade, the approaches to the stations were impassable. The river was dotted with people swimming or clinging to lifebuoys or fragments of wood, the barges anchored on the further side were hidden by men clustering like swarming bees, the outermost continually dragged down by others who struggled up from the water; the "President," the old Naval Volunteer training ship, lay low in the water, weighed down by the numbers aboard her, and dozens clung to her cables fore and aft. I saw one man maintaining possession of a packing-case, which barely supported him, with bloody knife; a dinghy drifted by, laden with women and one man, who threatened any who approached it with a revolver. As they neared the bridge the arch under which they must pass grew black, and though we shouted, the warning was unheard, or unheeded, the insect death rained down, the boat capsized, and we saw no more.

Nearly half an hour we stood there, hypnotised, the petroleum escaping from our saturated clothes and gathering in little pools around our feet, whilst the ants clustered thick in a semicircle behind and darted continually to and fro along the parapet in front, angry perhaps because we had so long escaped them. Then a river steamer without a living soul aboard, though her deck was piled, came in sight, her paddles revolving slowly, swinging uncertainly from side to side of the river, 'til she brought up with a crash on the piles of a wharf and began to settle down.

With the noise we awoke to a realisation of a new peril; London town was on fire. Heavy smoke clouds were drawing across the sun, rolling south-eastward before a rising breeze.

"Nobody to stop it," said I. "But at least some of those infernal things'll get roasted."

"They'll go underground 'til it's over," Vidal said.

"We'll go up with the first spark," said Mayence. "Can you swim?"

He shook his head.

"Not a stroke."

"And Tom is equal to about a hundred yards. We'll have to make a float of some kind and keep under water going through the bridges; we'll get below these for a start, anyhow. Come on."

With our abominable guard still in attendance we turned our backs on the river, and by great good fortune found the roadway underneath the railway viaduct passable, though we had to climb over many vehicles. The smoke grew even thicker, and we could scarce see our way, but it appeared noxious to the ants, who thinned away and had quite disappeared ere luck brought us to the end of a short street and a little wharf.

"Here we are," said Mayence. "And there are planks and rope. We'll make a raft of sorts. Hurry!"

Somehow, in no very workmanlike fashion to be sure, since we groped in pungent semi-darkness, we got our raft together and launched. It was high time; we were half suffocated, and the flames, spreading unchecked with frightful rapidity, roared near at hand as, sitting awash, we started on our voyage, Mayence, sitting aft, paddling with a short board 'til the mid stream caught us, and we were swept swiftly forward, unable to see more than a yard or two ahead.

Soon a dark mass loomed above us, the raft swerved, we shot through a bridge—Southwark—and never an ant materialised. Either we passed unseen or they had gone before the smother.

"Three more to pass, and we're all right," grunted Mayence.

"Look out! Shove off!" A barge drifting beam-on lay in our path. Vidal howled, thrust out a leg pushing with all his might. We bumped once, and went clear without receiving boarders. I needn't describe what we glimpsed in passing, nor what we presently saw as we circled in the swirl of the Cannon Street railway bridge; suffice it to say that many had sought refuge upon its floating fenders—in vain.

Below was a red flare of flaming warehouses belching showers of sparks, yet none reached us, and we whirled blindly on in the black, smothering smoke blanket, passed beneath London Bridge without seeing it, and narrowly missed running full tilt into an anchored boat, perilously laden with folks, who yelled in chorus as we rasped across their cable; two men with oars out tugged dementedly, another fool struck wildly with a boathook, smote his iron deep into one of our planks and nearly capsized the lot.

"Let go, you idiot!" roared Mayence, whilst the water licked their gunwale, and, fortunately for them, he obeyed, and we parted company, losing sight of them instantly.

Vidal levered the hook clear and crouched ready to fend off from what might come next. With ebb and current together the stream was a race, and we should have fared badly had we encountered anything moored; but our amazing good fortune held, and though we caught sight of many craft, and heard voices all about us, we kept clear of everything 'til, about the neighbourhood of Deptford, the smoke thinned and we could see our fellow-men once more.

Either margin of the river was lined with people standing in the water, knee-deep, waist-deep, up to the neck; beyond these a floating fringe, then boats and rafts, all loaded nearly to sinking; and the voice of their misery was a continuous giant groan, a deep, plaintive note of despair, such as I hope never to hear again. Of the people in boats around, none heeded us, except to curse when we fouled them; but after I had picked up the blade of a broken oar, we kept a better course, and had no more collisions.

"We must get as far down as we can before the tide turns," Mayence explained; and we paddled our best 'til in the broad reach a little below Greenwich, we met a flotilla of torpedo boats. Half dead with fatigue, blistered all over by the oil which had saved our lives at the expense of our skins, we were hauled aboard the first, and stowed in the narrow quarters below, already crowded with refugees, whilst the boats steamed into the smoky pall to rescue all they might, and when they were loaded, dropped down river and decanted us into the cruisers, battleships, and liners anchored about Tilbury.

All night the work went on, and all night and for many days thereafter London blazed unchecked. Of a forlorn hope of blue-jackets who went ashore with the intention of blowing up build-ings to stop its progress, only two returned, and by the end of a week a great part of the Empire city lay in ruins.

On the night of our rescue, our cruiser set out in company with a fleet of all kinds of vessels, and in the early morning we were landed at Yarmouth, which for the moment was out of the danger zone, and thence we went by train to Glasgow, where I had some friends. The journey took over two days, so you may guess the congestion and confusion that reigned everywhere. I believe that the Norfolk Broads, the Fen country, and many sheltered bays and estuaries grew populous, thousands of people returning to the primitive style of lake dwellings, and building themselves huts upon piles or rafts.

But the most part believed only in flight, and the roads were black with fugitive multitudes who could find no place on the overburdened railroads; if the ants had followed up their first onslaught with the speed of which they were capable, I think it probable that the whole island would have been depopulated.

Perhaps the burning of London disconcerted them, or they had the strategical sense to reduce the country in their rear before going further; at all events, they made no move northward for over a week, but during that time overran the country to the south of a line between the Thames and the Severn estuary, methodically slaughtering flocks, herds, and those unfortunates who had not escaped over the Channel or fortified themselves in some such fashion as we had done.

Then they flooded northward, but by that the country had been cleared before them, and at the Avon-Welland line they were brought to a full stop for a while. Every bridge was defended, and along the banks and in the gap about Naseby, where once a very different battle had been fought, hundreds of fire-engines pumping blazing petroleum went into action, and thousands of men fought right gallantly with hand-pumps and squirts. Surely it was the strangest battle that the world had seen, bloodless but deadly, so potent being the poison, that to be stung meant death before cautery or antidote could be used. For days it continued, the ants tunnelling beneath the rivers' beds at many points, emerging oftentimes amongst thickets or coverts far in the rear of the firing line, and there, ringed about by the reserves, to be driven to earth again.

Across the country from sea to sea was stretched a broad band of fire-scoured earth, miles wide, and by this frontier the invasion is for the moment stayed, at the price of constant, unremitting vigilance, though none knows what the future has in store. Even the most optimistic of our experts, Professor Guy Durham, is gloomy.

"Our real knowledge of the earth's crust is small," he remarks in his report "and a poor mile the limit of our shafts. What fissures, crevices, caverns, lie beneath us we know not at all, but it may very well be that, in the four thousand miles from surface to centre, many such occur. London, it is surmised, lies in part above a great subterranean lake, and it requires but a small effort to imagine such regions inhabited."

He goes on to details of our enemy's anatomy: *F. Horribilis*, as it has been dubbed, is in many respects entirely different from and vastly superior to its sun-loving brother, having a marvellously complex brain, excellent smelling apparatus, and, a somewhat unusual endowment for a subterranean creature, well developed eyes. In fact, the thing is altogether a super-ant, and he comes to a conclusion not hard to credit under the circumstances.

"I have no hesitation in announcing my conviction that *Horribilis* is an intellectual, a rational creature, able to plan, to reason, and, as we have so terribly experienced, to act in combination. I am of opinion that their aggression is a deliberate attack upon human supremacy, intolerable though such a suggestion may be to our self-satisfaction; but, taking into consideration their means of offence, their proved skill as miners, and the immense fecundity of such allied species as we know, I am forced to the forlorn conclusion that mankind may, at no very distant date, be compelled to struggle hard for very existence. And, lest we grow over-confident in our present defences, I am bound to point out that, if analogy holds good, our feeble barriers of fire and water may presently be passed, if not underground, then by the path of the air. Both the male and female of the ant, at one period of their lives, *are winged!*"

THE STORY OF THE STAIN

by Sophie Osmond

Phil May's Annual, Winter 1901

Sophie Osmond was a writer, journalist, and critic who published several popular novels set in Australia and New Zealand. She wrote three stories for *Phil May's Annual* between 1901-1904, all of which have supernatural elements.

We always thought there was something strange about the old kitchen attached to the homestead father bought at Carrap, even from the very first week we lived there.

It was mother who originally put the idea in our heads.

As we were settling and sorting things the morning after our arrival, mother suddenly left her work to examine a large stain in the earthen floor.

"I wonder what that can be!" she said.

"Something must have been spilt there," suggested Sis, who was two years younger than I.

"I'll try and scour it off," said mother, and presently she was scrubbing away at it. But all her work went for nothing, the stain seemed to stand out all the more.

"I hate the sight of it," she said.

"Well, don't worry, anyhow," put in father, because as soon as you get the house straight, I'm going to pull down this old shanty, and rebuild it."

I should say here that father, John Crosland, had added to, and rebuilt the old, tumble-down dwelling which was on the property when he purchased it, and now it was a six-roomed house, with a wide verandah all round.

We were some little distance off the road, so as to be near a never-failing creek—"Carrap" being the native equivalent for "plenty of water." The place had been lived on, and the land cultivated for many years, in a fitful kind of way, but it had latterly fallen into such neglect that father got it for next to nothing.

So soon as he and Uncle Ned had fixed up the house, mother and I and Sis joined them, taking with us all our belongings from the old home thirty miles away, and travelling in a bullock team, driven by our staunch friend and neighbour, James Bon, for that was the way folk did good turns to one another in those lonely parts.

True to his word, father and Uncle Ned commenced to pull down the old kitchen, that is, they made a start by trying to take out the window and door, but father sprained his ankle, and was laid up for several days.

When he was well enough he had another try, but again he met with a check, as Uncle Ned found the footbridge over the creek had been washed away in a flood, and they had to see to that before anything else.

About a week later they made their third attempt on the life of the old kitchen, when to their annoyance, and not a little to our astonishment, father was called away to attend an inquest at the township.

"That's three times we've been stopped," observed Uncle Ned. "Give it best, I say; it seems queer, the whole thing."

But there was much more "queerness" to come.

Father relinquished his idea of rebuilding, and decided to put down a new floor. But while he and Uncle Ned were working, they heard the noise of guns and shooting, as from a long distance, in the air, and yet next to them.

And when the floor was down, quite white and new, they

saw a dark place show in the wood, and just over the spot of the other stain. We all saw it, and wondered.

Next day it had grown larger and darker, and the next, and the next, until it had become the size and shape of the stain on the old earthen floor! And for all the scrubbing mother and I and Sis gave it, nothing would move it.

We were very curious to learn why, but father did not like us talking about the matter to strangers, so no one knew outside our home.

As we never heard the sound of shooting again, Uncle fancied it must have been due to some electric or other atmospheric influence in the locality, but father held to his own view of its being a peculiar echo of the hammering.

As for the stain, they put it down to the effect of damp, as the ground sloped towards the place where the kitchen stood.

Sis and I confidently expected a fresh development, but as none came, we felt in a measure disappointed.

"Never mind," said Sis, "you mark my words, when there's that, there's more."

But nothing "more" manifested itself, and we lived such a busy life that we grew accustomed to the dark stain, and seldom spoke about it.

When the general elections came round, James Bon asked father to put up a party of men working for their candidate. "Carrap" was the most central farm in the district; it was accessible to five adjacent roads.

An electioneering campaign was no light matter in that part of New South Wales, where the holdings were many miles apart.

Father was anxious to do what he could for his party, and, as James Bon had done, placed his house at the committee's disposal.

This meant much extra work for us women folk, for we would not be thought lacking in hospitality for the world; and yet we had to keep fresh and neat, having a certain pride of birth that father and Uncle Ned never allowed us to forget.

The visit of the election party upset the whole house. Every room was turned into a bedroom, and we Croslands had to cram ourselves wherever we found space.

Uncle Ned swung himself into a hammock in the verandah. Sis and I scraped together whatever we could in the way of spare rugs and cushions, and made beds for ourselves in the old kitchen. As I have already said, we had become so accustomed to the mark on the floor, that we never heeded it.

But that night it looked darker than usual, and Sis suggested it was an omen to the political party. So we drifted into joking about it, and Sis declared

"You're not game to sleep on that stain, Bess!"

"I am, though," I said.

And she dared me.

The end of it was, I spread my share of the rugs and cushions on the floor (the electioneers had all the available mattresses), and went to bed with my head directly over the mark, for further bravado.

And thus we fell asleep. At least I fancied I went off into a doze, but was awakened by the most dreadful noises, screaming, yelling, banging; yet I had no power to call out.

Something seemed to be pressing me down, down, down, until I sank out of sight; but all the time the awful clamour increased.

The window was full of ugly black faces glaring in; cruel hands were tearing down the woodwork, and brandishing spears. I could almost hear their teeth gnashing, and wherever I looked, there were more fiendish faces, more dark bodies, and those savage, ruthless hands.

I tried to cry out, in my terror, but no sound would pass my lips. My body did not seem to belong to me.

Then I became aware I was not alone in the hut. Three strange men, roughly dressed, were in the centre of the floor. Seizing their guns, they fired wildly at the attackers.

Two women rushed from somewhere at the back, carrying axes. At that moment the window gave with a crash, the blacks leapt in, one after another, 'til the room was full of fiends.

The women slashed at them with their axes, and the men fired, each shot taking effect.

Then it seemed that they could not have had time to re-load—so closely did their assailants press them—and they could only swing about the butt-ends of their guns, doing murderous work though the odds were against them.

One of the women fell, and was trampled underneath the feet of the blacks. Her heartrending screams rose above the din, and goaded the men on to redoubled efforts, and in their fury they laid about them with the strength of giants.

But still the blacks kept pouring in by door and window, and one of the white men fell dead.

And, oh! horrible that it was! the other woman seized a kerosene lamp that was fastened to a beam in the wall, and flung it on the fire, and the whole wall on that side burst into a blaze.

The two white men resolutely forced the blacks into the fire, and slowly victory was coming to their side. The noise was like the yelling of demons, but the two Englishmen never spoke, never opened their stern, set lips.

Such of the enemy as were away from the burning wall turned and fled, their shrieks of terror seeming to tear the very air.

The room was full of blacks, dying and wounded, and now the other two walls and the roof had caught, and were blazing.

The stronger of the Englishmen pulled out his friend who was wounded and the woman, and left the place to burn with all the bodies in it.

I made a last effort to scream, and to rouse myself, yet I only heard my own voice as the feeblest sob.

As I did so, I saw that the "dead" Englishman was not dead, but raising himself on one arm, crawled over to where I was lying, and scraped and clutched where my head lay.

"Find it! Find it!" he moaned. *"For God's sake! Send it to her! She has wailed all these years!"*

Then he fell back dead, and from his mouth there gushed blood, which ran into a pool underneath my head.

I awoke to see Sis bending over me, and crying with fright.

I suppose we awakened father and mother, for they rushed in to see what had happened. I told them of my vision, but they could not understand it, as less than half an hour had elapsed since Sis and I had bade them "Goodnight."

Sis had heard strange noises and shooting, but in a dim, far-off way, that might have come from the distant paddock.

Mother pacified us, and took us into her room, while father lay where I had been, lying with his head there, just as my head was. Yet he saw nothing, and heard nothing but a confusion of sounds.

Then Uncle Ned tried, but heard or saw nothing at all. By this time it was dawn, and everybody was up and astir.

Father said I must have had the nightmare, but that awful voice went on moaning in my ear—

"Find it! Find it! For God's sake! Send it to her! She has waited all these years."

It was with me all the day, and I begged mother to tear up the floor to see if there was anything under.

One or two of our visitors asked if anything had happened during the night, but father replied that one of his girls had had the nightmare, and had called out in her sleep.

The party of electioneering men dispersed on their different roads during the morning, and the household was quiet again.

Mother begged father to have the floor of the old kitchen taken up, and the earthen floor underneath broken into, to see if there were anything hidden. After thinking it over, father and Uncle Ned commenced work, more to set mother's mind at rest than for any other reason, for they grumbled at the waste of labour.

This time they heard no sound, either of guns or shooting, but when Uncle Ned drove his pick into the old clay floor, after the boards had been taken up, he suddenly started, and glanced at father.

"Did you hear that?" he said.

"No: what?"

"I distinctly heard someone draw a long, deep breath, as if

in relief."

"I heard it too," I said, for I was too fascinated to leave the spot.

Father looked dubious; he had heard nothing.

Two or three strokes of the pick soon showed Uncle Ned that there were stones under the clay floor. We were all on our knees in an instant, removing them.

Then came the earth, and there also the deep dark stain corresponding to the stain on the floor. This time father used his spade. We waited, scarcely daring to breathe. The ground seemed to slope to that particular spot.

Presently the spade scraped against something, and father brought up a tin "billy" of the kind that is used in the bush to this day. But it was black and discoloured, and of the same sodden hue as the earth.

"I scarcely like to touch it," said father, pausing in his work.

But Uncle Ned was not so squeamish. He prised the lid off at once with his clasp-knife, and revealed to our wondering gaze a small canvas bag, a bundle of letters, and some faded photographs.

They smelt horribly, and were, like the tin, discoloured.

He cut open the bag. It was full of sovereigns; tarnished-looking, but true enough, Uncle Ned said, as he examined them.

Then father opened the bundle of letters. It took some time to decipher the writing, but he made out they were all in the same hand, and from a woman named Mary Elwyn, living in Sonsea, England, for her name and address were on every letter, and the superscription on the envelopes ran: to "George Elwyn, Post Office, Goulburn, New South Wales."

I looked at the photographs, and dropped them with a gasp.

"What!" they all cried.

"The man I saw in my dream," I explained.

The photograph showed him standing beside a sweet-faced young woman in her wedding dress. The picture which portrayed the same girl holding a baby was less soiled than the others.

Father examined every paper, and found a deed, much obliterated, but distinctly showing the name "George Elwyn" as purchaser of some land at "Tandarra."

"Tandarra!" exclaimed Uncle Ned; "that's just over the road. 'No man's land,' they call it now."

"We must see into this," said father, as he replaced everything in the billy. "We must try and hunt up Mary Elwyn. Evidently she is George Elwyn's wife."

"Hadn't we better break up the whole floor while we are about it?" said Uncle Ned.

"Not yet," answered father; "we must get James Bon here as a witness. I wish to make the search honestly and thoroughly. God knows what poor widowed woman is waiting and hoping in England for the husband that can never return."

Father was a local justice of the peace, so was James Bon in his district, and they thought it would be an easy matter to get at the true nature of the discovery. But the date of the deed was thirty years ago, and the end of it was, father had to go up to Sydney, and Uncle Ned to Goulburn, to find traces of "George Elwyn" in the Government books of the time.

The affair created quite a stir, for father was anxious to make it as public as possible, to stimulate interest and talk, in the hope of learning anything about the first occupants of the place. Bit by bit the story pieced itself together.

Long ago a small family of settlers had taken up land at "Carrap" and "Tandarra." Skirmishes with the blacks were plentiful in those years ago, and the settlers were often called on to defend themselves.

One night the place was burnt down after a fierce fight; but it was the last attack the blacks made, for they lost so many men and met with so much slaughter, that they fled farther inland.

The two Englishmen—brothers, named Baxter—who survived, and one of their wives, left the district after selling "Carrap" to a man who had a craze for building, but knew nothing of land cultivation. His one idea was to have a house in the bush, and there he lived for several years.

On his death his widow gave the charge of the place to an

old shepherd, until a purchaser was found in John Crosland, my father.

But all this threw no light on the discovery of George Elwyn's property under the old kitchen at Carrap.

Father found the record of the purchase of the land at Tandarra, but there was neither stick nor stone, barring the remains of an old hut, to tell of George Elwyn. But as it was common enough in those days for settlers to band together as much as possible for protection, father concluded that George Elwyn must have concealed his treasure at the Baxters', for greater security. This was as near as we ever got to the heart of the mystery.

Father wrote to a solicitor he had known in London, asking him to make inquiries, and also wrote to Mrs Mary Elwyn, at Sonsea, in the chance hope that she might be still living there.

And she was! It seemed ages before we heard any news, but when the letters came, everything was cleared up.

George Elwyn had left his young wife with her people, while he went to make a home for her beyond the seas. Her one child, a son, was now her support, and dark days had settled on them.

The news of the property scarcely surprised the widow, who had waited thirty years.

"I knew George Elwyn would prove himself true to me," she said; "he said it so often in my dreams."

But there was a tremendous amount of time wasted, and many tedious delays, before Mary Elwyn could get her claim recognised.

If it had not been father, I doubt whether the affair, as far as the land was concerned, would have ever been made straight.

Eventually Mary Elwyn and her son came to New South Wales, and on to Carrap to stay with us.

The old kitchen was quite demolished by that time, and every bit of the ground it stood upon dug up; but I pointed out the spot where I saw her husband fall in my vision, and she knelt down and prayed, while the tears ran down her cheeks.

"That stain was his life-blood," she whispered.

And it seemed to me I once more heard that long, long sigh,

as of unutterable relief, and rest and peace, at last.

THE STRANGE CASES OF DR. WYCHERLEY: THE SORCERER OF ARJUZANX

by Max Rittenberg

The Blue Book Magazine, November 1911

Max Rittenberg (1880-1965) was born in Sydney and educated at Tonbridge and Cambridge University. He was a prolific author for several English magazines, but is best known as the creator of the character Dr Xavier Wycherley, a psychologist and psychic who helped solve crimes. Dr. Wycherley first appeared in *The London Magazine* in 1911 in the story "The Man Who Lived Again." Rittenberg wrote a total of eighteen Wycherley stories, a selection of which were later collected in *The Mind-Reader* (1913). He also wrote a series of stories about Magnum, a scientific detective, beginning with "The Mystery of the Sevenoaks Tunnel" in 1913. His other works include: *Potted Game: Some Triflings with the Highly Serious Subject of Sport* (1908), *How to Compose Business Letters* (1909), *Everyone Has Something to Sell* (1910), *Selling Schemes for Retailers* (1911), *Swirling Waters* (1913), *The Cockatoo: A Novel of Public-School Life* (1913), *The Modern Chesterfield* (1914), *Every Man His Price* (1914), *Gold and Thorns* (1915), *Modern*

Retailing (1915), *Effective Postal Publicity* (1923), *How to Finance a Business* (1923), *Practical Points in Postal Publicity* (1927), *Mail-Order Made Easy* (1928) and *Direct Mail and Mail-Order Principles and Practice* (1931).

She was climbing painfully on her knees the long flight of stone steps that leads from the Grotto of the Vision of Bernadette up to the great double Basilique of Lourdes. With her, helping and encouraging, was her parish priest, Père Bonivet.

"Courage, my child, and faith!" he was whispering. "Have faith, and all will be well. Only faith in Our Lady can cure you!"

Out of the crowd of the sick and the dying that had come to Lourdes—the lame, the blind, the palsied, the epileptic, the tuberculous, the cancerous—this peasant girl had above all attracted the attention of Dr. Wycherley. He was there in pursuit of his life-study, psychological research, for at Lourdes there gather a great multitude of those who are sick in mind. Apart from his study of the cures that earnest faith brings to pass at the Shrine of Notre Dame de Lourdes, many of his previous cases had been garnered there—cases where faith had been powerless to heal the injured mind.

This young peasant girl—scarcely more than a child—now on her knees on the long flight of stone steps, had attracted Dr. Wycherley's attention above all the rest. There was that in her face that lifted her out of the ruck of peasants. Not the beauty of her features, nor her soft, liquid eyes, nor her raven-black hair was it that first caught the attention of the observer but the spiritual light in her soul that shone through her face as a light shines through wax.

She might have posed as a model for a Joan of Arc when the call first came to her Domrémy.

Dr. Wycherley watched the girl and the on their painful climb to the Basilique, as he had watched them on many days previously; he waited outside the church until they came from their devotions. In Père Bonivet's face was a look of deep disappointment; in the eyes of the girl was a hardened look, a glitter that had not been there before. The light her soul no longer shone clear—it as though a marsh mist had dimmed it with a clammy film.

As the priest was hurrying her to their temporary home in the town, Dr. Wycherley raised his hat and addressed him.

"*Mon père*," he said, "I ask pardon for this intrusion if it is unwelcome. But I, like yourself, do my humble best to help the weak and the suffering and I see clearly that your pilgrimage to Lourdes has not brought the benefit you hoped for mademoiselle."

"We must be patient. In God's good time He will vouchsafe His mercies," returned the priest. "But I thank you—I see that you have the good heart."

"If you should need me...," said Dr. Wycherley, and wrote the name of his hotel on his card. Père Bonivet took the card and thanked him courteously.

* * * * * * *

On the evening of the next day the priest called on Dr. Wycherley in anxious distress of mind.

"I have come," he said, "because I fear that this case is beyond my powers. It may be that I am unworthy—that my soul is too stained with the cares and pettinesses of this world to take my prayers before the Most High. Tonight I can do nothing with Jeanne. She has blasphemed against the Holy Name—she will not listen to me! It is terrible, pitiable! And"—he lowered his voice to an impressive whisper—"the mark of the beast is coming upon her!" He shuddered at his own words.

Dr. Wycherley drew a chair forward for Père Bonivet. "Will you not sit down and tell me the trouble of mademoiselle? I have studied many cases of diseased mind, and it may be my knowledge can help. She is *hystérique*, is it not so?"

"So the doctor has told us, but in the Landes, where Jeanne Dorthez lives and where I go about the work of my Master, the peasants give it another name—a very terrible name. They say that she is possessed—bewitched!

"Myself I believe nothing of that," added the priest hastily. "I am of the modern school, and such things belong to the superstitions of the Middle Ages. So I laid the case of Jeanne Dorthez before Monseigneur the Bishop, and he advised me to take her on a pilgrimage to Lourdes. Out of his own purse our good bishop gave the money that was necessary for us, for Jeanne is but a poor peasant girl, the daughter of a woodcutter of the Landes, and myself I have little to spare."

"If they say she is bewitched, then they must have in mind some man or woman on whom they place suspicion of sorcery."

"You are right, monsieur. They say that Osper Camargo has bewitched her. They whisper many terrible things of Osper Camargo, that he is in league with the Evil One—but you and I, should we put belief in the superstitious chatter of peasants?"

The mental healer did not answer this. "Jeanne is a good girl," he said; "it is plain for all to read. When her attacks come upon her, she changes in mind, is it not so?"

"She changes terribly. Tonight she blasphemed against the Holy Name. I greatly fear that she may lose her reason."

"What other signs?"

Of course, monsieur, it is nonsense what I have now to tell you. But one day the women of the village forced her to be examined, and they whisper that upon her they found places where the prick of a pin was not felt!"

"Those places were of a definite and regular shape?"

"How did monsieur guess? Yes. The shape of the pentacle— that is what they whisper. The doctor at Mont de Marsan could find nothing, and myself I did not believe it. But tonight I have seen the mark of the beast upon her! Red upon her breast!" Again he shuddered, and crossed himself hastily.

Dr. Wycherley looked very thoughtful. "Let us go to see Jeanne," he suggested, and from a travelling medicine-chest slipped a few phials into his pocket.

The girl was lodging near at hand, and in a few minutes they had arrived at the house, a humble dwelling in a little back street of the town. When they were a few yards from the door the figure of a man slipped out quickly from the threshold and into the darkness of an alleyway.

The Priest started back. "For a moment I thought that was Osper Camargo! But the light is tricky in this narrow ruelle."

"He has a scrawny beard and a pair of evil-looking eyes?" asked Dr. Wycherley.

"Camargo has that and a nose crushed by the fall of a pine-tree upon his face. It was at the time of the accident—many years ago now—that he ceased to attend Mass, and after that he gradually became feared by the villagers. But of course it could not be Camargo, for he is far from here in the salt-marshes of the Landes—there would be no reason why he should come to Lourdes."

The woman who opened the door to them put her finger to her lips. "S'sh, *mon père*, she is at last asleep! It was with difficulty that we could quiet her."

They moved softly upstairs to the room, and at Dr. Wycherley's request the woman turned back the bedclothes and opened the girl's nightgown.

Above and between her breasts, distinct and unmistakable, was an angry reddish patch of the shape of a pentacle.

"Last night I saw it for the first time!" whispered the woman, with horror in her voice. "Tonight it is much redder! Monsieur le Curé, Monsieur le Docteur, what can it mean?"

Jeanne stirred in her sleep, and in her sleep murmured: "I will come. Oh, cease to torment me, for I will come!"

Dr. Wycherley stayed the night through in the girl's room—watching and studying her. Outside the window the Gave de Pau roared unceasingly down its torrential bed. There was menace in its voice.

* * * * * * *

Jeanne awoke in the morning with a curious dull glaze in her eyes. She expressed a strong desire to return home to her hamlet of Aureilhac, in spite of the counsels of Père Bonivet still to have patience and faith.

He appealed to Dr. Wycherley, but the latter drew him aside and suggested earnestly: "Let Jeanne have her way, *mon père*. I think it will be for the best.... It is upon your lips to tell me that if she will only have faith enough, she will be cured. Yes, but she has not the faith—she has lost heart.... Now you are about to ask me what can be hoped for if the pilgrimage to Lourdes has failed."

"You read my thoughts, monsieur!" said the priest in surprise.

"And you, *mon père*, read mine, for you see that I wish for Jeanne only what will be for her good."

"Yes, yes. But if she goes back to the Landes with her faith broken, who can save her from madness? I, alas, am not worthy to do this work for my Master—that I bow my head in sorrow to acknowledge."

"We must work together—I will return with you."

"But her father, Pierre Dorthez, is only a poor woodcutter. In the Landes we are all poor. How could we pay you, monsieur? No doubt you would need many francs—perhaps many hundred francs." To his simple mind the sum loomed vast.

"*Mon père*, you and I have both learnt that the true money lies in the grateful hearts of men and women."

The priest raised his hand in benediction. "I know not if you are of our faith, monsieur, but may the blessing of God be upon you!"

They travelled by slow, cross-country trains to the village of Labouheyre in the middle of the Landes district. It was a hot and sultry day, and the hundred-mile train journey seemed interminable.

Beyond Dax they had come into the true Landes country— great silent pine-forests alternating with wide stretches of sedgy marshland. At Labouheyre their arrival was unexpected, but one of the villagers at once offered to drive them in his ox-cart to Aureilhac. It was an honour to do a service for Père Bonivet.

But Dr. Wycherley noted that the villager took care that Jeanne should not touch him even with her garment.

The two oxen drew them along the great silent highway that runs level and straight northwards to Bordeaux, stone-paved like the streets of a town to bear the weight of the lumbering timber-wagons.

The oxen plodded along with the slow patience which is theirs.

The silence of the great forest fell upon them. Even in the full light of the afternoon the sombre forest carried something of the grim and awesome. No wonder that for the simple peasants there were still spirits of evil that lurked in its shadows and on Midsummer Eve gathered together for unholy revels out in the marsh of Arjuzanx.

From time to time they would pass a solitary goatherd lying down on his rough skin coat and dully guarding his little flock of longhaired goats. Once they caught sight of the local postman making his round on the stilts of the Landes to the outlying huts and farms, separated by stretches of marshland impassable on foot.

The ox-cart turned off the highway into a forest track deep-rutted from its winter traffic of heavy timber-wagons. The forest took them to its sombre heart. A grey film began to spread across the sky, shutting out the sunlight. But still it was hot and oppressive.

Late in the afternoon they reached the hamlet of Aureilhac—a few low roofed wooden houses in a clearing where lean hens scratched for food. Pierre Dorthez, returning from his day's work in the forest, raised his hat to Père Bonivet, and greeted them dully. He said little, either of comment or question, but ordered Jeanne to make ready a dinner for the visitors. Himself he would kill a fowl and gather vegetables for the soup.

As the girl set about her work, Dr. Wycherley watched her keenly from his seat in the kitchen that served also as living-room. She was intent on her duties by the *pot-au-feu*, but there was a suppressed excitement underlying her that showed in the twitchings of her hands and the pallor of her face. It was no longer translucent in its whiteness, but of a dull and clammy pallor like the colour of a marsh mist. And in her eyes there was once more the hard glitter. Now and again she would secretly put her hand to her bosom as though to satisfy herself that something of value hidden beneath her dress was still there.

When the simple dinner was over, Dr. Wycherley drew Père Bonivet aside.

"Where does this Osper Camargo live?" he asked. "I wish to see him."

"But surely you do not believe in the superstitions of the ignorant peasants, monsieur?"

"In my studies I have met many strange things, and I try to keep the open mind. I would see this man for myself."

"He lives in a solitary hut out on the marshes—on the marsh of Arjuzanx. But do not go tonight, for the way is treacherous!"

"I must go tonight, *mon père*—or it may be too late. Can one of the villagers show me the path?"

"At night-time they would not dare to."

"Can I find it for myself?"

"On the stilts there are many paths, but on foot only one that is safe. If you are determined to go, I must lead you there myself."

"Thank you—I accept your help willingly. But I shall ask you to return without me and keep guard over Jeanne while I am away."

The last gleams of the setting sun shone from between an angry bank of clouds as they came out of the forest on to the marshland. The pools, stagnant with slime, turned to blood, then grew dark and chill.

"It may be a bad night, monsieur," said the priest warningly. "See how the clouds have massed in the west, over the Bay of Biscay!"

"If necessary, I will spend the night with Osper Camargo," answered Dr. Wycherley quietly.

A tortuous path amongst the firmer parts of the marshland

brought them within sight of a low hut. It was surrounded by a few stunted trees on ground a little above the general level. Around them again were the dark sedges, whispering amongst themselves, and the chill, dank pools of slime. A marsh bird called to its mate with a strange, eerie cry.

"Is the way straight from here onwards?" asked Dr. Wycherley at length.

"Yes, you have but to follow the path. Only be careful that you sound around you with your stick should the foot tread on ground that gives."

"Then I would ask you to return at once to guard Jeanne. If necessary, give her bromide from the tablets in this phial. See to it that she does not leave the house tonight. *Au revoir, mon père.*"

* * * * * * *

The hut was silent and lightless. After knocking at the door fruitlessly, Dr. Wycherley lifted the latch and entered.

It was empty save for a lean grey cat that arched her back and spat at him. The bigger of the two rooms, serving as kitchen and bedroom, showed by small signs that it had been unoccupied for days. There was nothing to be done but to wait for the return of the owner, for no one at Aureilhac had been able to tell of his movements.

It was a lonesome, weary vigil. The cat, refusing overtures of friendship, had stalked out into the night. The clock over the fireplace was silent, for it had run down during the owner's absence. Around the room were tokens that this Osper Camargo worked on the superstitions of his neighbours, for conspicuous on the walls were a human skull, dead bats nailed up with outspread wings, snakes and blindworm preserved in spirit, and other devices common to the sorcerers of all ages. A heavy locked chest doubtless contained more of his paraphernalia.

But to Dr. Wycherley the most significant object in the room was hung above the bed where the peasant of the Landes would place his crucifix.

It was a small pentacle in hammered iron.

For many hours the doctor waited patiently in the lightless hut. For times such as this he had trained himself to a habit of deep thought that lost count of place and time, but yet was alert to the least unusual sign. He had made his brain his servant to an extent far beyond the usual with men.

His thoughts ran on the records in hieroglyphic that have come down to us of the sorcerers of ancient Egypt; the men who claimed that they could use the gods to work their will. He had spent many interesting hours with Professor Clovis Marnier, the great Egyptologist listening to his demonstration of the meaning of the hieroglyphs.

There was a sound out of the darkness—a plash in a distant pool. At the instant his watchful senses had flashed the message to his brain, and he was awake and alert. But he kept still in his chair.

The sounds came nearer. The door opened, and a man entered with a lantern, under his arm a pair of stilts slimy from the marsh pools. Placing the lantern on a table, he began to lay sticks on the dead ashes of the hearth, the grey cat rubbing affectionately round his legs. He had a ragged, scrawny beard and moustache, and his nose was crushed in the way Père Bonivet had described. A face with evil lines—an evil mind behind it.

He had not seen Dr. Wycherley. When at length he caught sight of him, sitting quietly in the chair in a corner of the room, he started violently and called out in the harsh, twanging dialect of the Landes: "*Sangrediable*, get on your knees!"

The doctor made no reply, but sat still.

"Who are you?" cried Camargo, flashing the lantern upon him.

"Peace, brother!" answered Dr. Wycherley. "Peace to you in the names of Khabbakhel and Knouriphariza, our masters."

"But I don't know you! What are you doing here?"

"We have met in the plane of the spirit," answered Dr. Wycherley courteously. "Though I live afar off, I have long wished to visit you and learn of your wisdom."

The man was clearly puzzled. Suspicion lay behind his narrow eyes. And yet his vanity was touched. Dr. Wycherley had allowed no trace of irony or ridicule to appear in his words—they had a tone of grave deference in them.

Osper Camargo twisted his hands uneasily. Finally he hit on a satisfactory answer: "You want to buy wisdom from me—*hein?*"

"Come!" remonstrated the doctor. "Payment between brothers of the craft?"

"If you want to learn, you pay!"

"Very well," answered the doctor, with assumed reluctance, and drew out a gold piece from his pocket.

The man's eyes glittered cunningly.

"Not enough!"

"This I will give you beforehand, and again a louis when you have shown me what I do not know already."

He showed a second gold piece.

"Do you know the incantation that brings the sickness upon the oxen? Or the incantation that drives the goats to madness? With them one can make money."

"Those," answered Dr. Wycherley, are elementary. I had hoped to see bigger proof of your powers. Even in my land they speak of the spells you can lay on man or woman."

Osper Camargo's pride was awakened.

"They speak well, for I have those powers, and I use them. But"—a cunning glitter came again into his eyes—"I work within the law. Whatever I do, it is such that the law cannot touch me. Oh, I am careful!"

"We have all to be prudent. A friend of mine, the great sorcerer, Smith—doubtless you have heard of him?—desired greatly a young girl of his neighbourhood, but she was of tender years, and the law of his country would not permit that he cast spells to bring her to his side. So he waited."

"As I have waited!" cried Camargo fiercely. "As I have waited these long years! If the mother would have none of me, the child shall—and willingly! It is my right! Everything is prepared!"

With a dramatic gesture he drew out a key from his pocket and opened the heavy oaken chest. The upper part of it was filled with dresses and dress material. There was silk and good cambric in the heap. He plunged his hands into it, fondling the garments, letting them rustle through his fingers.

"A fine trousseau for the bride," commented Dr. Wycherley. "She should be well pleased."

"A bride? Maybe yes or maybe no. Of one girl one may get tired. Why tie oneself up with the law?" He shut the lid of the chest and turned the key." But that is not the only reason why I desire her. No, no. There is another reason, a stronger reason—a reason that you of the craft should well know!"

Now it was Dr. Wycherley's turn to be puzzled. He thought he had gauged the man's mainspring of action. His motive was surely horrible enough—what worse could lie behind? And yet it must be something within the law, for the man was plainly stating truth as to his devilish prudence.

To gain time, Dr. Wycherley asked: "What is her name?"

"Ask at Aureilhac," answered Camargo. "They will tell you quickly enough!"

There was a note of triumph in his tone that expressed the near fulfilment of his desire. From the law he had nothing to fear, for the law takes no cognisance of wizardry as such, and it was plain that he had no fear of man's intervention. Perhaps they could keep the girl away from his hut for a week two weeks, a month even—but what of that? He had waited many long years—he could wait a little longer if necessary. Small wonder that Osper Camargo boasted openly of his desires.

"You do not know my second motive!" mocked the sorcerer.

Dr. Wycherley replied deferentially:

"No, I am but a learner at the craft, and you are a master. I have come from afar to drink of your wisdom."

"This much will I show you. Today I procured it, and it completes the preparations that are necessary."

He flashed a small corked glass tube from his pocket, and

quickly returned it to its shelter. In the fitful light from the lantern Dr. Wycherley could only gather the impression that it contained the dried ear of some cereal-barley or perhaps rye. It puzzled him still further. The thought of poison passed across his mind, but this he at once put aside—Osper Camargo was a coward at heart and would never risk the vengeance of the law in that way. But if not poison, what could it mean? A dried ear of barley—or perhaps rye.

"You speak of your powers," said Dr. Wycherley, "but you give me no proof. It may be that this girl is in love with you and will come willingly at your call."

"Ask at Aureilhac!" returned the sorcerer again, licking his lips. "Ask if she has been willing to come. But now I have her in my hands. When I crook my little finger, she will come."

From the west a flash of lightning filled the hut with light, showing with startling distinctness the fire of evil passion in the face of Osper Camargo.

"Shall I give you proof of my power?" he asked fiercely.

"For that I have journeyed from afar, and for that I will pay the further louis," returned the doctor.

The sorcerer set about his preparations quickly, while outside the storm gathered and the distant lightning flashed. First he lit a fire on the hearth and into it threw some powder that gave out a strong odour of balsam Next he took down the small iron pentacle from its nail over the bed, and hung it by a string round the neck of the grey cat. Then he scattered sand on the floor, and on the sand traced a magical enclosure fringed with mystic signs. In the enclosure he placed a small iron vessel containing a slow-burning pastille with a pungent odour, and next to it a rough wax doll which bore a certain resemblance to Jeanne Dorthez.

His preparations completed, the sorcerer began to recite strange incantations, swaying himself backwards and forwards in time to the words, beginning low and quietly and gradually working himself up to a pitch of hysterical frenzy. Finally he reached the stage where automatism of the lower centres holds sway in the brain. Writhing and foaming at the mouth, he fell in a fit upon the bed. After a little the jerking muscles quieted down—the sorcerer was in a trance.

Dr. Wycherley had watched with intense interest every detail of the fantastic operation, endeavouring to disentangle the essential and the significant from the gibberish of abracadabra and the puerilities of the wax doll. From the first there had been no doubt in his mind that this Ospar Camargo was a dangerous man. The problem in hand was: how far did his powers in the realm of the supernormal extend?

The anaesthetic patches on the body of Jeanne Dorthez which had seemed of such horrible significance to the goodwives of the neighbourhood—these were a not unusual symptom of a patient suffering from hysteria. The shape of the patches was probably the result of a post-hypnotic suggestion; the red mark on the breast of the girl could be produced by the same means. At the Salpêtrière Hospital in Paris many such experiments have been carried out. Dr. Wycherley had no doubt whatever that this Osper Camargo had gained influence over her mind and had been working to bend it to his own will—the appearance on her body of the symbolic pentacle would react on her mind and convince her that she belonged to him, body and soul.

But how would Camargo bring her over the marshes that night? How far did his telepathic powers extend, if he possessed them at all?

Dr. Wycherley searched the room for some indication that might have escaped him, and suddenly he found it. It was a negative indication—during the rigmarole of the incantations and the rhythmic swayings the grey cat had slipped out of the room.

At once a vivid mental picture came before his eyes of the cat padding swiftly over the dark path through the marshes—the forest to the hamlet of Aureilhac—reaching the low wooden house of the Dorthez—scratching at the bedroom window of the girl—Jeanne opening the window at the call and seeing the pentacle around its neck, the sign of her master—dressing swiftly and slipping out of the window—following it back to the marsh of Arjuzanx and the hut of the sorcerer.

How could he wrest the girl from the power of Osper Camargo? It would be difficult in the extreme. With her mind so under the power of the sorcerer, counter-suggestions might be of very little effect. Was there no way in which the law could step in, so that this man's power of working evil would be fettered?

Perhaps there might be some hope of this if he could discover the ulterior purpose at which Camargo had hinted. His eye turned to the oaken chest, and at once he went over to it. In his excitement, Camargo had forgotten to take away the key.

Dr. Wycherley swiftly opened it and turned over the pile of garments, seeking for something hidden in the box which might give him a clue to the great ulterior motive. His hand brushed against parchment, and he drew it out and took it over to the light—a parchment yellow with age and written in faded ink with words of French many centuries old. But it was possible to get its general purport, even if single words here and there conveyed no meaning:

The Potion
of Which Whosoever Shall Drink Shall
Become Immortal

It was a lengthy recipe full of such ingredients as the eyes of bats, the powdered forehand of a toad, broth of blindworms, and others nauseating in the extreme, but the culmination of the recipe sent a chill of horror coursing down the doctor's spine. Though he had watched by the bedside of raving madmen, he had never had to listen to imaginings so devilish as this. His eye ran over it hurriedly before he thrust it into his pocket to bring if necessary before a court of law:

"...*a maiden undefiled, a first-born...when she is with child... an infusion of the spotted rye...the left eye and the right ear... see to it that you both drink the potion together....*"

Dr. Wycherley realised as never before the feelings of our

ancestors when, centuries ago, they had had to deal with the sorcerers of their age. Small wonder that they had lynched at the stake men who put into practice what had been written on this old parchment. Small wonder that in their zeal to stamp out such devilish imaginings they had persecuted the innocent as well as the guilty.

Outside, the lightning flashed and the thunder tore across the swishing rain, but through the noise Dr. Wycherley sensed a footstep. He moved towards the door, but at the same moment the man on the bed stirred and rose up. He too had sensed the presence outside, the presence for which he in his trance was feverishly waiting.

Osper Camargo thrust back the doctor and strode to fling open the door. And as he did so, as he stepped out of the threshold to lay hand on the girl who had come at the call of the grey cat, a blinding flash of lightening, followed on the instant by the roar of thunder from directly overhead, struck upon him.

The sorcerer staggered back, his hands to his eyes, moaning horribly.

Groping, he blundered about the room, and a torrent of blasphemies poured from his lips as he realised what had come upon him. Then, little by little, the stream of imprecations died down, and as the girl moved to his side, shivering in her sodden clothes, Osper Camargo cried out pitifully, in a voice so changed from his previous tone that Dr. Wycherley started at it: "Keep away from me, for I am accursed! The judgment of God is upon me—He has struck me blind for my sins!"

He fell on his knees, and as from a little child there came from him the prayer of the Paternoster. One of those strange instantaneous conversions, the rationale of which is so veiled from us, had been witnessed. For a long hour, until exhaustion set in, the sorcerer laid bare his soul before his Maker and prayed for forgiveness. Let it be granted to him that he should work out his salvation in the cell of a monk, sworn to perpetual silence, and he would be content.

* * * * * * *

When the morning broke through the grey mists of the marshes, Dr. Wycherley and Jeanne Dorthez were leading by the hand over the marsh-path a blind man who murmured continuously the prayers he had learnt in his youth.

Behind them smoke curled up from the hut of the sorcerer that was. Dr. Wycherley had set fire to it so that the ghastly tokens and records it contained might never fall into the hands of any human being.

THE QUEER CASE OF CHRISTINE MADRIGAL

by A. E. Martin

The Shudder Show (194?)

Archibald Edward Martin (1885-1955) was born in South Australia and travelled widely in Australia. He managed circus artists from prizefighters to freaks before taking up writing full time. He is best known for his crime stories, but the chapbook in which the two stories published here originally appeared, *The Shudder Show* (NSW Bookstall Company, 194?), has the distinction of being the first Australian single author horror collection. The thirteen stories in it were clearly influenced by the American horror pulps, such as *Weird Tales*.

Christine Madrigal has relapsed into blessed unconsciousness. I do not think she will ever awaken. As her physician and her father's best friend, I hope not, for I would sooner know her dead than beset by those constant terrors which will surround her for the rest of her life.

This lovely girl has seen things which, praise God, are hidden from most mortals. I am setting them down while they are fresh in my memory, attesting that I believe every word....

In a little second-hand shop Christine Madrigal's hands

moved lightly along the backs of a row of books, her roving eyes seeking interesting titles. She found the pastime pleasurable, sometimes profitable. She was young, easy to look at, in love and loved, healthy in body and alert in mind.

It was a beautiful, sunny day—too beautiful, Christine knew, to be spent indoors, but she had no more than half-an-hour to put in. The half-hour was almost up. In a few minutes she would have to leave to meet her fiancé, she thought, with a glance at the wall clock. Her hand was stretched forward, her fingers idly drumming on the backs of books as she glimpsed the titles, when, all at once, the shop perceptibly darkened.

Christine, with a little feeling of disappointment, glanced down the aisle to the shop entrance.

"What a pity if it rains," she was thinking, and was surprised to see bright sunlight making shadow patterns on the roadway. She glanced upward, surmising some skylight illumination suddenly withdrawn, but there was no skylight, no window. A queer, cold draught touched her cheek, and involuntarily she shivered, and, preparing to pull her coat closer about her, fell to trembling, for, although she saw nothing, upon her wrist she felt the touch of cold, hard fingers.

She attempted to withdraw her arm, but the pressure increased, and she felt her hand drawn along the row of books, not haphazardly, but slowly and deliberately. The experience was to say the least, disturbing; but Christine was not the woman to be easily frightened. She choked back the exclamation which rose to her lips. The thing was too absurd. Again she attempted to withdraw her hand, and again the pressure of the unseen fingers increased, and, with more insistence than at first, continued to draw her hand along the row of books upon the table.

At length the pulling movement ceased. Christine felt her hand hovering, then the pressure was exerted downward 'til her fingers rested on a small volume in old-fashioned binding. Fearful, but curious, she lifted the book. As if their task had been completed the unseen fingers immediately released their hold, and, at the same instant, the light in the shop brightened.

With the book in her hand Christine glanced at the clock. The whole ridiculous incident had taken no more than a few moments. Without a glance at the title she took the volume to the bookseller, who peered at it disinterestedly over his spectacles, blew the dust from it, noted the price, and prepared to wrap it.

"Don't worry," Christine said, "I'm in rather a hurry. I'll take it as it is."

Outside the sun was so bright she had to shut her eyes against the sudden glare.

Within five minutes she was having tea with Rick Lamond. His eyes fell on the book at her side.

"Another opus," he smiled, picking it tip. "Gosh," he went on, as he skimmed the mildewed pages, "What are you going to do with this? Read it?"

Carelessly he threw the book on the table.

"Tell you what, Chris," he said. "When you and me's man and wife I'm going to burn down all the libraries within ten miles. Yes, sir. No rivals for me."

For a moment she considered telling him of her experience in the second-hand shop, but a glance at his rugged honest-to-goodness face beaming at her across the table negatived the idea. What was the use? He wouldn't believe. She didn't want him to think he might be marrying a crank. In any case, she hardly believed herself.

Nevertheless, she determined to forget the book in the bustle of leaving, but he caught sight of it, and tucked it under her arm.

"Just to prove I'm great-hearted Harry," he said. "Go ahead, honey! Read all you want. You won't find anyone in books as beautiful as yourself."

He grinned at her without opening his mouth, and squeezed her elbow.

Returning to her apartment late that afternoon, Christine threw the little book upon the table at her bedside, and made a quick change to a dinner-frock. Leaving her flat, she was annoyed to discover that the lift was not operating. Vexatiously she began the descent of the wide stone steps. It was the first time she had used them during her sojourn at this newly-built apartment house, and she noted that on the ground floor they faced the back of the building, looking out on to a courtyard she had never noticed before.

Curious, she stood on the last step and surveyed the scene, surprised to see not the spick-and-span newness that character-ised the rest of the building, but a squared space, floored with rough cobblestones, and surrounded with old stone buildings, picturesque enough in their way, but frightfully dirty. At one corner, sandwiched between what looked like unused and dilap-idated stables, a flight of stone steps ended at what she took to be the entrance to a store cellar.

Wondering a little, Christine turned and stepped into the carpeted lobby. Through the front doors she could see her waiting taxi, and was hurrying toward it when a slight sound at her rear made her glance over her shoulder.

The courtyard had been hidden from her view by a massive door. Christine's brow clouded. She had heard no one. And yet the big door was not only shut, but secured by a heavy iron bar and padlock. There was no one in sight except the porter in his little office ahead of her near the front door. She shook her head impatiently. There must be some plausible explanation, she thought. Nevertheless, the impatient honking of her taxi-driver was a comforting sound.

It was nearly midnight when she returned. Rick Lamond gave her his arm as she alighted from the cab, and they stood for a moment in the bright moonlight. He dismissed the taxi.

"It's too lovely to ride. I'll walk home," he announced, taking both her hands as the taxi drove off, and she faced the great white front of the apartment house.

"Let the old moon see your face as I kiss you goodnight," he suggested, and turned her round so that her features were illumined almost as in day, and he in turn faced the building. He was bending to caress her when he stopped suddenly and glanced over his shoulder.

"What is it?" she asked.

"Queer," he said, and pointed behind her. "The shadow... where does it come from?"

She turned her head and saw, on the white front of the building, a gigantic shadow shaped like the bent head and shoulders of a huge man. The shadow flickered as they looked, then began to diminish until it seemed it had squeezed itself through the open doors and into the entrance hall.

"Funny!" Rick glanced about curiously; then, feeling the tremble of Christine's hand on his, threw his arm about her. "What the devil was it?"

From across the road an old man shambled toward them.

"I guess you seen it, too," he quavered. He was very, very old, and, as they gazed at him in astonishment, he went on: "The shadow—where do it come from? Who's be it? *Why* do it come?"

Christine made an impatient gesture. Rick said: "It was an aeroplane, perhaps."

The old man shook his head.

"I'd a-heared a airyplane, alright."

"A glider, then?"

"Maybe, mister; but there be not many gliders, I'm thinkin'— and why should they come over this house every moonlight night, and me nor nobody not see 'em? Aye, mister, every moonlight night I sees that shadow come up and squeeze itself into yon pretty building—aye, ever since they pulled the old homes down to make way for their palaces."

Rick made a move. "It's a good yarn," he said lightly, "but I'm no mystery writer, gran'pa. Here's something for your trouble, anyway."

He thrust a shilling into the old man's hand, and steered Christine toward the entrance. She did not speak, and he looked down at her anxiously.

"Not scared, are you?" he grinned. "Don't let it get you down! Some cloud effect, maybe." He glanced at the cloudless, moonlit sky. "Perhaps I had better come up with you."

She shook her head.

"I'll be all right. It was a bit disconcerting. The old man...."

"Him? My dear, I bet he knows the answer, and it's paying him dividends. I think I'll give him a good swift kick in the pants after I've seen you to your flat."

"Just put me in the lift."

Together they entered the hall. Christine, as she passed the porter's little office, cast a quick glance toward the entrance to the courtyard. The big door was closed and secured as when she last saw it. Rick kissed her good-night.

"Sure you're all right?" She nodded, and he closed the lift door. "You've got my number—X3210. Ring if you feel you want me, and I'll come round and hold your hand," he called, as the lift ascended.

She kissed her hand to him, and pressed the button. "I'll be asleep and dreaming of you in half an hour, my dear," she thought, as the lift carried her upward.

But she wasn't. Even the familiar things in her rooms failed to rid her mind of its disturbing thoughts. Annoyed with herself, she disrobed quickly, bathed, and, jumping into bed, switched off the reading lamp.

The moonlight threw the pattern of the Venetian blind upon the carpet, and, with hands clasped behind her head, she watched it idly. Suddenly she caught her breath, and stared! Between two shadow lines cast by the blind the shape of a black hand intruded, its long, knotted fingers forcing the slats apart. Terrified, she turned to the window, but there was no movement, and the blind was motionless; the curtains still. From the table by her side she could hear the faint ticking of her watch, and then another sound—dull, closer. It was a moment before she recognised it as the beating of her heart.

With an effort, she forced herself to leave her bed and, her heart in her mouth, pulled up the blind. There was nothing. The window was open, as she had left it. Christine gazed down on the moonlit street, a sheer four floors below. Opposite, sitting in the gutter, was the figure of a man. She could not be sure, but she thought it was the old man who had spoken about the shadow.

She closed the window and locked it, let the blind fall and pulled the cord that closed the slats. She made sure the door was locked, and felt her way back to bed. The room was now quite dark, and she lay still, listening. Did she hear something? She was not sure. But there was something...something different. But it was not sound. All at once she knew. It was lack of sound. The ticking of her watch had stopped. And yet she had wound it before retiring.

For some reason Christine found this incident distressing. She tried to tell herself that perhaps, after all, she had only imagined winding the watch, but the thought persisted that the stopping of the watch, the touch of the fingers in the bookshop, the shadow on the wall, the closing of the courtyard door, and the hand at the blind were related...all part of some sinister purpose.

The dark room was deathly still now that the watch had stopped. Christine tried to think of Rick, tried to imagine him swinging along the moonlit road, but it was useless. Her nerves were shot to pieces. She felt her fingers stiff at her sides, the nails digging into her flesh; her palms were damp with sweat.

With a tremendous effort she moved them from under the bedclothes, determined to ring Rick and hear the comforting sound of his voice. She reached above her head, but for a moment could not find the light. At length she touched the switch. She sat up, looking fearfully about the room.

Her eyes moved to the table by her side, where her watch lay alongside the little volume she had purchased that afternoon. She put out her hand to take the telephone, and, at the same instant, felt on her bare wrist the pressure of unseen fingers. In startled horror, she looked down to see and feel her hand lifted and guided toward the book on the table. Her fingers were forced down and, unwillingly, she lifted the book and drew it toward her, holding it before her, wondering.

The book suddenly opened in her hand as if some unseen medium had acted impatiently, and, as she gazed at thick, black, old-fashioned type, the shadow of a finger followed the text down the mildewed borders and paused at words underlined in faded ink:

> There be devils and devils, but this is the master of all devils who liveth only by blood and calleth at his will. And it is written that he shall endure for life everlasting, for none can gainsay him, and he hath but to command and the young men and maidens rise at his beckoning and walk to his altar, which is in the earth, an unhallowed place. When he openeth, the doors of their chambers, though they be filled with a fearful fear and tremble in every limb, yet must they do his bidding and die at his say, for locks and double-locks and treble-locks cannot stay them, for he openeth them all and entereth into secret places as a shadow through a keyhole.

The shadow of the finger wavered, the book fell from Christine's fingers, and, with a half-smothered cry, she was out of bed groping for her dress, drawing it over her head, intent on one thing only—to be out and away from this horrid room. But even as the dress fell about her she was aware of the gigantic shadow on the wall before her—great stooping shoulders and bent head—and, as she gasped with terror, there came upon her shoulders the soft touch of urging hands. The door swung slowly open, while on the lighted wall the great shadow gradually diminished until it melted into the cavernous blackness of the passage into which the unseen hands were propelling her.

Slowly, her eyes staring, Christine Madrigal stepped from her room and, like a sleep-walker, moved toward and down the stairs. There was no light, no directing word, yet she knew with full certainty her dreadful destination. About her feet she sensed the scurry of horrid, accompanying Things that made faint, excited murmurings, and now and then uttered little cries of pain; and there were other noises beyond belief, as of unseen creatures jostling, which increased as she descended, until at length she felt in her face the foetid breath of larger horrors that touched her with pulpy paws, and gibbered and mouthed sounds that were not words at all, but indescribably loathsome.

Yet as she walked Christine felt that the loathsomeness about her was but the prelude to greater evil…the nauseous horrors were servant to some directing, malignant force. But she saw nothing 'til she was at the bottom of the steps of the apartment house and facing the great door leading to the courtyard.

Almost immediately this opened noiselessly. At once there was a rush of wings and sounds of scurrying, and crawling sounds and whimperings and moanings ahead of her and about the doorway. The noises ceased abruptly as again the huge shadow loomed upon the wall, for the lobby of the apartments was lit, though there was no one in it. The shadow dwindled and passed through the portals into the courtyard, and she was aware of a tall, cowled figure standing a little beyond the doorway, beckoning imperiously.

None saw her enter the courtyard. But an old man, gaping from the doorway of the apartment house, watched the shadows on the wall with terror in his eyes, his aged lips ashen and. trembling, for he had seen not one, but *two* shadows dwindle and disappear through the closed door. He was a very old man, indeed, and because he was standing on the doorstep of Death, perhaps it was vouchsafed to him to see and understand mysteries.

The cowled figure led the way swiftly and silently toward the stone steps set between the two old stable buildings, and began to descend. The touch of unseen, urging hands was at her shoulders once more, but Christine says no power on earth could have stayed her. When she reached the door at the bottom of the steps she could see a dimly-lit interior; the obscene mutterings and whinnyings, the fluttering and jostlings recommenced, to be quelled by a harsh voice from inside the cellar.

"Cease, little ones!"

Christine paused, framed in the doorway. The cellar was

long and narrow, and the ceiling low. The cowled figure stood behind, a rough stone table at the extreme end. He threw back his hood and extended his hands:

"Welcome, bride!"

The compelling fingers at her shoulders forced her forward, and, as she reached him, he took her two hands and held them— and his were as cold as death—while he regarded her silently, his gaze embracing her, his eyes preternaturally bright like those of some zealot who has fought sleep. His eyebrows were heavily tufted; his nose hooked and beak-like; his parchment skin so tight drawn that blue veins stood out like tattoo marks. His lips were thin and colourless; but suddenly his tongue appeared, and it was red like blood.

"Arthesus speaks, bride! Are you a-feared?"

His voice was hard and cruel. From the stone table he lifted a long-bladed knife.

"Do not answer," he went on. "I can see terror in your eyes. My little ones have done well."

Again there was that awful whimpering of unseen things. Arthesus held up his hand.

"Cease, evil ones!" he cried imperiously. "Stay silent 'til I command!"

At once all was quiet again. He looked down upon the girl once more.

"You see? Arthesus is master of all evil. He has silenced his little ones, but they are all about us, watching, feasting on your terror."

With a sudden movement, his free hand seized her gown and ripped it from her shoulder.

"*So!*" he hissed, and his red tongue again caressed his parched lips. Suddenly he turned and made a peremptory sign. Shrouded figures stepped from the shadow. Christine felt herself lifted. Cords passed swiftly about her, and she lay stretched on her back upon the altar-stone. Arthesus raised the knife and brought it down—inch by inch, until the point pressed lightly against the girl's breast.

"Soon you will die," he promised. "But not yet...not swiftly."

Christine uttered a shuddering sigh, and saw the gleam in his eye as her bosom rose against the prick of the knife.

"You bleed!" he cried. "So soon! It is too soon!" His voice rose in anger. "Then, if you must bleed—bleed in full!"

His teeth bared, he lifted the knife to plunge its crimson point into her body, but even as he raised it his eyes filled with dread, widening unbelievably, fixing themselves on her naked breast, upon which some trick of lighting had combined with the upraised dagger to throw the shadow of a cross.

The knife dropped from his hand, clattering on to the stone table. Christine felt the handle within grasp of her fingers and, at the same moment, from somewhere came a thunder of knocking and cries. Something snapped within her. Furiously she cut the bonds at her elbow. In a moment she was almost free, but Arthesus was glaring at her—pointing at her breast.

"The cross! It is gone! It was a trick! I am master!" His bare hands, with their knotted fingers, stretched toward her.

She heard the knocking above, and it nerved her. With a superhuman effort she drove the knife into the man's body, and, leaping up, raced to the door and up the stone steps.

* * * * * * *

Rick Lamond shook the sleepy porter.

"Miss Madrigal," he cried. "Ring her flat! Quick!"

The porter rubbed his eyes.

"It's very late," he demurred.

"Ring her!" Lamond repeated, and there was that in his voice that brooked no delay.

The porter rang. And rang again.

"She don't answer," he announced.

Rick strode quickly to the big door at the rear of the lobby, and began to pound upon it.

"Open this!" he shouted.

"But, sir—"

"Open it, I say!"

"I-I haven't the key. The manager—"

"Get the manager."

The porter made feeble resistance, but in a few moments was in excited conversation on the house 'phone. A minute later the manager appeared in his dressing-gown. Rick demanded the opening of the door.

"But, sir, that is absurd—"

"Listen," Rick told him, "Miss Madrigal is not in her room. I've rung her. The porter's rung her. She ought to be there, but she isn't. Ten minutes ago I received a telephone message imploring me for the love of God to go to her help. The voice told me to break down this door. Now do you understand? I am Miss Madrigal's fiancée, and if you don't open it I'll break it down myself."

The manager made a hopeless gesture.

"This door is never used," he said. "It is something to do with fire regulations. I don't quite know. I never remember it being opened. It leads nowhere."

Rick placed his hand wearily across his brow. Suddenly his gaze froze. He pointed to the floor at his feet.

Blood was oozing front under the closed door into the lobby.

The manager galvanised into action. With trembling hand he selected keys from his ring, and tried them one after the other, while Rick fumed and threatened. At last the padlock opened, Rick hooked it from the bolt, slammed the bar down, and flung the door open.

Less than two feet before him was the solid cement wall of the adjoining apartment house, but at his feet lay the blood-covered body of Christine Madrigal.

The manager raced to the telephone booth opposite the porter's office. He pulled the door open. Inside, kneeling on the floor, his hands clasped as if in prayer, his head resting against a corner of the booth, was a very old man.

He was quite dead, and between his fingers they found a crucifix.

* * * * * * *

I took the little volume which Christine Madrigal purchased in the second-hand shop, and without comment showed it to my friend, Professor Curtis.

He grimaced.

"Nice reading for a wet weekend," he grinned. "Arthesus, eh? Quite a boy in his day. I daresay there's a lot of pure legend mixed with fact, but there's enough evidence to prove that he lived a devil of a long time; and, funnily enough, there's no record to be found of his death. He had a pleasant little habit of drinking human blood. Just how many unfortunates were sacrificed to his lust nobody knows, but it's significant that over a period of a few years over a hundred young men and maids disappeared mysteriously in the locality where he was suspected of holding his séances."

"And," I asked, "where did he hold these…séances?"

"As a matter of fact," Professor Curtis said, lighting his pipe, "this city has changed so much architecturally in the last few decades that it's a little difficult to say." He looked up from his pipe with a grin. "I don't want to frighten you, old man, but at a rough guess I should say your monster lived in your own locality—probably did his dirty work in a cellar in the vicinity of the site on which they've built that awful new apartment house; you know, the one in which they found the old boy dead in the telephone booth."

THE HOLLMSDALE HORROR

by A. E. Martin

The Shudder Show (194?)

I had not seen George Jenner for thirty years. I remembered him vaguely at school—a moody boy, not in the least companionable, and by no means popular with the rest of us. Nevertheless, old school ties are binding, and when in the course of my job I found Jenner established in business at Hollmsdale, which is a long way from the centre of things, it seemed almost obligatory to have a proper reunion, and a talk about old times and the fellows we both knew.

As I met Jenner after he had closed his store and walked with him to his home, where I had been invited to dine, I suddenly recalled that he was one of the few schoolmates with whom I had completely lost touch. However, we had enough in common to keep the conversation going smoothly enough, and I looked forward to a home-cooked dinner with relish after a routine of country hotel meals.

Jenner opened his front door with a latchkey, and, as he stepped aside for me to enter, from somewhere at the rear of the house I heard the voice of a woman raised in altercation. Next moment Mrs. Jenner appeared. Her face was flushed with anger, but almost immediately she assumed her party manners, and came forward to greet me, smiling.

Her husband introduced us, and before long we were seated at dinner. The meal, unhappily, was a disappointment, and twice my host made disparaging remarks about the food that embarrassed me greatly, especially when I saw Mrs Jenner bite her lip in vexation. There were signs of tears, and I hurriedly changed the conversation.

They employed no help, and when his wife left the room for the purpose of bringing in the dessert, Jenner watched her go glumly, then turned to me with a shrug of his shoulders and apologised for the meal. I tried to pass it off, saying something to the effect that if he'd eaten as many hotel and restaurant concoctions as I had he'd cease being fussy. By the look in his eye I could tell he knew I was merely being polite, and when Mrs Jenner returned and began serving the dessert, at which her husband was already frowning, I said, more for something to say than because I believed it:

"Glorious air you have here in the country, Mrs Jenner. Believe me, I envy you! A chap like me, who spends so much time in sleeping-cars knows what he's talking about. It must be great, Jenner, to close up your business, come home, idle about a bit, and then go to bed, sure of a good night's rest."

To my great surprise, Jenner uttered an exclamation, and pushing his plate aside, rose abruptly. Tossing his serviette upon the table, he exclaimed: "Rest! Sleep!"

The next moment he had walked out of the room.

I looked at Mrs Jenner enquiringly, and half-rose from my seat, but her hand was on my arm, restraining me.

"Please," she said. "I'm sorry." Her handkerchief was at her eyes, and as she wiped away her tears she added: "I am afraid, Mr. Dent, ours is not a very happy household."

I made some fatuous reply meant to be consoling, and a moment or two later she rose.

"Maybe you would like to smoke," she suggested, and indicated the way to the verandah. I glanced at the clock as I left the room. Thank heaven, I thought, my train goes in an hour and I can make an early break. The evening promised to be singularly depressing.

I found Jenner pacing the verandah in the semi-darkness. He made a half-hearted apology for his rudeness, and offered me a cigar. I preferred my pipe. As we seated ourselves, he said: "The trouble, Dent, is that I can't sleep. At least, not healthily."

It was an unusual way of putting it, and I suppose he sensed my surprise, for he added immediately: "I dream too much."

I laughed. "Don't we all!"

"You don't understand," he said seriously. "My wife doesn't, or won't, understand. It's always the *same* dream."

"That, of course, is curious," I admitted, "but perhaps not as unusual as you imagine." I knocked the ash from my pipe against the verandah post, and said offhandedly: "Would it help at all to tell me about it?"

He pondered for a moment.

"Yes," he said, at length, "I think it might." He laughed a little self-consciously. "My wife is sick of hearing about it. She says it's an obsession. My God! An obsession!"

He was busy with his own secret thoughts for a few moments, but at last he pulled himself together, and continued.

"I dream I am in M—." He named a distant city. "I cannot tell you how I know this, but when I dream there is no doubt in my mind about it. I am in my pyjamas, and I am shut up in a stifling box. It is a very horrible sensation, and I make every effort to release myself, but I am queerly conscious that, despite my tremendous struggles, my body has not moved an inch. Worse than that, there has not been a single muscle movement nor a flicker of an eyelid, for my eyes are wide open and staring, though they see nothing. I am aware of an awful and disturbing rigidity. But I am also conscious that the box in which I am imprisoned is moving swiftly as if it were being carried swiftly by some vehicle along smooth roads."

In the half-light of the verandah, I saw Jenner's handkerchief mop his forehead before he went on:

"After a while the motion ceases, and I hear confused sounds. I am still stifling in the box, but powerless to move. I can only wait, stiff with terror, for what comes next. It is a coarse shout, followed by filthy imprecations. I feel the box falling; there is a crash, and I awake."

Jenner paused.

"Nightmare," I said weakly.

"Nightmare!" He spoke the word as if be had heard it before, but did not understand its meaning, and repeated it as something extraneous to the conversation. "Nightmare!" I made no further comment, waiting for him to continue.

"The dream doesn't end there, Dent," he said, at length. "I am so filled with horror that I fight against sleep. I walk about the house—but, my God, Dent, a man must have some sleep—and when it comes, Dent, *the dream goes on*."

I could see him leaning forward, his two hands resting on the knees of his outspread legs, his eyes staring at the floor.

"It will always go on," he repeated dully.

At that moment Mrs Jenner appeared with coffee. She placed her husband's cup on the chair beside him, after handing me mine, and seated herself in an armchair a little apart. Jenner looked across at her.

"Oh, for heaven's sake, Jenny," he cried, "go inside and do the washing-up."

I heard a teaspoon clatter with unnecessary violence, and saw Mrs Jenner rise and move swiftly into the house. I had risen, muttering protest, but Jenner had immediately relaxed into his former position.

"Say, old chap," I ventured, as he didn't speak, "you'll have to take hold of yourself."

I don't think he even heard me. With his head thrust forward, his gaze again on the floor, he went on as if there had been no interruption:

"When I fall asleep the dream goes on. I hear a wrenching sound as of nails being ripped from wood. But I still cannot move. I can see, but I cannot move—neither my arms nor legs nor my fingers, nor even my lips. I am to all intents and purposes dead and stiff, but my staring eyes see all, though they cannot move and must gaze endlessly before them.

"I feel myself lifted from the box and carried up a few steps into a brilliantly-painted building. It is like no building I have ever seen, it is so garish. But before I am carried inside I have time to notice that it is two-storied, and is close to the corner of a busy street—no more than ten or twelve yards away—and is sandwiched between two immensely tall buildings.

"I am carried through a hallway and then down a twisting stairway. It is gloomy and frightening in aspect, and I am left there, standing all alone, and yet not alone, for although I cannot turn my eyes, I know that on either side of me there is some unspeakable horror—that I am, indeed, set in the midst of horror unbelievable. This is the most awful part of my dream— to know that I am part of this dreadfulness, and must continue to be so everlastingly. I strain hopelessly trying to move—striving to shriek—but the rigidity continues until some blessed chance awakens me."

Jenner remained silent apace, then raised his head.

"That is my dream," he said. "That is what I have dreamed not once, but night after night for months. Always the same dream, except that sometimes countless faces swim before my vision, leering and smirking, with now and then one which mirrors the horror I feel." He waited a moment and added: "I shall dream it tonight."

I did not reply all at once. I didn't know what to say. When words came, they were commonplace. "You need a holiday. The thing's got you down. In any case, there's probably quite a reasonable explanation. Have you ever been in M—?"

"I know what you're driving at," he said testily. "No, I've never been in M—, nor was I ever taken there as a child. This is no infantile recollection resurrected from the subconscious. Psycho-analysis can't help."

"Anyway," I said, jumping up, "there's one thing I can do for you. I'm going to M— in a week or two, and I'll have a good look round. A garish, two-storied building, sandwiched between two skyscrapers and near the corner of a busy street, shouldn't be hard to locate. I'll bet you five to one no such animal exists."

He had not touched his coffee, but rose, too, and accompanied me inside, where I bade an embarrassed goodbye to Mrs. Jenner. I could not say "Thank you for a pleasant evening," or "It was a delightful dinner." I managed to stammer through some formality, and breathed a sigh of relief when the door shut behind me.

I had gone no more than a few yards on my way when I remembered I had left my tobacco pouch on the arm of the verandah chair on which I had been sitting. I returned at once, intent on retrieving it, and was about to knock upon the door when I heard an angry voice from within:

"You and your damned dream! Do you want me to go mad, too? I'm sick of it, I tell you! Sick of it! Sick of you! Next time you sleep you sleep alone, do you hear? And wake yourself up, d'you hear! When you dream, wake yourself up."

I couldn't face that household again.

A few weeks later I was in M——. I was rather busy, and confess that I had at least temporarily forgotten all about Jenner and his wretched dream. And he had evidently forgotten all about me, also. Anyway, he hadn't forwarded my tobacco pouch.

I had been in the city a couple of days when I received a 'phone message to call on a firm in J—Street, and during the late afternoon set off to keep my appointment. Enquiring my way, I was told that the office was in the big building immediately around the next corner, and upon the opposite side. When I turned into J— Street I glanced across the road, and my conversation with Jenner came to my mind with a rush, for I was staring at a two-storied building dwarfed between huge skyscrapers, one of which occupied the corner block.

The coincidence was a little startling, but that it was no more than a coincidence I was convinced after I had overcome my first shock, for the little building was frightfully dilapidated and looked as if it had been unoccupied for years.

Almost every agent in the city appeared to have "To Let" notices in its grimy windows, some of which were broken, and, my business completed, and consumed with curiosity, I selected the nearest of these, and said I would be interested to look over the premises with a view to rental.

As we walked to the building, I said to the agents' clerk accompanying me: "I suppose, in the event of a lease, the place would not be sold over my head?"

"There's no fear of that," he explained. "The building is part of an estate and is in some legal tangle which is preventing a straight-out sale. You'd be safe for years, I guess."

He turned the key in the padlock securing the heavy, front doors, and we passed up a few steps into a large, high front room. There were wide stairs immediately before us running up to the first floor, and these diverged left and right from a landing midway to the first floor. But what excited me somewhat was the sight of a row of stone steps descending to the basement, not straightly, but in a curve, so that from the top the door downstairs could not be seen.

"I'd like to look at the basement," I said, and the clerk led the way.

"I'm afraid it will be pretty dark," he said. "The light has been disconnected, of course, and it will be awfully grubby."

He turned the key in the padlock, swung back an iron bar, and opened the door. I remember it creaked on rusty hinges. In the dim light I could see that the place was reasonably big, though low-ceilinged. There was a stone floor, and around the walls at intervals were old-fashioned gas brackets. The place smelt dank, and I was glad to get out of it.

We ascended the curving stairway, and for appearance sake, I inspected the top floor, but gave no more than a perfunctory glance round.

"It certainly isn't modern," I commented.

The clerk sensed that I had lost interest in the proposition. He laughed shortly. "Lord knows what the old place could be used for," he said. "It's out of date as a Noah's Ark, and a civic eyesore."

I thanked him for his trouble, and bade him goodbye. From

the opposite side of the road I glanced back at the grimy building looking so ridiculously small between its giant neighbours. It certainly wasn't garish, and yet, I thought, recalling Jenner and his dream, the coincidence was queer.

A month later—on March 29th—George Jenner murdered his wife.

I read of it with consternation and horror. He had killed her in the middle of the night, and had then walked, in his pyjamas, to the police station and given himself up.

I followed the reports of the trial with the greatest interest, but there was nothing unusual in the evidence. Jenner maintained that she had nagged him and he had picked up a razor and deliberately ended her life. He pleaded guilty, asked for no mercy, made no appeal against his sentence, and was executed at S—on May 29th, just two months after his wife's murder.

I had occasion to visit M— several weeks later, and again called on the firm which had its office in the J— Street skyscraper. It was late afternoon and almost midwinter, and already dark, but as I turned the corner a blaze of light illumined the roadway, and, glancing across the street, I saw that the onetime grimy two-storey building had been miraculously transformed. It was now brilliantly lit. Neon signs bordered the facade, which had been painted in gaudy colours. Lights of various hue twinkled above the doorway, and stretching across the whole front there was a huge electric sign:

WAXWORKS

Something impelled me to enter. I paid my money and hurried in, turning immediately to the stairway leading to the basement. I ran quickly down the steps. Over the door there was a sign:

CHAMBER OF HORRORS

Almost the first sight I encountered inside was a life-like image, with staring eyes. It was clad in pyjamas, and between its waxen fingers it held a blood-stained razor. At its side was a sign:

GEORGE JENNER
The Hollmsdale Horror

An attendant came along and knelt by the figure. He pulled up the pyjamas, and busied himself with the calf of one leg. A moment or two later he looked up at me, grinning.

"We dropped the old boy's case off the lorry when we were bringing him in this morning," he said. "Fractured his leg." He adjusted the pyjamas again, and rose and stood surveying George Jenner's waxen face. "A fat lot he cares," he commented. Then, with a glance at the horrid figures on either side of him: "Well, he's in good company. I hope he likes it."

THE PYTHONESS

by Helen Simpson

Lovat Dickson's Magazine, January 1934

Helen de Guerry Simpson (1897-1940) was a gifted author who died tragically young of cancer in 1940. She was educated in Sydney and Oxford and wrote her first novel, *Acquittal* (1917), in a fortnight. An obituary in the *West Australian* described her as follows: "Dark in colouring, square in build and downright in manner, she was a good linguist, an expert cook, a talented pianist and a student of witchcraft. In pursuit of this last hobby she travelled to remote corners of Europe in quest of vampires." She is best known for her novels, *Boomerang* (1932) and *Under Capricorn* (1937), and she collaborated with Clemence Dane on a series of detective novels. Her rare first collection of stories, *The Baseless Fabric* (1925), contains a number of subtle supernatural tales clearly influenced by the work of Henry James.

Interest in Spiritualism need not imply that an inquirer has the religious temperament. He may attend meetings of a circle for half a dozen reasons; curiosity as to the next life, its habits and values; scientific inquiry; a mere taste for the marvellous; and occasionally, rather pitifully, a genuine and overwhelming desire to get in touch with some loved person lost.

All this is mere preliminary, to explain how I came to be sitting in circle with three men so entirely different from me and from each other as Tarrant, Pybus, Mortimer; and one woman so inexplicable as the medium, Mrs. Bain. Tarrant was one of those people that all the more showy religions cater for; he liked marvels. The blood of St. Januarius liquefies for such as these, and bullroarers whirl in African caves. Pybus was the earnest inquirer. He found spiritualism logical: it satisfied his intellect; having swallowed the camel of survival after death he ceased to strain at the gnat-like tactics of the spirits, who in their endeavours to resume contact with the world moved birdcages, rang bells, and brought from other climes such mementos as safety pins and faded flowers. (Apports was the technical term for these. They were diverse; their one common characteristic was portability. The spirits never, in my experience, astonished us by materialising a grand piano in my dining-room where we sat behind locked doors.)

Then there was the medium. Mrs. Bain had good looks of a large sort, but it would have been difficult to imagine falling in love with her—for me, at least; her natural voice, that most revealing attribute of man or woman, was tinny and self-assured, though it could put on a deeper note in the cabinet. Whether or no she was honest, she gave value for money. I believe the truth to be that she did possess certain powers which she eked out, poor creature, with safety pins and the like; destroying credibility by the very means she adopted to bolster it up.

I repeat that, diverse as were all our needs, she gave us good value, Lance Mortimer in particular. He had been going to her for some time, even before his wife's death; indeed, I believe it was Aileen, the wife, who induced him to attend this circle in the first place, and naturally after she died he gave it more of his time and interest than ever. Personally I was always a little sceptical about the messages Mrs. Bain obtained for him. She had known Aileen well, and the confection of detailed messages having the ring of truth seemed to me in the circumstances to be a little too easy. Possibly I wrong Mrs. Bain. At any rate

Mortimer seemed happy and reassured by the messages, which was the chief thing. He never missed a meeting, and three months after his wife's death had lost almost completely the dragged and haunted look which came on him during her illness.

I have said that to me it was impossible to imagine falling in love with Mrs. Bain; impossible that any man of education and intelligence should do so. She appeared to read nothing, to be interested in nothing; she was big and badly dressed. I admit that at moments she was impressive, while the trance was on; there was one occasion when she stripped off every rag of clothing in the cabinet and marched into the room stark, reciting something in a language none of us could follow, and making curious gestures—of libation, I imagine; her empty hands curved themselves to the handles of an imponderable beaker. There was some discussion among the five of us afterwards— this was in Aileen's lifetime—as to whether we should tell her the details of her performance when she came to, but eventually we decided not to embarrass her. On this occasion she was quite unconscious of her actions; the display was altogether too crude to have been the result of conscious deliberation; nakedness, after first youth has passed, and in a heavy muscular woman, lacks allure. We repeated to her so much as we could remember of what she had spoken—there was a refrain, like the "Pray for us" of a litany, which we were able to write down—and left it at that. I believe, personally, that for once some very old wine was poured into a new bottle.

But this was the performer; the woman was one who would terrify the average man, if he ever looked at her twice. And so I am quite unable to put into words my surprise when, strolling through Hyde Park one evening, in that unfrequented patch near the police station, I saw her sitting on the grass, with Mortimer beside her. She was unmistakable. It was summer and she had taken the hat from her heavy black hair, which had never been cut, and was never tidy; a coil of it had come down, and lay askew on her shoulder, while her dress, though it was of some light-coloured stuff, somehow looked frowsy. She had her back to me, but I could see Mortimer's face. It was the face you may see often enough in the Park of an evening, eyes intent, mouth restless, desire written plain on it for any passer-by to read. The sight sickened me, somehow. I had known gentle Aileen, his wife, rather well.

Mortimer was talking, urging something, looking steadily, as lovers do, at her mouth. She listened, not interrupting, but her right hand plucked at the grass, and when he seemed to have done she shook her head vigorously, so that the coil of hair slipped down further. When she answered, the timbre of her voice carried, though not the syllables; she seemed to be denying or refusing something, Mortimer became more urgent. On that her restless hand seized the discarded hat, and crammed it on anyhow; then, with an ugly, plunging movement like a cow, she got to her feet and, looking down on him rapped out something final. Unexpectedly she turned my way, and met my eyes. A cloud of red came over her sallow face, but she walked towards me.

"Quite a surprise," said she, in those tinny accent of hers, shaking her head; the coil of black hair tumbled forward over her shoulder. "I never!" said she, hastily stuffing it under the hat with her thick fingers. "What you must think of me—"

"Hello, Mortimer," I said, looking past her.

He had risen, and was coming towards the pair of us, seeming none too pleased at the interruption.

"We've been getting a breath of air," Mrs. Bain explained.

"Very wise," I said; "it's hot."

Then there was nothing more to say. I raised my hat to her, and started to move on; it was so very evident that Mortimer didn't want me. But as I took my first step Mrs. Bain fell in beside me, saying:

"I'm going your way, if you don't mind being seen with me."

I said something about my delight. She added, with what seemed deliberate intent:

"Mr Mortimer's had as much fresh air as he can stand. He ought to be getting home."

Mortimer said nothing whatever to either of us. He took off his hat and we walked on, leaving him standing on the path.

I had nothing in particular to say to Mrs. Bain, but I made some sort of conversation about the dresses and the grass. She answered absently and kept looking at me sideways. At last, just as we were halting to cross the Row, she suddenly spoke.

"I suppose you think there's something a bit funny going on."

I could not pretend to misunderstand, though I did not want confidences.

"There's no reason, you know, why you shouldn't sit in the Park with Mortimer."

She answered, in tones that sounded just a little shocked:

"Well, but he's only been a widower three months."

"Widowers don't have to shut themselves away from the world nowadays."

"No," said she dubiously; "only a person ought to show respect."

"Aileen Mortimer was a very generous and sane woman," I went on, "as you know. You might have sat in the Park with her husband in her lifetime with her full consent. Why should it be different now?"

"I don't know, I'm sure," said she; "only it isn't like the same—"

"Shall we get across?" I asked her, for really I found it intolerable to discuss Aileen with her, and I did not want to be drawn into any comment on Mortimer.

She made no answer, and I hurried her across, through a gap in the traffic. She came meekly enough, head well down as is the way of women; on the opposite, the Knightsbridge side, I stopped, meaning to leave her and walk down alone to Chelsea. To my horror and dismay she was crying. Her great eyes were welling, tears had overflowed, making channels through the brownish powder she used; in another minute she would have broken into noisy sobbing there on the public path. I could hardly leave her boo-hooing after me like a punished dog and so took action at once; gripped her elbow, and piloted her into a providential teashop that I had suddenly remembered—quiet, and no more than a hundred yards away. The place was nearly empty; it was getting on for six; shoppers were on their way home. Mrs. Bain gulped a "thank you" and disappeared without shame into the Ladies' Room. I was curious, and sorry for her in a detached sort of fashion. It is so difficult to realise that ugly women must have their emotions too.

She came out, powder renewed in a muddy mass on her nose, and sat down by me at the table. Without studying the menu she asked for chocolate—chocolate at a quarter to six—and while the waitress went for it, talked.

"I ought to be ashamed of myself, Mr Findlay; I know that. Making a fool of myself in public"—("And of me, too," I thought.)—"like a kid of ten. D'you know how old I am? I'm forty-three."

She looked it, certainly; she had never taken care, and nature had not been kind at the start. I said nothing. She was in the mood when a woman sees through the usual masculine futilities in the way of placation. She went on.

"Forty-three. Makes you think, doesn't it? I've been earning my living for twenty-five years, and you can believe me when I say I'm sick of it."

The chocolate came, hot enough to waft steam even on that summer afternoon. I poured out my tea and added lemon, while she sipped the boiling thick stuff, with a spoon.

"You're interested in your work, though, surely?"

"Look," said she, pointing her spoon at me; "I'm interested and it's as honest a way to make a living as most others. Only just—I'm sick of it."

She sipped more chocolate, and I could feel her waiting for me to make first move. No purpose was to be served by waiting, and I obliged her.

"Mortimer, I suppose, was suggesting an alternative."

"You're right, he was. And I refused. Refused dead, like that—" she made a slashing movement of her powerful hand— "and here I am, going on like a kid with a smashed toy."

The eyes had indeed started to well again. I said hastily:

"Mortimer didn't mean to offend you, I'm certain."

"Offend? Offend me? Oh, I suppose you think it was the other thing he wanted. It wasn't; it was marriage, flat out."

That did surprise me, and perhaps my face showed it.

"Oh, I know. Mrs Mortimer's only been in her grave three months. You think it's not respectful. Nor do I, and so I told him. But it was hard work saying it. I suppose I'm what they call, in love."

She said that as though it were some remote condition familiar perhaps to doctors, but her face contradicted her, or, rather, it underlined the words, gave them force and beauty, for all the clotted powder and the reddened eyes. I said, smothering my convictions, for I had no wish that she should marry Mortimer:

"Well, you know, there's really nothing against it. He's free."

She answered, staring into the cup, talking as if to herself:

"If only I could be sure—"

"Sure?"

"It's this way," she said, and paused to gulp down the rest of the chocolate. "I want to have a home of my own. And I'm fond of him. I don't deny. Fond—" she considered the word, and altered it. "I'm mad about him. But there's things to be considered. For one thing, I'm not his class."

There was no answer to that. It was pretty evident that they could have nothing in common, that there was not one chance in fifty of the marriage being a success.

"For another, I'm older than him. He's thirty-eight—five years—that makes a lot of difference. And I couldn't think of marrying him for a year; it wouldn't be right. That brings me up to forty-four. So, you see, looked at all round, it's silly. I see that as clear as you do. Only—"

I was sorry for her. This outburst was genuine, and in refusing Mortimer she had done the only possible thing; but the cost of the decision I could fairly estimate. After all, Mortimer made a fair amount of money, lived comfortably, had a position in the world. She was a vagabond, without a home or a future or any background save that which some psychic laboratory afforded. It was much to give up voluntarily, for the sake of common sense; I respected her, and told her so. She said, with a big, tremulous smile:

"Keep your bouquets a bit longer. I mayn't stick to it."

"I shan't blame you," I said, "if you don't. What about the circle? You'd better not be seeing him."

"No, that's right," she agreed with a sigh. "We'd better wash out the sittings for a while."

"How long will it take to—?"

Get over it, I meant, and though I left the actual words unsaid she answered them.

"I don't feel as if I ever should, come to that. Better say I'm going away."

"I'll tell Mortimer."

"Well, I'd be obliged. I don't want to get in touch with him, you see."

"How about money?" I said on an impulse. "Can you carry on?"

She looked vague, and said she could manage. We went together out of the shop, which was closing, and I saw her on to a bus before I walked thoughtfully home.

There was to have been a meeting next evening, but I sent out cards, with some invention about Mrs. Bain's having been called away suddenly to put off the others. These cards should all have been delivered next morning, in plenty of time to warn; nevertheless, at nine-thirty that night, our usual hour, Mortimer was shown in.

"No sitting tonight, I'm afraid," I said. "Didn't you get my notice?"

"I got it, thanks," he answered, "that's why I'm here."

He looked sick and dangerous, and I could easily trace the cause even before he spoke again.

"What did you say to her yesterday? I want to know."

There was no sense in refusing to discuss the matter, since he already knew all that she had told me. I let him have the whole of our interview in the teashop, ending with:

"And she's right, you know. What she says is unanswerable. She's thinking for both of you. I respect her, and her decision, and so will you if you're wise."

"What do you know about it?" He broke out in fury, not rowdy fury, but a deadly white quiet. "What do you know of what's behind it all? You with your respect, you're half dead!" He used a curious phrase then. "I've earned that woman, and I'm going to have her."

"That's your affair. I won't help."

"I don't want your help. Where's she gone?"

"I don't know."

This was true; I was surprised that she should so soon have cut herself adrift. He considered me, whistling softly through his teeth.

"You're a liar, but it doesn't matter. I'll find out."

"If you love her, you'll let her alone."

"I can't let her alone," said Mortimer, snarling, and turning to the door.

He might never have found her but for one thing; she had to live, and she knew only one way of earning money. If I had pressed a loan on her there in the teashop it might have prevented the whole tragedy—and yet, I don't know; I couldn't have kept on subsidising her, and she must, sooner or later, have gone back to her trade. She went far enough off, but mediums are easy to keep track of, especially such a woman as she was, well known and nearly honest. Mortimer ran her to earth in Edinburgh within three months of her departure from London, and began without delay or haste to make his siege.

Poor woman! She did resist as she had promised; fled the town, tried to get passage to America, and was brought up short, like a dog on a chain, by the imperious eternal need of money. He followed again and found her in some sort of dingy lodgings, where he fairly bullied her into consenting. All this I had from her long afterwards, and I remember the words she used:

"They say if a man gets thirsty enough he'll drink seawater

though he knows it'll send him off his head. I'd got to that state. I knew it was mad, but I was thirsty for him."

It would have been superhuman to expect her to put up yet another fight. She had done her best for the decencies, and for the ultimate happiness of both of them; he, and the world, and the circumstances of her life would have none of her best. She gave in.

Having yielded, she kept nothing back—no rashness, no absurdity of affection. She let herself go with his desire like a flower dropped on a quick stream; or, rather, since that comparison suggests something frail, like a whole tree swept towards Niagara. She would not marry him, so far she held out, until the year was past from the date of his wife's death, but she planned, doted, spent fifteen hours a day in his company, and with a snap of her big fingers gave her whole spiritualist connection the go-by.

She it was who wrote to me, for I believe that after those half-dozen sentences exchanged between us on the evening of her flight Mortimer would have seen me dead and damned before he put his foot over my door. She, on the other hand, remembered that I had understood both sides of the question. I wrote back congratulating, and suggesting that they should come one evening to dine. She accepted enthusiastically by telephone.

"Oh, please, Mr Findlay," I heard her unlovely voice; "if it isn't a rude question, will anybody else be coming?"

"That's as you choose," I answered. "Plain party, or coloured; you shall decide."

"Oh, then, just us, if you don't mind, Mr Findlay." She had that infuriating trick of using one's name at every sentence. "Unless—" the voice trailed off.

"Unless?" Then I suppose I must have caught her unspoken thought. "What about Pybus and Tarrant, if they're in London? A final meeting of the circle?"

"Oh, yes," said she, noisily glad; "that's what I was hoping you'd say. After all, it was with you all, and sitting for you, I met Lance. It would be nice to say sort of goodbye."

"You're giving up your work, I suppose?"

"Lance says I've got to," she answered, and the clumsy words, as she spoke them in her unbearable voice, gave an impression of joyous surrender difficult to describe.

So this was the party, four men, one woman, just as we had met often before. Pybus and Tarrant turned up first together, so that I was able to let them know the state of affairs. They were incredulous, as I had been when I came upon the ill-assorted couple in the Park.

"They say," said Tarrant, "a man always goes for the same type of woman. Here's proof he doesn't. You couldn't have two women less alike than the Bain and Aileen."

"Few husbands have energy enough to experiment in domesticity," I said, busy with the sherry. "If a man's happy with one type he'll stick to that."

Pybus, always literal, took up my words as he accepted his glass.

"Wasn't Mortimer happy, then, with Aileen?"

Tarrant jumped on him, of course. Aileen, so fine, such a darling, who wouldn't be happy with her? Pybus, making appreciative faces over his sherry, agreed that he had said something idiotic, and the topic dropped—dropped, and took root in my mind uncomfortably, like the barbed seed of some desert flower. They went back to the marvellous alliance.

"She's older than he is. And—how about Bain? Who and what was Bain?"

"He's dead, she told me once."

"Well, it's Mortimer's funeral. I wouldn't care for a wife myself that had been long on this job." Spiritualism, Pybus implied.

"She's giving it up."

Tarrant laughed.

"How can she give it up?" Which was just what Mortimer had said to me, concerning his pursuit of her. "She's—a sort of spirit right-of-way. After there's been going and coming for years you can't suddenly padlock a gate that people have got used to using."

"You can," said Pybus, the literal. "It's entirely a question of how long the trespassing has been permitted."

"She's been working as a medium for twenty-five years," I said, and Pybus' face fell.

"What I mean is," Tarrant went on, "she won't be able to help stuff coming through. It's a queer situation. Suppose Aileen wanted to get in touch with Lance?"

"Talk of something else," I said; "they're on the stairs."

A moment later they were in the room. She came first, untidy as ever, but grander. Her hair was wound up in a large bun, lop-sided already, and secured with a flashing slide of some kind at the back. Her dress was a savage orange colour which must have killed any clothing set near it save masculine blacks and whites—a terrific dress, but her face dominated it. Big and untended and uncouth as she was, there was about her a happiness so shining that it lent her almost beauty; as the two men congratulated, and she smiled with her eyes on Mortimer, I could read astonishment behind their civil masks. They were used to her as the medium, a powerful blank body, strong enough physically to stand the strain of the trances, having no very definite personality to oppose the entrance of the other-world forces, whatever they were. The instrument had become a woman, and though I was prepared for it, knowing the circumstances and having had that conversation in the tearoom, it was something of a revelation, even to me.

Mortimer, too, looked different, settled, as if at last he had come home. There had been hunger in that face when I last saw it snarling over his shoulder, and now that the hunger appeased he was again the pleasant-mannered fellow that his dub knew; the snarling face became something seen in nightmare, and which for her sake I hoped he might never show again.

Yet, despite the perfect contentment of the chief guests, or possibly because of it, our meal was not successful. The talk was spasmodic, gusty; it rose and died, and even the wine could not keep it to an even flow. The truth was, of course, that we were about the most ill-assorted party conceivable, having only one interest in common—a topic barred by the idiotic prejudice against talking shop. Somehow or other we laboured along, in friendly but difficult converse, to the moment of coffee, which at my suggestion we took at the table, all sitting together round the candles. It is a good moment, that after-dinner quarter hour's dawdle, wine circling, smoke ascending, and whether or no there is talk seems to matter little enough. I saw Mrs. Bain, as she stirred her coffee, gaze about her with kindliness. We had always held our circle in the dining-room, which lies at the back of the house, insulated from noise, and she was evidently remembering. I put it to her.

"A penny, Mrs. Bain?"

She came back to reality, looking a little puzzled.

"Penny? Oh, I see what you mean—for my thoughts. I was thinking about all that had happened in this room. We got grand results, didn't we?"

Everybody nodded, and there was a murmur of "That we did. Thanks to you. Wonderful phenomena."

She went on, looking steadily and lovingly at Mortimer:

"I'm giving it up, you know, for good."

"You won't be able to," said Tarrant, who, it must be remembered, was a believer born. "It will come over you sometimes, a rush of communication."

Mortimer laughed rather shortly.

I'll keep her to earth," he said, and glanced over at her for response. But for once she was not looking at him. She was staring down into her coffee cup, where the round of shining black liquid seemed to hold her eyes. Tarrant was going on with his argument, using over again his simile of the right-of-way.

"There aren't so many short cuts," he persisted, "and those there are get known; both sides of the fence they get known. How many mediums are there—proved, honest ones, I mean—in London? And how many wanting to use them on the other side? Do you suppose they're going to sit back and let—"

"Look out," I said sharply.

Mrs. Bain's head had fallen forward, though her eyes still were open, staring into the dark pool of the cup. Mortimer swore, and thrust back his chair. He was sitting on my left, opposite her, and I shoved him back and down. It is not healthy for sleepwalkers to wake them in mid-progress, and the same holds good for people entranced. I had, I may say, from the first moment, no doubt whatever that this was a genuine performance. Her colour was deathly, the breathing had slackened, the pupils of her eyes were contracted as if she had taken a stiff shot of morphia. She had looked like that once before, on the occasion when she stripped, and I remembered these preliminary signs most clearly.

Mortimer subsided under my hand, but spoke to her.

"Ruby, come back. You're having dinner with Findlay, not giving a sitting. Ruby!"

She took no notice at all, she who all the evening had been quiveringly alive to every glance and gesture of his. She stared into the cup, opening her mouth now and then. It was Tarrant who said, triumph in his whisper:

"Better let her get it over. What about the lights?"

"No!" said Mortimer loudly. "Ruby, listen to me."

"She doesn't hear you," Pybus told him unnecessarily; "something's coming through."

Tarrant got up quietly and, leaning over the table, blew out the candles, our only illuminants, one by one. We sat in the silence and dark, I with my hand still on Mortimer's arm, listening to strong sighs that came from her, seeming to shake her; great sighs, deep and endless, as though her whole trunk were hollow, a mere cavern for air. Then a voice sounded, broken and often half-lost, like some person speaking against the wind.

"Cruel," it said. "Oh, cruel! You hurt me so."

Nothing more for a minute. I took upon myself to be leader, since the others were silent.

"Who are you?" I asked. "Will you tell us who you are?"

"He knows," answered the voice; "Lance knows."

"Have you a message for Lance?"

A laugh; a pause; then a little husky sound of singing, an old song, familiar words, the folk-tune of "Lord Rendel."

"Oh, that was strong poison, Rendel my son;
Oh, that was strong poison, my pretty one—"

I felt the muscles contract in Mortimer's arm as involuntarily my fingers gripped tighter; we were both hearing the same thing, Aileen's light voice with a touch of County Kerry in it, singing an accustomed tune through the mouth of her supplanter. I remembered, troubled, that on this day a year ago she had died.

"Aileen," I said, "we know you now. What have you come to say?"

The voice fluttered on with its song.

"Oh, make my bed soon;
I'm sick to my heart, and fain would lie down."

Still Mortimer did not speak, and I supposed that the shock of the thing was keeping him quiet. We all of us know that voice and recognised it with the conviction that this was no trickery. Aileen spoke quite inimitably. This was herself.

"Lance, Lance," it went on. "What are you doing, my dear one? I'm sick, take that dope away. Must I have it, Lance? Ah, you've killed me, my poor creature, my dear lover; wasn't I dying fast enough—was that it? It's kind stuff you're using, gentle stuff, sleepy; but oh, the cruel pain at my heart! You wanted that big woman, did you? Poor Lance, and I was in the way, my sweet pretty one." Then the voice went wavering off into its tune again.

"I'm sick to my heart, and fain—and fain—"

It went away in ghostly heavings and sighs, cavernous breaths on which now and then a note of the song could still be heard riding. There was a pause, a deadly five seconds. Then the arm under my hand flexed, Mortimer's fist drove at me in the dark and caught me over the heart; there was the screech of a chair on the parquet, and a shaft of light struck in upon us through a door torn open. In an instant a wave of noise seemed to rise; feet scuffling, the voices, angrily loud, of Tarrant and Pybus in the hall, a struggle in which a mirror went down, and through which I could hear the scrape of steel. Mortimer's blow had been fierce enough to sicken me. I sat limp, hearing the struggle, which at the height of its din suddenly died away to silence, following the sound of a man's fall.

"He's done it. My God," from Tarrant; "how do you stop blood?"

"You'll never stop that," Pybus speaking. "Better than the hangman's trap, anyway."

I got to my feet with a groan, and pitched forward to the door, to whose handle I clung, looking out. Mortimer had made a job of it with one of the Chinese swords hung for ornament on the wall, my yellow wall that was streaked where blood had spurted towards it from the side of his neck. He died while I watched, with a writhing of the face, a rictus above clenched teeth that I do not now care to recall. We stood away from him, and stared down on him dying, without compassion of any sort for the man who had murdered Aileen. Not one of us doubted that; and if it may sound absurd wholly and instantly to believe a woman whom we knew to be not above using the tricks of her trade— well, we had seen the glow of her happiness before that voice came out of nowhere, singing and murmuring damnation to her hope. We looked down on him, and then round at each other, silently with a question. What to do?

Before there could be any consultation, a sound from the dining-room made me start and turn; that most ordinary of sounds, a long, untrammelled yawn. I went in at once, shutting the door behind me, and switched on the lights. Mrs. Bain was lying back in her chair, very white but conscious, and rubbing at her eyes with the heel of her hand like a child.

"Where's Lance?" she asked first, smiling. "And the others?

You look washed out, Mr Findlay. Whatever have I been up to?"

"Something came through," I began, stammering, for there were sounds outside as if they might be lifting him; "something rather shocking—"

She glanced down at once at her ornate and hideous dress, but it was not disarranged, she was clad as fully as its cut permitted.

"Fancy!" she said archly. "It must have been bad for you to look like that. I'm tired too; dead tired. But what's the odds, so long as you're happy? We always did get good results, didn't we, in this circle?"

THE EVIL THAT MEN DO
by Patience Tillyard

The Australian National Review, February 1939

Patience Tillyard was a Canberra-born educator who spent several years in the UK in the 1930s. Her father, Robin John Tillyard, was a world-renowned entomologist who founded the *Australian National Review*, and her mother, Patricia Tillyard, received a MBE in 1951.

I.

The last of the sunset light was pouring slantwise through the narrow windows of the little church when the Rev. Thomas Cochran pronounced the benediction and, gathering up his books, strode out into the vestry, the rustle of his cassock and surplice consorting oddly with the creak of the black leather riding boots he wore beneath. Dutifully clutching the plate, Mr MacWhirrter, the lawyer, padded out behind the parson, and his stout little middle-aged sister, breathing stertorously as she pumped at the organ pedals, broke into somewhat wheezy variations on the closing hymn.

Julia Thorpe, the Bank Manager's wife, rose from her knees and, taking her husband's disengaged arm, proceeded with him down the church, out into the dusty golden light that was flooding the west door. Round it the black-coated, black-frocked congregation gathered.

They were a strange pair, the Thorpes: Julia tall and stately, with a haughty aquiline nose and a grim twist to her thin lips; James short and square, slightly bow-legged from many years of riding, his eyes blue and kindly and crinkled at the corners. But though Wangawarra had smiled when they first came to the Bank, seven years before, and though the knowing ones had said: "Ah, it's easy to see who's lord and master in *that* house!" they knew better now, having learnt that James was the only man on earth for whom the downright, hard-headed Julia had any considerable respect at all.

As they took up their stand to the left of the porch, there were salutations for them from every group: for James Thorpe in Wangawarra was as much of a power as was the Reverend Thomas in his mining parish of Mount Clancy, and Julia was as popular as such a blunt-spoken woman could be.

Though they acknowledged the greetings, it was obvious that they were thinking of other things; for they stood silently, arm-in-arm, and James now and again stole a sideways glance up at the handsome profile of his wife, who was still looking thoughtful, just as she had done during the peroration of the Reverend Thomas's fine forty minute sermon.

"Generally," said James to himself, "she looks politely heretical. But I believe that this time Tom got home somewhere."

Julia turned her eyes severely upon him.

"James, don't look at me like that. I know quite well what you're thinking. Yes, for once there was something in that sermon, and I shall tell him so."

The old verger, Ruffie Gilligan, on week-days custodian of the least disreputable of Wangawarra's three public houses, had closed half the double door and stood lugubriously beside it, swinging his bunch of large keys. In the year of grace 1865, church property had to be carefully guarded, or it was liable to be put to unhallowed uses, especially in townships which lay, like Wangawarra, on the direct route from Sydney to the great goldfields.

"'Avin' a reel 'unt, they is," announced Ruffie mournfully. "The Reverend dropped a penny on the floor, and Mr MacWhirrter's down on 'ands and knees with 'im lookin' for it. Show's 'e's Scotch, that does," and he cackled rustily.

Julia heard the vestry door flung open, and from where she stood she could see the Reverend Thomas emerge into the dim church with a small canvas bag on the palm of his left hand. Poor stout MacWhirrter, panting slightly from his exertions on the vestry floor, followed the parson down the aisle.

Ruffle clanged the door to triumphantly behind them and locked it with much jangling of keys.

"That which was lost is found," said the Reverend Thomas. "Eh, Mac? Sorry we've kept you waiting, everybody, but I dropped the penny, and Mac quite rightly wouldn't let me go until we'd found it. Here you are, James," and he handed the bag to the Manager, in whose private safe the day's spoils would repose until the Bank opened the next morning.

The parson went round shaking hands, asking questions and bidding friendly farewells; for he came only twice a year from Mount Clancy to preach at Wangawarra. As he left it, each group dispersed, this one across the dusty, grass-grown churchyard to the straggling main street of the little town, that to collect children and put into the shafts of buggies horses which had been tied beneath the pine trees since the eleven o'clock morning service; many people drove thirty miles to hear the Reverend Thomas and spend, between the services, some happy social hours among their friends.

"Now supper," said James, steering his wife down the path. "You'll come in too, won't you, Mac? And Miss MacWhirrter?"

II.

Supper over, the Thorpes and their guests were sitting out on the deep verandah of the Bank House. They had left the lamps inside, and the thick darkness had brought relief from the flies, though very little from the heat, which was still intense. Two red points of light marked the long chairs in which the parson and James Thorpe reclined, puffing slowly at pipes, another the spot where the little lawyer and his cigar were perched on the verandah edge. Now and again there was an uneasy stir from the straight-backed chair where Miss MacWhirrter primly sat, her feet dangling uncomfortably just above the floor. Julia was sitting equally erect upon another stiff chair, but her presence was betrayed only by the brisk click of the knitting needles which she had brought out in defiance of the Sabbath day. Poor Miss MacWhirrter. Scots-bred, had long ago ceased to be shocked by Mrs Thorpe, whose practical Christianity she had to admit was unimpeachable, if unconventional.

Suddenly in the silence the tempo of the knitting needles accelerated, and James gave a little chuckle.

"Julia's making up for lost time, aren't you, my love?"

"Nonsense, James," was the tart rejoinder. "I've merely changed from ribbing to plain. 'Lost time,' if you like, but I must say not so much wasted as usually is by the Sunday evening sermon."

"Ma'am," came the Reverend Thomas's voice, "were I not so comfortable, I should feel it my duty to arise and bow. I ask you to take the will for the deed. So my dissertation entertained you?"

"Thomas," observed Julia, "your attitude, for one of the cloth, is refreshing in the extreme. But no, I was not entertained. I was, for once, completely interested."

There was a grunt of assent from her husband, a gentle "Yes, indeed" from Miss MacWhirrter, and from the lawyer a vigorous nod, indicated by the movement of his cigar-end.

"Instead of your Hebrews text," said James, "you might even have taken 'There are more things in heaven and earth, Horatio,' were Shakespeare permitted in the pulpit instead of the Scriptures."

"Um," agreed the parson thoughtfully. "I might."

"Clouds of witnesses, ghosts, what you will," announced

Julia decisively, "I've no time for. I hope the dead have better things to do than supervise our wretched goings-on. But most certainly I agree with casting away the works of darkness in this land of light."

"What I said about our responsibilities," explained the parson, "is one of my firmest beliefs. It stands to reason that the thoughts and actions which go into this young land in its early years are going largely to determine its future—shall we say?—atmosphere, and there's no doubt about it that the start hasn't been a good one on the whole, has it?"

"Nae doot whitever," came in a grunt from the verandah edge. The little that Alexander MacWhirrter spoke was in the Scots of his boyhood.

"That's why I always try to push home the point about the greater responsibility of those few people who are willing to cast aside the works of darkness."

Julia moved restlessly, and the click of the needles stopped for a minute.

"Works, yes," she said emphatically, "and actions, yes. But, Thomas, you'll never convince me that thoughts, good or bad, hang about unseen, like ghosts, to influence us. It's too fantastic."

"'The evil that men do lives after them'," said James softly. "I'm good on Shakespeare tonight."

"Yes, but that's concrete evil, James" maintained Julia. "Come, Thomas, you don't really believe in principalities and powers, do you? Weren't you speaking metaphorically about the works of darkness?"

"Yes to the first question," replied the Reverend Thomas slowly, "no to the second. My twenty years in Australia have shown me some queer things, Julia, and I can't for the life of me explain them all away on rational grounds. Seriously, sometimes I can feel evil preponderating round me—"

"Overwork," diagnosed Mrs Thorpe. "Or liver."

James gave a crack of laughter, and the parson chuckled.

"'Help thou mine unbelief'," said the Manager. "Julia is a

confirmed sceptic."

"No, but really," went on the Reverend Thomas, "I do often feel it. Tonight, for instance, with all due deference to the Sabbath and to your hospitality, Ma'am, I should say was one on which the powers of darkness are balancing the scales fairly evenly with those of light."

"It's the weather," said Julia firmly.

As she spoke there was a resounding crash from above. Simultaneously, Miss MacWhirrter let out a frightened squeak, and the Reverend Thomas sat bolt upright in his chair. There was a dismal wail the next second.

Julia imperturbably gathered up her knitting.

"John has fallen out of bed," she said. "He often does. Too much Sunday tea is the rational explanation of *that*."

III.

Since Sunday there had been no relief from the heat, which had steadily grown more oppressive. All day Wednesday the blue sky had arched, with a glow like an overheated oven, above the dusty, breathless earth. In the afternoon, the western sky thickened, and the sun went down, a hot red ball, into murky clouds that were climbing slowly out of the plains.

After an early breakfast on Monday morning, James and the Reverend Thomas had set off together on horseback for Mount Clancy, eighty-seven miles distant. On Tuesday the Manager had business to transact at the branch there and would ride back alone on Wednesday, leaving the parson to another six months' work among his miners. Excursions like this were frequent; for Wangawarra had a more important branch of the Bank than Mount Clancy, which, ever since it had been Clancy's Claim, a collection of prospectors' shacks, had had a bad history. Two of its Bank Managers had been murdered, one actually outside the Wangawarra Bank, whither he had ridden for his life with a store of gold. Another had been badly man-handled, and the Bank itself had been robbed four times, so that many Mount Clancy people did their business, whenever possible, at Wangawarra, a farming centre with a clean sheet.

Julia had had a trying day. The three children had not been to the parsonage for lessons, as the Vicar was away. Their good humour was exhausted by lunch-time, when a violent triangular scrap ended in floods of tears and bed for them all. At tea, there was further trouble, when John dipped Katharine's pigtails in the milk jug, and they bawled again. By 6.30 they were all back again in their beds for the night, and Julia was free to take a book to the angle of the verandah whence she could watch the storm clouds mounting, at the same time command the short drive and, through a gap in the pepper trees, most of the street down which James would come clattering home.

The light she found was too bad for reading, and she was too weary to go in for a lamp, so she sat quietly in her tall chair, pushing back with both hands the depression that she had felt all day, but with especial force now that darkness was falling and she had nothing active to do.

So abstracted was she that the sudden hurried crunch of the gravel in the drive made her jump sharply to her feet.

"Who's there?" she called sharply and immediately upbraided herself for her lack of self-command.

"Only I" answered the timid voice of Miss MacWhirrter, who emerged, puffing, from the shadows of the drive.

"Oh, Julia"—and she stood looking beseechingly up from the bottom of the steps—"I had to come over and see you. Alexander is working in his office, and we aren't having supper 'til eight, and I couldn't stand it any longer!" Her voice rose, and she wrung her hands.

"Come, come, Annie," said Julia briskly. "Pull yourself together, and come inside."

She helped her up the steps and led the way in, steering the breathless little woman firmly by one arm.

"Wait," she ordered, "'til I light the lamp."

As her groping fingers found the tinder-box on the hall table, there was a sudden squeak of fear from Miss MacWhirrter, and Julia promptly dropped the box with a clatter on the stone floor.

"Well, what is it?" she exclaimed, all the more sharply because her nervousness made her angry with herself.

Miss MacWhirrter stood clutching the doorpost and staring down the drive. As Julia came out, she seized her arm in a grip of surprising strength.

"S-someone by the gate!" she gasped.

Julia gazed into the black shadows along the lightness of the drive until her eyes ached.

"Nonsense," she said finally. "I can't see a thing, and I don't see how you could in such darkness. Now, Annie, don't be silly. Come along in with me, and tell me what's the matter."

"But I did see someone!" almost sobbed Miss MacWhirrter, as she was towed into the hall by Julia, to whose arm she still clung so tightly that she had to bend down with her to grope for the lost tinder-box. "Down by the gate, in the bushes to the left. It *moved.*"

Julia allowed the light to sputter before she answered.

"All imagination! You're overwrought, Annie. I'll just light the verandah lantern for James, and then we'll go into the parlour."

Miss MacWhirrter followed her fearfully to the door.

Julia stretched up to light the lantern, high on one of the verandah posts; it flung a feeble circle of yellow light a few yards down the drive, whose darkness it only accentuated. She had another good look towards the gate, partly to reassure Miss MacWhirrter, partly to steady her own nerves, which were strangely jerky.

"Really, Annie, I can't see a thing," she repeated, turning and stepping inside. "Just your imagination. Though what's come over you I can't think."

Bearing the hall-lamp, she led the way into the parlour, where she lit the big central lamp and firmly but kindly pushed Miss MacWhirrter, still shivering and shaking, into a chair.

"Now," she said, "just what is the matter?"

The little woman gave a gulp and then poured out an incoherent story.

"It's *all* the Reverend Thomas' fault. I've never felt like this since I was a small girl out on the moors at night. He shouldn't have talked about powers of darkness. You can't see them, but you can feel them, if you think about it. And I never had 'til Sunday night. Oh, it was dreadful going home! And Alexander said it was all havers, but it wasn't—I *knew* they were there. And I didn't sleep a wink, and it wasn't any better in the morning, and it's got worse ever since, and I couldn't come over and see you before because I thought you'd laugh. And then when I did come, I saw—" Her voice rose hysterically, then broke in a sob. "It's *all* the Reverend Thomas's fault!"

Julia, standing beside her, listened with her fine brows drawn together. She put her hand on Miss MacWhirrter's fat little shoulder and gave her a kindly shake.

"Now I expect you feel better. There's quite a lot in confession for some people, you know, Annie. I think myself it's the weather. No one feels quite normal in heat like this. Also you have been overworking—haven't you? Without any help in that barracks of a place of Alexander's?"

Miss MacWhirrter looked up at her with comfort dawning in her eyes.

"Do you really think that's what it is? Oh, I do hope so. Yes, I suppose I have been doing too much." She gave a final hiccup into her handkerchief. "Oh, Julia, you are a comfort. And thank you for not laughing at me. I was so afraid you might."

"Rubbish! I'll go and make a cup of tea for you, and then you'll be all right. Will you come with me, or stay here?"

She looked down with kindly eyes on the short conflict revealed in Miss MacWhirrter's ingenuous round face.

"Oh, I think—I'll stay here. You've made me feel so much better, Julia. Yes, I shall be all right here."

"Good!"

With a reassuring pat, Julia took up the hall lamp and walked across the parlour to the dining-room, which led to the kitchen.

She half-turned at the threshold to smile at Miss MacWhirrter, huddled in her chair opposite, and so she did not see, until she had passed through the doorway, the figure of a man in riding kit, standing with his back to her and leaning on the mantelpiece over the empty fireplace.

Her fingers tightened convulsively on the lamp handle, and she bit back by a colossal effort of will the shriek that rose to her lips.

The second she stood there getting a grip on herself seemed an eternity. The man at the mantelpiece must suddenly have realized she was there; for he spun round on his booted heel and looked full at her, his face illuminated in the warm glow of the lamp. She saw a queer crooked mouth and a great beak of a nose beneath brows that were inordinately thick and dark. It was a frightening face, yet somehow, strangely, a friendly one. Behind it, the clock said twenty-one minutes past seven.

"The shotgun!" Julia thought frantically. "James's shotgun is in the corner by the sideboard just behind you. Get that, and you may be able to move him quietly, without alarming Annie."

Keeping her gaze fixed on the eyes that stared unwinkingly at her, she stepped almost imperceptibly backwards, raising the lamp gradually as she did so, to keep the man in the circle of its light. Then in a flash she set down the lamp on the sideboard, seized the gun and levelled it.

The putting down of the lamp had unfortunately shortened its range, but she was able to see, with a sickening thump of the heart, that the man was no longer there. A glance across the room showed her the kitchen door fast, and the shutters across the windows, while no scream had come from Miss MacWhirrter in the parlour.

"He must be under the table," She told herself desperately. "And I haven't a hand to lift the lamp!"

She stood there gathering her strength for what seemed another eternity. Then she moved slowly sideways and forwards, covering the room with the gun and the parlour door with her person. There was enough light for her to see that he was not behind any of the chairs, which were the only other furniture in the room, and with her finger still on the trigger, her eyes alert, she pushed the door slowly back on its hinges until it was flush with the wall.

"He can't he behind there," she breathed. "Then he must be under the table." Gritting her teeth, she advanced grimly to bend and prod the miscreant in the ribs with the gun. But all she saw was the oblong shadow cast by the table and the lamplight beyond it.

"No one!" she whispered; then straightened swiftly, fearing that her eyes must have played her false in their search and she was about to be attacked in the rear. Still the room was bare, and a further stoop convinced her that the table sheltered no one.

Slowly she uncocked the gun and dropped it into her right hand for use as a club, if necessary. Then she stepped over to the lamp, took it up and thoroughly searched the room, even peering up the great chimney.

"Well," she said to herself, as she finished up weakly by the sideboard, "it must have been imagination. I'm as had as Annie MacWhirrter." Though she was shaking all over and wet with perspiration, this admission made her give a grim little chuckle.

"Julia!" said Miss MacWhirrter's voice from the parlour. "What are you laughing at?"

"I'm not," lied Julia promptly. "I'm just getting the cups. The fire's in, and I won't be long."

The clock showed her astonished eyes that only four minutes had passed since she came into the room.

Before she went through into the kitchen, she took from the sideboard James's brandy decanter and poured into a teacup a stiff peg, which she drank off at a gulp.

"I must keep away from Annie," she told herself with a shaky little laugh, "or she'll smell spirits, and the fat will be in the fire."

IV.

Half an hour later a distant mutter of thunder made Julia rise, on legs that still did not seem quite her own, to look out into the blackness through the window which she had had reluctantly to leave open, for fear of again scaring Miss MacWhirrter, miraculously restored by two cups of strong tea. The darkness was, if anything, thicker, but the heat was not quite so heavy; for now and again puffs of warm air, precursors of the storm, rustled in the pepper trees and stirred the lace curtains. Over in the west, as she looked, there were swift flickers of lightning. Then came another growl of thunder, perceptibly louder than the first.

"Annie," she said, "unless you want to spend the night here, you'd better be getting home. It will probably be pouring in ten minutes' time."

"Oh, dear," fluttered Miss MacWhirrter, heaving herself to her feet. "I must go, Alexander's supper will be late as it is." She peered fearfully past Julia. "But that dreadful drive!"

"I'll come with you, of course," interposed Julia swiftly.

"Oh, thank you!" The answer was full of relief and gratitude. "You are brave, Julia. I couldn't face that drive alone. And Alexander will bring you home.... I do hope we don't see anything."

"Rubbish!" said Julia with a briskness she was far from feeling. "Of course we shan't. Put on your cape. Mine is in the hall."

As she lifted the cape to Miss MacWhirrter's shoulders, the faint beat of hooves some distance up the street came to her tense ears on a sudden sough of wind.

"Hark!" she said. "A horse! That must be James. We'll be at the gate by the time he is, because he always walks the mare the last mile home."

She gathered her cloak from its peg in the hall, pushed Miss MacWhirrter out of the door and slipped the lantern off its hook. She had to stop, clutching her cloak about her in the rising wind, to help the stout little lady down the steps. Then she realized, in a disquieting flash, that she did not feel the relief she had expected to feel at the sound of James's horse; rather, she was filled with an inexplicable sense of urgency.

"Oh, *hurry*, Annie!" she snapped, losing patience. "Fall down them if you can't walk. Only hurry!"

"Well, really, Julia!" Miss MacWhirrter's injured puffing changed to a shriek of terror; for outside the gate there was a sudden commotion that made Julia release her arm and go flying down the drive between the dark trees that were now bending and roaring before the storm.

She shot out of the gate on to the road, and a brilliant flash of lightning revealed her husband, half-unseated on his rearing bay and beset by three assailants. A short man was leaping, pistol in hand, for the snaffle-ring of the terrified mare; another, a tall fellow, was wrestling with the arm that strove to whip the pistol from its holster; the third was staggering back from a kick James had dealt him with his stirruped foot. Julia halted half a second in sheer horror, the lantern held above her head. Dazzled as she was by the lightning, she felt, rather than saw, the short man trying to train his pistol on James amid the plunges of the mare and near her, the third, recovering his balance, jerk his weapon up. Involuntarily she leapt forward and brought the lantern down with a swinging blow on the fellow's head. He gave a sharp gasp and fell like a stone, while the pistol exploded harmlessly into the dust and the lantern crashed on to the road in a flare of burning oil. Simultaneously the second gun went off, somewhere near the mare's head, and there was a yell of anguish, followed by a string of oaths and fresh snortings from the maddened mare.

"James!" shrieked Julia. "Are you alive?"

"He is and a'," came the unmistakable accents of Mr MacWhirrter. "But by the grace of the Lord alone. Ha, wad ye, ye scoondrel?" and another flash of lightning revealed the decorous little church-warden knocking on the head the tall assailant who had bitten the dust, while the little man, the back of his skull smashed by the bay's lashing hooves, lay motionless beyond. James, tight-lipped, was dealing with the plunging animal, on whose back he had somehow regained his seat. With a sigh of thankfulness, Julia staggered back against the Bank wall.

The next instant there were lights and voices all round them; for the uproar had penetrated Ruffie Gilligan's bar, a hundred yards down the street, and out had rushed a score of men, who stood round clutching pistols, lanterns and heavy pewter mugs, while Ruffie himself, a genius with animals, seized the bay's bridle and quieted her with pats and melancholy soothing noises. Julia heard James's voice, and then he was by her side, with his arms round her.

"The closest shave I've ever had, my dear," he said, "and it's thanks to you and Mac and, as he says, the grace of the Lord that I'm not like that fellow there." He jerked his head towards the still, dusty figure, the face of which a big man was about to cover with a grimy handkerchief.

Julia could not for the life of her say a word, but the tears were running down her cheeks as she kissed her husband, and the men who saw her there in the lantern-light revised their opinion of the Manager's grim lady.

The big man was stooping excitedly over the body.

"'Old the light, Ben!" they heard him say. "God, if that ain't Black Randolph! Sir!" he called to James. "Yer mare's been an' killed Black Randolph! I'd know 'im anywheres—a little cove with that long scar on 'is chin!"

"Black Randolph!" said James thoughtfully. "Whew! The first and last time he ever bungled a job." He propelled his wife gently towards the gate. "Shove those two in the lock-up, Ruffie, and get someone to rug the mare and give her a bran mash. I'll see to her later. I'll be over soon, boys, to tell you the story, if you want to hear it. Come on up to the house, Mac, and have blessings heaped upon your head."

They moved up the drive through a night that had become strangely silent, despite the roar of the wind and the thunder overhead and the excited voices in the street behind them. Though she leant on James's arm, Julia realized it was more for the sheer joy of knowing he was there, and safe, than for support; now she felt perfectly calm and steady, and the air that the wind drove round them was no longer oppressive, but cool with the first heavy raindrops.

On the bottom step, where Julia had left her, sat Miss MacWhirrter, huddled like a ruffled hen in her cape.

"Annie!" exclaimed Julia, stricken with remorse.

"I didn't even faint!" announced the little lady triumphantly. "I just sat here and shut my eyes and listened in case the children should be frightened. Julia, I knew there was someone in those bushes!"

"I believe," said Julia, with a return of her old acidity, "that the fact you've proved me wrong for once is all that matters to you. Come on in and have some more tea."

V.

According to his promise, James had visited Ruffie's crowded bar and recounted his story; the mare was comfortably stabled; the storm was over; the MacWhirrters had just taken their leave. Julia stood arm-in-arm with her husband on the verandah, listening to the rain hissing down steadily on the hot earth.

James gave a little chuckle.

"I believe Annie will gloat all her days," he said, "because she didn't faint."

"Let her," replied Julia briefly. "You're safe."

"Yes, my dear," was the grave answer. "How Providence worked it all out so neatly amazes me. Somehow Black Randolph must have found out in Mount Clancy about the gold I was to carry back with me, and if those two fellows of Tom's hadn't come with me I'd have been neatly disposed of somewhere on the way. Randolph knew they'd be staying at the Vicarage, so laid his little ambush for me out in the street, between there and here, when the chances were I'd be alone. All very nice—but my arrival was set for the exact moment that Mac came for Annie and you were about to bring her home." He paused, then went on gently: "It really looks, Julia, as though the assault of Tom's powers of darkness was repulsed at every turn by the armour of light, doesn't it?"

She could not speak for a moment.

"I've been wrong at least twice today, James," she got out at length, "and I might have known I was wrong, because it's been a terrible day, full of warnings."

She could see the sympathy in his blue eyes, as he half turned to her.

"Yes," she said. "Only I could feel them, not interpret them." She stopped, grappling with her self-command.

"Well?" he asked.

She too half turned and put her other hand on his rough sleeve.

"James, you won't laugh at me, I know, but I must tell you this: before I took Annie home, there was a man in the dining-room, and he just disappeared."

James's eyebrows went up.

"Julia, he couldn't have."

"But he did," she insisted. "I got the shotgun without taking my eyes off him, and he simply vanished."

"Didn't he go into the kitchen?"

"No, the door was shut."

"Past you, then, into the parlour?"

"Annie was facing the door. And the windows were shut, and I looked in the cupboards and under the table and up the chimney."

"Queer," he said meditatively.

Julia was watching him appealingly.

"James, was it my imagination?"

"Perhaps," he answered absently, his brows puckered as he gazed down the drive. They stood in silence for half a minute.

Suddenly she saw his head go back, and he turned sharply

to face her.

"Julia," he said urgently, "I've just had an idea. This man—what did he look like? Can you describe him? His face?"

"Yes," she replied, "of course I can. My lamp was shining full on him. He had a big curved nose, a queer lop-sided mouth and the thickest black eyebrows I've ever seen."

James nodded very gravely and took both her hands in his.

"I thought as much," he said. "My dear, this will be another shock for you, but beyond all doubt the man you've just described was Pengelly, that very good fellow the Bank Manager of Mount Clancy, who was murdered thirteen years ago outside the Wangawarra Bank."

She looked at him uncomprehendingly. Then, as the words slowly pierced her consciousness, like missiles whose force is almost spent, she felt herself swaying.

For the first time in her life she fainted.

ABOUT THE EDITOR

JAMES DOIG works at the National Archives of Australia in Canberra. He has edited several volumes of colonial Australian supernatural fiction, including *Australian Ghost Stories* (Wordsworth Editions, 2010). He has also edited single-author collections by H. B. Marriott Watson and J. S. Leatherbarrow, and has published articles on obscure authors of horror and the supernatural, including R. R. Ryan, Keith Fleming, and H. T. W. Bousfield. He has a Ph.D. in medieval history from Swansea University in Wales.